# THE PRICE OF INNOCENCE

## BRYAN DEVORE

ISBN-10: 0-9852413-3-0
ISBN-13: 978-0-9852413-3-9

Also available as an e-book.

# PART ONE

*This sometimes happened: from time to time, Dantès,
driven out of solitude into the world, felt an imperative
need for solitude.*
—Alexandre Dumas, *The Count of Monte Cristo,* 1844

# 1

---※---

*February 14, Leipzig, Germany*

IAN LAWRENCE'S EYES were tired from scanning through hundreds of Internet articles. Sitting alone in the Handelshochschule Leipzig university computer lab, he couldn't believe it was already two in the morning. He had chosen ten terms related to the economics of organized crime and translated each from English into German, French, Russian, Polish, Czech, Slovak, Croatian, Armenian, Romanian, and Hungarian. For each translation of each word, he searched the Web for articles or sites that might be useful to his research. Even though he couldn't read any of the articles he found, he copied and pasted those with numerous key words into an online translator program so he could read a rough translation.

It was an article from a Krakow newspaper, with a picture of two women, that captured his attention. Both of them could have been models. They looked like sisters: one about 15 years old, the other about 20. The caption under the picture read, "*Siostry Zoe i Miska w Krakowie cztery miesiące przed domniemanym porwaniem Miska przez handlarza kobietami.*"

Ian stared at their picture. Something horrible must have happened to them, because his Web search included only horrible words. He copied the article into the online program to get a rough Polish-to-English translation. As he read the translated article, his worst fears about the girls were confirmed. They were sisters from Krakow. The oldest, Zoe, was twenty-three, and the younger, Miska, was fifteen. Nearly three months ago, Miska had vanished. The police opened a major investigation, and the story got a lot of publicity in the regional papers around Krakow for a month after the disappearance, but slowly, as days turned into weeks with no breakthroughs, the story faded from the press. According to this article, the whole thing would have been forgotten if not for Zoe's continued efforts to discover what happened to her sister. Zoe believed her sister had been abducted by human traffickers and put to work as a sex slave. The investigating authorities had uncovered an eyewitness testimony and some credit card data that seemed to support the likelihood that Miska had been kidnapped. Because their family didn't have much money and there had been no contact from those responsible, the authorities believed that sex traffickers were to blame.

Ian tried not to imagine what had happened to young Miska during the past three months if she really had been forced into the sex slavery trade. Every ounce of humanity inside him fought against the notion of thinking about this fifteen-year-old child suffering such horrible abuse for so long. He clicked back to the article and looked again at the picture of the sisters. He turned his focus to the older sister, Zoe. He thought about her losing her kid sister to crime, just as he had lost Jessica.

That was when he realized he was going about his research all wrong. He had already read every book, paper, and interview in the academic community about organized crime. He needed to do his research on the ground level. With the people. In the dark alleys of the world, where the crimes were committed and the victims suffered. And he would start with this woman Zoe and her missing sister.

He spent the next fifteen minutes typing a long e-mail to the journalist who had written the article. It was four in the morning when he finally sent the message.

He had five hours before he and the professor's friend, Marcus Gottschalk, met at the Leipzig train station and headed to Prague. Logging off the computer, he grabbed his leather satchel with the papers he had printed from the Internet, and walked up to the twenty-four-hour library. Like a physicist looking for evidence of dark matter in the universe, he was obsessed with discovering the theoretical link between the operations of organized crime and the legitimate corporate world. He would stay up all night if he had to. How could he even consider the luxury of sleep when so many victims were suffering at this very moment?

When the sun came up three hours later, he left the library to return to the computer lab. Logging on to his account, he saw the e-mail reply from Zoe Karminski.

*   *   *

Ian had come into Prague from the north, circling up around Hradčany Castle, which gave his first clear view of the ancient city below him. From his vantage point on Letná Hill, he could see much of the city across the Vltava River. There seemed to be an old stone bridge every hundred yards along the river. He could see the famous Charles Bridge, permanently closed to automobiles, packed with painters and meandering pedestrians. Red roofs with a dusting of snow stood along the old city walls. Looking out over a sea of Gothic and Renaissance churches, clock towers, stone bridges, monasteries, and graveyards, he felt as if he had gone back in time.

A week ago he had given the professor his dissertation proposal regarding an unexplored research gap: economic policies and strategies that governments could implement to diminish organized crime. The professor had loved it but added that this wasn't a topic one could research in the comfort and safety of a university library. That's when the professor told him about his former MBA student Marcus and said they should go to Prague to research his dissertation topic.

Now that he was in Prague with Marcus, he couldn't wait to delve into the kind of research the professor was talking about.

They took a green BMW taxi to Nový Svět, to a long twenty-foot-high wall set with brightly painted residential doorways. Marcus led him up the sloping cobblestone street that curved into Loreto Square.

"This has long been a working-class neighborhood," Marcus said. "But it has memories of greatness as well. We are very near where Einstein taught physics for years before defecting to your America, just before Hitler's blight swept this land."

Marcus opened a red door and waved Ian into the shadowy interior.

Inside the dim, dank chamber, Ian felt as if he had entered a vampire's lair. Dust motes floated in the plank of light slanting in from a high window. They descended a narrow stone staircase that might have wound down to a fairy-tale castle dungeon.

With each step he took into the darkness, Ian grew more excited. But when he reached the basement's dirt floor, his excitement turned to unease. Without needing to take another step into the underground chamber, he saw ten faces staring back at him in the flickering candlelight.

"What is this?" he asked Marcus.

But Marcus had stepped away from Ian and vanished into the shadows like a phantom. And at that moment, it occurred to Ian that he had just walked into an ambush of some sort.

Then, without warning, a dim red light turned on overhead, illuminating the ten faces. From the corner of his eye, he saw Marcus standing next to a light switch. Marcus nodded toward the group sitting around the large wooden table that Ian could now make out. "Ian, I'd like to introduce you to some people from the White Rose."

"I . . . recognize a few of you from the university," Ian said. "Are you all students at HHL?"

"No," Marcus answered. "Some are; some aren't. Some are alumni, and others have no affiliation with the school."

"So what do you have in common?"

"Only this," said a girl Ian knew as Florence. "The professor found us all. Just as he found you."

"I'm taking him to the factory tonight," Marcus said.

They seemed surprised.

"Is that smart?" Florence asked.

"He's ready for it," Marcus said.

"Ready for what?" Ian asked.

"You'll see."

*   *   *

"I've already forgotten half their names," Ian said. Marcus and he had left the dungeon meeting for the cool open air of the small courtyard.

"You'll get to know them in time."

"And there are others?"

"Oh, yes."

"Where are they?"

Marcus looked down and smiled. "Everywhere."

"What's that supposed to mean?"

"Quebec, New York, Tokyo, Shanghai, Bangkok, Moscow, Paris, London, Istanbul, Dubai, Barcelona, Rome, Mexico City,

Helsinki, Rio, Cairo, Buenos Aires, San Francisco, Miami, Sydney, Los Angeles."

"What is this, some kind of conspiracy?" Ian asked as they left the courtyard through a narrow walkway between two buildings. He could see people walking in the street up ahead.

"It's a network."

"A *secret* network," Ian added.

"We have to operate the same way they do if we expect to damage their operations."

"*They*? You mean criminal organizations?"

"Yes."

"So your ambitions are global?"

"Very much so."

A cold gust shot down the alleyway. Ian zipped up his black leather jacket, and Marcus buttoned his cashmere coat. From somewhere in the distance came the two-tone high-low siren of a police car.

"And all the groups are like this?" Ian asked. "Ten to fifteen people? Mostly students?"

"Mostly students, yes. Change has often begun with mostly students. The size of group varies. We're the Berlin group and we're the largest in the world. That's because we were the first to organize, and we helped the others recruit and develop their own chapters. But our chapter's size is closer to fifty people. You just met a few of them. Most are still in Berlin."

"Why are these in Prague?"

"I'll show you tonight."

It made surprising sense that at some point a group like this should develop from the same youthful, rebellious passions that had been at or near the heart of every revolutionary change throughout history. Still, he could scarcely believe his luck, after a youth spent troublemaking and adventuring in Kansas, to have stumbled onto what could be the great revolution of his generation. A people's revolution against global criminal enterprise. His heart raced with excitement.

"And Dr. Hampdenstein helped put all this together," Ian said. "Incredible."

"He's one of the world's top economic professors, at one of the world's top universities. Lots of brilliant, ambitious students come here from all over the world. Some come for a degree, some for a semester abroad, some for one of the many global seminars. And the professor travels frequently as a guest lecturer to other top schools. Many of the places he's been, he's found committed students eager to start their own local chapter of the White Rose."

"How long has this been going on?"

"I was one of the first few he recruited," Marcus said proudly. "That was five years ago."

They left Nový Svět through a maze of uneven cobblestone streets centuries old, under a stone archway into Staré Město, the oldest part of the city. Ian felt a camaraderie with Marcus that he hadn't felt since chasing tornadoes in Kansas with his brother. But that was nothing more than a thrill with the excuse of capturing some interesting film footage. This was different. Now he was trying to help save the world.

"You understand this could be dangerous?" Marcus said.

"I've been in worse."

They went up a stairway to a large pedestrian bridge of ancient stones. Medieval gargoyles lit by antique glass lamps lined the parapets, staring out of the fog like phantoms. Ian loved everything about this world that Marcus was taking him into, though he felt a lingering sense of foreboding. He knew that whatever Marcus had in mind for him, whatever the details of the White Rose's activities, he was ultimately being led into a world of darkness. Beneath all this beauty and history and the flocks of gawking tourists was an underworld of crime.

They had walked over a mile and were now beyond the castles and bridges and historic beauty that most visitors thought of as Prague. There were no more cafés or museums or concert halls. Marcus stopped near a large wooden doorway. Beyond this street lay furrowed fields and, in the distance, what looked like a very old factory.

Marcus led him inside the doorway, where once again a narrow stone staircase spiraled down into blackness, as if someone had carved little steps into the inner wall of a deep well. As he felt his way down the uneven steps, he held out one hand to brush against the cold stones of the wall, while his other hand slid down the iron rail bolted to the steps. At the bottom, Ian could see the dim red glow of an open doorway.

Entering, he found a dark tavern perhaps a quarter the size of a basketball court, packed with at least thirty pale-faced, black-clad Goths. Small wooden tables lined the stone walls and floors.

Marcus squeezed Ian's shoulder and said, "You saw that factory outside?"

"Across the field?"

"Yes. There's something there I need to show you."

"Well, then, let's go."

"No, it's not time yet. We got here too early." He looked at his watch. "It won't really start for at least another thirty minutes."

"What won't start?"

"Let's get a drink," Marcus said, pulling him toward the bar. "Professor Hampdenstein told me a little about your work at the university. I know you have an approach to fighting organized crime through economics—an approach never attempted before. The White Rose can help you develop and test those ideas. And in return, you can help us take the White Rose to the next level. We both want the same thing. We can help each other fight organized crime." Marcus paused. "How long does it take to implement your ideas and bankrupt a cartel?"

"It depends," Ian said. "If it works, two to four years."

They found a gap in the crowd at the edge of the bar. A thin bartender with long jet-black hair was pouring shots of tequila. Her dark, sleeveless shirt exposed bare white arms with spiraling tattoos. Marcus caught her eye and ordered two vodka shots and two Denkle beers.

"The professor said that you think, with the right simulation, it could be tested in a few months," Marcus said after the bartender moved down the line of patrons, collecting more drink orders.

"If you picked the right two criminal organizations and were directly involved, you could accelerate the process," Ian said, leaning back on the underground tavern's cold stone wall. "You would have to choose two organizations that already have a history of competition, preferably with some violent encounters—you'd need that underlying animosity and tension. Even then, starting a war between them will be complicated. And starting a war is only the first phase."

"We don't have that much time," Marcus said.

The tavern was already a very live room, with loud ambient chatter bouncing off lots of hard surfaces, but now a Swedish death-metal song spilled from the surrounding speakers. It must be a hit in this part of Europe, because several enthusiastic patrons were screaming out the lyrics. Marcus leaned closer to Ian so they could hear each other over the angry-sounding music.

"If my theorem works, it could change the world," Ian said. "But I need a real case study to prove it to the academic community. Otherwise, they'll just read it with interest and debate its merit and analyze it to death and write discussion papers, but nothing will change."

The bartender set their drinks on the wooden bar top, and Marcus paid her. When she walked back to a cluster of chatty patrons in the far shadows, Marcus said, "You sound like you believe you can get rid of organized crime." He grinned. "I suppose the world needs dreamers." Taking a long drink, he then set his beer down and grabbed the vodka shots, handing one to Ian. "Lucky for you, I like dreamers." He held his oblong shot glass up to the light. *"Prost und trinken."*

"To what?" Ian asked.

"This vodka we drink to forget."

"To forget what?"

"Everything! Our childhoods and first loves and parents' warm care and hopeful teachers and those faithful few friends we all had in our youth."

"You think I can't handle it—this world of darkness and crime?" Ian asked. "You think that just because I've studied it in books I can't handle seeing the real, ugly thing."

"Trust me," Marcus said, still holding his drink up. "It's better if we pretend to forget everything before going forward."

"I don't *want* to pretend to forget."

"Ian, you may not realize it yet, but if you continue with me on this path, you won't be the same person an hour from now that you are in this moment. You need to understand this before we go any further."

Ian looked at the shot of vodka in his hand and thought about Kansas and all his family and friends still there. For the first time since leaving the States, he felt homesick. The pain and emptiness came upon him as quickly and stealthily as a nightmare can intrude on the sleeping. He wanted the feeling to go away. Marcus was right: he didn't want to think of home. Not here. Not while journeying into the darkness to do what he felt he was born to do.

He clinked his glass against Marcus's. "All right," he said. "To forgetting everything." He tipped back the shot and felt it burn his throat. His eyes watered, and his heart felt strong. He pounded the bar top twice and looked at Marcus with a sense of liberation.

Marcus finished his shot and grabbed Ian by the arm. "Now that we're free, I can show you the factory."

They left their beers, leaving the underground bar for the moonlit shadows of Prague's outskirts above.

\*    \*    \*

"Stay low and be quiet," Marcus whispered. They were hunched over like monkeys, with their hands touching the ground as they moved up a grassy slope. The dim lights of the factory created a hazy illumination rimming the top of the final rise in front of them. The grass was wet and cold. The whole world was cold.

"What do they make in this factory?" Ian asked.

"Sh-h-h! Just keep following me. And for God's sake, stay close!"

"What about security?"

"Not out here," Marcus said. "They own enough police and politicians to protect themselves. They have guards near the traffic routes. They also have security around the sensitive areas of the factory. We're safe here, but we can't go any closer."

They stopped at the edge of the final hill, still a hundred yards from the grounds below. Down at the large square gravel parking lot at the back of the factory, Ian could see seven pearl white limousines lined up. No people were in sight.

"What's going on in there?" he asked.

"Just wait for it. You'll see."

"A meeting?"

Marcus looked at him with a volatile, almost hateful gaze. "Look, I promise you again, you're about to see something you will wish you could burn from your memory."

Six pairs of headlights were moving toward the factory. The vehicles pulled through the open gate, and maybe two dozen men got out. Ten men came out a sliding steel door of the factory and met them.

"It's a meeting, all right," Ian said. "Managers from the various business units of one organization? I can't tell. Maybe it's a multicartel meeting of regional bosses from different outfits."

"That's not what this is . . . Just watch."

Another door opened, for a brief moment revealing the silhouettes of several people inside the factory. Three of the men by the car were laughing and motioning toward the door. Then out of the shadows stumbled three women in matching gray sweatpants and white T-shirts. They should be freezing in the cool night air, but their lowered heads and shuffling gait told Ian their senses were numbed.

"What is this?" Ian whispered.

Marcus remained silent as one of the men moved toward the nearest woman and ripped off her T-shirt. Her pale skin and large breasts were briefly visible until she fell to the dirt. He stood above her, waving her torn shirt like a victory flag and laughing to the other men.

"Oh, my God," Ian said. "Is that what this is? Please tell me that's not what this is."

"I told you I would show you the greatest crime being committed in the world today."

"No . . . not this," Ian said. His anger was boiling inside him. "I could have handled almost anything, but not that." His gaze fell to the dark, wet grass between his hands. "I can't watch. Please tell me it's not about this."

"I told you the factory doesn't make anything. It's just one of the places they keep their girls. The men aren't mafia bosses or capos here for a meeting; they're just customers."

"We have to stop them. We need to call the Prague police."

"That won't solve anything. You've studied organized crime. You know that law enforcement and political corruption is a large expense item on criminal operations' income statements. Even if the police do come, it won't fix the problem. We have something bigger in mind—something that could help stop these crimes. But if we tried to do anything tonight, we would only be jeopardizing our future plans."

A deep pain burned in Ian's chest. The girls looked weak and disoriented, dressed in rags that had been torn to look skimpy. Tears filled his eyes. "We have to do something," he said.

"We *are* doing something."

"What?"

"We're watching. And we're learning."

"We're just going to sit here as those men rape those girls!" Ian gasped.

"That's exactly what we're going to do." Marcus laid a hand on his shoulder. "Look, do you think this is the first time those girls have been raped? Huh? Do you think they'll even remember any of this tomorrow morning? They're so drugged up, they don't remember their own names. And you think these are the only girls those bastards are doing it to? Trying to stop them tonight won't do a damned thing to stop this from happening all across the world."

"You're crazy."

"No. Not crazy. I told you, we've been planning a big operation."

"Why'd you bring me here?"

Marcus sat cross-legged next to Ian. "We want to combine our plan with the plan you outlined in your dissertation. That's why the professor arranged for us to meet: your economic theories can be combined with what the White Rose is planning, and together we could really hurt organized crime."

"The professor believes this?" Trying to imagine what those girls went through every night was too much for him.

"Yes," Marcus said. "But the question is, what exactly would you like the White Rose to do to help you prove your theories?"

"You don't want to know."

"Trust me," Marcus said. "We're willing to consider anything, no matter how unorthodox."

In a stony voice, Ian said, "I want to start a war between the Geryon Mafia and the Malacoda gang. A war that will bring a revolution."

# 2

*April 15 (2 months later), Kansas City, Missouri*

JAMES LAWRENCE FELT a sudden surge of frustration and annoyance. "What do you mean, '*missing*'?"

He had stopped being concerned about his brother's activities years ago, and looking back at the party in full swing behind him, he just wanted to get back to his well-deserved celebration for making it through tax season.

"No one knows where he is," his mother said through the phone. "Not the university, not the U.S. consulate, not the German police . . . no one."

He set his beer bottle on the wrought-iron table and rubbed his forehead. His mother had a knack for choosing the worst times to call. Here he was, trying to enjoy the after-busy-season party the firm threw annually after the last client tax return went out the door. The firm had rented the Have a Nice Day Café bar in Kansas City's Westport district, and already the place looked like a small Mardi Gras festival. While all the other tax accountants were drinking and laughing inside, James stood out on a balcony in the cold spring night air, listening to his ever-fretful mother rant on and on about the latest trouble that his younger brother may or may not be in.

"Mom, listen, nothing's happened to Ian. He always does this. You know how he is: he runs off to God knows where, doing God knows what, without telling anyone. Just give him a week. He'll turn up; he always does."

"No, James, you listen to me!" His mother's voice had taken on a piercing intensity that he couldn't dismiss. "This isn't like before. He's in a foreign county. We have no way to get in touch with him, and who knows what might have happened to him over there!"

"Aw, Mom, he's twenty-four years old."

"He's still your little brother!"

James sighed, realizing that there was only one way to calm her down. "Mom, I'm in the middle of my firm's after-busy-season party. What is it you want me to do?"

"I want you to come home. We need your help *here*. Your father and I have been trying to talk with the exchange program coordinator at K-State, but we're not getting any answers that help us."

"I can't believe this!" James groaned, tensing his grip on the phone. "I've been working myself to death for the past three months while Ian's been off screwing around in Europe, and now *I* have to drop everything just because he's run off on a road trip without telling anyone. This is *unbelievable.*"

"James, please. We don't know what to do. He may need your help!"

He closed his eyes. He couldn't refuse his mother's request, no matter how overwrought she was. "Okay," he said. "Fine. I can drive to Manhattan tomorrow."

"Can't you come tonight?"

"Mom, I'm at a party, and I've been drinking." He was stalling. "It's a two-hour drive—you really want me to try it tonight? I can be there early in the morning. Then I can meet with the coordinator at K-State. We'll get this figured out, okay? Everything'll be fine."

"Your father and I have tried talking to the coordinator, but he's not concerned—says American students skip classes to travel around Europe all the time when studying abroad."

"I agree with him," James said. "I'm telling you, Ian probably just went skiing in the Alps with some French girl he met at a party in Berlin. You know how . . . *random* he is."

"We think you need to go to Germany, to make sure he's okay."

"*What?* Mom, there's no way!"

"James, please! We don't know what else to do! You know your father can't travel, and I have to stay here to take care of him."

James felt sick and frustrated. "But *Germany?* This can't be that serious!"

"Ian sent me an e-mail," she whispered through the phone, as if unburdening herself of some great secret.

"What! When?"

"Two weeks ago."

"Two weeks? But you said he's been missing for a week."

"Oh, James, you have to read it. You have to understand. Here, I'll send it to your phone. Just hold on."

James took a long swig from his wheat beer. An old Motown song was blaring from inside. He tried to think about the volume of tax returns that he and his coworkers had prepared over the past three months for their seemingly endless list of clients. The hours had been brutal—between seventy and eighty billable hours a week—and it had been mandatory to work on Saturdays for more weekends than he could remember. Oddly, though, James had actually enjoyed busy season. He was well into his third year out of college, and happy to be settling into the steady routine of a long-term career in public accounting. The more work he had on his desk, the more secure he felt, the more constant seemed the pulse of his job, and the more satisfied he felt with his professional life. And his professional life was what he lived for.

It was a far cry from his and Ian's rebellious high school days. They had been inseparable daredevils, endlessly seeking one thrill after another. It was always about another party lived, another harmless crime gotten away with, another adventure survived. But so much had changed since those heady high school days. Even though Ian had stayed a free spirit—as they both had once been—James had found comfort in the safety and security of a steady, reliable career. Public accounting had seemed the perfect solution at the time. And it would still feel like the right choice if not for the image of Ian living the free, adventurous life that he himself had given up long ago. Ever since Jessica's death, there seemed to be a deep and growing chasm between them as their lives had gradually drifted apart.

The flood of memories now brought James the nostalgic pain he had hoped to avoid. He hadn't wanted to be reminded of all they had lost.

The message hit his phone, and he opened Ian's e-mail:

*My time in Germany has always been an adventure, but recently it's more than that. Much more!*

*I want to tell you everything, but I'm afraid you wouldn't understand unless you saw what I've seen. There is so much happening that people don't know about! Or so much that they choose not to see. We've all heard stories, but until you see it with your own eyes it doesn't feel real. But it is real! It's terribly real!!! And I've finally discovered*

*my purpose for coming to Germany. This
never could have happened in Kansas!*

*I feel guilty about it, but I can't tell you
how exciting it is to have such a sense of
purpose. I know exactly what I have to do.
You see, it will all be in my dissertation. I
will reveal everything, expose everything,
and all through an academic paper! It will
change the way the entire world looks at
business and finance and trade. I will open
their eyes to what's happening. The whole
world will see, and they will never again
be able to look away. And then, finally,
things will change forever!!!"*

The e-mail ended abruptly, as if Ian had sent it on the spur of
the moment. But now it was the last communication anyone in
the family had from him, so James could see why their mother
hung on its every word.

"What do you think it means?" she asked.

"I don't know," he said into the cell phone, now on speaker.
"Ian's smart as hell, but he's always been a little crazy. It's hard
to say."

What he didn't tell her was that the message's tone reminded
him of the last time he and Ian had gone storm chasing: an
adrenaline-fueled pastime they had pursued together many times
during high school. They had been tracking an F4 tornado
approaching Dodge City when the giant funnel suddenly veered
from a steady path, straight toward the highway they were racing
on. James had screamed for Ian to turn back, but Ian had turned
to him with a crazy look in his eyes and yelled, "No! I've got
this motherfucker!" The enormous funnel had gotten within two
hundred yards of them, roaring like a thousand freight trains,

before turning back onto its original path at the last moment. And as it pulled away from the road, James would never forget the sound of his brother slapping the steering wheel and laughing like a madman.

Staring at the e-mail, he could only imagine what new danger his adventurous, daredevil brother may have found at the edge of Eastern Europe. But one thing he did know: when Ian went looking for trouble he had a knack for finding it. James didn't know what his brother had been up to for the past few months, but he was starting to get a bad feeling. Maybe their mother was right after all: maybe something bad really had happened to Ian.

The day the tornado turned away from them, Ian had thought they somehow won, as if anything could win against an F4 twister. But James believed it was because God had shown mercy on them at the last second. It had been a long time since he felt that his life was saved for a reason. Perhaps Ian really had found his purpose in Germany. And maybe now it really was James's purpose to save him from whatever trouble he may have gotten himself into. Perhaps James's entire life, since that day the nightmare funnel cloud passed them by outside Dodge City, had been one long, meaningless lingering until this moment, when he must follow his reckless brother toward unknown dangers in a foreign land.

His mother's words echoed in his mind: *He's still your little brother . . . He may need your help!* He pursed his lips and nodded as if giving a delayed answer to her comments. Ending the call, he killed the rest of his beer, pitched the bottle in the trash can, and headed down the balcony steps toward the alley, without a word to anyone at the party roaring inside. And for the first time in years, James felt uneasy about what the future held.

# 3

────────※────────

*International airspace, North Atlantic*

THE HUM OF the Boeing 757-200's jet engines filled the cabin with ambient delta waves that had already soothed the other passengers around James to sleep. He leaned his forehead against the cool Plexiglas window, looking at the stars above the dark and quiet world below. Occasionally, he would spot a cluster of lights thirty thousand feet below—a solitary freighter or oil tanker plying between continents across the black ocean.

He had left Chicago four hours ago and was now probably halfway to Amsterdam. This was the longest flight of his life, and he felt a little nervous being outside the United States for the first time.

With tax season over, it had been easy enough to get a week or two off to go chasing after Ian. But he hadn't wanted to take off any time at all. He liked his life in Kansas City, liked his steady, peaceful routine of jogging around Mill Creek Park each morning before getting to work on the Plaza at seven sharp. He enjoyed his thirty-minute lunches, sitting outside on the white stone terrace overlooking the giant fountain with its meadowlarks and squabbling blue jays. There was always a sense of achievement when he left work after everyone else, with the entire evening before him to watch his weekly shows, rent a newly released movie, or read. He loved the simplicity and order of his routines, so it was with some trepidation and frustration that he had left his comfy life in Kansas City for a journey into the unknown.

In his inside jacket pocket, next to his own passport, he had Ian's duplicate passport. Duplicates were sometimes issued to process long-term student visas, and their mom had gotten Ian's in the mail just before he vanished, so she had sent it with James in case Ian should need it to get back home.

Turning away from the window, he reached up to flick on the reading light, pulled out his bag, and began reading the pages his mom had printed for him before he left. They were the first three of the four e-mails Ian had sent their parents, and maybe they held some clue to what had happened to his brother in Germany.

He read the first e-mail:

*Mom and Dad,*

*Life here is good. Sorry it took me so long to email. It's been interesting getting used to life in Germany. The language is hard to learn, but I'm making progress. Many Germans under the age of thirty know English as a second language, which helps. Those who are older learned Russian instead.*

*I'm the only American at the university, which is exactly what I had hoped for. One of my professors was last year's runner-up for the Nobel Prize in Economics! I plan to go to Berlin this weekend. I've read that Berliners, due to the city's unique past, are very liberal. Some of the parks even have sections reserved for nude sunbathing. You've gotta love Europe!*

*I'm always trying to tell the other students about how great college football is, but they still prefer soccer. Next week I'm taking a day trip to Dresden with some other students to visit a castle just outside the city. I've never been to a castle before! And a few days ago, we visited a German brewery in the countryside for my strategic management course. We were there to study the production and distribution operations of the business, but we also found time to sample the different beers and got a bit drunk.*

*Well, I need to run. I'm meeting some students at a Biergarten for a few drinks before we head to a club in the city center. Looks like it could be another fun night. Carpe diem, right!*

*Cheers,*
*Ian*

James smiled, hearing Ian's voice in his head as he read the e-mail. He could only imagine how much fun his brother must be having. He sometimes wondered if he had made a mistake in his own life by being so cautious and calculating. His brother just seemed to float through life with such ease, never making sacrifices for the future, always having fun. His own life could easily have followed a similar path if he had made different decisions.

He read the next e-mail:

*Mom and Dad,*

*Sorry it's been so long since I wrote. I've just completed my first week of the "Transitional Economies" course. Tomorrow I'm visiting Prague with a new friend I met at a dinner party thrown by one of my professors. There's a group of people that have a pretty different way of looking at the world. I'm looking forward to spending more time with them, and they promised they would show me a side of Prague that would "open my eyes." The professor is helping me iron out a fairly ambitious concept for my dissertation, and he thought some of the folks in this group could help my research.*

*The professor also said it would be a good city to visit while considering my dissertation. He really likes my idea and thinks it has the potential to be one of the most controversial and important academic papers in years. And he's one of the most brilliant and connected professors I've ever known.*

*Anyway, I need to get back to finishing this case study. Hope everything is going well back in Kansas.*

*Cheers,*
*Ian*

Typical Ian: he had found a way to continue putting off a career by hiding in an exchange program that seemed more of an extended vacation than a serious academic effort. But something bothered James: the slight change in focus during the message. There was still the sense of adventure and discovery, but he couldn't help noticing Ian's infatuation with the professor who had thrown the dinner party, and the mysterious group of people he was going to see in Prague.

He flipped to the final e-mail:

*Mom and Dad,*

*The world is a dark place. Not for everyone, of course, but certainly for too many people. And in Prague I saw the darkest of nights that I could have imagined. Not for me but for others: a forgotten group of victims.*

*Now I know exactly what I have to focus on for my dissertation. It will be like no academic paper ever written. I will research its dire themes firsthand—not in the libraries of the world but in the very streets and alleys of a sinister world that has hidden in the shadows for too long. I have it within my power to do something no one has ever done before.*

*The people I met in Prague are the most passionate and honorable I've known. The things they're trying to do are revolutionary. I feel the same way Thomas Jefferson must have felt when attending the Continental Congress. My professor was right: I have a unique opportunity to help them achieve what they've been struggling for all these years. And I realize, this is what I've been searching for my entire life. Everything I've ever done has been specifically designed by fate to prepare me for this moment. I can't tell you any more right now, but some day I'll be able to tell you everything. And I promise that you will be proud of everything I'm about to do.*

*Love,*
*Ian*

Proud of *what*? James wondered. What the hell was Ian up to? He closed his eyes and thought about the e-mail. It was the next level, evolving from the second message but not quite as excited and passionate as the one their parents got right before Ian disappeared. There was a pattern here. Each message seemed to progress toward the unknown theme of Ian's dissertation. Perhaps the doctoral research could shed light on his disappearance. Once James arrived in Leipzig he would need to figure out what this mysterious academic paper was all about. He knew his brother well enough to know that he would risk everything on something he was excited about. And James had never seen him more excited than he seemed to be in those messages. Whatever Ian's plans had been, something must have gone seriously wrong.

James turned out his reading light. All traces of distant ship lights on the black ocean below had vanished. It was as if he were traveling across an undefined no-man's-land, being pulled toward a dark world that now beckoned him only a week after it took his brother.

# 4

———————•❋•———————

*November 9, 1989, West Berlin*

THOMAS HENZOLLERN SAT in the little café, staring
across the wooden table at the only woman he had ever
loved. He smiled as he watched Maria Köpf raise her coffee cup
to her lips. But his smile met only her worried glance over the
rim of the cup.

He leaned back in his chair and scanned the faces at the two
nearest tables. Satisfied that this conversation would remain
private, he said in German, "This week's demonstration will be
twice as large as last week's." He spoke fast, revealing his
excitement. They were both studying law at the Humboldt-
Universität zu Berlin and had been dating ever since being paired
up for a corporate liabilities case study a year ago. Thomas's
strong jaw, piercing eyes, and easy charm had made him a
natural womanizer. But his romantic conquests were behind him
ever since the night he first stayed with Maria.

Maria was quite different from Thomas. She was naturally
shy, and her smooth, beautiful skin glowed with a tan
complexion uncommon in the often-overcast climate of central

Europe. Perhaps there was some Italian or Turkish blood in her ancestry, Thomas thought.

"The resistance . . . it's growing so fast," she replied quietly.

But he could tell she was distracted by something else. For over two months, they had been involved in organizing peaceful protests against the Communist regime. Two months of hard work with energetic, idealistic student activists. The activities had soon spread from overt protest in West Berlin to covert aid to trapped protesters in Leipzig and other East German cities. Both Thomas and Maria believed it was the great cause of their generation. However, Thomas now found himself looking with concern at Maria. Her lips trembled.

"What is it?" he asked.

"Sorry?" She set her coffee down and brushed back her bangs. Her deep, brown eyes looked up and studied him with a vulnerability he had never seen in her.

He pushed his beer aside and put his hand over hers. "What's bothering you? What is it? Tell me."

Perhaps it was the frank insistence in his voice that gave her the strength to answer.

"I'm pregnant."

Thomas's eyes widened as his mind scrambled to reclassify and reorganize his entire life. Everything changed for him in that one moment. In an eyeblink, his ambitious, self-centered life had grown larger than himself. He was going to be a father.

"How long have you known?" he asked, now looking at her with that same quivering passion he had felt the first time they were together. He loved her now more than ever. He would marry her, and their unborn child would be the first of many. With any other woman in the world, he would have been terrified at the news. But not with Maria.

"A week," she said quietly.

"A *week*? Darling, you shouldn't have waited to tell me. My God, you should never live through anything like that without telling me."

"Thomas, what will we do?" she asked, her voice breaking.

"It will be all right," he said. "I love you. We will be married. The child will make us a family. It will be beautiful and smart and strong."

"A family?" she said with a look of wonder that betrayed how young they both were. "Beautiful and smart," she whispered.

"And strong," he said. "We could name him Hans, after his grandfather."

"Oh, a boy, is it?" she replied, grinning. "And you're so sure because . . . ?"

He laughed. "All right. I suppose it is possible."

She grabbed his hand. "If it's a girl, we should name her Hanna so that it is still inspired by her grandfather's name."

"Hanna," he said. "She would be as beautiful as you and as much trouble as I. Yes, 'Hanna' would be perfect if it's a girl. Beautiful Hanna."

He felt that something was wrong even before he noticed the frightened look from Maria. She was looking over his shoulder at the street behind him. Half the café had jolted upright and was looking in that direction, the way a herd of antelope stiffens at the smell of a predator. He rotated in his chair, twisting to look behind him, and saw two people run past the café, their shoes clomping rapidly on the cobblestone street. A few seconds later, another half-dozen people ran past as if pursuing the first two. Mumbling began to rise from the other patrons of the café. Seeing another group rush past, Thomas jumped to his feet, knocking over his chair. Everyone in the café was now startled to their feet as a constant flow of people rushed past, always in the same direction.

THE PRICE OF INNOCENCE

Thomas turned to Maria. "Come on," he said, grabbing her hand. They moved toward the street and were shocked to find even more people rushing out of pubs and side streets, all running into this great river of human beings flowing toward some unseen destination. Before they knew what they were doing, Thomas and Maria were running in the group. He held her hand to keep her close as he leaned into a man and yelled, "What's going on?"

"It's over!" the man yelled back with excitement.

"What's over?!" Thomas yelled, trying to keep up without losing Maria.

"The wall! It's opened! People are coming through! It's over! They're letting people out!"

"*What!* How?" But Thomas was too excited to care about the answer.

And the man didn't answer but ran on ahead with the crowd until Thomas couldn't keep up with him without losing Maria. It was chaos.

"Come on!" he yelled to her.

On they ran with the growing mob, through the city park. They were nearly exhausted as they emerged from the line of trees and saw the breathtaking view behind the towering Brandenburg Gate. It stood at the midpoint of the eighty-seven-mile Berlin Wall, which had split the city in two for nearly three decades and currently held over a million East Berliners prisoner. Underneath the gate, dozens of weathered Trabants were queued up and driving into West Berlin for the first time. Windows were down and horns were honking as people from the mobs leaned in to touch the extended hands of the people inside the cars, welcoming them with jubilation. Strangers greeted strangers with an inexplicable bond of joyous reunion that seemed the very personification of humanity's potential. Television cameras from worldwide news correspondents were already filming every image they could capture, realizing that this was a defining moment in the history of the world.

Thomas pulled Maria away from the street, and they rushed along the park's pathway toward the growing cluster of people crowding against the wall next to the gate. "They did it!" he yelled back at her, thrilled at the culmination of all the protests they had helped organize over the past few months. "I can't believe it! Can it really be over?"

When they reached the wall, Thomas turned to Maria, kissed her on the lips, then bent down to kiss her stomach. "It's a new world now! It will be a new Germany!"

As she smiled back at him he felt something hard hit his shoulder. He turned to find a man slapping him on the back. "Help me up!" he said, pointing toward the ridge of the wall. Thomas leaned into the cold concrete of the wall and interlaced his fingers to make a foothold for the stranger. "Thank you, brother," the man said as he put one foot into Thomas's hands and slid halfway up the wall. Putting the other foot on Thomas's shoulder, he pulled himself up onto the wall, then rolled onto his side and extended his arm down toward Thomas. "Come on, brother! Climb!"

Thomas's eyes widened with excitement. Grinning, he reached up and grabbed the hand stretching down to him. Two other men moved in and helped lift him into the air. His elbows were soon stretching over the top of the wall, pressing hard to mantel him up, while the stranger pulled up on the back of his jacket. Laughing together, the two men stood alone on the wall while countless others scrambled up to join them.

He stared out at the amazing scene. On the west side of the wall, the crowd had grown as hordes of West Berliners rushed toward it. As far as the eye could see, arms were waving and reaching up from the masses that swarmed toward the Berlin Wall, eager to bind their great city back together again. Thomas looked down the top of the wall, which snaked off into a vanishing point somewhere in the distance. He couldn't believe it was over. Tears of joy filled his eyes as he realized what it meant to be standing here after all the protests, all the suppression, all the courageous people who had given their lives trying to surmount the barrier he now stood on. What they would have given to see this sight! The checkpoint towers still stood manned, but the guards and riflemen merely watched the scene in baffled silence. On the east side of the wall, he could see the stark no-man's-land stretching like a dead river of torched earth. For so long a ground of death and despair, it now seemed no more than the last vestige of a regime that could no longer survive in Europe.

Somewhere in the crowd, an impromptu orchestra began playing a modified version of Beethoven's Ninth Symphony. As the music carried over the crowd, someone below Thomas's perch swung a sledgehammer at the base of the wall, chipping off a small piece of concrete. When the man looked up and met his eyes, Thomas felt consumed by the excitement. He pointed at the man, then at the hammer, and lay flat on the wall to reach the upheld hammer.

Grasping it, Thomas stood up again on the wall and held the sledgehammer high in the air. All in the crowd who could see him began to cheer, and the television cameras and photographers quickly turned their attention to him. He pumped the hammer a few times to soak up everyone's excitement, then—after giving notice to the people below him to move—he swung downward with all his might, knocking off a large chunk. Everyone screamed with jubilation. The stranger next to him laughed with uncontained, delirious joy.

Looking down, Thomas found Maria in the crowd, watching him. He beamed a smile at her, then turned back and continued banging away, to the roaring delight of the crowd, as television cameras broadcast the scene of freedom to the entire world.

\*   \*   \*

Twenty-five years after the fall of the Berlin Wall, while James Lawrence was on an airplane somewhere over the Atlantic, the forty-eight-year-old German senator Thomas Henzollern got out of bed and walked across the spacious floor of his Berlin penthouse. As he poured an inch of scotch into a tumbler at the side kitchenette, he heard a woman moan beneath the bedcovers. Returning to the bedroom, he saw that the woman had moved from the bed to his desk, covering her naked body with a spare bathrobe. He sat at the foot of the bed and watched her as he took a drink.

"Look how young you are here," the woman said, peering at the picture that showed him standing on the Berlin Wall with a raised sledgehammer.

He mumbled into his glass, "I was twenty-three and in my last year of law school."

"*Ages* ago!" she laughed. "So this was the famous moment when you made world news."

"The news wasn't about me. It was about the Wall; it was about Germany. It was about the beginning of the end for Communist rule in Eastern Europe. I was insignificant compared to these things."

"But you were the image they grabbed on to. One of the first iconic pictures of that transition to freedom. That's why you were able to get elected to the new Senate at such a young age. Weren't you the youngest ever elected?"

He smiled. "As you said, that was ages ago."

The woman looked at another picture on the desk. It was also of Thomas, looking about the same age as in the first picture—this time smiling as he held a young woman close to him in an impulsive pose for the camera. The young woman looked elated and was hugging him while turning her head toward the camera. A mountain town festival was frozen in the background.

"This was your wife?" she asked him.

"Yes."

"So tragic what happened to her."

"Yes," Thomas said, looking out the window with a thousand-mile stare "Yes, it is." He closed his eyes and listened for any sound he could latch on to. When he heard nothing but the woman's faint rustling in the chair, he took another drink of scotch.

"And this is your daughter?" the woman asked, now looking at a picture of a teenage girl with long, wavy blond hair, sitting astride a horse with green mountains in the background.

"Yes. That's Hanna."

"Your only child?"

"Yes, of course."

"She's very beautiful, like her mother."

"Yes, she is. Beautiful Hanna." He took another drink.

"Does she live in Berlin?"

"She's at university in Leipzig." He stood and walked toward the balcony, drawn by the city lights.

"Do you see her often?"

But before Thomas could answer, the phone on the desk rang. The woman glanced at him as if asking permission to answer it. He moved toward the phone. As one of the senior ranking senators in the German Parliament, he had received his share of late-night phone calls. They seldom bore good news.

"Herr Henzollern!" Thomas's chief of staff spoke frantically through the phone.

"*Ja,* what is it, Joseph?"

"It's the chancellor, sir! He's had a heart attack!"

"What!" Thomas said, his shoulders rising as his body tensed. The woman had moved away from him, back toward the bed, noticeably concerned.

"Yes sir. He was rushed immediately to Berlin Hospital. He's alive, but his condition is weak. They don't expect him to live through the night. But he is awake, and he's asking for *you*."

Thomas closed his eyes as his mind tried to process the dire news of the chancellor's health, and the terrible ripples that would spread across Germany should their great leader die.

"I'll be there at once," Thomas said.

"Sir, I've had a car sent to you. It will be there in five minutes."

"Thank you, Joseph. Please meet me at the hospital. This could be one of the darkest nights for Germany in decades. We need to prepare for the worst."

# 5

THOMAS'S ASSISTANT GUIDED him through the Berlin Hospital's emergency ward, passing the doorways of patients fighting some of the most difficult battles of their lives. Many people couldn't truly understand or appreciate these patients' struggles until the day came when they, too, must fight that battle. But Thomas's memories allowed him to understand the pain and the courage and the suffering only too well. Through the prolonged surgery after complications during Hanna's childbirth, his Maria had suffered for two hours before dying. And although she had never set eyes on her baby Hanna, Thomas had felt the pain for her. And as he now walked through the hospital, he was reminded once again of all the pain that he had taken on since his wife's death.

He arrived at a closed door guarded by two burly men in suits. They glanced briefly at him and waved him through the door.

Stepping into the small hospital room, he found himself alone with the chancellor. Thomas looked at the IV tubes connected to fluid bags hanging on a chromed frame, then looked down at the chancellor's old, bearded face. Although the man was beloved by all Germany, Thomas would always be able to look past the fame and prestige and power and see the younger man his friend had been twenty-five years ago, when they worked together during the resistance against the Communist regime that had blighted half their country after the war.

Long before Volker Schlarmann was elected chancellor of a reunified Germany, he had been district leader of the White Rose anticommunist party's rebel operations in West Berlin. And it was through the White Rose that Thomas had first met and worked with him. Now most traces of those days were gone. The first to go had been Maria. And now, a quarter century later, the only other remaining survivor from their group of impassioned young rebels was on the verge of death. Soon Thomas would be the only one left of their old revolutionary group.

"Thomas," the chancellor said in a croaking whisper.

"Yes, I'm here," he said.

"Thomas, it's up to you now. You must finish it for me."

"Finish what?" he asked, wondering if perhaps the man was confused from the medications.

"The journey. You are one of the few who can understand. They're out there now, trying to find the solution to *the crime.* But they will need your help."

"Who needs my help?"

"The White Rose!"

Thomas's blood chilled. "What do you speak of?" he asked, trying to confirm the words he thought he had heard.

"The White Rose," the chancellor rasped again.

"But it hasn't existed since the Wall came down."

"It *has* existed," the chancellor replied.

"Impossible! We disbanded it."

A knock at the door interrupted them. Thomas's head jerked toward it as it opened, revealing a slender doctor dressed in white.

"Not now!" the chancellor hissed.

"But, Herr Chancellor, it's time for your—"

*"Eine moment! Bitte!"*

The doctor nodded and stepped back out of the room, and the chancellor stretched out his left arm and grabbed Thomas's wrist. "We've been bringing it back for years, Thomas. But it's not finished. Not yet. I need *you* to finish for me now."

"You said, '*we*'?"

"*Ja,* me and someone else from those days."

"But who? Everyone else is now dead. You and I are the last."

"No, there is still Friedrich."

"Friedrich Hampdenstein? No. I'm certain he is dead."

"No, but he did make himself *seem* dead. After the Gulags, he went into seclusion for years. Not even I knew this at the time. But he resurfaced ten years ago and has been teaching . . . at the university in Leipzig."

"This cannot be true."

"He's a professor of economics, Thomas. He contacted me not long after he began teaching."

"And the White Rose? It exists again because of *him*?"

The door opened again. The doctor was now accompanied by a nurse and a man pushing a tall machine with wheels. "I'm sorry, Herr Chancellor, but this time I must insist on interrupting. We need to transfer you to the IC wards for your scan. It's imperative that we transmit your data to Hamburg for analysis before midnight."

"Agh!" the chancellor groaned. "I'm supposedly the most powerful person in Germany, but one little heart attack, and everyone starts bossing me around."

"It wasn't so little, Chancellor," the doctor replied while marking something on the patient's chart.

"We can't talk anymore," the chancellor said, turning his head back to Thomas. "But find him. He can explain everything.

And he can tell you what you must do in my place. It's as important today as it was back then."

Thomas shook his head. "Whatever it is, it can't possibly be as bad as it was back then."

"In many ways, it's worse. It will make you weep. Now, go, old friend. You'll find him in Leipzig. Everything we fought for back then is once again at risk."

Thomas shook his old friend's hand, perhaps for the last time, and left the room. He walked down the white and green striped hallway. The hospital had a clear yet cold feel, and as he walked down the corridor, thinking of the life and struggles he had borne all those years ago with a group of people who were all but extinct, he found himself avoiding the view through each doorway he walked past. He could hear patients in each room, living, dying, fighting for whatever little victory they could manage. *Friedrich Hampdenstein!* he thought to himself. *How the hell did you manage to stay alive all those years?*

# 6

———✻———

JAMES STEPPED OFF the twin-engine Fokker turboprop
with the twenty other passengers, onto the tarmac of the
modest airport on the outskirts of Leipzig. Through the distant
chain-link fence, a lush green hillside glistened with morning
dew. The two pilots were smoking cigarettes with the blond
flight attendant. A green-uniformed guard with a machine pistol
stood next to the electronic glass doors that opened with a loud
hiss for the passengers. *So this is Germany,* James mused. *Let
the adventure begin.*

Picking up his travel bag from the luggage sitting on the
tarmac, he walked passed the armed guard and handed his
passport through a glass casing to the middle-aged woman in a
dark blue uniform.

*"Willkommen in Deutschland,"* she said. *"Ist Ihr Besuch
geschäftlicher oder privater Natur?"*

"I'm sorry, I don't speak German," James said.

"Welcome to Germany," she said in heavily accented
English. "Is your visit for business or pleasure?"

"I'm visiting my brother at HHL," he said.

"Pleasure, then," she said.

"I hope so."

"How long is your trip in Germany?"

"As short as possible."

"HHL. So your brother is a student here?"

"He's supposed to be, but I'm not sure he knows that," James said bitterly.

She scrunched her eyes and made a funny face at him, then looked down to the crisp new passport and stamped it on the same page but a different square, just below the stamp he had gotten when changing planes in Amsterdam. She slid his passport back under the Plexiglas. "Enjoy your time in Germany, Herr Lawrence. *Auf Wiedersehen.*"

"Off-feet-a-sing," he replied.

*   *   *

James stepped off the train onto one of the five platforms that stretched out from the Hauptbahnhof station toward the tracks he had just traveled on from the Leipzig airport into the city. An enormous roof arched above the area like a dome over a football stadium. Moving through the crowds with his travel bag over his shoulder, he was surprised at the excitement he felt. He had never traveled to a foreign country before, but only now that he had finally reached his destination city would he let himself slow down and marvel at where he was. Leipzig, eastern Germany, formally part of the Soviet bloc, a place that had seen history-changing battles, from Germanic barbarians taking on the Roman legions, to the Napoleonic Wars to the First and Second World Wars.

As he moved off the platform and through one of the many entrances to the station, he was taken aback by the scene he found. The inside opened up into a spacious, bustling atmosphere that seemed right out of an old movie scene shot in New York's Grand Central Station, with only the clothing styles changed. And in that moment, James realized how little his life had prepared him for this journey.

He walked through the main vestibule of the Hauptbahnhof station, through the heavy glass doors, and suddenly he was in the bustling city of Leipzig. A line of green and white Mercedes taxis waited outside the station, and beyond these, more tram lines than he had ever seen. Beyond the tram lines was a busy six-lane street, full of little cars and medium-size commercial trucks.

James grinned at the sight of everything. This complex, smooth-running insanity was almost what he had expected. But as he stepped out onto the wide concrete slab to walk across the six rail tracks to the travel station on the other side, he froze at the electronic scream from a tall, rustic tram that blurred past him, missing him by maybe two feet. Shaken, he stepped back and saw all the other pedestrians, waiting behind the faded yellow line that he had crossed without recognizing it as the demarcation line between living and dying.

After taking a moment to gather his wits and look carefully both ways, he walked on, looking at the tram signs and following their zigzag routes through the city. The number 15 line went to the Sportforum stop, where the university was.

Once aboard the tram, he tried to study the other passengers without making eye contact. As a foreigner in their land, he felt out of place and a little insecure. If he could avoid having to say anything, then maybe they would just think he was one of them.

# 7

———◦◦※◦◦———

THE BLACK RANGE Rover with government plates stopped next to a red Lamborghini and a Rolls-Royce Silver Phantom in the small VIP parking area in Leipzig's old town hall market square. Thomas Henzollern looked out the backseat window at the pedestrians strolling about the square or sitting at outside cafés near the yellow and brown Renaissance building with its famous stair-step gables, stone arcades, and blue clock tower.

"Stay here, please," Thomas said in German to the two bodyguards in front, who had picked him up at the airport twenty minutes ago after his flight from Berlin. "I'll just be in Auerbachs Keller."

"At least take this, sir?" one of the bodyguards said, offering Thomas a black device the size of a lighter. "It's a panic button. Press it and we'll be there in less than thirty seconds."

Thomas took the device, got out of the SUV, and entered an obscure stone doorway across the square. Inside, he went down the stone steps to the cellar that Goethe had made famous two centuries ago with *Faust*.

He walked into the elegant old restaurant feeling both on edge and light-headed, as if in a dream that could, at any moment, turn into a nightmare. He was meeting Friedrich Hampdenstein just twelve hours after learning from the chancellor that the man still lived. He stood looking out on the vast, low-ceilinged dining area with its patterned wood floors and its stone-columned archways dividing it into five sections.

He entered one of the rooms and scanned every face, looking for one he hadn't seen in twenty-five years. Moving through the cavernous room, he stepped around a stone column to find a man with a close-cropped gray beard, sitting at a small table. Unseen, Thomas gazed at the man. He had last seen Friedrich in East Berlin, six months before the wall fell. It was just a few blocks from Friedrichstrasse Checkpoint, where, as a student activist, Thomas had made frequent crossings between West and East Berlin, under the cloak of an internship at a West Berlin law firm doing business with the East.

He had met with Friedrich in their usual park, walking along the gravel paths by the duck pond as they planned another protest. Friedrich was to leave for Leipzig that evening to coordinate the "building peace" protests outside Thomaskirche, the very church where Bach composed music in the last decades of his life. But Friedrich never made it to the rally. No one knew exactly what happened to him, but the rumors were not good: the Stasi, the KGB, or someone else had taken him someplace that people never came back from. Now Thomas found himself staring at a face that still bore many hints of the old Friedrich. And yet, it had changed so much, he couldn't be sure this was his old friend.

"Friedrich?" he asked after walking to the table.

The man raised his head and looked at him. "Thomas," he replied, with gleaming eyes and a smile half-hidden in his gray beard.

Thomas slapped a hand onto the man's shoulder and squeezed it. "We thought you were *dead*," he whispered, tears welling in his eyes.

"I *was* dead, my old friend." He gestured for Thomas to sit.

Thomas shook his head and sat down across from him. "What happened to you?"

Friedrich raised a hand and flagged a passing waitress. "Two Einsiedler Hefeweizens, please," he said to her. After she left, he returned his gaze to Thomas. "This is still your drink, *ja*?"

Thomas half-laughed in amazement. He couldn't believe that after all these years he was sitting down, about to drink Hefeweizen with his old friend.

"It happened the night before the second Leipzig protest," Friedrich said. "It was only a few hours after we met in that little park. The Stasi arrested me before I could leave to catch the train to Leipzig. Apparently, one of our new recruits had been arrested a few days earlier because his neighbor informed on him about some unrelated thing. The recruit then told them everything he knew about me, to save his own neck. He didn't know much, but it was enough to create suspicion." He shook his head. "Back then they could turn almost anyone into their damned informants. Stasi sons of bitches—they were the devil's own police."

"But they couldn't turn *you*," Thomas said. "If they had, you wouldn't have been the one to disappear. It would have been me—and a great many others."

Friedrich nodded, and his eyes grew glossy.

"Why didn't you contact any of us after you were freed?" Thomas asked.

Friedrich looked down at the thousand sparkles of light in the varnished wood table. "I had to travel after I was freed," he said, sounding almost apologetic.

"Why?"

"I don't know. It was just something I needed to do. And I was right. It has helped make me the man I am today . . . A good man?" he shrugged. "A bad man?" He chuckled. "Both, I think. But I hope St. Peter thinks I was more good than bad—or at least good enough."

"I can't imagine what it must have been like for you."

"I learned to stop questioning life years ago. Bad things happen to good people all the time. There is no logic, no universal plan, no natural equilibrium. People's lives are destroyed every day—everybody knows this." His eyebrows rose. "*You* certainly know this. I was sorry to hear about Maria. She was a remarkable woman."

"Thank you," Thomas replied, nodding also at the waitress, who had just brought their beers.

"Your daughter . . . I've seen her at the university, but I've been able to avoid actually meeting her. Would you say she's more like you or more like Maria?"

Thomas smiled. "She looks like her mother, but she acts too much like her father."

"Ah. Unfortunate for you."

"Oh, yes," Thomas replied, and they both laughed and took a drink of beer.

Thomas decided to shift gears. His voice took a certain edge as he said, "The chancellor told me the White Rose has returned."

"Please," Friedrich said. "You must understand. I know what you are thinking, but you're wrong. It's necessary."

"How can it be! Necessary for *what*? There are no more Nazis, no more Stasi! Germany is a free, democratic country. We're the largest economy in Europe. We have the best engineers, some of the best banking institutions. Our citizens are smart and hardworking and are interested only in justice and peace and prosperity for ourselves and the entire world. So I don't understand why the White Rose has returned. What possible need is there for it?"

"It has the power to do things that cannot normally be done."

Thomas's eyes stared past Friedrich to fall in an unfocused gaze on a row of empty tables against the stone wall. "I don't understand how any of this is possible. Why is this happening? And why now?"

"This is the time for change, Thomas. For too long the world has let this crime exist."

"What crime? What the hell are you *talking* about?"

"The chancellor didn't tell you?"

"No."

The features of the old man's face sagged, as if everything in his life had been taken from him in that one moment. But somehow, Thomas read it as the summation of all his friend's darkest memories from an unspeakable past.

"You wouldn't believe what my eyes have seen," Friedrich said. "I've walked past the tombs of kings . . . slept on stone floors of third-world prisons. I've had automatic rifles pointed at my forehead by screaming soldiers a third my age. I've been in more interrogation rooms than I can remember, and there were times I was tortured that I would give all I own to forget. I have not just seen hell—I have lived there."

He paused before continuing. "After the Soviet Union collapsed it took the new government four years to find out that I even existed. At the time of my release, I was in a Siberian prison. Once I was out, I spent years traveling the world, perhaps in some hope of rediscovering my own humanity. I worked for a time on a fishing boat with a crew of ten, drifting all over the Mediterranean in search of bluefin tuna for the Asian black market. I've camped in the deserts of Egypt and climbed mountains in Chile whose peaks rose up into the jet stream. I've ridden a mule down the south ridge of the Grand Canyon and motorcycled from Cape Town to Cairo. After a time, I went back to school and finished the PhD in economics that I started before my imprisonment. I had developed a keen interest in combining the disciplines of game theory with case studies of corruption. My research took me all over the world. I've drunk champagne with corrupt officials in Beijing, and vodka with corrupt businessmen in Moscow. I've been to opium parties in Manhattan penthouses, hosted by corrupt Wall Street bankers with an endless supply of call girls. Early on, I realized that my time in hell had now made me an eternal student of it. I researched hell everywhere on earth that I could find it. And to my surprise, I found it *everywhere!*"

Friedrich stopped speaking and took a long drink of his beer.

"You're talking about worldwide corruption?" Thomas asked. "*This* is why you and the chancellor brought back the White Rose? It's the responsibility of the local authorities, and most local agencies in the world are fairly good at dealing with their own culture's crime and corruption."

"Ah, like Germany?"

"Absolutely, like Germany. Our government is as good as any at safeguarding our domestic security, and we're also as generous as any country when it comes to international conflicts that threaten the lives of defenseless people. Whether it's nuclear proliferation or global environmental concerns or military conflicts in unstable regions of the world, Germany has been a noble and compassionate country ever since the end of World War Two. We have tried to distance ourselves from our Nazi ancestors the way the Americans distance themselves from their ancestors who slaughtered the Native peoples and stole their land."

"Years ago, the chancellor and I met in Frankfurt, just after the Bundestag elected him. I had more research and theories about international criminal organizations than I had ever considered publishing to the world. I didn't just want to heighten the academic debate on crime. I wanted to show that crime can be *stopped*."

Thomas's face was now stony, and his dark eyes ablaze. "These are not the old days," he said. "Germany is at peace. There is no need for a resistance like before. Things are balanced now. The government is working. And all our citizens have their rights and freedoms."

Friedrich sighed. "Would that it were so! But not everyone in Germany has these things. Criminals have made victims of those who had every right to enjoy a peaceful life, before life was taken from them. And until we end this crime, society can never be safe. We *had* to bring back the White Rose. The chancellor and I decided that we had to act."

"But . . . you speak as if you were still in the *resistance*."

"Am I not?"

"But the resistance is over, Friedrich. Look around. We won. The Wall fell, the East was freed, Germany was reunified, and the Soviet Union died. It's over. What you're fighting now is something different."

"No! They are one and the same, Thomas! Can't you see that? One and the same!"

Thomas shook his head. "The chancellor wanted me to contact you. But I don't see how I can become involved in this. The world works differently now. And we're too old to protest in the streets or smuggle information across borders. There are political channels we can use now. I can't get involved in some illegal, underground activist cause as if I were twenty-two again."

"We don't have *time* to do this legally. Every month things are getting worse. My data shows this."

"No," Thomas said. "I don't want to hear any more. I can't help you."

Thomas's phone rang. He held up his finger while answering the call. After listening for a few seconds, he ended the call.

With moist eyes, he looked at Friedrich. "The chancellor has died."

Both men were silent. Finally, Friedrich raised his beer in front of him, holding it over the center of the table without a word. Thomas raised his as well, and their glasses touched in a delicate, somber toast for the great politician who had been an old friend to them both. They knew that every citizen of the country would feel the man's death.

Friedrich was the first to speak again after the silence. "Thomas, please. I can't do this without you. Just let me show you my data. Let me give you all the details of exactly what the White Rose is doing. You said yourself that it was the chancellor's dying wish."

Thomas looked at Friedrich and saw in his eyes the rebellious protestor and fighter he remembered from their days in the resistance. And even though he couldn't answer his old friend immediately, he could already feel the revolutionary fire rising again in him after a long dormancy.

# 8

JAMES STEPPED OFF the tram at the Sportforum stop. He
felt tired and had trouble concentrating. It was the first hint of
jet lag he had felt since jumping seven time zones in one night.
He hoped it would soon pass. Swinging the travel bag over his
shoulder, he walked into the square, toward the familiar three-
story yellow building he had seen in the brochure. So this was
Handelshochschule Leipzig, the mysterious university that had
so captured Ian's imagination.

Entering the building, he went up the stairs to the third floor
and walked down the hallway, past several doors, until he found
the brass nameplate for Dr. Kauker: the university's international
exchange coordinator. He knocked.

"*Ja, willkommen,*" a man's voice boomed from inside.

"Dr. Kauker?" James said, stepping inside. A thin blond man
sat behind a white desk that curved around him like a command
pod in a science fiction movie.

"Awe," the man said, recognizing an American accent. "You
must be Ian Lawrence's brother. Please take a seat. I trust you
had a good flight."

A ten-minute discussion with Kauker accomplished nothing more than a plan to wait until some news about Ian surfaced. But along with his commiserations on the long journey, the man gave James a pass to the university, and access to Ian's student e-mail account. James was glad he had thought to get written authorization from his parents and Dr. Bristle at K-State, asking the HHL administrator for the e-mail access. Herr Kauker said that because Ian's status was considered "unknown but suspected as tourist at large," there was nothing more he could do.

After the talk with Dr. Bristle before leaving Kansas, James hadn't expected much from this meeting, but he needed to establish his presence at the university before exploring any leads about Ian. Ian had gotten involved with a group of people here—the same people he had traveled to Prague with—but James didn't know who they were. There was also Friedrich Hampdenstein, the professor who was advising Ian on a dissertation that seemed to be at the very heart of his disappearance.

James returned to the main floor of the building, which was now full of students. Energetic students zipped through the hall. The chatter sounded mostly German, but he caught a male voice calling out to someone in English. *Ian?* Could he be *here*? Standing on his toes, he looked over the tall crowd in time to see a short-haired brunette reply in German to a male student wearing glasses. *No Ian.* His head began to swirl.

Leaning back against a door, he caught himself, accidentally pushing down on the handle with his hand, and stumbled backward into a classroom. Three students were discussing something around a large table.

"*Können wir Ihnen helfen?*" the gangly, freckled young man asked.

"Uh . . . I'm, um, sorry," James said.

"*Du bist kein Student?*" a pretty girl asked.

"Sorry. I'm, uh, not sure . . ."

"No," said the first student, interrupting James's stuttering. "No, I don't think he is a student here," he said. "You look lost."

"I'm American. I'm looking for my brother, Ian Lawrence. He's an exchange student at the university."

"Ah, Ian," said the girl. "Yes, of course. You look like him."

"Ian?" said the student who hadn't yet spoken, directing his question to the girl.

"*Ja,* the American from Kansas. He brought Jake Daniels to International Festival, remember."

"Ah, of course. Tornado chaser," another said.

James blinked hard, scrunching his face as he struggled to concentrate. The jet lag was kicking in. "I can't find my brother," he said. "I need to speak with Professor Hampdenstein. Where can I find him?"

The girl pursed her lips. "I will show you," she offered.

She led him to the top floor of the university, to an unmarked door in the center of the hallway. Entering, they found an older woman sitting behind a small desk.

"*Wir würden gern Herr Professor Hampdenstein sprechen,*" the girl said. "*Ist er im Büro?*"

"*Nein Herr Professor ist leider nicht da,*" the woman replied.

The girl frowned. "*Das ist der Bruder von Ian Lawrence,*" she said, gesturing toward James. "*Er möchte sich mit Herr Professor treffen.*"

James felt frustrated at his inability to understand them.

"*Der Bruder von Ian Lawrence,*" the woman said, staring at James. "*Einen Moment, bitte.*" She moved the mouse on her computer. "Mr. Lawrence," she said, now switching to English, "the professor is not at the university today, but if you would like, you can find him at his house this evening for a dinner party he is having. Many of the other students will be there. It's a weekly event for him. I can give you the address and time if you wish."

"That would be great. Thank you," James replied. He was annoyed that he couldn't speak with the professor right now, but the woman seemed to be genuinely doing everything she could to help him. He took the note from the assistant and left the room.

"Can you show me where the computer labs are?" he asked the girl once they were back in the hallway. "Herr Krauker gave me access to Ian's university e-mail, and I'm hoping it will have some information about where he is."

She took him back to the first floor and stopped in front of the doorway. "One of the computer labs is in here," she said.

"Thank you," James said. "I appreciate your help. I don't even know your name."

She smiled. "Hanna Henzollern," she said, shaking his hand in mock formality. "I'll be working in the same room you stumbled into earlier, if you need any help. *Tschuss.*"

"*Tschuss,*" he replied, not really knowing what it meant.

He went inside the computer room. It was small, with three tables, each containing four computer workstations with short divider walls. Finding an open station, he clicked on the menu screen and logged into Ian's e-mail account. It took him three tries because some of the letters on the keyboard were in different locations from those on an American keyboard. After logging in, he found sixty-nine unread e-mails.

James blinked slowly, suddenly feeling sleepier than ever. With fading concentration, he stared at the list of e-mails. No matter how badly he wanted to dive in, searching for any hint about his brother's mysterious life for the past three months, he just couldn't keep his eyes open any longer. If he could just close his eyes for five minutes . . . He locked the computer screen and laid his head down on his folded arms on the table. *Just five minutes,* he said to himself.

# 9

JAMES COULD FEEL someone looking at him. Lifting his head off the desk, he stared at the screensaver's looping, hypnotic lines winding out in front of him. It took him a moment to remember where he was: *Germany, Leipzig, Handelshochschule, a computer lab*. Once his memory had caught up with reality, he turned in his chair to look around the room.

"Have a nice nap?" a female voice asked.

Hanna Henzollern was sitting up straight, with one hand folded over the other on her lap. Her face was slender, like a model's, and her blue eyes hinted at an intelligence and strength that captured his attention as much as her long golden hair. He must have been feeling the jet lag when they first met, because he hadn't realized how strikingly beautiful she was.

"How long was I asleep?" he asked.

"Over an hour. So you came to visit your brother, and he never met you at the airport?"

"Not exactly," he said. "I think he went missing two weeks ago. No one figured it out until a few days ago. I came to find him, to make sure he's okay."

"What?" she asked, pulling her chair closer to his inside the computer cubicle. Their jeans touched as her thigh pressed against his.

Her excitement with his story made her treat him as if they were old friends. He found himself wanting to reveal everything to her, perhaps because he felt so alone in a foreign country. And maybe it was because he himself felt a little lost in life, in his journey, and in his desperate search for his brother. So he told her everything. And with each word, he felt his burden grow a little lighter.

"So what are you going to do?" she asked after he was finished.

"Right now I'm going to look through his e-mails. I think his disappearance has something to do with his dissertation. I'm hoping that if I can figure out what he was working on, it might give me some clue to where he is. From the e-mails he sent our mom, it almost seemed as if he was doing some sort of investigation. Like a journalist on a story. He mentioned traveling to Hamburg and Berlin and Prague. He mentioned a new group of friends he had made outside the university."

"Hanna, time to go," another female student said after moving away from a computer terminal.

"I'm not going, Pauline," Hanna replied.

"But this is the class discussion on the principle-agent theory case study. You *have* to go!"

"I'm busy. But please don't tell Herr Brushkett you saw me."

The young woman left the room.

"You have class starting now?" James asked.

"It's not important. I'm more interested in your mystery."

He perked up. "Hanna, I really could use your help translating Ian's messages. Some of them are in German, but I don't want you to get in trouble for missing class."

"I want to help you find your brother," she said.

James was no fool; he knew he needed all the help he could get. And there was something in her that he trusted. "Wow," he said. "That would be an enormous help. When are you done with classes today?"

"This is my last one. I could be back here in an hour."

James nodded.

"What will you do while you wait?" she asked.

"I could go check out Ian's apartment. There might be some clues there."

"Where is it?" she asked.

He pulled a folded piece of paper from a side pocket of his backpack. "*Studentunstowerkracken*?" he said, assuming he had slaughtered the pronunciation.

She giggled. "It's a student dorm on the other side of Leipzig. You can get there on the tram in twenty minutes." She showed him on his folded city map, which had all the tram lines in varying colors, running through Leipzig like a network of little intertwining pipes. "You'll need to go in the main entrance and find the *Hausmeister's* door. *Hausmeisters* supervise the student living areas. They are usually old ladies, and they are often very rude. They generally hate foreigners, too—mean old women. Smile a lot and try to look stupid; then maybe she'll help you."

"Great," he said with a sigh. "Sounds like fun."

Hanna stood up, grabbed her book bag, and headed for the door. Turning to look back at him, her long golden hair hid the left side of her face. "I see you back here in one hour, okay? Try not to get lost!"

"Too late," James said with a weak smile.

"Hey, we'll find your brother, okay? It's just a mystery. An adventure. Cheer up—this is going to be fun." And she left.

He looked again at the map. It was time to continue the journey into his brother's mysterious recent past.

# 10

V LASTOS DIMITRIOU STEPPED off the train onto one of five station platforms within the train shed of the Leipzig Hauptbahnhof. Looping the strap of his leather duffel bag over his broad shoulders, he walked leaning forward on the balls of his feet, like a cat, maneuvering through the crowds with relative speed and grace. He had just come from Berlin, and he was not happy about the assignment he had been given.

Once outside the train station, he waited impatiently near the bustling tram stop while trying to blend into the crowd. His shifty eyes continually checked the people around him for anything suspicious. He didn't think there was much chance he was being tracked, but he knew from experience that someone in his profession could never be too careful. He was relieved when the tram arrived after only a four-minute wait.

Getting on the tram, he kept his back to the wall so that no one would bump into his duffel bag. If anyone even suspected what he carried inside it, they would call the police, and he couldn't let anything jeopardize his assignment.

Looking at his watch, Vlastos figured he should arrive at the Johannisallee stop within fifteen minutes. And from there, it should be only a five-minute walk to Ian Lawrence's student apartment.

*   *   *

James felt a little twinge of excitement at riding on Leipzig's rustic tram system. The divide between the old and new Germany was obvious: modern glass high-rises alongside soot-blackened stone vestiges of the suppressed economic life under Communism.

Closing his eyes, he mentally ran through everything: Ian's personality and background, his desire to study abroad in Germany instead of some other country, his strange e-mails to their mother, the timing of his disappearance, his comments about his dissertation and the professor and the unknown group he had gotten involved with. Then there was the "unthinkable" crime that seemed to have him so worked up and that he had apparently witnessed during his trip to Prague with these unknown people. Though all this information seemed relevant, in the end there had been one thing that stood out as the potential key to everything: Ian's trip to Prague.

The tram jostled around a curve, reminding him of the way a roller coaster shook at the start of the ride, just before the screams began. Then a robotic-sounding voice from the overhead speakers announced, "Johannisallee." Getting off, he saw a cluster of five orange and green buildings about ten stories high reaching above the drab gray structures a block over. They must be the student housing buildings, because they were far bigger than anything else around. He crossed the street halfway down the block to enter a wide alleyway that headed toward the buildings. An open second-story window had a small dog leaning on the sill, its head resting on its front paws, looking seriously at him. Small pots of geraniums flanked the dog's furry face.

Rounding the corner, James found himself staring at a vast open lawn the size of two football fields. He had never seen so many student dorms bundled together, and the blocky architecture with its ridged lines and bland design screamed of the old Communist society. Even the off-color orange and green sections made the buildings look more like outdated factories than places where people lived. He found building 9-A and entered through the creaky steel doors.

Inside the front hallway, near the elevator, were the mailboxes for all the units in the building. Scanning the tiny numbers on the boxes, he found 1016, with "I. Lawrence" taped inside the plastic. "Ian," he murmured, touching the mailbox's small aluminum door.

He took the elevator to the tenth floor and found the door to room 1016. Standing in front of it, he listened for a few seconds and, hearing nothing from inside, knocked. He stepped back, his breath deepening and his heart quickening as he waited. He stared at the thick metal handle, watching it for any movement. His ears pricked, trying to catch even the slightest rustle from the other side of the door. He hoped and waited for anything that might hint that Ian was here, as if nothing at all was wrong and this whole thing had all been just one big, unnecessary scare. He prayed that the door would rattle and then swing open, revealing his energetic younger brother's cool gray eyes and astonished smile. *"James! What are you doing here?"* he would say. *"My God, you came all the way here looking for me? I'm so sorry! Mom's always so paranoid. Come on, I'll buy you a beer. Least I can do. How do you like Germany so far?"*

But nothing happened. There was no sound, no movement . . . no Ian.

With his latest hopes deflated, James felt ridiculous. Shoulders slumping, he fished in his pocket for the key that the *Hausmeister* had given him after he showed her the letter from Herr Kauker, allowing him access to Ian's apartment. He stepped through the doorway, feeling as if he were practically walking in his brother's shadow.

*    *    *

Vlastos stepped off the tram at Johannisallee and walked beside an ivy-covered stone wall that paralleled the street. Walking around the tram as it crawled away, he crossed the street to a wide alleyway leading toward the student housing complex.

As he walked, he pondered Strobviok's instructions for dealing with Ian Lawrence. Vlastos knew Strobviok as well as anyone did, which was why he couldn't help feeling sorry for anyone foolish enough to get on the man's bad side. Strobviok was not someone you wanted to enrage. Even so, Vlastos couldn't help feeling insulted at getting the lame job fobbed off on him. Dealing with a defenseless grad student was a task for a low-level soldier.

Near the end of the alleyway, Vlastos saw an open second-floor window with a small, shaggy dog peering out at him. He turned the corner and headed for building 9-A, to find apartment 1016.

*    *    *

Ian's room was a studio apartment twice the size of a two-person dorm room at an American university. A small bed was pressed against the wall across from the door, and a wide stretch of huge windows spanned the long wall to the right. A small desk, small stove, and small bookshelf were the only other things in the room. Off the far left corner of the room was a doorway to a bathroom with just enough room for a toilet, sink, and small shower. The enormous windows gave a sweeping view of the broad lawn in the center of the cluster of buildings.

James remembered from Ian's e-mails how the windows in this dorm had twist handles that could unlatch them either to vent from the top or to swing open from the side. Ian had said he couldn't open the windows anymore, because he had accidentally jammed the latch one night, causing the entire 150-pound window to come off the frame and fall into the room. He had gotten a neighbor's help wedging it back on the sill. Already on bad terms with the Hausmeister, he had decided not to tell her about the broken window latch.

There were no clothes or travel bags in sight. It was really beginning to seem as if Ian had packed up and left. James moved toward the bookshelf to examine the two-dozen books scrunched together along the top shelf. There he found titles by Welsh, Høeg, Amis, Ishiguro, Le Carré, Greene, García Márquez, Kafka, and Kundera. Half of them he had read. Then his eye caught the cover on a thick pink volume he had never heard of. Pulling it off the shelf, he read the enlarged red words on the front cover: *The Economics of Organized Crime,* edited by Gianluca Fiorentini and Sam Peltzman, published by the Centre for Economic Policy Research.

He flipped through the pages. Ian had marked many sentences and entire paragraphs. The book seemed full of highlighted passages, but the first one he noticed was in the first pages. *"The core of organized crime activity is the supplying of illegal goods and services—gambling, loan-sharking, narcotics, and other forms of vice—to countless numbers of citizen customers. This definition clearly establishes a direct link between the core activities of organized crime and the management of illegal markets."*

Farther down the page was another underlined sentence: *"Indeed, according to this view, the criminal organization looks very much like a (highly structured) corporation whose business is that of producing illegal goods and services for the consumer."*

"Brother, what the hell were you working on?" James wondered aloud. Flipping through the rest of the book, he saw countless underlines and notations that Ian had made. Then he looked at his watch and realized he needed to get back to the university to meet Hanna. He could study the book in more detail on the tram.

He put Ian's book in his small backpack, slung it over his shoulder, and left the room. Waiting for the elevator, he looked at his watch. If he remembered right, the next Line 42 tram heading toward the university would arrive at the stop outside in six minutes.

The elevator door opened, and James was startled to find a tall man in a raincoat standing inside the car. The man squinted as if recognizing something in his face. "Herr Lawrence?" the man asked.

"Uh, yeah, but . . ." James replied, figuring that the man must be confusing him with his brother.

Without another word, the man pulled a small black semiautomatic pistol from a holster concealed inside his waistband, and pointed it at him.

"Hey, wait. No, I'm not—"

The gun fired, hitting him in the chest. His brain felt on fire as he jerked backward and hit the floor. He couldn't understand the pain. Why was this happening? He stared up at the bland off-white ceiling. Then the pain intensified as if he had been shot again. He stiffened and tensed and thought he saw the hallway grow brighter. Then all his pain and thoughts ended as the world around him darkened out.

# 11

THOMAS HENZOLLERN ARRIVED back in Berlin in time for the emergency session vote at the Reichstag building. While he sat waiting in the parliamentary chamber, ambient chatter filled the room, as it might in an opera house minutes before the curtain went up. He watched as the leader of the proceedings stood and walked toward the center podium below the glass-domed ceiling. The other parliament members ceased their conversations and took their seats. "Let the vote begin!" the leader said.

The members reached toward the individual voting consoles attached to their desktops. Thomas spent a moment staring absently at his desk, listening to the white noise from the air circulators hidden behind the cherrywood vents. Then he entered his vote.

Once the twenty-minute clock had run down, the vote was closed. The senate leader read the tally on the electronic counter and looked out at the members surrounding him in the chamber.

"The results are final," he said. "There is a majority vote selection, and it is my honor to announce that Senator Thomas

Henzollern will be Germany's new chancellor." The leader looked at Thomas. "Congratulations, Chancellor Henzollern."

A wave of applause and supporting cries rose up in the senate chamber. Thomas looked down, exhaled a deep breath, and then raised his head. Nodding with gratitude, he stood and made his way to the podium, where the senate leader would swear him into the highest political office in Germany.

# 12

THE PAIN JOLTED James awake, and his eyes went wide with terror as he tried to sort out what was happening. He was back inside Ian's dorm room, sitting in a chair. His arms, legs, and waist were somehow strapped to the chair, and duct tape covered his mouth.

Sitting cross-legged on Ian's bed and staring at him was the man who had shot him in the elevator. A tan raincoat was hanging like a wet towel on the single hook by the door. The man wore dark jeans and a heavy brown sweater. His eyes were bright and smiling, as if he was very excited that James had woken up. His hands rested palms-up on his knees, making him look like a meditating Buddha, but then, a Buddha wouldn't have two handguns beside him on the bed. One gun was silver; the other was the black Taser that James remembered from the elevator.

"I'm glad we could finally meet," the man said, tipping his head sideways without moving from the bed. "I've heard so much about you. The things you're doing are really quite impressive." His smile faded. "Of course, lately we've gotten a better understanding about some of the *other* things you're doing. It seems you haven't been entirely honest with us. You've had an ulterior motive—been playing both sides. But we found out, and now I'm afraid things are going to go very badly for you."

He tapped the silver gun on the bed without taking his eyes off James. "So," he continued, "I hate to do this to you, Ian, but I'm afraid there is some information I need to get from you. It's buried deep inside you, but you should know, I'm willing to cut it out of you if I must."

James tried to pull his arms to his chest, but they tensed helplessly against the duct tape that held them. He mumbled frantically at first, trying to tell this man that he was not Ian, that he had no idea where Ian was or what he had done. But the tape over his mouth prevented him from saying anything.

The man put both hands on the edge of the bed, lifted himself up to let his legs unfold and his feet drop to the floor. The motion was slow and carefully controlled, as if he were a gymnast dismounting from the rings. Every movement he made was economical and fluid. He bent over James and ripped the tape away from his mouth.

James felt a flash of anger from the sudden pain. He was about to plead with this man, to tell him there had been a mistake, but his instincts told him this was not the time to divulge the truth—at least, not yet. The truth was a magic card that he could hold and then play anytime he wanted. It might kill him or save his life, but if this man thought he really was Ian, with important information, then he just might let him live a little longer than if he knew the truth. It might even somehow help James learn more about what Ian had been up to.

"So, Ian, why don't you tell me everything?"

"I can't," James replied.

The man whacked him on the knee with the gun. James groaned, taking quick breaths to process this new, exploding pain. His eyes teared up.

"I really must insist," the man said.

"Okay," James said. "You want to know about my research?" he asked, trying to recall anything from Ian's e-mails that might satisfy his inquisitor. "You want to know about Prague?"

The man gave a quick snap kick to the inside of James's right shin. "You talked to them in *Prague*? Are you kidding me!"

James was terrified. He had no idea what he could say that would satisfy this man. He had made a mistake; he was going to have to tell him the truth.

The man casually dropped his hand to his hip and pulled out what looked like a military tactical knife. His left hand firmly gripped James's throat while his right hand flicked open the four-inch razor-edged blade and held its tip inches away from James's left eye.

"I presume your right eye is the dominant one. Am I correct, Ian?"

"Wait, please," James begged in panic.

"I'm not working for a fucking charity here, Ian. I cut out eleven eyes last year." He waved the knife side to side a few inches in front of his captive's eyes.

And then it happened: James felt the fearlessness he had once felt with Ian, before Jessica's death. He remembered what it felt like to believe that fate was protecting him from dying before he could accomplish something meaningful with his life. Just as fate had saved him and his brother from the twister outside Dodge City so many years ago. James felt the sleeping daredevil awakening inside him. *What was this man compared to nature's wrath? What was a four-inch blade compared to a monster tornado?*

"What the fuck are you doing!" James growled. "This isn't how you talk to me. You want answers? Fine! I'll give you answers. I'll tell you anything I know. I have nothing to hide.

But you won't get reliable information from me if you start jabbing me with that fucking knife!"

The man grinned as he pulled the blade away, twisting it in his hand so that it reflected the bright world outside the big windows. "Very good, Ian. I'm impressed. Nine out of ten people I blind are already crying pathetically and begging for mercy by this point. I admire you for not doing that. They said you would be strong, so I'm glad you have lived up to your reputation. But unfortunately for you, Strobviok is not happy with you at the moment."

"I can work things out with Strobviok," James said, grabbing on to the name for credibility.

"God, it's hot in here," the man said, wiping his forehead. Then, looking at James, he said, "You're very good at pretending, aren't you. You pretended you were interested in helping our organization. You remember that, Ian? You sought us out, for God's sake. You sent Strobviok your proposal, remember? You claimed to have a revolutionary idea for increasing profits. A new business model. And Strobviok was very interested in your proposal."

Walking around behind James, he continued. "But then we learned some very disturbing information, Ian. We learned that you had become involved with an organization known as the White Rose. You see, we are not as ignorant as you seem to think. We also learned you've been trying to contact Manchevski. And once we learned that, we knew you couldn't be loyal to us. And that is why Strobviok has sent me to you."

"Look," James said. "This is a misunderstanding about Manchevski. Strobviok can trust me. I'll do what I promised him. The White Rose has nothing to do with this." He had no idea what he was saying, so he hoped his reply made sense. He was desperately trying to piece together the puzzle behind these past few months of Ian's life.

"Well, I'm glad to hear we're finally on the same page, Ian. Now, tell me about Prague." He moved toward the window. "Why do you keep it so damned hot in here?" He tried to turn the handle, but the window didn't budge. After struggling with it for a few seconds, he said, "How do you open this damn thing, anyway?"

Grasping on to this thin whisker of an opportunity, James focused. "Rotate the handle clockwise and pull out hard," he said, recalling the exact words from Ian's e-mail describing the night he broke the window's latch.

The man turned the handle and yanked hard. The metal hinges groaned as the 150-pound window slipped off its bolts, shifting with a sudden bang as it fell off the sill and slid down the wall. The edge of the heavy window slammed down on the man's right foot before he could react. With his foot pinned to the floor, his whole body tensed. The window tipped away from the wall, falling sideways on top of him, knocking him down and pinning him to the floor.

Amazed that his slapdash idea had worked out so well, James threw his weight to one side, tipping the chair sideways onto the floor. He moved with his elbows and knees just enough to inch his back up against the corner of the bookshelf.

He was able to position himself to scrape the tape binding his right wrist against the rough horizontal metal edge of the bookcase. He could rub the tape only an inch each way along the edge, but it was enough to start cutting into the tape. As he sawed awkwardly at the tape, he could see, from his ground-level view, the man's struggles as he tried to push the giant window off himself.

With his back to the floor, the man did an upside-down pushup against the top of the window, but this put more of its weight on his foot. The agony was too great, and he swore in an unknown tongue as he was forced to lower the top of the window back to his chest. He took quick breaths to gather his will for another painful try.

The tape around his right wrist was finally giving way, and he ripped his arm free. Then he could free his other arm. Then his legs.

As James got to his feet, the man managed to position the gun across his chest while pushing the window up a few inches with his elbows. Aiming it in James's direction, he fired, and the bullet lodged just above the floor, in the metal bookcase.

Panicked because the bullet had passed between his ankles, James scampered awkwardly across the floor as if running barefoot over mousetraps. Because the window still held the man down, any more shots fired would also be close to the tiled floor. Jumping awkwardly toward the bed, he grabbed his backpack and book bag. Two more shots went off, each splintering pieces of the wooden bedstead near the floor, only inches from his left foot. He bounded toward the door, anticipating more shots at any time. Swinging the door wide, he dashed out of the room as two more shots rang out behind him.

He got to the top of the stairs before stopping. Turning his head back toward Ian's door, he heard more groaning from inside. His instincts told him to run, but part of him was hesitant to flee from this man who seemed to know so many of Ian's secrets. What if he never saw the guy again? If Ian's disappearance turned out to be permanent, would he regret, years from now, that he had run away from the best lead he would ever get?

Dropping his bags, he ran back to the apartment, leaned against the doorjamb, and peeked inside the room. His attacker had pulled himself halfway out from under the window. Seeing motion at the door, the man fired again.

James pulled his head back just as the bullet struck the open door. "Shit!" he yelled, now more angry than scared. "What the fuck is your problem, man! What did I do to you?"

Then he heard the unmistakable sound of the heavy window thudding onto the tile floor. The man must have finally gotten free. James ran back to the stairs and pounded down them to the lobby and out the door. Racing along the sunlit alley until he was back on the main street, he reached the tram stop just as a tram arrived.

He jumped on, and as the tram pulled away, he looked back at the alley. He watched as long as he could while the tram slowly gathered speed, pulling him farther away. His adrenaline was still pumping, but after two blocks, a smile broke on his face. The man never came around the corner—his injured foot must have prevented the man from giving chase. James had no idea who the guy was or how many people he had hurt or killed—only that he had been damned lucky to get away. Once the adrenaline subsided, his thoughts turned to Ian. Wherever his brother was, he was in serious danger.

# 13

HANNA WAS READING another e-mail when James burst into the computer lab with a look of horror on his face. He knelt beside her in the small enclosed computer desk and whispered to avoid drawing any more attention from the other students in the lab. "I'm in real trouble, and I need your help," he said. "I can't stay here. Can we leave?"

"Wait," Hanna said. "I've been looking through your brother's e-mails. I need to show you something."

James leaned in closer. "You are *never* going to believe what just happened to me."

"And you are never going to believe what I found," she replied. She tapped the monitor. "Your brother is *crazy*. Did you know that?"

"Look," James said, "I really have to get out of here. If they knew about his apartment, then they know he was a student here. They could be watching the university. I'm not safe here. I have to go somewhere else—now."

"Why aren't you safe here?"

"Because they think I'm *him*!" James gestured toward Ian's opened e-mail account on the screen. "They think I'm Ian."

"Who are *they*?"

"Can we please just leave?"

She could see the sweat beading on his forehead. "Okay," she said, then turned back to the computer and logged off Ian's e-mail account. "We can go to my flat. I've forwarded the e-mails that you will want to see to my personal account. You won't believe what I found. It seems Ian has a lot of friends who aren't afraid to hurt people."

"You really found something in his e-mails?"

"Oh, you have no idea. You told me your brother has done some crazy things in the past. Well, whatever those things were, they're nothing compared to what he's been doing lately."

* * *

"You're lucky you're not dead!" Hanna said as she punched him in the chest. "Why would you pretend you were Ian?"

"I don't know," James said. "It felt like a good idea at the time."

He was sitting with her near the back of a tram moving south along Windmühlenstrasse. He had just told her everything that happened at Ian's apartment. No one else was in the car.

"You read through his e-mails?" he asked.

"Many of them, but not all."

"Did they give you any idea where he is?"

She nodded. "I think he might be in Berlin."

"Berlin! Why?"

"Well, you know the group that the man was asking you about?"

"The White Rose? Yeah."

"Ian talks about them in his e-mails."

"Who does he talk about it to?"

"A number of people. I don't know the names. They're in the e-mails."

"What is this White Rose?" he asked.

"I don't know. It seemed like it might be some sort of protest group."

"You mean like some sort of activist group?"

"Maybe," she said. "But the e-mails made a lot of references to violence, almost like they were some sort of environmental terrorist group. Like those stories of people who blow up science labs because they do animal testing."

James grimaced. "God, I hope not. If Ian got involved with an outfit like that, it would be like throwing gasoline on a small fire—Ian being the fire."

"You also mentioned you were interested in his dissertation," Hanna said. "It was in his e-mail folders."

"You *saw* it?" James asked excitedly.

"I couldn't open it. It was password protected and stored in his draft folder. He hadn't even e-mailed it to anyone."

He grinned. "Password protected, huh? Well, I know a few things he might have used for his password."

The tram stopped, and the ancient metal doors rattled open. A teenage girl stepped aboard from the concrete platform and sat down gingerly a few seats away from them. She seemed drained of energy, another weary traveler in life, much the way James felt. Another lost soul who had lost heart. He knew that look from many evenings staring into the mirror before he went to bed. Evenings that ended with him trying to figure out where he had gone wrong, where he had lost hope for the dreams of his youth, and when he had tired of the adventure.

"Are you all right?" Hanna asked.

He nodded.

"When was the last time you slept?"

"In the computer lab, remember?"

"No, I mean when was the last time you got some *real* sleep?"

"More than forty-eight hours ago. I've been catnapping ever since my mom called to tell me Ian was missing. Never more than an hour or two at a time. And the jet lag's been hard."

"You won't be able to last much longer," she said. "I'm amazed you've lasted this long. Sooner or later, you're going to crash. You can't avoid it. Your body has to be able to adjust to the time zone shift. There's no way to cheat it."

"I don't have time. Every hour counts. I have to find Ian."

Hanna looked at him skeptically. "Is this your first time traveling overseas?"

He nodded.

"Then you don't know what you're talking about. Thinking you can just nap through a jet lag spanning eight time zones is like thinking you can just skip eating for a week and feel fine. Trust me, you're going to crash sooner or later."

The tram slowed, and she looked out the window, then patted him on the shoulder. "This is our stop."

With a hiss, the orange doors folded open. They walked down a cobblestone path that curved around the road and went up to a pedestrian bridge overhead. Crossing it, they walked into a park of lush trees and with flowerbeds lining the gravel path. Three teenagers in a grassy meadow were kicking a soccer ball around in a triangle. Two men in matching balaclavas played chess on one of a half-dozen stone tables designed for the game. One old woman lingered along the riverbank, throwing crumbs at the wading ducks that trailed her in the water.

Reaching the other side of the park, they walked along a courtyard near the city center. James was surprised to see so many people sitting outside this early in the afternoon, drinking beers in the cafés and pubs.

They walked across a street bordering the park. A large concrete apartment building loomed above them. He supposed that many buildings like this were still scattered throughout the former Soviet bloc. To him there was something romantic about the struggles of the past. The fallen Soviet Union was a fading echo in this part of Germany. He almost couldn't believe that his life had taken him here. He had never felt this alive in Kansas City.

He followed Hanna into a hallway with a checkerboard floor of black and gray tiles. The elevator door rattled as they rose a dozen floors to the top level, and they walked on plush red carpeting down the hallway to Hanna's apartment.

"Where can I read the e-mails?" he asked.

She pointed to the laptop sitting on a table in the corner of the main room. A worn couch was next to the computer table.

But even as James headed toward her computer he felt his body grow leaden. The fatigue came more suddenly and stronger than before, and suddenly, he didn't care what Ian's e-mails said. He just wanted to sleep.

"Maybe I should lie down for a bit first."

Hanna pulled some sheets and a pillow from the hall closet and put them on her couch. "Get some sleep," she said. "I'll wake you in a few hours."

As James lay down, he mumbled, "We can't forget the dinner party at the professor's."

"We won't."

"Or the after-party that any students go to. They could know something about the White Rose."

"I know; we won't."

"I need time to look at the e-mails, also. Ian said his dissertation would change the world."

"Go to sleep, James."

His eyes closed. His body relaxed, and he began to fade into the backwoods of his mind.

"I admire you," she said. "Your loyalty toward your brother. Your love for him. I'm an only child, so I don't really know what it's like."

"Love makes people equal," James said, recalling the words from a novel by Peter Høeg. "My brother and I are equals." He was drifting toward sleep.

"I've never had an equal," she said.

"I could be your equal," he mumbled with his last conscious breath.

As he drifted in half-waking twilight, he thought he felt a light kiss on his forehead.

# 14

————⸙————

JAMES AND HANNA walked across a pedestrian overpass, with vehicles zipping by underneath them. After crossing over the street, they walked a dozen blocks until they had entered a quiet neighborhood that felt far from the city center.

She had woken him a few hours before they left for the professor's party, and in that time James had scanned through all of Ian's e-mails. He had tried to break the password with everything he could think of from Ian's life back in Kansas, which at this moment felt like a faraway world from another life. In the end, he had run out of time before they had to leave to meet the professor. But James had learned a lot from the messages.

"What you said about the e-mails was right," he said as they walked through the shadowy neighborhood. "Ian kept referring to 'Devil's Night,' but he never explained what it was. Maybe another group, like the White Rose. There was some mention of weapons, and activities that hinted of something illegal. It looked like some messages had been deleted from his account. There were chains of correspondence followed by large gaps where I thought something should have been. Whole days were absent."

Hanna stopped walking, as if their journey was coming to an end.

"Yeah, Ian was definitely up to something illegal," he said. "But I think it's more complicated than that. Nothing about the White Rose seems illegal, or at least not as bad as some of the other stuff. I can't figure it out. It's almost like he was living two lives in addition to being a student. Three lives . . . How's that even possible? He must have lost his mind."

Hanna gestured with her eyes at the two-story house directly across the street. "This is the professor's house."

It appeared small from the entryway, but the distant echo of guests hinted that the place was bigger than it seemed. They were greeted at the door by a tall, slender woman with sharp eyes. She led them through the opulent apartment, to a large room with leather couches and chairs, and maybe forty people sipping cocktails and chatting in the German language that James was pretty sure he would never understand.

Through another doorway, he could see a den with an antique walnut desk and library bookshelves that stretched from floor to ceiling. Hanna looked at him and nodded, so they went in. A rolling ladder stood just behind the desk. Two leather chairs sat in the opposite corner just below a magnificent painting of a battlefield with hundreds of cavalry scattered across a valley, with gunsmoke sitting low like thick, dark fog. Death and chaos were everywhere. It reminded him of a painting in his father's old study, though it was very different.

"Life is such a struggle," said a voice behind him.

James and Hanna turned to find a tall man in a dark suit, standing in the doorway and holding a large glass of blood red wine. With a well-trimmed beard, a bulbous nose, and cheekbones that looked strong as wrought iron, the man had a strangely captivating quality.

"*The Battle of Leipzig*," he said, motioning toward the painting with his eyes. "By the Russian painter A. I. Zauerweid.

The first major battle that Napoleon's army lost. That was the turning point in Europe in 1813. Had he won that battle, all Europe might be speaking French today as its first language."

James looked first at the man and then back at the painting. "It reminds me of *The Battle of Little Bighorn,* by the American painter Charles Russell."

"Ah, yes," the man said. "Custer's last fight against the American Indians. You know, he was so desperate when surrounded by the Indians, he ordered his men to shoot their own horses and stack the carcasses to form a protective wall. Pretty clever, really, but it only delayed the inevitable. In the end, he and all his men in the five main cavalries were killed—over two hundred and fifty soldiers."

"How do you know so much about it?" James asked. He was suspicious of anyone with a German accent telling him something about America that he didn't know.

"I've made it my life's work to study violence. Things that different governments consider legal and illegal violence— history is full of both."

"Custer's men were slaughtered," James said. "Do you think that was legal?"

"Depends who's making the laws," the man said, taking a drink from his wine. "I know it is American folklore to praise the courage of Custer and his men, and to glorify battles like Little Big Horn and the Alamo. And to be sure, those men fought courageously and died courageously. But Custer and his men were not the only victims. People forget that most of the American Indians at the Battle of Little Bighorn were chased down and killed by U.S. cavalry reinforcements not long afterward. It's the perfect example of violence in history. I've seen it time and time again. The thesis is simple: with violence, everyone loses."

The man took another drink from his wineglass. "But there's another part to the story. In that case, as in many others, the violence was inevitable. People grow; societies evolve and move; groups clash; violence resolves. This is true whether one looks at the U.S. expansion into the West, early imperialism by Britain, France, Spain, Portugal, the Netherlands, and Denmark, or the many belligerent invasions in history, whether by the Roman Empire or Napoleon's France or Hitler's Nazi Germany." The man's cold eyes glared at James. "And you don't even want to get me started on the Soviet Union's violent record."

"You're Professor Hampdenstein," James said.

"And you're Ian Lawrence's brother. You look a lot like him."

"*He* looks a lot like *me*," James said. "I was born first."

"Are you sure?" the professor asked in a way that made him believe it was a genuine question.

"Of course I'm sure! What kind of question is that?"

"Well, it depends on one's definition of *life,* really. And if one hasn't really lived life, can they really be said to have been born?"

He looked at the man without knowing what to say. The professor had turned a question of fact into a philosophical debate. But more importantly, he had given James a glimpse into the relationship between Ian and the professor. The professor wouldn't have made such a comment unless Ian had told him about James and some of the decisions each brother had made after Jessica's death.

"Do you know where my brother is?" he asked.

The professor stepped forward as if to console him. "I'm afraid I can't give you the answers you want."

James's eyes narrowed. "And what exactly does that mean? I've come all the way from Kansas to find my brother."

"And yet, you've not come far enough."

James stepped forward, shortening the distance between the two men. "Professor Hampdenstein, if you have any idea where my brother is, you'd better tell me now. I know Ian was working with you on his dissertation. And I also know he was meeting with a number of *questionable* people for research purposes before he disappeared. He must have discussed this with you. I'll take all this to the U.S. consulate if you don't help me. And the American newspapers might be very interested in a story of an American student missing in a foreign country."

"Mr. Lawrence, I spent five years in a Siberian gulag for 'crimes against the state.' During that time, I was beaten once a week—twice a week when there were Western holidays. The Fourth of July was the worst day of the year for me. You're an American; you know Patrick Henry's words, 'Give me liberty or give me death'? Well, for those five years, I prayed for either one and was denied. So please, don't try to threaten me with *bad publicity*."

Despite their verbal sparring, there was something in the professor that James trusted. According to the e-mails, Ian admired this man more than anyone else he had met in Germany.

"I'm just trying to find my little brother," he said.

"What makes you think he wants to be found?"

"Maybe not by just anyone, but he would want to be found by me."

"Are you sure?"

"Damn it, Ian and I have a history! Don't you understand that? We're not just brothers! We're best friends! We've been through *everything* together. Whatever might have happened here in Germany, it doesn't matter. He would love to see me!"

The professor smiled. "You're so like him, you know that? All calm, intelligent rationality until something triggers an impulsive passion that you can't control. Ninety percent brilliant logic, ten percent instinctive rage or passion. I don't know how either of you made it to adulthood, but I'm glad you did. The world needs people like you and your brother."

"Professor, please," James said. "I need to know what my brother is up to. I know he's obsessed with his dissertation, that he believes he's writing something that will cast a spotlight on what he believes people need to see. He's trying to expose something. I don't know what it is, but I found a book in his apartment about the economics of organized crime, so now I'm terrified that he's gotten involved in something really dangerous. I'm sure you've spent a lot of time talking with him since he's been here in Germany, but you don't understand his history. He's not just some ambitious grad student. He can be really crazy, like nothing you've ever seen. Words like 'risk' and 'danger' mean nothing to him. He actually gets a thrill pushing life to the edge. He probably should have been killed a dozen times in his life so far, by one thing or another. Sooner or later, the odds are going to catch up with him, but as his brother, it's my responsibility to protect him if I can."

"What do you know about organized crime?" the professor asked.

"Only what I've seen in movies."

"The movies are shit. They usually get it wrong. Except for the Godfather trilogy. Brilliant films. Puzo and Coppola are geniuses. Also, everything by Scorsese: *Goodfellas. Casino.* Most people wouldn't believe how realistic those films are. Nicholas Pileggi is brilliant. But the Italian-American Mafia is merely one of many types of criminal organization. In America in the 1950s and '60s there were about twenty-four major crime families of this type, not the hundreds that many people suppose. Very large, centrally governed families, from a strategic management point of view, but their operations were highly segmented. Prohibition gave rise to the influence of the Italian-American Mafia because illegal markets established by government legislation are one of the three fundamental scenarios that can stimulate the growth of organized crime in an economy. The Sicilian Mafia was stimulated by a power vacuum after the unification of Italy during the 1860s. Various families protected and controlled specific communities because no strong governmental agencies had yet developed."

"What does this have to do with my brother?" James asked.

"As I said, I specialize in the study of violence. I'm one of the world's dozen or so leading experts on the economics surrounding illegal activities—specifically, organized crime activities. Without a doubt, highly sophisticated illegal business activities that are every bit as professionally structured as the world's top corporations and firms. The main difference between criminal organizations and legitimate firms—besides the more complicated business models and financing structures of criminal organizations—is the enormous amount of violence required to maintain a successful flow of regular business operations."

"You talk about organized crime as if it's just another business," James said.

"That's precisely what it is," the professor replied. "Do you think people are involved in organized crime because they like to kill people or cause suffering or break the law? Do you think they like to risk going to prison? No. They do it for the same reason a person gets an MBA and becomes an investment banker. They do it for the same reason someone gets a bank loan to start a restaurant. They do it because they want to make money; they want to make a profit. It's a business to them—a business that offers high profit yields and opportunity if they are willing to accept higher risks and ignore standard ethical considerations. But that is why the most successful criminal organizations are large, extended families instead of conventional organizations. The family allows the criminals to culturally raise future members in an environment that helps them instinctively accept the higher risks and low morals. After all, blood is thicker than water, and often it is thicker than money. Loyalty is strong. I know that you understand this—after all, you are here to find your brother. You don't care about anything else."

"Why would my brother want to study criminal organizations? He's never had any interest in them in the past."

"I've had many conversations with your brother. He's always been fascinated by dangerous things: driving fast, daring someone to fight him, chasing tornados only a few hundred yards away from towns that were being ripped apart. I told him about some of the things I had seen in my life through my study of violence. It fascinated him. I think he realized that no matter how violent or indiscriminate Mother Nature could be, human nature could be just as violent and ten times more cruel. And he was looking for a dissertation topic that would be interesting and hadn't already been saturated with research. So I helped him get an understanding of the history of different criminal organizations. I told him about the history of the American Mafia, the Sicilian Cosa Nostra, the Neopolitan Camorra, the Calabrian 'Ndrangheta, the Apulian Sacra Corona Unita, the Russian mafia, the Israeli mafia, the Albanian mafia, Mexican and Colombian drug cartels, the Indian mafia, the Chinese triads, the Irish mob, the Japanese yakuza, and the Turkish mafia, to name a few."

James's facial expression fell as every muscle in his body seemed to lose strength. He could only imagine how Ian would have been seduced by stories of the dangerous world of organized crime. "You gave him the idea to study organized crime from an economic point of view for his *dissertation?*" James said. He felt sick.

"Your brother was trying to understand how regular business models and analytical formulas relate to organized crime. He wanted to see how standard sophisticated business strategies could improve and advance illegal business operations. He was looking at their business models in relation to advanced financial theory concepts, contract theory, strategic management, principal-agent theory, and game theory. He was even exploring concepts of advanced tax strategies related to legal businesses that criminal organizations owned for money-laundering operations. You should have seen him. Your brother was brilliant in his approach. He believed that criminal organizations, as developed and sophisticated as they are, still have a lot they could learn from the academic world about the business strategy concepts that companies like General Electric, Procter and Gamble, Goldman Sachs, and the Boston Consulting Group have used for decades."

"Why would he want to figure out how criminal organizations could increase profits?" Hanna asked, jumping into the conversation after minutes of listening in silence. "Wouldn't that only hurt the world's economies? Wouldn't that only increase violence in certain cultures?"

"*Ja,* of course. You are exactly right. But Ian wasn't really trying to figure out how to make criminal organizations more profitable. He was actually trying to figure out how to destroy them. Or if he couldn't knock them out altogether, he was at least hoping to develop strategies to weaken their business operations."

"I don't understand," James said.

"He wanted to sink them," the professor said. "But in order to figure out their weaknesses, he wanted to get as close to their operations as possible. And to do that, he had to pretend he could help them. He used his initial research and studies of their illegal businesses to advise them how to increase profits. This helped him get in contact with some members of the Geryon Mafia in Berlin. As he learned more about their organization and operations, his ultimate hope was to find a critical weakness within the organization, which he could then exploit to destroy their operations. Ian knew that he would be gaining unique and authentic research material for what could be one of the leading papers in the academic world on the economics of organized crime."

"And you *encouraged* this?" James gasped.

"I encouraged him to explore a research topic that fascinated both him and me. Why not? Few people have this opportunity."

"What opportunity? To get killed?"

"To study the activities and effects of organized crime in such a way. Do you have any idea how much Ian's paper could help the world? Small, individual acts of violence—even larger terrorist activities—are nothing compared to the enormous damage to societies and economies that results from the consistent illegal activities of criminal organizations across the world."

"Terrorists commit crimes, and they're sometimes very organized. They're not considered criminal organizations?"

"No," the professor said, "not in the academic definition of the term. Terrorist organizations are not businesses; they don't operate for a profit. They act strictly on ideological beliefs. They obtain financing to carry out activities with no expected monetary reward, much like an NGO—albeit an *evil* NGO. And terrorist groups have an organizational structure more like a military. Criminal organizations are structured more like business firms or government bureaucracies, usually like a dictatorship, with a strong alpha male as the top boss. Different criminal organizations will often come together to form a *copula,* or a commission of different families and organizations, so they can have business agreements regarding their various monopolies. This helps the different organizations avoid warring with each other. This is what Lucky Luciano did in America in the 1940s, and then again in Italy in the 1950s. Because money is the key focus of criminal organizations, they select their operations based on risk and reward. Terrorists, on the other hand, don't care about risks; often their greatest reward is to die violently. Criminal organizations hate violence because it's expensive and disruptive to regular business operations. But because they are conducting illegal business, they cannot rely on justice from law enforcement or legislators or the court system. In the legal business world, if someone steals from you, unjustly damages your reputation, or fails to honor their end of a negotiated contract, the business can sue the party that has damaged them. If these things happen in the illegal business world, then the criminal organization, with no protection from the legal system, has no choice but to resolve the situation with violence. Violence is not personal for them. It is merely a necessary business activity to maintain successful operations and profits."

"Violence is always a business decision?" James asked.

"Most certainly. Sometimes the temptation for personal revenge will exist. But all significant acts of violence within a well-structured criminal organization need the approval of the crime boss. It has been this way since the first mafia was formed in Sicily in the 1860s."

"What if I told you that a criminal organization is trying to kill Ian?"

The professor raised his chin. "What makes you think this?"

"I went to Ian's apartment this afternoon. When I was there a man with a gun confused me with Ian. He tried to kill me. I got lucky."

"I don't understand," the professor said. "You're sure he was a professional? A mafioso?"

"He mentioned the name Strobviok," James said.

The professor's eyes widened slightly. He stared at James for a moment with a silent intensity. It was as if the man was measuring James—as if, for the first time, this young man in front of him had said something he hadn't anticipated.

"He also mentioned the White Rose," James added.

"No," the professor whispered.

"Professor, what the hell is going on here? What have you gotten my brother into? What is the White Rose?"

The professor seemed to consider this before replying. "The White Rose is both an idea and an organization. The idea is simple: exposure is the most effective weapon against oppression. But the organization is complex. It first existed during World War Two. A group, made up mostly of medical students in Berlin, formed the White Rose to publish and distribute pamphlets protesting Hitler's political and military activities. This was highly illegal and extremely dangerous. Although many in Germany shared these students' opinions privately, no one was doing a clandestine operation of peaceful protests on such a scale. They worked in secret with one small printing press to create the pamphlets they would distribute throughout the city at night. Eventually, they were discovered by the SS and publicly executed. Only a few members escaped discovery and survived."

The professor continued. "The original White Rose group was then the inspiration for a second group by the same name, formed during the late 1980s to organize protests against the oppressive Communist regimes of the GDR and the Soviet Union. We organized protests in both West and East Germany against the Berlin Wall and other forms of oppression from the Communists."

"You said *we*," James said.

"Yes. I was a part of this second White Rose." He glanced at Hanna before quickly looking away.

"You were *what*?" James asked.

"It was one of the best things I've done with my life. Probably the best thing."

"What does your group do these days?" James asked. "This is not the 1930s or the 1980s."

The professor held his eye for a few seconds, then said, "We explore ways to disrupt the operations of criminal organizations—especially organizations specializing in money laundering, human trafficking, and pharmaceutical counterfeiting. This includes corruption and bribery of government officials, law enforcement authorities, and those responsible for monitoring cross-border travel and importation of goods."

James shook his head as tears welled in his eyes. "And my brother was involved with *this*?"

"Your brother had a natural gift for coming up with creative and original ideas about economic modeling for criminal organizations. He didn't just look at various government policies of deterrence—he had actually developed a three-phased economic equation explaining how to destroy any criminal organization through manipulating market demand and pricing and other economic factors. He didn't look at them as criminals. He studied them as if they were corporations seeking to maximize profits, and he designed a method for how to use economics to destroy those profits. Few people have ever thought to study criminal organizations from such a business point of view. And no one has ever done it to the extent that your brother did. He actually proves that organized crime relies on government-generated economic climates more than anyone has ever realized, and this makes the black market more vulnerable to government manipulation than anyone ever imagined. I was so impressed with his early research, I thought it might even have a chance to catch the attention of the committee for the Noble Prize in Economics. Your brother's dissertation could change the world, Mr. Lawrence. And he knew it."

"So what happened to him?"

"Once I could see the impressive caliber of his paper, and his passion for the research, I introduced him to the White Rose. He traveled to Prague to see some of the things the group was involved in. Illegal things, yes, but things that were designed to hurt various criminal organizations that we've been tracking for years."

Hanna stood gaping at the professor. When James caught her glance, she shook her head as if she shared his concerns about this dangerous web the professor had brought his brother into.

"How many are in the group?" James asked.

"We have four hundred people, Mr. Lawrence—four hundred and counting. We're very organized, as are the criminal organizations we're pursing."

"So if my brother's working with you, why don't you know where he is?" James demanded.

With a wistful look, the professor slowly shook his head. "I don't know what happened. A week ago, he just disappeared. No one in our group has any idea what happened to him or where he might be."

"This is bullshit!" James yelled, pacing in front of the bookshelves. "You claim to be his mentor, yet you pull him into something this dangerous!"

"He pulled *himself* in, Mr. Lawrence," the professor said. "The more I showed him just how dangerous his line of investigation was, the more excited he got. He feared nothing. He was more courageous than anyone in the group. He wanted them to get more aggressive against the criminal organizations they were monitoring. He said the White Rose wasn't doing enough. He wanted them to take direct action." He slapped the top of the leather armchair beside him, making a sharp snap in the little room. "But it's too dangerous! And some in the group worried that he was motivated by the pursuit of his research. He knew that the closer he could get to these organizations, the better his research would be."

"So he went off the reservation," James said, feeling as if he was understanding things for the first time.

"We don't know that," the professor said.

James laughed. "Trust me, Dr. Hampdenstein: he left you in the dust. That's what he does when he doesn't think people can keep up with him—just forges ahead without them."

"Are you speaking from experience?"

"What if I am?" James snapped. "My point is, you don't know him like I do."

"I understand that," the professor said. "That is why I need your help."

"What kind of help?"

"It appears that Ian was trying to contact some men from one of the criminal organizations. They have operations all over Eastern Europe, but he was specifically trying to meet them in Berlin."

"And you think these men might be responsible for Ian's disappearance?"

"No. We're certain they don't know about it."

"How can you be so sure?"

"Because they keep sending e-mails to a private account Ian had set up. They still want to meet with him, but he isn't responding—possibly because he *can't* respond."

James looked hard at the professor, standing a few feet away with only the desk between them. Was there something the man wasn't telling him? Something about his last comment hinted that he wasn't revealing everything.

"The e-mail account isn't through the university?"

"No, it isn't."

"So what do you need me for?"

"We have access to Ian's account. The men were getting impatient, and we were afraid we would lose contact with them. Your brother was obviously up to something that he wasn't telling anyone about. And I believe that if we could meet with these men, we might be able to find out what he was up to. And that might help us find him."

"So we go meet with them," James said. The convivial chatter outside the study had grown louder, and the party seemed ready to spill over into the den at any moment.

"It's not that simple. They want to meet with Ian. He has offered them something—we don't know what. But whatever it is, they won't want to get it from anyone else except him."

"So what can you do?"

"We sent them an e-mail pretending to be Ian. Once I heard you were coming to Germany, I was able to set up the meeting with them."

"You want me to be Ian?" James said.

"Your brother believes that an underground battle is beginning to rage in the world today. He believes that Germany could give him a doorway into that battle. And he believes that it is a battle worth fighting. He has courage like I have never seen. And I think he was prepared to make the ultimate sacrifice if he needed to. I pray that you have some of that same courage. We need your help. We need you to be willing to sacrifice."

"Just a minute!" Hanna snapped, eyes blazing. "You have no right to ask that of him!"

"I don't know if I can do this," James said, staring at the professor.

"Your brother did this kind of thing all the time," the professor replied.

"I'm not like my brother."

"You used to be."

James nodded. "I'll do what I can. But I'm not willing to start making sacrifices for your cause—I don't give a great heap of shit what you and your people are up to. I just want to find my brother. He's the only one I'm willing to make any sacrifices for."

"I understand."

"So what do I do?"

"The e-mail chains are on this," the professor said, handing him a thumb drive from his pocket. "The meeting location is in the most recent e-mail. It's at the Berghain nightclub in Berlin, at eight tomorrow night. A train leaves from Leipzig to Berlin every few hours. You should have plenty of time to make it."

"You want me to go alone?"

"You have to."

"No, he doesn't," Hanna said. "I'm going with him."

"He has to go alone," the professor insisted.

"No one will know I'm with him," she said. "I'm good at blending into a crowd of people. Besides, I can help him. He doesn't know the country. I can drive him to Berlin. I can make sure he's at the right place at the right time."

"I need her help," James confirmed.

The professor looked at Hanna, then James. "Okay," he said. "But be careful. This is probably the best lead we're going to get about your brother. If it doesn't work, I'm not sure what to do next."

James stared hard at the professor. "There's something you need to promise me . . . something I might need you to do."

"Go on."

"If something happens to me, I want you to travel to Kansas. I want you to go to my parents' house, and I want you to tell them everything. It'll kill them if they lose both Ian and me. But it will be even more painful for them to live without knowing what happened to us or why. You understand? Promise me this."

"Incredible," the professor said.

"What?"

"What you just said . . . it's exactly what Ian said to me a week before he disappeared."

James prayed the professor was right, for it might be the only advantage he had in discovering the truth behind Ian's disappearance. So much else was stacked against him. Even the professor seemed to be withholding part of the truth. Hanna was the only one he trusted, and he was thankful to have her with him as he prepared to journey deeper into this dark world that had taken his brother.

# 15

JAMES OPENED HIS eyes to the sunlight and found that he was still in Hanna's apartment. The memories from last night were blurry in his mind, and he half wished they were just a dream. A shower was running somewhere nearby. Down the hall. It turned off. Then a blow dryer turned on. He sat up and swung his feet down to the floor. The bathroom door opened. Hanna stepped into the hallway with a white towel wrapped around her. Her blond hair was darkened because it was still damp. "Did you sleep okay?" she asked.

"Yeah," he said, ruffling his hair. "I cracked Ian's password last night after you went to bed."

She brightened. "Really?"

He nodded. "I stayed up half the night reading his dissertation. The professor was right: it's incredible. Ian goes into the history of organized crime, how they operate financially, their management styles, how to improve their operations, and in the final part he outlines a rather complex process that he believes can cripple or destroy any criminal organization."

"Can I read it?"

"Yeah. I wouldn't have found it so fast if it wasn't for you." He paused. "Can I use your phone? I need to call the university to tell Kauker I'm leaving Leipzig. He wanted me to inform him if I planned to travel outside the city, and we're leaving for Berlin this afternoon."

"Yes, of course," she said. "I need to change anyway. You can have the bathroom and shower now if you want."

As she padded barefoot down the tiled hallway, he went to the kitchen. Picking up the phone, he dialed HHL's main number, written on the scrap of paper stuffed in his wallet.

*"Dies ist die Geschäftsstelle des Handelshochschule. Wie kann ich Ihnen helfen?"*

*"Sprechen Sie Englisch?"* he asked.

"Yes."

"This is James Lawrence. Could I speak with Herr Kauker?"

"Oh, Herr Lawrence! It's good you called. Herr Kauker has an important message for you. Please hold, and I'll transfer you to him."

James closed his eyes and leaned his head against the kitchen wall.

"Herr Lawrence?" Kauker's voice burst from the silence.

"Hello, Mr. Kauker," he said.

"Herr Lawrence, you are still in Leipzig?"

"Yes."

"You were not in your hotel room last night?"

"No. I found someplace else to stay," James said, feeling a little alarmed. "How did you know I didn't stay there?"

"We tried to contact you. I had the police enter your room. The hotel manager assisted them."

"Why?"

"Oh, Herr Lawrence, I'm afraid I have some terrible news to tell you. We have found your brother. Ian has been killed. I'm so, so sorry. His body was found very early this morning."

James felt as if his brain were contracting, squeezing in on itself. "What?" he whispered, unable to wrap his mind around what the man was saying.

"Your brother is dead," Kauker said.

Time froze. The whole world was frozen. Every last expanding particle of energy in the universe was frozen.

"Could you please repeat that?" James whispered, his eyes watering, his mind spinning.

"Your brother is dead, Herr Lawrence. I'm so sorry to tell you this. We are all shocked."

James's throat felt dry, and his stomach tightened. It made him feel sick, but he forced himself to concentrate. It wasn't real. It was only a voice on the telephone. The voice couldn't change anything. He had to concentrate. He didn't have all the information. He wasn't being told everything. This couldn't be true.

"You're positive?" James asked.

"They found him in his apartment this morning. He had been shot. The police need someone to officially identify the body. I told them you were here in the city."

"The police are positive it's him?"

"They're positive. The building's Hausmeister was there. She confirmed it was Ian. But the police still feel he should be identified by a family member, for the record. Ian's face was beaten."

James shook his head and banged the phone against his temple. "It isn't him—it can't be. Ian wouldn't let anyone kill him." A little whimper escaped his lips. "Do you understand? He's smarter than anyone. He has so much life in him . . . so much energy. Nothing could take that away from him. Nothing! He wouldn't let anyone do that to him." James had felt that he was going to pass out, but now the anger was giving him strength. "I won't believe it until I've seen the body. Where is it?"

"Martin Luther Hospital. It's near the university. I can meet you there."

"Go, then. I'm leaving right away. I'll be there soon."

James ended the call and looked up to see Hanna standing at the edge of the kitchen. She was dressed and had car keys in her hand.

"They could be wrong," she said.

"You know where Martin Luther Hospital is?"

"Yes, of course."

"Can you take me?"

"Let's go."

# 16

JAMES WALKED INTO the hospital with Hanna in tow and saw Kauker waiting in a dark suit at the front admissions counter. A nurse had her head down behind the workstation as she flipped through a patient's insurance forms.

"Where is he?" James asked.

"They're coming. They'll be here in a minute."

"The body is being brought out here?"

"No. The doctor—he's been called. He's coming out to take us back to the morgue."

James saw two men walking down the hallway toward him. The one in the white uniform looked like a doctor; the other was in a gray wool suit covered by a trench coat. A policeman, James thought. Plainclothes—the kind of person who would be assigned a homicide case. Both were looking directly at him as they walked. They weren't speaking to each other, as if they had already rehearsed everything that needed to be said. He searched their faces for anything that would give him hope, but all he saw was the sympathy they were prepared to offer him.

"Herr Lawrence, I'm Detective Reeland from the Leipzig Police Department," the man said in barely accented English.

"This is Doctor Kirsch. Thank you for coming down. We're very sorry about your brother."

James nodded. "I'm ready to see the body."

The detective and the doctor led James down the long corridor. Kauker and Hanna followed. They turned a corner and kept walking. Then they took another corner and got in an extra-large metal elevator, which took them one floor belowground. The air was cold. No one spoke. They stopped at two metal doors at the far end of the basement hallway. The detective stepped aside to let the doctor enter first. The room was long and bare of any pictures or wall decorations. Three metal tables were evenly positioned in the room, with white sheets over them covering what were obviously bodies. The doctor led James inside. The detective followed, while Hanna and Kauker stayed near the door.

The moment James saw they were going to the last table, his eyes locked on to it. His imagination was going wild. Even though they had grown apart during the past few years, he couldn't envision what his life would be like without Ian. He had always believed their current disagreements about life were temporary. Sooner or later, Ian would have changed, just as James had changed. And their relationship would have been repaired. After all, they were brothers, and they had been through so much together growing up.

But they had waited too long.

"Are you ready, Herr Lawrence?" the doctor asked. He pinched the top of the white sheet at each corner at the head of the table.

James's heart raced. Anxiety flooded him. But he was as prepared as he would ever be to face the truth.

"Herr Lawrence?" the doctor asked patiently.

"Yes. I'm ready. Let's do it."

The doctor pulled back the sheet, revealing the pale, beaten face.

James's eyes widened as he stared at the familiar-looking face. He stiffened. It was beaten badly around the eyes and nose. *Ian,* he thought. He fought to control his mind so he could look more closely. It didn't look like his brother in life, but it was difficult to imagine what he might look like after suffering such a beating. And then he saw the truth, and there was no longer any question. He started to shake, and his hand came to his mouth. He let out a whimper and stepped away from the table. Everyone was silent as the doctor redraped the body. James's free hand was shaking violently as he backed into the corner, knelt on the floor, and began to weep.

Hanna rushed toward him, knelt down, and threw her arms around him while burying her face in his neck. "I'm so sorry," she said. "I'm so, so sorry."

"Oh, my God," James croaked through his tears. He couldn't stop shaking. "I haven't lost him. My God, I actually thought I'd lost him. I almost believed it. But I haven't. I haven't lost Ian. Jesus, what is going on here? I'm going crazy . . ."

"You'll be okay," Hanna said. "I'm so sorry."

"No. Please, listen." He had regained a little control as the shock began to subside. "It's not Ian. It's *not him.* Oh, Christ, I'm losing it. I can't take this anymore."

"What!" Detective Reeland asked. Everyone stared at him. Hanna jerked her head back to look at him.

James tightened both fists and pressed them to his forehead. "It's not Ian. It's not him. *Not him!*" He was shaking all over, as if he had just survived a catastrophic accident.

The doctor was silent. Detective Reeland stepped forward and jerked his head first toward the corpse and then back at James.

"James, you're okay?" Hanna said.

He gave a high, hysterical laugh, like a hyena's titter, as the tears ran down his face. "That isn't my brother."

"You're positive?" Reeland asked.

James pulled his fists away from his forehead. Without looking up, he said, "Positive."

"You can tell from the face?" the detective asked. "That's very good. I'm happy it isn't your brother. But, please, the woman in his apartment building identified him as your brother, so I must ask you one last time: you are absolutely positive this is not your brother, Ian Lawrence?"

"I'm absolutely positive," James said. "I can tell by his face. The jaw isn't right. His eye sockets aren't that close together. The face is close to Ian's, but not close enough. It took me a second to see it, but it's definitely not him. If you are concerned about the bruises and need additional proof, just look at his chin. Ian has a slight dimple in his chin, just like mine. See this?" He pointed to his own chin. "I have no idea who that corpse is—or, was—but the chin has no dimple at all—not even a hint of one. It's not Ian."

Reeland pulled the sheet back enough to confirm James's description. "Okay," he said, stepping away from the table. "I'm very happy for you, Herr Lawrence, but this is peculiar. We find a body in your brother's apartment. The body closely resembles him. The door to his apartment was left open, probably to ensure that the body would be discovered soon. It would appear that someone was trying to make it look as though your brother had been murdered. If you weren't in Leipzig, Herr Lawrence, then we very well may have concluded, at least for the moment, that this was Ian Lawrence."

"But it would eventually have been cleared up," James said.

"Yes, but the question is, why would someone want people to temporarily think Ian was dead?" Reeland asked. "We've determined that six shots were fired in your brother's apartment, from a twenty-two-caliber pistol: three in the door frame, one in the baseboard by the bookshelf, and two in the side of the bed frame. But we didn't recover any rounds. Each bullet had been dug out. And there's some confusion about that anyway, because it was a twenty-six-caliber bullet that killed this man." The detective gestured with his eyes toward the body.

"My parents have tried unsuccessfully to work with the U.S. consulate and the Leipzig police to start a missing-person search for my brother," James said. "I expect you'll take us more seriously now."

The detective glared at him while nodding. "We had opened a murder investigation for your brother. Since this isn't him, we'll open a missing-person case for him and link it to the murder investigation for whoever this guy is." He stepped back and looked at the body again. "The Leipzig Police Department will set up jurisdictional contacts with the U.S. consulate to initiate a countrywide search for your brother as a person of interest relating to this homicide. Chances are good your brother might know who could have done this. We'll send his profile to Interpol, to put out a wire to all authorities and customs officials within Europe."

"Anything I can do to help?" James asked.

"I'd like you to come to the police station and tell me everything you know, on the record. It may help us find your brother."

"I'm coming, too," Hanna said. When Reeland opened his mouth as if to protest, she quickly added, "He's a foreigner and needs someone there he can trust."

The detective's gaze drifted sideways into a vacant part of the room; then he gave the doctor a nod, to return the body to the drawer.

# 17

H ANNA PULLED HER red Mercedes convertible through another turn on the highway outside Leipzig. The car's top was open, and the wind was whisking around her and James as if they were on motorcycles. Trees on the edge of green fields lined the road. In the distance, across the fields, slowly spinning wind turbines looked like giant white flowers scattered along the horizon.

A half hour ago, they had left the Leipzig police station after being inside for over two hours. There, James had told Detective Reeland everything he knew about Ian's disappearance: their mother's worried phone call, Ian's daredevil nature, the e-mails, and the stranger James had escaped from in Ian's apartment— everything but the conversation with the professor, and the nature of Ian's dissertation.

Though he had felt exhausted when they finally left the police station, he had quickly reenergized as Hanna raced the convertible through the German countryside.

"I have a friend in Berlin," she said over the wind. "We can stay with him."

"Didn't you say your father lives in Berlin?"

"He does, but we don't need to see him. Besides, my friend can help me keep an eye on you at the club tonight, in case there's trouble. He has . . . What do you Americans call it in the movies? 'A wrapped sheet'?"

James frowned. "Wrapped sheet . . ." Then he chuckled. "You mean a *rap sheet.* Like a criminal record?"

"Yes, that's it. A rap sheet. A record of his crimes."

"What kind of crimes?"

"Nothing violent. He was one of my friends when I lived in Berlin before starting university. We used to get into a lot of trouble. But just kid stuff, okay? Nothing bad."

"Okay," James said. "Can't wait to meet him."

They drove across a bridge and then turned to merge onto a large divided highway with two lanes each direction. "Yesterday was your first time in Germany, yes?" Hanna asked, speeding up quickly.

"Yes," James said, feeling a little uneasy as the wind ripped past them. He could barely hear her now over the roaring engine. Glancing at the speedometer, he saw that they were driving 160 kilometers an hour—about a hundred miles an hour.

"Then this is your first time on the autobahn!"

"This is the autobahn? It looks like a regular highway. I thought it would be wider, but it's no different from Interstate Seventy in Kansas."

"There is one difference," she said, accelerating the Mercedes.

He looked at the speedometer again and calculated that they were just passing 120 miles per hour. He stiffened. "Will you slow down, please?" he yelled over the noise.

"Why?" Hanna asked, continuing to accelerate.

"You're going to get us killed, that's why!"

She laughed. "Oh, so you're afraid you might die?"

"Of course I'm afraid!"

She smiled as the speedometer needle edged higher. James tightened his hands on the sides of his seat. The faster they went, the more his eyes were drawn to the vanishing point in front of them. They must be driving close to 150 miles per hour, but he didn't want to take his eyes off the road to verify their speed. The engine was screaming at such a high pitch, it sounded on the verge of flying apart.

Then something strange happened: he felt himself accept that they were going to die. He even felt suspense because they had not yet died. At first a large smile grew on his face. Then a quiet laughter shook his chest, and finally he screamed out in jubilation. He felt insane, as if he were spitting in Death's eye and getting away with it. He glanced at the speedometer and saw they were racing along at just above 150 miles per hour.

"Who-o-o-a-a-ah!" he screamed until his lungs were empty and he had to inhale.

"Who-o-o-a-a-ah!" Hanna yelled back.

"Whoa!" James screamed again. "Holy shit!"

"Do you feel alive now?" Hanna yelled.

"Yes!"

"Do you like feeling alive?"

"Yes! Yes! Whoa!"

"Then you'd better hold on!" She pressed the accelerator to the floor. The Mercedes climbed past 250—over 170 miles per hour.

Hanna kept it at its maximum speed for over a minute before bringing it back down twenty percent to a fast cruising speed. James hadn't felt so exhilarated in years, and again he found himself wondering why he hadn't found time for more adventures in his life.

They were on pace to reach Berlin by sundown.

\*   \*   \*

Thomas Henzollern felt as if his entire country was spinning below him. He was now responsible for the people of Germany. As the newly appointed chancellor, he was Germany's representative to the world.

A knock came from the door, and his chief of staff entered his office. "Herr Chancellor, we've had a request from Washington. The president of the United States wishes to attend the funeral for Chancellor Schlarmann."

"Has the ceremony been set?"

"Yes sir. The funeral will take place in St. Hedwig's Cathedral, at noon Thursday. Many of the world's leaders have extended their sympathies and plan to attend."

"Thank you, Joseph. The chancellor would have been honored. Please see that everything is taken care of."

When his chief of staff left, Thomas picked up the phone. He sat on the corner of his large desk and dialed a number.

"Dr. Hampdenstein," a voice answered.

"It's Thomas. I've decided to help you with the White Rose."

"That's wonderful! Thank you. It's the right thing."

Thomas closed his eyes and massaged his forehead. "There's something you should know. In three days, at Chancellor Schlarmann's funeral, I will have the opportunity to meet individually with many world leaders, including the president of the United States. I'm considering telling them about the White Rose."

After a moment of silence, the professor replied, "I think that is exactly what Schlarmann would have wanted: to communicate his dreams and ambitions to his closest friends in the international community."

"Everything is moving fast here. Can you come to Berlin tonight so we can discuss things before the world turns its eyes to Germany for the funeral?"

"I'll fly there tonight."

# 18

JAMES FELT UNEASY as he entered the apartment. The cluttered living room had three old couches bunched together around a large oblong coffee table. Several ashtrays were scattered around the room. Clothes and blankets were draped over the couches; some had fallen to the floor. A television sat on the wood floor, against a bare wall. Without even entering the kitchen, James could see the handles of pots and pans sticking out of the sink. A narrow hallway ran from the living room back toward bathrooms and bedrooms, and James could only imagine the disarray they must be in. He tried to hide his disgust with Hanna's friend Victor's domestic habits.

"Take a seat," Victor said to them both. "Want some coffee?"

"We can't stay long," James said, which got him an angry look from Hanna.

"Really," Victor said, looking at James as if taking an interest in him for the first time. He turned to Hanna. "Just popping in and out? What is it—you just need some pizza?"

"No, it's not like that. I was hoping we could crash here tonight, but there is someplace we have to be within the hour."

"Sure, sure. Let me get some coffee." He glanced back at James. "I'll be very fast. I *promise*." He left the room.

"Pizza?" James asked.

"He means marijuana," she said.

"He thought we came here to score some pot?"

"He's a dealer, James. That's why people come here."

"He's a *what*?"

"Just calm down. He can help us."

"How can you be friends with a drug dealer?" he hissed.

Standing up, she snapped, "Come here," and pulled him toward the back hallway. She pressed her palm to his chest and leaned in close. "We were friends growing up. Victor and I and a few others were what you'd consider 'troubled' kids. We were immature and a little anarchistic and loved raising hell: vandalism, theft, disturbing the peace. We had a lot of fun causing trouble and breaking minor laws. We were young and crazy, and we partied like there was no tomorrow. Alcohol and drugs and sex. Okay?"

"I don't even know you," James said.

"Stop it. You *do* know me. I'm not like that anymore. I was young, and I was looking for excitement. Life was boring, and I didn't like living up to people's expectations of me: a senator's daughter, goddaughter of the chancellor. My parents got to grow up free because they had anonymous lives. I never had that freedom, so I had to find a way to make my own."

"By hanging out with drug dealers?"

"Victor wasn't dealing back then. We were all users, but that's it. He got into dealing about the time I was starting to think about moving on. It was his dealing that encouraged me to leave when I did. I couldn't be a part of that. He knows I hate that part of him."

"Not as much as I do," James hissed. "I don't want his help."

"Listen to me, James. Victor has seen a lot of things in his time. We don't know what we might be walking into tonight. We don't know who these men are. I don't care what you think—this is going to be very dangerous. Having Victor with us will make it less so."

"You don't get it. I *hate* drug dealers."

"Everyone does."

"No, not like me they don't."

She saw his hands clutched in fists. "Why?" she asked. "What happened to you?"

"Coffee, coffee!" a voice bellowed from the living room. "You guys still here?"

"We're back here!" Hanna shouted. "Hold on!" She put a hand on James's shoulder, her finger brushing along the side of his neck. "Look," she whispered, "if you don't want my friend's help, we can leave right now. It's your choice. If you can't get past whatever your real problem is, we can run right now. But I think it's smart if he comes with us. You don't know how good a person he can be to have on your side. Come on, we don't have much time. This is my city; you need to trust me." She moved down the hallway, leaving him standing against the wall.

James could hear her talking to Victor. She was right. He was supposed to be at the club in an hour. And Victor could help him make sure that nothing went wrong at the club. But Hanna was wrong to think she understood James's situation. Only Ian could understand the deep-seated loathing he felt for all drug dealers. Only Ian knew how much a drug dealer had cost them seven years ago.

He stared blankly at the white wall in front of him. And within the wall, he saw that vignette from his past. Ian and he were riding in their grandpa's brown 1973 Ford pickup. Their ten-year-old sister, Jessica, was sitting between them, smiling as the wind breezed through the cab. James, driving, had looked over and smiled when he saw her eyes closed, the sun on her little round face, the wind whisking around her blond curls. Everything was peaceful until Ian sat forward and jerked his head left. Then James could hear it, too: distant sirens somewhere down the tree-shaded neighborhood street in Manhattan, Kansas. The sirens were getting louder. He slowed the truck, pulling to the side of the street. The sirens were loud now, but still he could see nothing. Jessica was alert and startled, looking at her two big brothers. James saw flashing lights reflect off the window of a house across the four-stop intersection. Then a green Oldsmobile raced around the corner, with two police cars in hot pursuit. It came straight at them, swerved up onto the sidewalk, clipped a tree, and was deflected back toward the street, where it slammed into the front of their truck. The last thing James remembered before his head hit the steering wheel, knocking him out, was Jessica's high-pitched scream.

"Okay," Hanna said. "I've told him what we're doing. He's going to help us."

James was still staring at the blank wall. He wiped away the tears.

"Hey, what's wrong?"

"Nothing."

She held his hand. "Are you okay?" she asked gently.

"Yeah," he said. "Come on, let's go. We have to keep going."

# 19

THE CITY LIGHTS of Berlin reflected off the wet streets as Hanna drove the three of them along Budapester Strasse. They passed the old Gedächtniskirche with its badly damaged spire from a wartime bombing raid. The ruined spire had been turned into a memorial, with a separate modern belfry next to it for the new church. Berlin seemed a mystery to James. Even the traffic lights, which turned from red to yellow before turning green, reminded him that despite its similarities with the United States, Europe was still a different world.

"It finally stopped raining," she said. "Has the storm passed?"

Victor frowned. "I don't think so—clouds are too dark. Lightning strikes hit the city hard; half the city center had its power knocked out. It's been a crazy night—even before you showed up." He grinned. "But don't worry: where we're heading, there will be plenty of lights and flashing lasers."

"What can you tell me about this club we're going to?" James asked.

"It's massive!" Victor said. "Biggest nightclub in Berlin. Many floors, and many rooms on each floor. Themed rooms, you know, like eighties and techno and American rap and punk rock and pop music. Very dark, smoke, flashing lights everywhere. You know how dance clubs are. And beautiful women. My God, the women can kill you with just a glance. You'll love it."

"I'm not going there for the women. Hanna told you what we're doing."

Victor shrugged. "Sure, I know what we're doing. But there's no reason we can't have some fun, too. You're too serious. At least *try* to have fun—you're in Berlin, after all!"

They parked and walked toward a line of people that stretched half the block. Victor motioned for them to follow him, and they waited near the front of the line as he spoke to one of three bouncers. Then he waved for them to follow him as the bouncer lifted the red rope so they could enter the club ahead of those waiting in line.

The entry room was dark, with a floor of black stone tiles, and felt cold, like a cellar. A wire-gated elevator shaft rose up in front of them, with a wide staircase wrapped around it, with people moving up and down the segments between floors.

"We shouldn't stay together much longer," Victor said. "They might be watching, and you said you were supposed to come alone."

James knew he was right. "Let me go up ahead of you," he said to Hanna. "I'm supposed to wait on the forth floor, by one of the bars." He pulled his passport and wallet out of his pocket. Keeping only the few euros he had on him, he handed everything else to Hanna, though he kept the copy of Ian's duplicate passport that his mom had given him. "You'd better keep these for now. If I'm supposed to be Ian, it's better if I don't have anything on me that says otherwise."

She took everything from him, then leaned closer and gave him a tight hug. "Be careful," she said. "If you can't learn anything that will help us find your brother, get away from them as soon as you can."

"I will. As long as I'm in the club, I should be safe. Just don't lose sight of me."

She let go of him. Her face was motionless except for her eyes, which followed him as he walked away.

Going up the stairs, James stopped at the opening to the second floor and looked around at the faint blue lighting, the standing tables without chairs, and a halogen-lighted bar with two women serving drinks. There were maybe thirty people in the room, and he got the feeling that this was nothing compared to how busy it would get later. The room was more of a hallway, really: open on the opposite end, which seemed to lead into another room and then another after that, stretching and branching out farther and farther. Standing in the vestibule to the third floor, he could see a flushed room with hundreds of people drinking and dancing to flashing lights and loud electronic music.

He continued up the stairs to the fourth floor. Leaning over the railing, he looked down the chain-link cage around the elevator shaft. It was mostly dark, with sporadic flashing lights from the floors below. Though he couldn't see them, he knew that Hanna and Victor were somewhere below. Their presence made him feel as though he had an ace up his sleeve.

He moved into the front room of the fourth floor. There was no one around, not even behind the bar. Lingering smoke drifted along the floor in the next room, creating a low fog that settled at his ankles, hiding his feet. A dozen figures drifted in the dark shadows by the walls.

He moved into the next room and saw, amid maybe thirty people, three men in black leather jackets who hadn't a trace of enjoyment on their faces. They must be the men he was meeting, but they didn't know what he looked like. So he went to the bar first and ordered a Jack and Coke—Ian's favorite drink. While waiting for his drink, he watched the three men in the bar's mirror. All three looked tough and athletic in their own way. One had a shaved head and a strange dark marking, maybe a tattoo, down his right cheek. The second man looked like a small bear and constantly shifted his weight from one foot to the other. The third had dark, wavy hair and was younger than the other two: maybe about James's age.

The drink arrived, and James couldn't delay any longer. Closing his eyes, he took a drink of whiskey and Coke and imagined he was Ian. No longer a tax accountant from Kansas City, he was instead an adventurous daredevil in search of an academic understanding of the economics of organized crime. He imagined that he had written the e-mails and dissertation drafts he had found in Ian's account. He imagined all the hours of study and research it must have taken to link organized crime to such concepts as balanced scorecards, strategic vertical integration, end-run offensives, multinational diversification, the nine-cell matrix, Modigliani-Miller and the financial structure puzzle, enterprise risk management, free cash flow, Brander and Lewis's Cournot analysis, the Diamond-Dybvig model, the Kiyotaki-Moore model, and game theory analysis. Then he thought about the concepts and strategies and arguments outlined in the notes of Ian's dissertations—*his* dissertations, for he was now Ian. Fiscal evasion, administrative and political corruption, bribery, access to black markets, commercial and financial frauds, violations of antitrust and other regulatory legislation, money laundering, violence, assassinations, and gang wars. He recalled Ian's—his—studies of Grossman's analysis of the kleptocratic state, the history of the first criminal organization—the Sicilian Mafia—from the formation of the first *cupola* to the U.S. deportation of Lucky Luciano to Sicily, to the mob's eventual expansion into narcotics trafficking. He closed his eyes and drank his whiskey and Coke and imagined his brother's recent months in Germany until, when he opened his eyes, he saw Ian staring back at him in the mirror.

*I am Ian Lawrence,* he told himself. *I'm obsessed with the economics of organized crime, and I've been wanting for months to talk to these men—to talk to anyone who can help me finish my research. I want to open people's eyes. I want to change the world. And I'm not afraid to die. I've never been afraid of dying.*

He was ready.

He moved through the clusters of people toward the three men he had been watching. The man with the tattooed cheek noticed him first; then the other two were watching him. He held their eyes and walked with Ian's confidence until he was standing in front of them. He didn't say anything at first. He didn't need to. They were already communicating with each other just with their stares.

"*Können wir Ihnen helfen?*" the tattooed one asked him.

"I prefer *Englisch*, gentlemen," James said, thankful that Ian spoke only a little German and had always e-mailed them in English.

"What do you want?" the man asked, switching to English but pronouncing his "w's" more like "v's."

"I'm Ian Lawrence. You asked me to meet you here."

"So you the one thinks he can advise us how to better run our business?" the heavy man in the center asked.

"That's my gift."

"A gift which is not free," the man said.

"That's right," James said. "Nothing valuable ever is. That's the first principle of economics."

"And how much you expect us to pay you?"

"That depends on what I find. But I promise you, I will find a lot. Organizations like yours are impressively efficient considering the lack of academic discipline within your ranks. But make no mistake, there are enormous opportunities for improving supply chain management and strategic pricing, based on the economic models I will present to you. These also concern you men directly because higher profit margins for the

organization mean increased proportional earnings for everyone
*in* that organization. There is no reason why I can't increase your
organization's profits by half and, through the implementation of
various employee scorecards and incentive programs, increase
each of your annual earnings by twenty-five percent or more."

He could tell he had the men's interest. It was an exhilarating
feeling, as if he were swimming with sharks and just realized
that they might not be interested in eating him after all. But just
as he felt the surge of confidence, he realized that something was
wrong.

The big man grabbed his arm and squeezed tight. "Excuse
me, Mr. Lawrence, but you must come with us."

"Where?"

"Outside the club," the man said, tightening his grip.

James saw that he had no choice. He looked at the younger
man, who was now ignoring him and talking on a cell phone.
The tattooed man was already moving a few paces to their side,
as if to flank him should trouble arise. All four moved in a
cluster toward the other room. He had foreseen this. All the
organizational charts in the dissertation notes had shown the
complex layered structure in which capos and soldiers operated
within criminal organizations. He knew that the meeting in the
club wasn't going to be conclusive; they had just made their
screening decision either to take him to meet their boss or to kill
him outside the club. It all depended on what Ian had originally
promised these men and whether James could deliver it.

They reached the stairs and headed down. James prayed that
Hanna would see him. If she and Victor could somehow follow
him, they may be able to help him escape. As they got to the
bottom of the stairs and rejoined the loud chaos of the club's
main floor, his eyes searched desperately for Hanna. Then he
saw her standing with Victor at the elevated bar across the room.
*See me!* he thought, as if he somehow had the ability to
communicate telepathically. *Please, God, let her see me.* And at

that moment her eyes met his. She stiffened and nudged Victor. *She has me,* he thought with an upwelling of hope.

But in that moment, the entire club went dark. A surge of groans and cries of surprise rose up from the crowd. People bumped into each other unexpectedly, pushing back, tripping and falling to the floor, where others trod on or tripped over them. The panic quickly grew, and everyone wanted to make for the nearest exits, marked by red "Ausgang" signs that hovered like phantoms in the darkness.

A strong hand clamped down on James's arm. It must be the big man. These were pros who knew exactly how to get him out of a pitch black nightclub that had fallen into chaos. They could have been the Secret Service. As they pushed him through the crowd, elbowing people out of their way, he was terrified that Hanna wouldn't be able to see any of this in the darkness and chaos.

\* \* \*

Hanna nudged Victor. "Here he comes," she said. "He's with them . . . Looks like they're leaving."

But just as she said this, all the lights in the club went out and they were thrown into darkness. A few people hollered as if ringing in the New Year. Others panicked. Soon enough, the place was bedlam.

Hanna grabbed Victor's arm as the confusion and panic grew. "There!" She was looking at the five emergency doors along the far side of the club, with glowing exit signs that faintly illuminated the tide of heads flowing beneath them.

She pushed frantically past the dark blurs of people, pulling Victor along in her wake. Somewhere nearby, a bottle shattered on the floor. People cursed. A fight broke out, and a girl screamed. Somewhere else, several voices were laughing. She could hear the bartenders trying in vain to maintain order as a drunken patron yelled for another drink. She pushed forward hard, shoving, ducking, elbowing, desperate to make it outside before the men took James away. Letting go of Victor's hand, she rushed across the dance floor. Then someone bumped her hard in the darkness. Her foot clipped something, and she fell to the floor, where someone tripped over her, kicking her in the side. The sudden pain made her cry out. Then a strong arm wrapped around her waist and lifted her to her feet.

"Slow down," Victor said. "We have to be careful. You can get trampled in this kind of thing."

"We have to get to him!"

"You have to relax!"

"NO! We can't lose James!" She took off again, bucking the crowd and wishing she were twenty kilos heavier.

Finally, she was at the exit. Pushing her way out onto the crowded sidewalk, she scanned for any sign of James. It was raining lightly, and a loud lightning strike above told her that the storm wasn't winding down just yet. Then, peering around a knot of people on the street corner, she saw two men pushing someone into the back of a black Mercedes while another man limped around to the front passenger side and got in. The next moment, the car took off and sped down an alley.

"Do you see him?" Victor asked, arriving at her side after fighting his way through the crowd.

"He's gone," she said. "A car . . . they took him. I can't believe it. I've lost him."

\*    \*    \*

Vlastos Dimitriou sat in the front passenger seat of the Mercedes and watched the sporadic lightning from the massive storm reflect off the building walls. *"Meantime we shall express our darker purpose. Give me the map there. Know that we have divided in three our kingdom; and 'tis our fast intent to shake all cares and business from our age, conferring them on younger strengths, while we unburthened crawl toward death."*

The driver looked at him. "More of your Shakespeare, sir?"

"*King Lear,*" Vlastos replied. He looked to the heavens as another jagged thread of lightning zipped across the sky. "It's about having secrets—dark secrets—and then passing those sins on to the next generation of the world."

A lightning bolt brighter than a welder's arc split the sky with a deafening bang.

"I'm getting outside," Vlastos said to the driver. "They'll be here soon."

Outside the car, he could sense an uneasy tension in the city. The people pouring out of the nightclub's exits were glad to trade the darkness and chaos inside for the inconvenience of a little rain.

Vlastos grinned. He couldn't understand why so many people were afraid of the dark. It was there that he always felt safest and strongest. All the storm-caused blackouts had given him the idea to cut the nightclub's power. Along with concealing the snatch job, it was always fun to cause a bit of havoc.

Then he saw his men pushing through the crowds, coming toward him. And with them was the man he was anxious to see again: the same man who had broken his foot inside the small apartment in Leipzig yesterday. Reaching the car, his three men stopped in a semicircle around their captive.

"Here he is," the younger man with glasses said. "His passport says 'Ian Lawrence,' and he seems to know everything the contact was supposed to know."

Vlastos smiled at James's shocked expression. "Yes, I've met him before. I was trying to have a nice conversation with him in Leipzig, but he ran away."

"You were threatening to cut my eyes out," James said.

Vlastos looked away and pursed his lips, as if pondering a fair point. "You see this?" he said, nodding at his right foot, which was in a thin cast. "You broke two bones." He grinned as if this amused him. "Not only did you get away from me in the middle of our conversation—which never happens, trust me— you also managed to break my foot. Do you realize how rare that is? How many people were applauding in their graves when you did that? Most impressive. I was told in advance that you were smart and probably capable of causing a good deal of trouble. But I had no idea you could pull off what you did. I haven't had that much excitement in months. And now we're *really* going to have some fun."

Vlastos said to his men, "You did well. This is Ian Lawrence. I've seen him before and can vouch for his identity. Get in the car, Ian."

"Wait," James said. "Where are we going?"

Vlastos limped forward and said softly, "Listen very carefully, Ian Lawrence. I'm told that you have a mother and father and older brother back in Kansas. If you don't do exactly as I say, I promise you they won't be alive twenty-four hours from now. We have a man in Chicago who can make good on my promise. Do you want me to give him a call?"

"Okay," James said. "My family has nothing to do with any of this. Take me anywhere you want."

Without another word, the men pushed him into the backseat of the Mercedes while Vlastos limped around and got in the front passenger door. The car accelerated and turned down the alley.

# 20

PROFESSOR HAMPDENSTEIN LOOKED out the jet window at the sea of lights below. Less than an hour after taking off from Leipzig, his flight was on its descent over the outskirts of Berlin. The cabin was quiet. He looked around him at the other passengers, sitting in quiet decorum.

These were the good people that made the world go around. The kind of people he no longer understood. He understood students, because he had once been one, and he understood criminals and their victims because he studied both. But he no longer understood the average, normal, basically good person. They were a mystery to him. Because of years being tortured and abused as a prisoner, there was now a distance he would always feel, a disconnection from society. In some ways, he knew that not being able to let go of those darkest days of his life was crippling him today. A psychologist would probably try to help him move on. But he couldn't move on. He didn't *want* to forget what evil men were capable of doing.

He turned back to the window. As the jet came over Berlin, he noticed large black swaths within the briar patch of lights below. He couldn't see landmarks such as the Reichstag, the

Heuer Lehrter Bahnhof, and Pariser Platz—they must be in the pockets of darkness below him. Half of Berlin seemed to be blacked out except for the occasional brief glimpses provided by lightning. Other passengers on the flight had noticed, too, and a growing buzz of excitement and concern spread throughout the cabin.

Friedrich plugged his headphones into the seat outlet and toggled to the cockpit call station. He heard the pilot and copilot talking to the tower. The airport was on its own energy grid, so despite the blackouts they could land the jet safely.

"Are we going to die?" asked the little boy sitting next to him, whom he had all but ignored through most of the flight.

"Not today, we won't," Friedrich answered.

"How do you know?"

The kid was a little precocious, so Friedrich liked him immediately. "Planes fly through these things all the time," he said. "It might get a little exciting, but we won't die. It'll probably be fun."

But the little boy was not convinced; he was too quiet.

"Where are your parents?" Friedrich asked.

"In Berlin. They're meeting me at the airport. I was visiting Grandma."

"You're a big boy to travel by yourself."

"The airport people have been helping me."

"Still, it's a brave thing to do at your age. I wasn't strong enough to do it when I was your age."

"You weren't?"

"Oh, heavens no. Definitely not. It wasn't until I grew much older that I got stronger."

"How did you get stronger?" the boy asked with the innocent curiosity that children so often showed.

"Well, first of all, I read a lot. Then later I traveled a lot. And while traveling, I met a lot of people who were strong—some of them *very* strong—and they tested me and made me realize my own strength. Just as you are being tested now by the fear some people on this plane have because of the city blackouts below."

"What's a blackout?"

"The storm made a lot of the city lights go out—Berlin hasn't seen darkness like this since your grandma was a little girl."

"So I'm being tested?" the boy asked. "Like you were?"

"That's exactly what this is: a test. It's okay to be a little afraid. That's only natural. But the test is if you can be brave and control that fear. Look around you. See all the people who are terrified about something they don't understand and can't control anyway? It isn't always easy, but you have to try to be stronger than everyone around you."

"And you're not at all afraid?"

"No. I know I will live through this. I've lived through much worse."

The boy nodded. "I trust you," he said. "And if you will live, then I will, too, because I'm sitting right next to you. It's a game, like you said. I'll be strong now, and that will make me even stronger the next time. Thank you."

"You're welcome, my friend."

When Friedrich turned back to the window, he was smiling. Berlin was still a patchwork of light and dark below, but he no longer looked into the darkness. Instead, he watched the boy in the reflection of the window. The professor who specialized in studying bad people engaged in horrific business dealings had been reminded of the decency of youth, and the ever-present hope for a better future. But most of all, he smiled because he had been reminded that even the most lost of all human beings—he himself—could still, occasionally, find his way back to connection within a world of normal human beings. Perhaps there was still a chance that he could rejoin the world and live as if none of the horrors he had witnessed had ever happened.

Perhaps there was still a way for him to learn to love life, even while living with the darkness.

*  *  *

Thomas Henzollern stepped out onto the viewing platform atop the massive glass dome of the Reichstag building. He loved the building's mix of ancient and modern architecture. And once a year, on his wife's birthday, he allowed himself this small abuse of his power and had a security man guard the entrance to the balcony so that he could have a few moments' solitude here to honor his Maria.

Though the storm had left parts of the city in darkness, the Reichstag building and surrounding area still had power.

Located only half a block from the Brandenburg Gate, the Reichstag balcony looked out on the eastern edge of Tiergarten—the central park—where the Berlin Wall had once cut the city in two. He clasped his hands behind his back and stepped out to the edge of the viewing platform. Sparkling city lights glittered below, divided only by the occasional dark blot of a park.

As he gazed out at the Brandenburg Gate, he remembered that November day in 1989 when the Berlin Wall had opened and, later, been ripped down by German citizens. He could see the spot where he and Maria had run through the crowd. Tears welled in his eyes as he thought of that tragic day, eight months later, when Maria left this world after bringing their daughter into it.

"I'm sorry if I failed Hanna as a father," he said. "I needed you to be there. Why couldn't you be there? It wasn't supposed to be like that. We had so many plans together, so many things we were going to do. Hanna was only going to be the beginning, remember? You wanted three children. I wanted six. We could never agree . . ."

As he wept, a strong wind blew across the balcony, shaking the trees in Tiergarten across the street. Lightning flashed a mile away. Light rain kicked up again.

"Are you out there?" he asked the heavens, hoping his wife would somehow answer him. His faith had weakened over the years, but he finally found the courage to doubt out loud. "Maria! Are you there? Have I lost you?" he cried out. "Tell me that you can hear me! Tell me that what I've been doing for Germany is right! Tell me that what I'm about to do is right! And that Hanna will be all right despite my failings as a father! Please, I need to know that you are really there . . . that *someone* is there!"

Just then a dazzling lightning bolt stabbed the earth only blocks away, flickering brightly for almost a second before vanishing. The thunderclap sounded like a rifle shot in his ear. And to Thomas's amazement, his entire field of view vanished. Like a tidal wave, the blackness rushed toward him, vast tracts of city winking out until, within seconds, all was dark but the starlit heavens.

The timing of the area blackout with his pleas was the closest thing to a divine answer he had ever witnessed. It was beyond coincidence: Maria *was* still with him, listening to him, after all these years. He believed it now, and he swore he would never doubt it again.

He stood and wept as the rain fell and lightning continued above the darkened city.

# 21

⸻⸻⸻·❁·⸻⸻⸻

A S IAN LAWRENCE left the building with his friend
Marcus Gottschalk, something caught his peripheral vision.
He turned to see the dome of the Parliament building now aglow
above the darkened city. The first light to come back on during
the blackouts, it now stood like a beacon over the dark city
center.

"That's a good sign," Ian said. "Every country wants a good
working government. It's a symbol as much as anything,
especially this soon after the chancellor's death."

He put on his helmet and swung a leg over the Kawasaki
Ninja ZX-14. Turning the key, he revved the engine. The sound
reminded him of all the times he and James had taken their dirt
bikes out on the hills around Tuttle Creek, just outside
Manhattan, Kansas. After gearing up in pads and helmet, they
would race through the junipers along the sloping trails with
wide banked turns, tabletops, and gap jumps. He missed his
brother and the adventurous times of their youth. But he didn't
have time to indulge in nostalgia at the moment, so he flipped up
his visor and shouted at Marcus, "Is it safe to ride through Berlin
before they get the power on?"

Marcus nodded. "If we don't go too fast, we'll be fine. Traffic will be blocked everywhere, but we can slide through." Then Marcus took off on his bike.

Ian smiled, flipped his visor down, and raced after him. It felt exhilarating to race through the blacked-out streets of a big city half immobilized in darkness.

\* \* \*

The men led James up a concrete staircase dimly illuminated by red emergency lighting. They had just past the fifteenth floor, and he assumed they were going all the way to the top. Every minute that these dangerous men let him live emboldened him. His bluff was working—he was Ian Lawrence, and they wanted to talk.

"You didn't need to threaten me about my family," James said as they reached the top floor.

"I thought it necessary," his captor replied.

"Since we're getting to know each other, what should I call you?"

"Vlastos," the man said.

They walked through a vestibule into a grand room that stretched the length of a swimming pool. The penthouse's beige marble floor looked so heavy, it was easy to forget that they were two hundred feet up. Vlastos put a finger on James's upper back and pushed him forward. There was no sound here but their own. Even the dark city below seemed silent.

At the far end of the long room, the glass wall opened onto a vast balcony that stretched along half the building's roof. Dozens of candles, set in glass lamp chimneys, gave off a dim, flickering illumination. Near what looked like the edge of the balcony, some thirty feet in front of him, a man seemed to float above a city dimly lit by a pale gibbous moon.

He approached the figure.

"I've stood out here thousands of nights in my life," the man said, "but never once have I seen such a sight as this. Half the city is as black as the sea at night. The storm has moved east. As the cloud cover drifts away from Berlin, it pulls back a curtain from across the sky, revealing the stars that early civilizations believed were their ancestors. And since life comes from star particles, I suppose they were correct."

"Interesting," James growled.

"A lot of things are interesting about tonight," the man said. "Do you know what else is interesting? What you see is an illusion."

"How's that?"

"The stars. It takes their light thousands of years or longer to travel here. What you're seeing above you right now is the universe as it was thousands of years ago. You're looking directly into the past. Theoretically, something catastrophic could have destroyed any number of these stars centuries ago, and we wouldn't know it. This entire night sky, with all these stars, could be one grand illusion."

"Hmm."

The man glared at him. "An illusion, perhaps, like one brother pretending to be another."

James felt a sudden chill. "Why do you say that?"

"It wasn't your fault. You were dealt a losing hand. My name is Strobviok, and I met your brother over a month ago in Prague." He grinned. "I'm impressed you made it this far, past all my men. *Good* men. But from the beginning, you never had a chance."

"I just want to find my brother."

"Unfortunately, I think I need to have you killed."

"We share the same goal," James said, doing his best to rein in the rising fear. "I can help you."

"I don't need your help. We can find your brother without you."

"You don't know my brother very well, do you?"

"You have wasted your time coming to Germany to look for him. And you should never have taken the risks you did to come as far as you have. I'm afraid it has now cost you your life."

James was silent. He felt sick.

"Out of courtesy—for we are courteous people—we will have some vague message delivered to your parents. Something kind, humane, so they are not forever haunted by the mystery of their loss. We will make sure that your body is found, so that you can have a proper funeral. And when I do find your brother, I will make sure he knows of the foolish sacrifice you made for him. You should understand that all this is a gesture of respect for you. Almost none of our victims are so honored."

"So I should thank you?" James asked angrily. "What right do you have to take my life?"

"I have no *right,* Mr. Lawrence. What I have is the power—and the incentive. It's in my best interest, because what you know and what you have seen now make you a risk to me." Strobviok gave a tired sigh. "You think I'm some monster? That would make it easier, but alas, I'm as human as the next man. I'm good to my family. Good to those who are loyal to me. My business may seem reprehensible to you, but it's not as bad as others. How much of the world is worse off because of large corporations that operate in *legal* industries?"

"They don't murder people," James said, angry at this man who had decided it was good business to kill him.

"What about large agricultural companies with their processed foods and preservatives?" Strobviok asked. "How many people develop diabetes, heart disease, cancer, because of their products? How about cigarette or alcohol companies? Gun manufacturers legally produce the very weapons that kill innocents. Health insurance companies deny coverage or treatments that could save a person's life, just so they can make a better profit. Big oil buys small alternative energy companies just to keep their technological breakthroughs off the market. Chemical companies poison water supplies. Manufacturing companies exploit cheap labor in plants with poor safety standards in developing countries so they can increase their profits. Big pharma charges outrageous prices for medications that either bankrupt the patients or leave them unable to afford lifesaving treatment. In the long run, many of these companies are little different from illegal enterprises. The biggest difference is merely that politicians have been able to give them legal status."

"That's a twisted way to look at business," James said.

"Perhaps, but it's all true. People just forget it. You see, once a business becomes illegal, the way it must be structured changes completely. There are additional costs—bribery, money laundering, and higher wages—because the management and workers must take greater risks. There is occasional loss of product through law enforcement raids. And then there is the cost of violence—an unfortunate but necessary business expenditure. Also, we can't take advantage of the synergies available to legal corporations, because illegal businesses must be very segmented, so that if one business is busted by the police, then at least the others are not compromised."

"If it's such a tough business, why don't you make a change? Start a legal one. You obviously have the money."

As James said this, he was trying to find a way to escape. It was impossible to see the entire layout of the large rooftop patio in the dim candlelight. Maybe four or five men, including Vlastos, were inside the penthouse. There seemed no way for him to get out.

"There are some advantages, though," Strobviok continued, his dark silhouette moving along the edge of the balcony. "Because we are already illegal, we don't need to abide by any regulatory restrictions. Indeed, Monopolies are encouraged so that individual organizations can control pricing in various markets. And because of the additional cost and the monopolistic tendencies, organizations can control supply enough to keep it always out of sync with demand, so that the prices for illegal goods and services are substantially higher than they would be if those same goods and services existed in a legal market. This helps ensure high profit margins."

James couldn't believe how similar Strobviok's ideas were to the descriptions in Ian's dissertation. All this was in the beginning of his first draft, before any of the good stuff. Ian had them all figured out, and he knew how to make them thrive or die. And at that moment, it dawned on him just how dangerous Ian was for criminals like Strobviok. He had to get out of here now—this man would kill him just to send Ian a message. Feeling his pulse quicken, he fought to keep any sign of his growing fear from showing.

Strobviok looked out at the dark city. "Brothers are often alike," he said. "You didn't have any trouble pretending to be him to get past my men. Are you a *lot* like your brother?"

"I used to be," James said. "We were very close."

"But not anymore?"

"It's complicated. But no, not anymore."

"Things change," Strobviok said.

"They do." James didn't know how much longer he could keep up the calm front. Maybe the darkness of the rooftop balcony and the penthouse could work to his advantage. Maybe he could dart through the shadows of the inside room and make it past the men before they could catch him in the low light.

"Do you know much about what your brother was doing since he arrived in Germany?"

"I know a lot about his dissertation. I've read an early draft. And I've learned about a group he was involved with."

"The White Rose?" Strobviok asked. "You don't care about them?"

"No."

"Even if your brother does?"

"I just want to find my brother before he does anything else risky."

Strobviok stepped closer to him, his face half illuminated in the flickering candlelight. "Are you haunted by the American dream, Mr. Lawrence?" he asked. "I think many of your countrymen are. Your culture puts too much pressure on people to succeed. Growing up, you all believe you will become astronauts or movie stars or millionaires. Ninety-nine percent of your citizens over the age of forty are brokenhearted because, deep down, they feel their life is a failure. The only thing that keeps them sane is that almost everyone they know is also a failure. So they get married and take out loans to buy a house and a nice car. Then they have children and spend the rest of their lives pretending that it will be their children who live the American dream. Then, if they live long enough to see their children fail, their hope turns to their grandchildren. That's why they call it the American dream instead of the American reality."

"I don't think anyone in Germany has a lot of room to criticize America's past," James said. He couldn't wait much longer. If he wanted to live, he was going to have to make a run for it soon.

Strobviok laughed and waved a finger at him. "Careful, Mr. Lawrence. I'm still trying to decide . . . There may be a way I can use you."

"For your business?"

"To find your brother."

"You aren't confident I can help you."

"Your brother is the one who can help us, not you. You only want to find him."

"Is that a crime?"

"No, of course not. Too bad, though—there are good profits in crime."

James was distracted by what looked like a suddenly illuminated dome only two or three blocks from them. "What is that?" he said.

Strobviok saw it, too. "That is the dome of the Parliament building. It seems that power has been restored to those in *power*."

The familiar sound of a motorcycle engine erupted from somewhere in the darkness below them. James looked over the parapet and saw the lights of two motorcycles racing through the streets. He hadn't been on a motorcycle in years, and he realized just how much he missed the thrill of revving the engine, releasing the clutch, and sprinting after Ian's lead.

"Maybe you could be useful to me," Strobviok said.

James hated feeling so vulnerable and helpless. He had to make his move, but it would likely only hasten his death.

"But no," Strobviok said, shaking his head. "I'm sorry. I just can't. It's too risky. As much as I like you, Mr. Lawrence, I must have you killed."

"I can find my brother for you," James said. "I'm close. I just know it."

"You won't turn your brother over to me."

"No, but I won't have to. I think he wants to come to you. He's the one that first made contact with your people. But he sure as hell won't meet with you if he finds out you killed me."

"You pretended well," Strobviok mused. "If I hadn't already met him, I may have been fooled along with the rest of my men. Do you think you can do that again?"

"I don't understand."

"I'm not the only one looking for your brother," he said. "Why didn't I think of this before? Maybe I can kill two birds with one stone . . . Yes, it's perfect."

"What?" James said.

"You're going to help me find someone."

"You mean my brother?"

Strobviok laughed. "No. Someone else. From this moment forward, you are Ian Lawrence, and you're going to do everything for me that I was going to have your brother do. And in the process, you just may find your brother."

"How?"

"It's all connected, Mr. Lawrence: you, me, your brother, my enemies, the government, the White Rose. So this is what I'll do. I won't kill you tonight. You'll leave here with my top man to help find and kill my worst enemy, who also happens to be looking for your brother. If you can't find him, you will die. If you can't find him and you run from me, I'll send a man from Chicago to Kansas to kill your parents. If you try to hide your parents, I'll find ten people very close to you—family and friends—and they will die badly. So I promise that if you can't pay the price for failure, many others whom you love will pay the price for you."

James wanted nothing more than to shove the man backward off the rooftop and send him hurtling to the sidewalk below, but he knew he would never succeed.

"Don't be angry," Strobviok said. "This is not what will happen. It is only a threat so that you honor this agreement. None of your loved ones will be harmed, because you will do this one thing for me. Am I right?"

"And if I do this for you, you'll let me and my brother live?"

"Would you believe me if I promised?"

"I suppose not."

"Then don't waste your breath. For a lot of people, hope is enough. I suggest you find a way to make it enough for you. But I can promise you one thing: if you *don't* help me, there is no hope."

Strobviok motioned for him to move back inside the penthouse, where the other men were waiting. "After you, *Ian Lawrence*."

# 22

IAN RODE INTO the underground garage and raced to the far end, where Marcus had stopped. Leaving the bikes, they went up the enclosed stairs to a now mostly lit Berlin.

Looking at the electronic board inside the terminal, he said, "We'd better hurry."

"We have time," Marcus replied. "We're an hour early."

Ian shook his head. "There's been a slight change. We're not going straight to Prague. I need to make a detour to Krakow first. Our train leaves in thirty minutes."

"You're kidding, right?" Marcus grabbed Ian's arm. "She can't go with us. You know that."

Ian looked down at the hand on his arm. "I know, but I still need to see her. It might be the last time."

The elevator pulled them up to the cavernous halls of Berlin Central Station, and they headed toward the platform. Ian had to go to Krakow. She had turned into his greatest strength, and he needed that strength before going back to Prague.

\* \* \*

"You can't just take me," James said to Vlastos, who was driving them toward the Berlin train station. "People will be looking for me."

"They won't find you."

"Where are we going?"

"Prague."

The word struck James with a strange sense of excitement that momentarily pushed his fear aside. His journey was taking him farther than he had imagined. Prague: the city that figured so ominously in his brother's correspondence.

Had Ian returned to the darkness? James wondered if he was being pulled by fate toward whatever hell his brother had been sucked into.

"I bet you're not so impressed with me anymore, are you, Vlastos?"

"Oh, quite the contrary, Mr. Lawrence. I'm extremely impressed. You may think your situation dire, but I can assure you, most of the last fifty men I've brought to Mr. Strobviok at a similar hour of night have fared much worse than you. In fact, now that I think about it, you are the only one who has ever lived beyond such a meeting. So congratulations, Mr. Lawrence. You may not entirely understand the danger you have been in, but once again you have cheated death where all others before you have not. I couldn't be more impressed. But now everything is different. We are going to Prague, a city not known for giving quarter."

"Are you saying I'll die in Prague?" James asked.

Vlastos shrugged. "I can't predict the future, kid. But Hamlet said it best: '*All that live must die, passing through nature to eternity.*'"

As Vlastos drove him through Berlin's dark night, James sensed that in his blind pursuit of Ian, he had walked into a demonic world that gave scant hope of escape. But he couldn't fight it. He had to see this hell that his brother had tried to penetrate.

# PART TWO

*If I betray my friends and our family, I and*
*my soul will burn in hell like this saint.*
—oath of la Cosa Nostra

# 23

HANNA HENZOLLERN WALKED through the senate chamber of the German parliament hall, past the giant glass eagle that hung behind the podium. Across the chamber, she entered another hall that led her to the glass dome of the parliament building. The lights were dim, and she knew it was because her father was paying his respects to the mother she had never had the chance to know.

She made her way to the top of the observation deck and climbed the short metal staircase to the open-air platform atop the glass dome.

"My beautiful Hanna," Thomas said when he turned to see her.

"Chancellor," she replied. She glanced over the side toward the Brandenburg Gate. "You've come a long ways, Dad, since you stood on that wall with a sledgehammer. I wish Mom could see this."

"Oh, she can see it," Thomas said. "Where is that American you said you were bringing to Berlin?"

"I don't know, Daddy." Her lips trembled, and she began to cry.

"Hanna, what happened?"

"I . . . *lost* him, Daddy." The sobs shook her, so she could barely pronounce the word. She hated being so weak. So vulnerable. Especially in front of her father. "I—lost him."

"Hey, sh-h-h-h. It's okay. Just tell me what happened."

"I was supposed to watch him, Daddy . . . to always have eyes on him. I was supposed to follow him and call the police if things looked too dangerous."

"The *police*? What's going on?"

"I was too far away!" She slapped her forehead with both palms. "I had him, but the lights went out and he vanished in the darkness. They took him. I tried, Daddy."

He wrapped both arms around her, and she pressed her face to his chest and wept. "He trusted me, Daddy. And now he's all alone."

"Who took him?"

"I don't know," she whispered. "They're bad people. Really bad."

"It's okay, my love. It will be all right. We'll find him." Thomas held her the way he had when she was a little girl growing up. "It's okay, Hanna. Just slow down and tell me what's happened."

And then, between sobs and choking tears, she told her father everything.

\*   \*   \*

Thomas could feel eyes following him as he entered the luxurious Gelt Hotel on Wilhelmstrasse, less than a mile from the Reichstag Building. His security team of ten was as professional as America's Secret Service, and another fifty men on reserve at the Reichstag Building could be on-site within two minutes if needed. But they also made it impossible for him to keep a low profile.

Within minutes, he was in the Presidential Suite, which security had swept and locked down for him. Inside, Friedrich Hampdenstein was waiting for him.

"How's your daughter?" Friedrich asked as Thomas sat down across from him.

"Distraught. The American's brother, James—the one she's become friends with—has been taken by whoever he was meeting tonight."

"Doesn't surprise me," Friedrich said.

Thomas glared at him. "You speak of people as if they were your personal pawns. What happened to the Friedrich I once knew, who would have sacrificed everything he had to save the life of just one person?"

"That man died in a Soviet gulag when the world forgot about him."

"Bullshit! People change, but not that much. You must be able to remember the compassion you felt in your youth. I remember how we used to talk during the early days of our White Rose." Thomas leaned forward. "Don't you remember?"

"I remember almost everything," Friedrich said. "I remember what I felt back then, but what I don't remember is why I felt it. Maybe I was just young and stupid."

"You don't really believe that," Thomas said. "You were one of the greatest student activists this country ever had." He shook his head. "I don't believe for one second that you would intentionally put your students in harm's way."

"But you do think I could be so blinded by obsession that I don't understand the dangers."

"Well, it's gotten out of control and now things are going to change," Thomas said. "You can't keep doing what you've been doing. Right now we're going to focus on these two American brothers. We're going to find them both and send them home. I'm getting Interpol and all levels of the German law enforcement and intelligence agencies involved in the search."

Friedrich sat up in his chair, gripping the wooden armrests as if he had just got an electric shock. "You can't do that! Things aren't that simple."

"Why not?"

The professor pursed his lips and seemed to ponder what he was about to say. "There are elements of large criminal organizations involved. Bringing law enforcement into this too early could spark a wildfire of violence across the region."

"Organized crime?" Thomas whispered. "This is what you've involved these *kids* in? How could you!"

"How could I *not*?" Friedrich hissed. "Do you know what these cartels do?"

"Of course."

"Do you really?" Friedrich asked. "Do you close your eyes at night and think about their crimes? Do you ever try to imagine their victims? These syndicates commit crimes just as evil as anything Hitler or Stalin did. Their financial power and operational reach are so enormous, they make the worst terrorist networks in the world look like nothing more than small gangs of angry teenagers. We're not talking about the occasional bomb set off by a group of religious fanatics. These people mass-produce routine, daily suffering with the efficiency of a production line. The sheer volume of their crimes staggers the imagination."

There was a moment of silence in the palatial hotel room as both men stared at each other. Thomas trusted Friedrich as much as anyone he knew, but he couldn't let his old friend talk him out of what was most important.

"Listen, Friedrich," he said. "We need to get the authorities involved in this right now. I want these brothers found."

Friedrich got up from his chair. "You'd risk everything I've done to cripple organized crime in Eastern Europe, just to save two Americans? Do you have any idea how many lives would be saved each year if we could destroy even one of the major crime syndicates in Eastern Europe?"

"We find these boys first, Friedrich! Then we can worry about how to continue your plans."

"It's taken years for us to get an understanding of these groups. To get everything in place. You're going to undo everything Chancellor Schlarmann worked so hard for during the last few years of his life."

"Don't you care about these boys? Has prison really stolen your compassion?"

A spark of anger flashed in Friedrich's eyes. "How dare you," he said softly. "Do you remember Mary Brungart?"

In his mind's eye, Thomas saw a skinny woman with wavy black hair, whom he had known nearly thirty years ago. "Yes."

"Do you know where she is today?"

"No. I lost track of everyone except the chancellor years ago."

"She's in a small cemetery in the forest outside Salzburg. Buried next to her parents. Never had a family of her own. Died in a hiking accident in the Alps."

Thomas said nothing.

"Do you remember Sasha Winwickstein?"

"Sasha? Yes, of course."

"He's buried in Paris, in the Père Lachaise Cemetery. College kids walk past his grave every day while searching for Jim Morrison's tombstone. But no one ever notices him. The world will never know the small but brave part he played in freeing East Germany."

"You've been to their graves?" Thomas asked.

"I've been to *everyone's* grave. All sixteen who were in The White Rose with you and the chancellor and me. I had to find each one of them, if only to see them one last time."

"You've been to Maria's grave?" Thomas asked.

"Yes. You see, Thomas, prison only made my compassion for people stronger."

Tears welled in Thomas's eyes. "She would have been pleased that you honored what we all had back then."

Friedrich grasped the chancellor by the shoulders. "We can have it again, Thomas! We can reclaim our youth."

"Is that what this is about? You're trying to relive the glory days?"

"I'm trying to finish what I was prevented from finishing. All of you got to see the Wall fall. But not I—I couldn't see over the walls they put up around me for five years. Germany was set free while my freedom was taken away. I don't have time to take life for granted anymore. If I'm ever going to change the world, I need to do it now!"

Thomas scrunched his eyebrows. "I may be able to wait on involving the authorities, but we have to do something to help these American brothers. I have a good friend who can help us find them. Just one man can keep things discreet so that your plans are not disrupted."

"A private investigator?"

Thomas shook his head. "Much better. An ex-soldier. He was special forces for seven years, military intelligence before that. He's a hero of Germany. The man saved my life once, fifteen years ago."

Friedrich nodded. "Just please make sure he's careful. We don't want anyone in these crime syndicates realizing what we're about to do to them. They can be very quick to react when they sense a threat to their business operations."

"He'll be careful," Thomas said. "Neither he nor I would be alive today if he weren't very good at what he does."

# 24

WOLFGANG JÄGER SAW headlights approaching through the rain, slowing as the car passed him. He watched in the mirror as it turned around and pulled up to a stop beside him. It was a large black Mercedes with heavily tinted windows. He took the keys out of the ignition and stepped out into the cold rain pounding the dark street. Opening the back door, he got into the Mercedes.

"Thank you for meeting on such a night, Wolfgang," Thomas said.

"It's good to see you, Thomas—or I suppose I should call you 'Chancellor' now."

Thomas smiled. "You only ever need to call me Thomas. How is the family?"

"My son is fifteen. He wants to join the army, but my wife and I are trying to get him thinking about university."

Thomas patted his friend on the shoulder. "Wolfgang, I'm afraid I have to ask a favor."

"Of course."

"It will mean travel, and it could be dangerous."

"Anything you need, Thomas. You know that."

Thomas nodded. "I know. And I appreciate it. But you can still say no if you want. I'll understand. You have a family to think about now."

"Please, just tell me what you need me to do."

"I need you to find two American brothers who have disappeared."

Wolfgang listened for the next ten minutes as his old friend told him everything known about the separate disappearances of the brothers, and the professor's plans to use Ian's theories and the White Rose against organized crime. With each word, he felt his energy rise.

"And these brothers were involved with the student activist group?" he asked when Thomas finished.

"One of them was. He went missing a week ago. The other came to Germany to find him. He was kidnapped earlier tonight."

Wolfgang's gaze fell to his knees. "Have you considered they might be dead?"

"We have reason to hope they're both still alive."

Wolfgang looked past his old friend and out at the cold rain washing over the Berlin night. "I'm not as young as I once was. Something like this could be difficult for me."

"I wouldn't ask you if I didn't think it was important for Germany," Thomas said. "The professor is planning something important, and he can't risk having the criminal organizations feel increased pressure from law enforcement in the next few days. I need the brothers found, but I need this done quickly and quietly. You're the only one I trust for this."

Wolfgang knew he couldn't say no to Thomas. For the past fifteen years he had been living the dream life with his wife and son, and the only person in the world he would risk losing that for was Thomas: the man who had first made that dream life possible. But his wife would never understand why, fifteen years after leaving Germany's KSK Kommando Spezialkräfte elite military unit, he was being asked to embark on one last quest for the greater good.

# 25

JAMES LAWRENCE COULD tell that Vlastos was watching him through the reflection in the window. "What do you want with my brother?" he asked, swishing his beer.

Vlastos didn't answer.

"Ever regretted killing someone?" James asked.

Vlastos nodded. "My parents," he said. "I realized later that they didn't deserve it."

James shot him a blank stare. So many questions sprang to mind. How long had Vlastos been a monster? When did he become evil incarnate? Then, to his surprise, he saw the man's face break into an open grin of white teeth.

"Oh, fuck you," James muttered, irritated at his own gullibility.

"You really thought I could do that, didn't you," Vlastos said, trying to contain his laughter.

James didn't answer. "What do you know about my brother?" he asked.

"Your brother is a nobody," Vlastos said. "Just like you. But somehow, he has become dangerous to our business operations." He smiled. "Just like you."

"So my brother is still alive?"

"Yes, I believe so."

"Why don't you just leave him alone? Why do you all think he's so damned important? Huh? He doesn't know what the fuck he's doing. He reads and studies and listens to some crazy professor who's obsessed with turning every academic study paper into something that can change the world. But it's all bullshit. Nothing's going to change just because of some PhD student with a crazy equation in his head."

Vlastos smiled as his eyes cut through the glass tumbler he held in his hand. "Albert Einstein was just some nobody with an equation in his head, yet he eventually helped create the atomic bomb—still the most powerful and destructive weapon the world has ever known."

"You think my brother's another Einstein?" James asked.

"We've heard about his dissertation. When it comes to the economics of organized crime, your brother is indeed a genius. One of the big advantages we've always had is that few people truly understand the details of how we run our business. But your brother has figured it out and even expanded on it. We're not sure how he got so familiar with our business structure."

"So you're going to kill him," James said. "You're going to kill my brother, and you think I'll help lead you to him."

"We won't kill him."

"And I'm supposed to believe that because . . . ?"

"We've found another use for your brother—for you. Just like any other business, we have competitors. Currently, the one giving us the most trouble is called the Malacoda gang. And we know that they, too, want to meet your brother. That is how we plan to get close enough for me to kill their boss, a man named Aleksander Manchevski. Strobviok told you this in Berlin."

James looked hard at Vlastos. "I know how these things play out. I've read a draft of my brother's dissertation in detail. You're going to end up starting a war?"

"We think one may be coming regardless."

"A war between your organization and the Malacoda gang?"

"Yes."

James couldn't believe what he was hearing. Somehow, Ian had gotten himself into something more dangerous than he ever could have imagined when their mother first told him Ian had "found trouble in Europe." And now, while trying to find Ian, James had found troubles of his own.

# 26

WOLFGANG JÄGER CONCENTRATED on the narrow stream of illumination his car headlights cast on the winding road. He had crossed the German-Czech border a few miles back and was now driving through dense forest. For the older brother, James, he had little to go on other than what Thomas's daughter had mentioned about the nightclub meeting. All he could do was have someone from his security firm start working with the Berlin *Polizei* in hopes of identifying the men who had taken James, using images from the nightclub's video surveillance footage before it lost power.

But Wolfgang was more optimistic about the younger brother, Ian. The professor had given Thomas some contact names and locations in Prague, and Wolfgang had obtained the younger brother's credit card information through an old Interpol contact. The analysis of the charge activity showed that he had made four trips to Prague within a two-month period, even though the professor had said he went there only twice.

Two trips unaccounted for—two trips that Wolfgang believed held the answers to Ian's disappearance.

Rounding a turn, the car cast its headlights on a roadside brothel. Four women stood on the long wooden front porch and waved excitedly at his car. He honked twice and smiled as he drove past. In his years of travel for special forces operations—usually to very poor and unstable regions—he had seen many forms of prostitution. He had also seen men and women suffer in environments that offered no opportunity for income. And after all he had seen of refugee camps, burned villages, and families surviving only because of the World Food Program and other organizations, he knew that those four women waving eagerly at him from a battered brothel in the wooded Czech countryside were the lucky ones compared to many.

Hearing a sudden loud pop from under the car, he felt the immediate sluggishness in the steering wheel and knew that a tire had blown. He let off the accelerator, resisted the temptation to brake, and tightened his grip on the wheel. Despite his efforts, the car began to slip off the road and slid into the ditch, where another tire went flat before the car jolted to a crunching halt.

Although jarred, Wolfgang was not injured, just disappointed that he hadn't been able to control the situation a little better. Once again he feared that he may have lost more of his edge than he reckoned on since his prime fifteen years ago.

He got out and checked the damage. His cell phone had slid off the center console and hit the metal bar under the passenger seat, cracking its touch screen into pixel rainbows. It was useless. Grabbing his travel bag from the backseat, he started walking on the highway, back in the direction he had driven from. He had passed the brothel only a quarter mile back. They would have the closest phone.

*   *   *

Wolfgang approached the brothel as if sneaking up on an enemy target, unable to break the instinct that it was always better if people didn't see him coming until the last possible moment. In all his travels, he had never been inside such a place. And he had never been with a prostitute, though he had known many soldiers who had. Now five women were standing on the porch. They hadn't yet noticed him silently approaching from the darkness.

"Hello," he said in Czech just before emerging from the shadows.

Four of the women were startled; the other didn't so much as flinch. She had voluptuous curves and long, curly blond hair. Her big blue eyes stared at him as he came up the steps.

"Pardon me," he continued in Czech. "I had a car accident a half kilometer down the road. Now I'm stranded. May I use your phone?"

The woman nodded while the others around her smiled at him. This was not a place that turned away men. They invited him inside the thick wooden door that looked a century older than the house itself.

It was hard for Wolfgang to feel that these women were doing anything wrong: their smiles were so genuine, their eyes so bright with excitement, and their voices full of joy and good humor. Apparently satisfied with the business of selling pleasure by the hour, they were as full of life and energy as anyone he had ever met.

The blonde led him to a small room in the back, where he found a phone. She helped him find the number he needed in the directory and then left him alone to make his call. When he finished, he found her waiting on a red couch outside the room. She looked at him with eyes that were warm and seductive.

"You will be leaving soon?" she asked.

He nodded. "Someone's coming to tow my car into Telnice. They can probably fix it in the morning."

"Do you want to stay here?" she asked. It was clear what she was really asking.

"What's your name?"

"Neniska."

"Well, Neniska, I wish I could," he said. And for one moment, he wished he had met this woman years ago, when he was a young man and free from responsibilities.

"You can stay for a little while," she said. Her sparkly blue eyes made refusing difficult.

"I can stay until the man I called arrives."

"So you have time to keep me company."

He smiled. "Yes, but not in the way you are accustomed."

She gave a little pout. "You don't like me?"

"Not enough to dishonor my wife and son," he said. "But I do like you enough to have a drink or two. I can pay."

She patted his cheek flirtatiously, then tapped his nose. "You pay for nothing. Keep us lonely girls company. Sit with us outside so when customers come they don't feel guilty, and maybe you can even give us help if there is trouble. You look like someone who can handle trouble."

"And you look like someone who can *cause* trouble," he said with a grin.

"My whole life, baby. That's why I need you for as long as I can have you. Come, I get you a drink and you can keep me company until your help comes."

Wolfgang followed as she led him through the first floor. They passed the narrow staircase near the front door and moved into a lounge room that was empty except for several red and purple couches.

Beyond the lounge was another room, illuminated almost entirely by thousands of little Christmas lights strung along the ceiling in chaotic, crisscrossing grids.

At the bar were three women. Wolfgang had seen them talking and even laughing when he first entered the room, but once they noticed him they calmed into a more soothing, nuanced speech that must be the professional tradecraft they used around clients. But he wasn't a client, and he was glad to have Neniska with him, letting him move within this world as a friend.

"Vodka?" Neniska asked, walking behind the self-serve bar.

"Yes, thank you." He sat on the padded fur-topped bar stool beside the other three women.

"So where are you from?" she asked after sliding two filled shot glasses between him and herself.

"Berlin."

"And what do you do there?"

"I work in the security business."

Her painted eyebrows rose with interest. "Whose security?"

"Corporations, politicians, celebrities—whoever can afford me. I'm a consultant."

"Are you good at what you do?"

"Yes."

"So then, you must be very expensive."

"Not to the kind of people I work for."

She raised her glass to him. "That is something we have in common," she said with a smile. "Who knows? Maybe we have some of the same clients."

Wolfgang chuckled. "It wouldn't surprise me."

A distant sound of voices came from the front of the brothel. Wolfgang's ears twitched as he heard the sounds, but it was too difficult to make out anything other than that it was the sound of men.

Neniska didn't seem to notice. "Where are you traveling to?"

"Prague."

"Everyone traveling east on this road travels to Prague," she said. "But is that your final destination?"

"I won't know until I get there."

"Why are you going?"

"To find someone."

"For work?"

"For a friend."

"And what if you don't find them?"

"I will find them. I have to."

He could hear the bantering voices of several men growing louder. They seemed to be coming this way.

"And where are you from?" he asked.

"Bereznik, Russia. It is a town a thousand miles northeast of Moscow."

"A thousand miles from the closest place sounds like it's a world away from everything."

"This is why I left," she said. "Growing up in Bereznik was nice. It is a good community, you know. Good Russian people— best in the world. A very happy childhood. But most of my friends and I were looking for more when we got older. We see pictures, read magazines, watch movies, and we see a lot of different young people living exciting lives and having adventures in big cities in Europe and America. So we fantasized a lot about moving west. You know, it was some kind of dream life we thought about all the time, and we always figured that one day we would be old enough to leave home and travel west, where our future lives would just open up for us." She beamed, recalling the feelings of her youth in central Russia. "We always had happy life growing up in Bereznik, so we were naturally very optimist about life in general. Bad things did not happen there. We had no real idea or experience with the horrible things some people can do to the innocent. We had no reason not to have hope."

"Neniska, what happened?" he asked.

The room exploded with loud voices and laughter as four burly men stomped through the doorway.

"I have to work now," she said.

"Wait. What happened? Please . . ."

"I'm sorry. Clients now." She set her drink down on the bar and, to his surprise, gave him a warm, genuine hug. "I'm glad I met you, Wolfgang. I hope you find the people you're looking for."

He grabbed her arm gently. "Wait. Please stay with me."

"I have clients," she said.

"It's okay. I'll pay you."

At first this seemed to make her uncomfortable, but then she nodded.

He handed her money before continuing their conversation. "When did you leave Russia?"

"I left when I was eighteen, to work as a secretary for an export company in Istanbul. It was good pay and only for the summer. I needed money for the science academy in Moscow the next year."

"What happened?"

"Things were not as promised in Turkey." She looked away from him and stared at the red Victorian wallpaper.

Wolfgang didn't need her to spell it out for him. He was well aware of the problems for young women in the East, and he suspected that he knew the horrible answer to the mystery of her story. Like so many damaged souls he had met in his long career touring the forgotten hell holes of the world, he found himself caring deeply for this girl who had had her youthful dreams stolen and her body bought and sold. He had to understand her story; he had to know if he could help.

"You were trafficked?" he said.

She nodded, her eyes dry but filled with pain. "They kept me in Istanbul, in a building with other girls. This is where I was forced to work for them."

"How long?"

"Three years," she said matter-of-factly, as if time didn't mean much after the first few weeks of her enslavement.

"Are you a prisoner here?" he asked. If she was here against her will, he would do whatever he must to save her.

Her eyes widened as she turned her head back toward him. Studying him for a moment, she smiled and shook her head. "No, not now. I choose to be here."

"You're sure? I can help you if you're being forced."

She must not have expected his kindness, and her lips trembled slightly. But she never lost her smile. "Where was someone like you five years ago?" she asked, her eyes shiny with tears.

The festive chatter and laughter seemed louder. More women had come into the room, no doubt drawn by the prospect of business with another group of men that had joined the first. The night's trade was starting up.

"I'm sorry," Neniska said. "I can't talk about the past anymore. I will need to work soon, so I need to seem happy."

"Wait, please," Wolfgang pleaded. "I'm sorry. I don't mean to cause you pain. But I wish to know, why do you do this now after what happened to you."

"I have a daughter to think of," she said.

A woman approached them. She had short blond hair that hung straight, catching the gleam of the overdone Christmas lights. She was attractive for her age, which Wolfgang guessed to be early forties. But he could tell she had to work hard to make herself up before surrounding herself with the natural beauty of these women who still had the youthful glow that she once had twenty years ago. The crow's-feet at the corners of her shining eyes hinted at the hard life she had lived.

"You the one that called the tow truck?" the woman asked politely.

He nodded.

"It's here." Turning to Neniska, she said, "We have many clients now." Then, glancing back to Wolfgang, "Of course, you're more than welcome to stay if you wish."

"Thank you," he replied. He gazed at her until she turned and left them.

"I must get to work," Neniska said.

"Please stay," he said. "I'll pay you more for your time."

She shook her head. "Your mechanic is here."

"I'll pay him to wait until we're done talking."

"I don't want to take any more of your money. I have to work." She stood up. "And you need to go find the people you are looking for."

He stood up with her. "Thank you for your help, Neniska. And thank you for telling part of your story. Someday I'll return to hear the rest."

"You won't return," she said. "Besides, there's nothing else to tell."

Wolfgang looked tenderly at her. "What is your daughter's name?"

She hesitated at first, then answered, "Ana Natasha Baronova."

Wolfgang kissed her on both cheeks the way he would an old friend. "I always return to a place if I say I will. Always, Neniska."

He then left the room unescorted, walked down the lively hallway, onto the festive front porch, and out into the dark night. He could see the mechanic's gangly frame waiting in the tow truck's headlights. As he walked across the graveled lot, he tried not to think of what the rest of Neniska's night would be like.

# 27

WHEN JAMES WOKE in the private room on the train, he felt the cold window against his left arm, and the gentle rocking as the train cut through the dark European countryside. The wooden racks above him smelled of pine. Then he saw Vlastos, lying on the opposite bench with eyes closed and a face as relaxed as if he were a corpse.

Without making a sound, James sat up and, as quietly as possible, rose from the bench. A sliver of moonlight cut across the floor. He looked down and wondered if he had the strength to kill the sleeping Vlastos. His fist tightened as his eyes locked onto the man's Adam's apple. A strong punch there was all it would take to kill him. How many lives would he be saving in future years if he ended this killer's life tonight? Perhaps this was the real reason fate had taken him on this journey. Maybe he wasn't supposed to find Ian after all. Maybe everything had happened, the entire sequence of events and chance meetings, just so he would meet this man, discover his evil, and have this opportunity to kill him.

But James couldn't. He was too afraid of getting it wrong. And part of him wondered if he was also afraid of getting it right. He had never killed a man before. It might have been different in a decisive moment of kill or be killed, but this man was sleeping. And some instinct inside him warned of great danger in trying to kill someone as deadly as Vlastos.

Turning from the bench, he moved toward the cabin's doorway. As he touched the handle, a voice behind him said, "Don't wander too far."

A chill shot down his spine. He turned to look at Vlastos and saw the devil's eyes staring back at him. *"Come, thick night,"* Vlastos said, *"and pall thee in the dunnest smoke of hell, that my keen knife see not the wound it makes."*

James nodded. "I'll stay close," he replied. Then he opened the door and went down the hallway, dizzy from the realization of how close he had come to getting himself killed.

*   *   *

James passed through three cars before arriving in one of the train's lounge cars. It was lined on both sides by benches with red cushions and small tables covered with thin white tablecloths detailed in tiny white flower patterns. He was developing an appreciation for the Eastern European attention to detail in things that would have been much more standardized in America.

*"Was möchten Sie trinken?"* the barman asked.

*"Eine Bier, bitte,"* James replied, guessing what the man had asked and having learned a few words in the past couple of days.

The barman came back with a Pilsner in a tall, thin glass, with a flower-shaped European-style paper coaster rimming the lower stem. James took a drink of the cold beer and immediately felt a little more relaxed.

"You went to Kansas State?" a voice asked from his left.

James almost spilled his drink. He turned to find a young man sitting two bar stools over. "How did you . . . ?" He paused, looking at the jeweled gold class ring on his left hand. "You saw the Power Cat. You're American?"

The man nodded. "Isaac Shelton," he said, putting out his hand. "From Kansas City."

"*I'm* from Kansas City," James said, shaking the man's hand. "I didn't grow up there, but I live there now. Down on the Plaza."

"I love the Plaza," Isaac said. "Especially at Christmastime."

James laughed. "I can't believe there's someone else from Kansas City on this train. We're a third of the way around the world and I haven't even met another American since I got here. What are you doing this far from home?"

"On a mission to Prague for the Christ Community Church. I'm in the process of getting my Master's in Divinity from Midwest Baptist Theological Seminary in KC."

"You're traveling alone?"

"I'm with people in Prague. I went to Berlin this past week for a short trip."

"I thought Americans only went on church missions to places like China or Southeast Asia or Africa."

"We go wherever we're called to go."

"Well, please don't try to come after me—I'm already a very happy Christian," James said, raising his beer as if to toast this accomplishment.

Isaac grinned. "Don't worry, I wouldn't try to convert a fellow Kansan even if you weren't—not while we're relaxing at the bar, anyway."

"Much appreciated. So what do you do? Just come over here for a few months and go door-to-door looking for lost or drifting souls?"

"Pretty much."

"And how's the business for *that* these days?"

"Well, you find a lot of people interested in listening," Isaac said. "Lot of people searching for something in life that they can't put a finger on. A road to peace or happiness. Some end up being interested, but most aren't. But many *are* interested in listening, or considering taking their lives down a new path. Anyway, what are *you* doing so far from Kansas?"

"Visiting my brother," James replied.

"And what's he doing here?"

"My brother . . . like you said: searching for something in his life."

"Does he know what he's searching for?"

"Yeah, I'm pretty sure he's finally found it, too. That's what worries me."

"Why?"

James grinned nervously. "You'd have to understand my brother to know that."

"Do *you* understand him?" Isaac asked.

"Yeah. I'm the only one that does." He took a long drink from his beer.

"Sounds like the two of you are lucky to have each other."

James studied the man's calm composure and reflected on how quickly this stranger had earned his trust and gotten him to the edge of talking about personal things. "Isaac, I think you're going to be a natural religious leader someday for a very lucky community."

Then movement caught his eye and he turned to see Vlastos standing in the far doorway, watching him. The killer tipped his head, gesturing back down the train toward their private room. Then he locked his expression into a stony stare and held it on James for what felt like an eternity before disappearing back into the shadows.

"I'm sorry, but I need to go," James said.

"You sure?" Isaac asked. "I can't tell you how nice it is to meet someone from back home all the way out here. I had to spend two months in a language program in Prague before I was even fluent enough in Czech to meet people."

Leaning forward to meet the stranger's raised glass halfway, James thought of Vlastos. "Isaac, do you believe that some men are instinctively evil?"

"I believe that man is complicated."

"What does that mean?"

"I believe that all men have good and evil inside them. Not just the *potential* for good or evil, but the ever-present combination of both. This is where much religion comes from. It's also were much religion comes into play as men and women try to understand the complexities of society and even of themselves."

"But you don't believe that a man can *become* pure evil? Maybe they've had a naturally evil instinct their entire life and have eventually found themselves living within a secluded world of terrible things: a world so dark, they've forgotten everything good."

"I can only tell you what I believe," Isaac said. "And what I believe is that man is complicated beyond understanding. A seemingly evil man can retain good elements inside him that can, at any time, turn him back onto the road of good. And a seemingly good man can find himself drifting off course, an inch at a time, into a world of darkness that may eventually make him a stranger to everyone he's ever known in his life—even, possibly, himself. But these are extremes. In most cases, you can find good and evil in everyone. To what degree these two elements are balanced within a man or woman are for only God and the devil to know."

"You don't think man will know if he himself is good or evil?"

"I think man is the last to know these things."

James stuck out his hand. "It's been a real pleasure meeting you, Isaac Shelton."

"Give your brother my best," Isaac said with a grin. "Tell him I'm glad to know I'm not the only one who's drifted so far from home."

James went back to the private room. When he opened the door, he saw Vlastos staring out the black window.

"I told you not to speak to anyone," Vlastos said. "The trail needed to stay invisible. Now you've made a mess for me to clean up."

"No!" James said with sudden horror. "You can't hurt him."

"Hurt him?" Vlastos said.

"He hasn't done anything. He's not a part of any of this. He's an American, from Kansas City. Like me. It would have seemed suspicious if I hadn't talked to him. We just talked about home. Nothing about you or . . . any of this."

Vlastos pulled a leather Dopp kit from his luggage, unfolded the table from the wall, and opened the kit on it. From the kit he removed a white rag, a small glass vial with a medical stopper that allowed for needles to be inserted through the rubber center, and a cubical tin box the size of a billiards chalk.

"What are you doing?" James asked.

"You spoke with him," Vlastos said as he removed the cap from the vial, held the rag over the opening, and turned the vial upside down three times to make triangular dabs on the rag. "He knows who you are now. He knows you were on this train. And he might have seen you with me at some point before tonight, and he might see us briefly after tonight." He put the cap back on and returned the vial to the Dopp kit. Then he opened the tin box and removed one of three green chemical tablets the size of aspirin and set it next to the rag.

"No, you can't," James said. "He's on a religious mission, for heaven's sake!"

"Then his god can protect him if he wishes."

"No," James said. "There's no fucking way. I won't let you."

With uncanny speed, Vlastos uncoiled from the bench and hit him in the solar plexus. James dropped to his knees before he even realized he'd been hit. Panting on his hands and knees with tears welling in his eyes, he could do nothing as Vlastos circled behind him and held the rag over his mouth and nose. He tried not to breathe in, but the potent vapors of the chemical gave him no choice, and within seconds he fell into unconsciousness.

# 28

IAN LISTENED TO the quick, rhythmic snaps of the high-speed train as it rolled across the sleeping Polish countryside somewhere between Berlin and Krakow. Marcus would find a café near the station in Krakow to wait while he visited Zoe. He needed to see her one last time before they journeyed on to Prague.

"Can't sleep?" Marcus asked.

Ian shook his head without looking up from his whiskey. "You think we're wasting time, don't you?"

Four other people sat at the far end of the dining car, out of earshot. "I think we should be going straight to Prague."

"I told you, I need to see Zoe first."

"How did you find her, anyway?"

"Through the Internet," Ian said. He smiled. "I know how that sounds, but it was for my research."

"That was two months ago, when you first discovered her and her sister's story?"

"Yeah."

"And how many times have you been to Krakow since then?"

"Seven times."

Marcus gave him a skeptical look. "For research?"

"It's more than that now."

"Oh, man! I don't believe it! You fell for her, didn't you?"

Ian nodded solemnly. "We fell for each other."

"And her sister is still missing."

Ian nodded. "We both hope my dissertation can prevent future victims."

"Picked out a name for it yet?"

He nodded. "'An Economic Case Study for the Destruction of Organized Crime Syndicates Using Advanced Game Theory.'" He paused, then asked the question that had been haunting him for months. "Is it possible to find one specific girl that's been taken?"

"Doubtful you'd find anyone specific," Marcus replied. "Once a girl has been taken, she just disappears. No one can find them."

"So they will die?"

"No, no," Marcus said. "Not usually, anyway. Often they release them when they're no longer profitable. You know, too old, too used up or drugged up. There comes a time when a girl who is held captive and raped and abused by thousands of different men will become undesirable. Once they get like that, they're not worth the space and upkeep, and they get replaced by fresh, younger women."

"How long until they're 'used up'?"

Marcus looked sadly at him. "Maybe three or four years. Maybe they're on drugs most of that time, and maybe they are raped—I don't know—by a dozen different men a day. Sometimes more. Maybe they get pregnant from time to time and are forced to have abortions. After a while, things take their toll on what was once a beautiful young woman."

"They're still beautiful inside," Ian said, "no matter what's been done to them."

"You might be surprised," Marcus replied.

He tried not to think of what this meant for Zoe's sister. "So there's not much hope?"

"For Zoe's sister?" Marcus shook his head. "No. Even if we did somehow find her, it's been over five months since she disappeared. She will have been—"

"I know!" Ian hissed. "Don't you think I've thought of that? I know exactly what will have happened to her, what they will have done to her. But we can't think about that! We can't allow ourselves to imagine *that*. We have to be practical, not emotional. You tried to teach me that back in Prague two months ago, remember? It just took me a while to see that you were right."

"I remember. It's hard to understand at first. You've learned a lot since then."

"And now here we are, getting ready to start a war," Ian said. He stood up. "I need to get some air." He left the dining car.

The train noise increased when he opened the far door to walk into the enclosed section between cars. It was his favorite part of any train, and he found himself standing in between the two cars, listening to the metallic thumping over the rail joints, feeling the rhythmic jostle in his feet as the train raced along the tracks.

Looking past his reflection in the window, he could see the faint countryside in the dim moonlight. Tears welled in his eyes as he thought about *her*.

*       *       *

When the train arrived in Krakow, Ian grabbed a taxi in front of the station while Marcus found a café to wait in.

Thirty minutes later, he stood in the gray courtyard outside the enormous mass housing network of concrete buildings that held the hidden lives of two thousand Krakow citizens. Zoe's face appeared inside the little square window just before the metal door clicked open and she walked into the courtyard toward him.

"You look worried," she said when she reached him.

*Do I?* he wondered. He liked that she could read him better than anyone he had ever known besides James.

"I just wanted to see you before I went back to Prague."

"Because you're afraid you might not return?"

"I'll return."

"But it *is* dangerous—what you will be doing?"

"I've been there before and made it out all right."

"But this time is different," she said. "You will try to do more. You're willing to take more risks this time. I can see the eagerness for danger in your eyes."

Ian held her gaze for a moment. Neither said another word until he stepped forward and wrapped his strong arms around her. "I'll come back, Zoe." He squeezed her tightly, exciting them both as their bodies pressed together. He turned his head down toward her and kissed her jawline and then the side of her neck. She moaned in a whisper.

"I'll come back," he repeated in her ear.

She wrapped her arms around him and squeezed him harder than she ever had before. They held each other for what felt like an eternity. Then he let her go.

Walking back to the train station alone, he thought about how natural and familiar all the sights and sounds and smells felt to him. Somehow, even though this place was completely different from where he had been raised, Poland now felt as familiar to him as Kansas had always felt. He heard light Polish chatter from inside a small café as he walked past. Fresh rainfall gave a clean, wet smell to the cobblestones he walked on. And the sight of a church spire reaching up above the buildings in front of him added a sense of ancient peace and calm to everything. All this and Zoe, too . . . It made him wonder whether he might wish to live the rest of his life here when his quest was over.

Arriving at the train station, he saw Marcus sitting at a café reading a paper. Approaching from behind, he tapped his friend on the shoulder. It was time to leave for Prague.

# 29

VLASTOS LOCKED THE sleeper cabin and moved down the train car, toward the lounge. He limped through the hallway, but not even the weight and awkwardness of his foot cast upset his perfect balance. Opening the exit door, he stepped into the sealed section between cars and was instantly immersed in the roar and clatter of the high-speed train. He then hobbled through the two remaining cars.

The lounge was more crowded now. The man James had spoken with was still sitting alone at the bar, still looking for a conversation to shorten his journey.

Vlastos sidled past the other passengers and sat at the bar, next to the man whose life he would take. He ordered a Pils in German, then, when the barman turned away, mumbled to himself in English, "Can this night get any longer?"

"South African, by any chance?" the American asked.

"No, no," Vlastos said with an amused smile. "German. I just learned to speak from a proper Englishman. But *your* accent is not English. Canadian?"

"American," the man said. "Isaac Shelton." He stuck out his hand.

"I'm Jörgen Wiedemann," Vlastos said, shaking hands. "What brings you out here to the precise middle of nowhere? Nothing out here but emptiness and trouble. It is a bit like your old American West in that regard."

"There was a lot of opportunity in the Old West," Isaac said.

"Perhaps, but also a lot of death, no? A lot of wasted lives, I think."

"I don't believe any life is wasted," Isaac said. "Everything happens for a reason."

"You are a philosopher, then?" Vlastos asked, nodding as the barman delivered his beer.

"It's just what I believe," Isaac said. "I have no more of life's answers than anyone else."

"A *modest* philosopher," Vlastos said, raising his pint to Isaac. "All the more convincing."

Isaac laughed. "So what brings you to Prague?" he asked.

"Biz-ness," Vlastos said slowly.

"What sort?"

"Mmm, I work for a private organization headquartered in Berlin, which provides a wide range of products and services to a diverse client mix. I'm a . . . operational consultant, and I work on special projects for the organization's president. We have an operational division based in Prague, and I'm making a visit to ensure we are addressing all risks associated with potential market loss from our main competitor in the region."

"Sounds really interesting," Isaac said. "I have a brother at the University of Missouri business school back in the States. He's studying international finance. Maybe he could interview with your company when he graduates, if you're both interested."

Vlastos smiled like the devil in the early stages of bartering for an unsuspecting soul. "If he studies hard and learns finance and banking well, I wouldn't be surprised if we could find a place for him in our organization." He laughed to himself. "It's a tough environment to work in. Lot of pressure. Many people don't survive it. We don't tolerate mistakes. It's the kind of job that can kill someone if they can't keep up. But if they're good at it, we offer the kind of financial compensation they won't find anywhere else."

"Sounds like it's not for the faint of heart."

With his left hand, Vlastos took the tablet from his pocket and palmed it carefully. It was one of the most diabolical weapons he had ever discovered for his assassination toolbox. Inside the capsule was a small amount of a liquefied radioactive compound—too little to be harmful by mere touch. But if it got in your eyes, it would immediately blind you. And if it got into your digestive system, it would start burning holes in the large intestine within ten hours of ingestion. For Vlastos, it was the perfect killer in any situation where he wanted ten hours' lead time before any symptoms began, and another ten hours before the victim died. He merely had to drop the tablet into someone's drink, knowing there would be no easily traceable connection when the victim finally died and he had long vanished. The only disadvantage was that it was a very expensive way to kill someone. Still, Vlastos always kept a few tablets in his luggage for occasions like this, which required a touch of delicacy.

"Can I buy you another drink?" Vlastos asked Isaac after they both had finished their beers.

"Why not?" Isaac replied.

Vlastos motioned to the barman and ordered two more Pilsners. As the drinks were set in front of them, he felt his heart quicken with the cold thrill of an imminent kill.

"*Prost!*" he said, raising his glass.

"What's that?" Isaac asked with visible amusement, raising his glass. "Like 'Cheers' or something?"

The man seemed truly innocent of all bad things—not that Vlastos had any problem killing the innocent along with everyone else. One of the fringe benefits of living to take so many lives was that he understood the truth about how insignificant an individual life truly was. For as long as he could remember, every time he had killed someone, bad or good, he had woken the next day to find the world operating with the same jaded self-interest as ever. For him, the lesson was simple: no one person was important enough to make any difference in this world.

"Yes," Vlastos said. "'*Prost*' means 'toast.' So *Prost*!"

The two men raised their glasses.

Vlastos nodded toward two attractive young women sitting in the corner of the lounge car. "Goddesses," he said. "You know them?"

As Isaac turned to look at the women, Vlastos moved his right hand from his chest to an outstretched position, subtly dropping the small capsule into Isaac's drink. "Lovely . . . lovely," he whispered as if the women might hear them. "Not married?" he asked, glancing at Isaac's hand in the half-light.

"No," Isaac replied. "Just haven't met the right one yet."

"You're not planning to find her out here, are you?"

"Goodness, no! Too far from home."

Vlastos smiled. "Home," he murmured, as if saying the name of a long-lost love he hadn't thought of in ages.

Isaac lifted his glass to his lips, and Vlastos's hand snapped up, quick as a striking cobra, and latched on to his wrist.

"Wait," he said. "We can't drink until we toast something."

"What shall we toast?" Isaac asked.

"Oh, no, sir. It must be your toast, not mine. Your choice. It's the least I can do. Anything you wish for in life—wish for it now."

"And what if I already have everything in my life that I could want?" Isaac asked.

"Then you should wish to keep it," Vlastos said. Then, after a second's pause, thinking of the coming death of this innocent and seemingly good man, he couldn't resist reciting a few lines of Shakespeare that came to mind: "'*Thou seest the heavens, as troubled with man's act, threatens his bloody stage. By th' clock 'tis day, and yet dark night strangles the traveling lamp: Is't night's predominance, or the day's shame, that darkness does the face of earth entomb, when living light should kiss it?*'"

"'Tis unnatural,'" Isaac said, cutting in with a dramatic flourish, "'even like the deed that's done. On Tuesday last a falcon, tow'ring in her pride of place, was by a mousing owl hawked at and killed.'"

Vlastos stared in awe at the man who had answered his words with the very next lines from *Macbeth*. Not since his father's death had he encountered another soul with such intimate knowledge of the only writer who mattered to him. And he, as much as anyone, understood the haunting portent of the lines Isaac had spoken.

"*Prost*," Isaac said, raising his glass again as if eager to drink his own death.

Vlastos grabbed his own glass, hesitating a moment, eyes in a downward gaze lost somewhere in the swirling grain of the wooden bar top. He thought of James's plea that he spare this man's life. Then he thought of all the tragic elements of Shakespeare's writing, with its timeless beauty often hidden beneath the words. Vlastos nodded, knowing the choice he had in front of him and the difficult decision he had just decided he could live with.

He lifted his glass as his eyes met Isaac's. "*Prost!*" he replied, clinking his glass against Isaac's so hard that both glasses broke, spilling shards and beer between them.

"Oh, *Scheiße!*" Vlastos said, laughing a little tipsily. "Look what you've done."

"What *I've* done?" Isaac replied, still surprised.

"Right, right. No sense pointing fingers. A man can hardly be blamed for not knowing another's strength. Let me resolve the matter. Sir, two replacements, please. And charge *me* for the broken glasses if you must."

A minute later, the mess was cleaned up and the two men were holding their new drinks. Vlastos raised his glass to Isaac's. "*Prost* once again," he said. "Easy, now . . ."

Their glasses touched, and they drank. He needed to finish his drink as quickly as he could without raising suspicions. Then he would excuse himself and return to the cabin to free James, who should still be unconscious. His decision not to poison Isaac left him vulnerable once they arrived in Prague, and the only way he could mitigate the risk now was by leaving the train at the next stop, even though they were somewhere in the Czech countryside, at night. He couldn't risk having any more encounters with Isaac lest the man learn more about James and his journey.

Seeing his own cold eyes in the mirror in front of him, Vlastos couldn't believe he was going to leave such a loose end dangling. He was uncomfortable with the entire situation now, feeling vulnerable about the job, which made him even angrier with himself than he had been when he first let James escape him a few days ago in Ian's apartment.

Vlastos emptied his glass and stood up from his bar stool. "I'm afraid my time in this place is finished," he said, laying some euros on the bar top as carefully as if he were presenting a straight flush.

Isaac reached out his hand to shake. "Well, it was really nice to meet you, Jörgen," he said. "Maybe we'll bump into each other again sometime."

"Maybe," Vlastos said, shaking the man's hand and knowing that this would be the first and last time they would ever see each other—as was the case with nearly everyone Vlastos had come across during the past twenty years. In another life, he might have had a few more beers with the man while discussing Shakespeare, until they decided to relocate to a table closer to the two goddesses in the corner. But he had a job to do, and he worked in a profession that required absolute discipline to keep the odds of success high.

He knocked twice on the bar top, gave Isaac a farewell nod, and moved toward the door. With each step he took, he felt himself growing more powerful as his focus on the job turned him back into the same killer he had been for the past twenty years.

# 30

JAMES LAWRENCE WAS back in Manhattan, Kansas, yet it wasn't real, somehow. It was Saturday night, and he was drinking at Rusty's Last Chance Saloon with his girlfriend, Julie Sherman, although he hadn't seen her since their relationship ended more than five years ago. He was surrounded by old friends. Some had faces he didn't recognize, yet somehow, they were still his friends. Everything was very familiar, even though his mind was alert enough to warn him that none of it was real: it was part memory and part imagination. He half realized he was dreaming, yet he didn't want it to end, so his mind made no attempt to jolt him from this comfy, familiar place.

He looked at Julie, and she smiled in return. Her thin lips and big teeth reminded him of a horse when she laughed. It was something he hadn't found attractive when they first started dating, but he realized now that it was one of the things he missed most in the years since he had seen her. Now, in this dream world from his past, he found himself laughing with her as if no space or time had ever separated them.

Her hand fell onto his thigh, and they both pretended not to notice. It must be summer, because they were wearing shorts. He said something into her ear over the loud Jimmy Buffett song, but the scent of her tempted him to start kissing her neck before he could finish what he wanted to tell her. He could hear his friends discussing how many more pitchers of beer to order from a waitress. And in this moment, he couldn't remember a time in his life when he had felt more surrounded by happiness.

As he pulled away from Julie, he felt the light brush of her golden hair across his face. The large wooden double doors to the bar's front entrance were attached to a sailor's rope that stretched across the ceiling on a visible pulley system, tied to a separate empty beer keg for each door. Every time either door was pulled open from the outside, one of the hanging kegs would rise a few feet. James now focused hypnotically on the rising metal keg, pulled toward the ceiling of the bar on a rope as thick as his forearm. And as if the rising keg were the sound of a doorbell, he looked toward the front entrance of Last Chance. A crowd was clustered incuriously around the front entrance, as if they were standing there only because everywhere else in the saloon was occupied. Much of college drinking was standing around waiting for something interesting to happen.

As the door closed and the keg lowered from the ceiling, James saw Ian emerge from the crowd clustered at the entrance, and walk to the bar. His brother was alone, as he often chose to be, yet many eyes followed him with interest. When Ian got to the bar, he was able to order beer from the bartender, ahead of others who had waited much longer. James watched as his brother shook hands and said a few words to some strangers, smiled, and motioned for the bartender to put a round of drinks on *his* tab, before moving away.

James was so distracted by Ian's activities, it took him a moment to notice that Julie had vanished. So had all his friends around the table. But as often happened in dreams, even the strangest things seemed quite natural, so he thought little of it and turned his attention back to his brother.

Ian looked young and healthy. Life, it seemed, was good to those who shirked responsibility. *It's good for a while, anyway. But sooner or later, life will catch up to you, Ian. You can't avoid it forever. You'll have to grow up. You'll have to accept that she died and I moved on and our parents found a way to live with it, and you will need to pretend that there was never any future for her if you want to have one yourself. She was never meant to grow up. She was always destined to die when she was only ten years old. It was our fault for thinking that because our life was so great, it would be good forever—our fault for not realizing how vulnerable we all truly were.*

James couldn't feel the tears running down his face, yet somehow, as can happen in dreams, he knew he was crying. He and Ian had shared her affection equally, as brothers often did. Yet despite that love, they both had been helpless to protect their little sister when she was in the greatest danger of her life.

Something had changed that did not seem natural even in this dream. He sensed an outside intrusion. Ian noticed him from the bar, grabbed his half-finished beer, and came toward him, unsmiling, through the crowd. James watched as his brother approached, past some wooden cable-reel tables, past a cluster of college girls eyeing him, past a big bearded man with a machine gun playing a card game with two guys who looked like clones from some fraternity house. Ian moved with ease through the sea of people, toward James. The bar grew steadily brighter, blotting out the patrons along the walls, yet Ian had a dark outline that made him impervious to the blinding whiteout. Only twenty feet away now, James saw a slight smile form on his brother's face, his eyes gleaming with the thrill of their reunion after what suddenly felt like a lifetime apart.

"James," the voice said, shaking him.

His eyes opened, and he jerked when he saw Vlastos standing over him with their bags. Dazed, he jolted upright and leaned back into the corner of the sleeper car's bed. "Fuck . . .

shit!" he muttered, rubbing his wet eyes and ruffling his hair in a desperate attempt to snap back into this dark world that he suddenly found himself back inside. Gazing around the cabin, his off-balance mind took a few seconds to recall that he was on a night train in the eastern European countryside, somewhere between Berlin and Prague.

"We're leaving," Vlastos said, tossing one of the bags to his feet.

"What?" James mumbled, still confused. "Are we there?"

"We're getting there a different way. Now, come on. The next stop is soon."

"I don't understand," James said. He leaned forward to grab the bag, and it hit him that he had been sleeping in the bed fully dressed. Even his shoes were still on. Then, with a flash of horror, he remembered the argument he had been having with Vlastos.

"What happened?" James demanded. "What did you do? Tell me you stayed away from the guy from KC!"

Vlastos grabbed James's throat and squeezed. "Don't ever question me," he said softly. "Don't ever hesitate when I give you a command. You made a deal with Strobviok that binds you to what *I* say."

James struggled to resist Vlastos's overpowering strength. "What did you do to him?" he croaked.

Vlastos released him and took a few hobbling steps back, toward the door. His sudden rage had calmed. "Nothing. That's why we're leaving the train at the next stop." Then he said, "I didn't do it for you. I don't want you to be confused and think I spared his life because of something *you* said. It had nothing to do with that. His life was saved by someone else: someone much more important than you could ever dream of being." He stepped toward the door and opened it. "Now, follow me this second!"

James had no choice but to follow. "Where are we, anyway?" he said. "Where is the next stop?"

"Somewhere out there—in the darkness," Vlastos said, glaring back at him. The man's world seemed to have turned suddenly toward death, as if he was embarrassed to have connected momentarily with the living. "Everything out there right now is darkness. We had our opportunity to ride this train into a city with enough lights to blind the gods, but now we are forced to step out into the empty darkness in this forgotten land."

James hadn't realized until now that the man had a certain air of exaggerated, self-indulgent poetry in his occasionally bizarre style of speaking. Perhaps this might have struck fear, or at least uneasiness, into the many men Vlastos had tormented in the past. But verbal parlor tricks wouldn't work on him: James had been with his little sister when she was killed, he had chased monster tornados across the prairies, and he was now on a journey, in a foreign land, to find his brother—the one person in the world who understood him. James stared hard at Vlastos, making no attempt to hide his hatred for the man.

Knowing he had little choice except to continue following Vlastos on his brother's path, James slung the heavy duffel bag over his shoulder and moved toward the door. As they walked down the narrow passageway, he could feel the train slowing. A voice came over the speaker and announced in a heavy foreign language something that made him feel once again as if he were the only foreigner on the train.

James tried to steady his breathing, to slow his racing heart, and told himself that if he just kept going, then somewhere, through all this darkness, he would find Ian.

# 31

---◦✳◦---

CHANCELLOR THOMAS HENZOLLERN opened the file that Professor Friedrich Hampdenstein had forwarded him. It was written by the missing American, Ian Lawrence. He focused on the paper, and the world around him faded away. As the leader of Germany, he felt his skin tingle at the implications of the introductory paragraphs:

> There are dark places in the deep ocean—places where light cannot penetrate—but there is nothing darker than the hearts of evil men whose souls have been poisoned by a life in organized crime.
>
> Criminal organizations—sharing most attributes of any large, sophisticated corporation—are nothing more than illegal corporate entities operating in such illegal markets that mitigating government regulations are nonexistent. This prevents governments from controlling any aspect of

*the business activities except by throwing the weight of law enforcement at them. Such measures, while sometimes successful in disrupting certain operations of a criminal organization, have a history of severe limitations in disrupting the illegal market as a whole.*

*This paper will explore the past theoretical errors governments have made in attempting to stop criminal organizations. In addition, it will explore a new theoretical outline of specific procedures, economic actions, and timelines in arguments— governments approaching the issue as they would the regulating of a legal corporation attempting to build a monopoly, fix prices, evade taxes, etc. This paper will show how it is possible for any government to peacefully bankrupt any criminal organization operating within its municipality, state, or country within a two- to-four-year time frame, using advanced game theory and innovative economic policies.*

Thomas stared at the computer screen as if the American's words were a swinging gold medallion in front of his face, sinking him into a deep hypnosis. Had this American really discovered an economic theorem that governments could use to peacefully destroy any criminal organization on the planet? Was something like that even possible? Under other circumstances, he would never have believed it. But the American had the help of Professor Hampdenstein, who seemed to know as much about the economics of organized crime as anyone in academia.

He scrolled to the next page and kept reading. He could scarcely believe what the American had discovered. Everything was so interconnected. He was combining the same management strategies that MBAs had been using for decades—the same high-level corporate finance strategies that the world's top investment bankers used to rule the legitimate economies of the world. The same economic principles that explained recessions and depreciations and every historic asset bubble known to humankind. It was at times complicated, at other times brilliantly simple. The American had given a careful history of all the fundamentals he needed before exploring his concise theory backed by what looked like a detailed working copy of two case studies to prove his point. And as Thomas read through the pages, he found himself believing it was really possible. Perhaps Ian really had discovered how to destroy as many of the world's criminal organizations as its governments chose to take on—as long as they could be patient and, at times, ignore interorganizational violence.

After he finished reading it, he closed his laptop, stood up, and walked across the room to the telephone.

*   *   *

James and Vlastos waited two hours before the next train arrived. The outskirts of Prague revealed nothing more than vast empty fields and small vacant train stations. Then there were glimpses of ancient, decrepit factories, with broken windows and overgrown with weeds, in an echo of a time before depression, war, and Communism in turn had plagued this economy. Then James saw little neighborhood clusters of red and brown brick houses lining the tracks before the train slid into an enormous glass station with people everywhere. Prague looked like a

Medieval European city that had somehow managed to thrive in the modern world.

The sunlight inside the car dimmed as the train entered the shadows of Prague's main hub. They were barely moving now, and he could see passengers standing on the platforms jutting out between sets of tracks. The train emitted a high shriek as its brakes locked and metal rubbed against metal for the last twenty feet before stopping.

Vlastos stood and pointed toward the door.

Stepping off the train, James walked with Vlastos while taking in the sights around him. He was now farther from home than he had ever been in his life. Here was a city older even than Berlin. How the hell was he going to find Ian here? And what was going to happen with Vlastos? The unknown dangers made him feel sick. This wasn't what he did for a living: he was a tax accountant, usually dealing with certainties, rules, and well-outlined planning. He wasn't trained to troubleshoot a fast-changing problem on the fly. He didn't just make things up as he went along, or wing it as he dived into a sea of unknowns. His mind kept trying to catch up, to think its way out of this problem. But his thoughts were only making him crazy. He couldn't control a thing that was happening. He was drifting in the ocean, helpless to control his fate.

The professor had been right: he really didn't have any control over his life, as he had thought for so long. He was at the mercy of forces that didn't care about him.

\* \* \*

Wolfgang turned the BMW hard right on the narrow cobblestone street in the Old City district. The road wound down the hill from Prague Castle toward the Vltava River. The view to his left was obstructed by a tall stone wall that snaked alongside the street. It was surely part of the old city's fortification wall from centuries ago. To his right, a hill seemed to wrap around the Czech capital below. The hillside was scattered with stone buildings, including a large monastery that he recognized from his first visit here many years ago.

Driving across a short bridge, he entered a maze of narrow cobblestone streets walled by crowded old stone buildings. Following the GPS device on his windshield, he parked on the street and walked to the small red door of an antique bookstore.

Inside was an old friend who would know everything about crimes in the city.

# 32

JAMES AND VLASTOS were in a café near the Prague Museum of Medieval Torture Instruments. Vlastos had stepped away to make a phone call, and James was using the free moment to ponder why Ian would have tried to live a split life between HHL, the White Rose, the Geryon Mafia, and the Malacoda gang. The same brain that was accustomed to tabulating and conceptualizing countless numbers and scenarios and memorizing tax rules and pending tax code legislation was now compiling all the pieces to the real-world Rubik's cube that Ian had pulled him into.

He closed his eyes and concentrated on all the pieces he knew of Ian's mystery, so that he could imagine the missing pieces to the puzzle. He saw his brother and himself as adventurous, rebellious youths. Then he saw Ian and himself on different paths, drifting apart. And then Ian was in Germany, seeking a purpose in his life for the first time but still always attracted to anything dangerous. He saw the professor who specialized in the economics of organized crime after living the kind of mysterious, dangerous life that would have attracted his brother like a moth to a flame. Then he saw Ian's e-mails and dissertation and the mention of using economics to destroy criminal organizations from the inside out.

He saw everything. He understood how everything was playing out. Then the answer came to him: Ian was trying to start a war between the Geryon Mafia and the Malacoda gang!

Vlastos returned to the table. "I've made the arrangement for the first meeting," he said, looking at his watch. "But it's time to go. There's an introduction chain—a protocol we need to follow. That means there are some people we need to meet before we can meet the ones who will introduce us to those who can get us close to the top men in the Malacoda gang."

"So we're four levels away from the top," James said. He was used to navigating complex U.S. tax regulations and could quickly visualize the abstract command structure of the criminal organization.

"That's right," Vlastos said. He put money on the table and got up. "Come on. If we're late, we may not get another chance. If that happens, my boss just might have us both killed."

They left the café, and Vlastos lead James over the uneven cobblestones that arched down to the Vltava River and into the water. They were moving toward a man in a long, black leather jacket, who knelt at the edge of the river and was dipping his fingers in the water as if trying to wash his hands. When they were still thirty yards away, Vlastos whispered to James, "Remember, from this point forward, you are your brother. They will try to kill us if they suspect you are not Ian Lawrence."

*But I'm not Ian,* James thought. *Not even close.*

He saw the ancient Charles Bridge only a hundred yards away, and the imposing Prague Castle rising up on the mountainous skyline that rimmed the city.

"Ramos," Vlastos said.

The man took his fingers out of the river and stood up straight. His jacket was rumpled around his shoulders and biceps, as if he were made of rock or bronze hidden under the black leather. His neck was bunched with muscles.

James also noticed that Vlastos's demeanor had changed. The killer had become reserved in his movements, polite and respectful as he shook the man's hand, as if following some sort of etiquette understood between men in organized crime.

The man shook Vlastos's hand without smiling. Then his eyes shifted to James.

"Ramos," Vlastos said, "this is Ian Lawrence. He's been helping Strobviok with some business in Berlin. He's now interested in helping Manchevski here in Prague."

The man gave a slow nod as his stony face and sharp, gleaming eyes studied James.

"You know Mr. Lawrence's reputation?" Vlastos asked.

"No, but I've heard the name mentioned." He was still staring at James, as if watching him for any hint that something was not as advertised.

"He has ideas that could make your boss a lot of money. Manchevski will want to hear these ideas."

"And what do *you* get out of this?" Ramos asked.

Vlastos looked at him hard. "That is for Manchevski and me to discuss."

"So you are vouching for this man?"

"Yes," Vlastos said in a way that made James understand the serious implications of this for all future introductions of Mr. Lawrence into the Malacoda gang.

The man nodded again. "And I'll vouch for you. Let me go meet with someone. I'll be back in an hour with their decision."

Ramos walked away from them, along the sloping cobblestone steps only feet from the lapping river water.

"That wasn't so bad," James said.

"That was just the first of four doors. The next one will be harder, as will the next one after that—if we make it that far.

And just so you know, when he was staring at you he was studying you carefully for anything funny. You did good."

This surprised James. It hadn't occurred to him that people working in organized crime were accustomed to reading people's hidden agendas for a living, but now he realized that it was probably a most important trait to have if one hoped for a successful career in organized crime.

"So now what?" James asked.

"Now we wait. When he returns with the decision, he'll either invite us to the next meeting or try to put a bullet in both our heads."

"If that happens, you'll protect me, right?"

"I think that if that's what happens, I'll have my hands full just trying to save myself. But if it's any comfort, I'll try to save you, too, if I can."

"Gee, that's great," James muttered. "What more could I ask for?"

Vlastos chuckled for the first time since the start of their journey.

# 33

LOUD ALTERNATIVE ROCK music echoed through the upper floors of the old Prague warehouse. The man sat in front of two computer monitors at a long makeshift table of plywood on four metal drums. With the mouse, he scrolled down the text on the screen, grunted, and opened a message box to reply to the intranet post. The other monitor had a word document on half the screen, and a map of Prague with embedded flags and tracker marks on the other half.

His cell phone, sitting next to the keyboard, suddenly glowed, announcing an incoming call. No name appeared—only a number. But it was a number he knew: a pay phone on the corner of Svobodova and Rasinovo Nabrezi, which his informant always used.

"Hello," he said.

"Something's happening that you might be interested in," the voice said.

"Okay."

"One of Strobviok's men has come to Prague. His name is Vlastos. And he has with him someone who is supposed to give advice on how to make certain illegal business practices more profitable."

"Who's the man?" he asked.

"His name is Ian Lawrence."

*Impossible!* The man hunched over the keyboard, tightening his grip on the cell phone. "What else can you tell me about him?"

"He's an American. I'm not sure how he got in contact with the Geryon Mafia. White, about one point nine meters, blue eyes, athletic build."

"You're sure he's an American?" the man asked.

"The contact checked his passport."

"And it said 'Ian Lawrence'?"

"Yes."

"The picture matched and everything."

"Yes, it was him."

The man gasped. He knew that it couldn't be the *real* Ian Lawrence. "Okay, thank you. This is very valuable information for us. We'll need to verify what you're saying before we can transfer anything for this information."

"I understand."

"Where are these men now?"

"They're being called to a meeting with some soldiers."

*Jesus,* the man thought.

"Okay. Let us check on some things here. Then I'll have someone get you a message. And let me know if you learn anything else—especially about this Ian Lawrence. You did good. Really good."

When the call ended, Marcus jumped up from his chair and ran down the corridor of the warehouse. As he rounded a banister and raced down a rickety old staircase, he yelled excitedly, "Ian! Ian, you're not going to believe this!"

# 34

———————•≡✴≡•———————

A N HOUR AFTER Ramos left them, James saw the man returning along the river. His expression was stony, impossible to read. James feared that he was about to learn more about the criminal world than he ever wanted to know.

"Get ready," Vlastos said to him. Ramos was still fifty yards away, approaching. "He's not going to try to kill us. We're going to the next level."

"How do you know?"

"He came alone."

The further James was pulled toward the Malacoda gang, the more he thought of Vlastos as his protector. He realized how ridiculous this was, but he was desperate to hold on to some thin sliver of security, even if it was false. So he could only hope that if things got violent, Vlastos would find some reason in the moment of chaos to try to save James.

Ramos arrived. "Come with me," he said, then turned on the cobblestones and lumbered back in the direction he had come.

They followed the man for fifteen minutes through the warren of narrow streets. The more they walked, the less they saw of other people. There were no tourists in this part of the city. Eventually, Ramos led them into a stone walkway through a building before opening a thick wooden door and leading them into a black void. James's eyes adapted to the dim light from an old cigarette machine and the few dim lightbulbs lining the room, which, he could now tell, was a pub—though not a normal pub that was open to the public. This was a shady, private pub, removed from civilization, unknown to any who were not supposed to be here. A place to drink and meet but not to make money. It seemed like the kind of establishment the owners kept for privacy rather than profit. He was now on the edge of a criminal organization's reception lobby.

He felt goose bumps on his arms as Ramos led them into the back room of the pub. It looked like a kitchen, with a concrete floor, metal slabs and counters, ovens, dangling pots and pans, and blocks full of large knives, which at this moment felt more like weaponry than cutlery. In the center of the room stood two men, both in jeans and dress shirts and black leather jackets.

The first, James learned as Ramos introduced everyone, was named Artani. It was an Albanian name, apparently, and James got the sense from Artani's reaction to Ramos's pronunciation of his name that in Albania it meant something that showed how proud of him his parents must have been minutes after he was born. Artani shuffled quickly on the balls of his feet as he made a gesture toward James and Vlastos—a sort of phantom shaking of hands—before sliding back into place like a boxer ducking and weaving in the ring to confuse his opponent. The man's eyes had an energetic sparkle that hinted at a daring, challenging spirit.

The second man was named Kreshnik. He stood motionless, though he somehow seemed to James more dangerous than anyone else in the room besides Vlastos. The man's short gray hair seemed to contradict the hopeful way his sad eyes widened slightly during the introduction.

"I've heard of you," Kreshnik said to him.

"What have you heard?" James asked, a little more interested in the answer than the real Ian probably would have been.

Kreshnik let the question hang for a moment, as if to intimidate him. "I heard you have ideas about how we can do our jobs better."

"I'm not here because I know how you can do your job better. From what I assume, there is no one who can do your job better than you. But what I can offer is consultation on a few strategies that will help you and your colleagues operate this business even more profitably than it is already being run."

"We know Ramos," Kreshnik said. "If Ramos vouches for Vlastos here and Vlastos vouches for you, then we will listen to what you have to say. But we need to ask you a few questions first, to make sure you really are who you say you are."

"Do you want to see my passport?" James said. Ian's duplicate passport had worked on Ramos and everyone else so far, so he was as confident in it as if it were his own.

"Passports can be forged," Artani said.

"Don't get us wrong," Kreshnik said, interrupting Artani. "Our boss is very interested in hearing what you have to say. But we have a responsibility here, a chain."

Vlastos hadn't said anything in minutes, and James realized that he wouldn't be speaking in this meeting. It was now up to James alone to convince these men he was Ian.

"Well, I'm here," he said. "Just tell me what you need me to do."

"First, you need to tell us why you're here," Kreshnik said.

"I'm here to offer your boss some ideas that he might like," James replied.

"No, I mean why have you decided to do this? Why contact us?" Kreshnik's dark eyes now gleamed with the kind of dangerous, challenging intelligence that hinted at a deeper power and a greater evil. "Why involve yourself in our world?" His index finger tapped the butt of the pistol in his concealed waistband holster.

Resisting the urge to throw up or pass out, James felt himself overcome by a flood of memories of his brother. He had studied Ian's life for a long time, but in this moment even that wouldn't be enough. Vlastos had been right. He needed to *become* Ian.

"I was born to be in this world," James said, feeling Ian's answer more than thinking it. "I was born in Kansas, and even though I raised as much hell as I could growing up, it wasn't the kind of real action I needed. It's taken me a lifetime to discover my path here, but I'm here now. And I'm telling you, this is what I was born to do."

James could tell by Artani's and Kreshnik's looks that he was wearing Ian's daredevil craziness convincingly. It was a craziness that James had often felt in his own blood, but not until now had he ever been forced to strip away his restraint and become as crazy as Ian.

"Tell me, Mr. Lawrence," Kreshnik said. "What makes you think you can add any 'efficiencies' to our business that we have not already thought of?"

James nodded as if appreciating the question the way that Ian would have appreciated it. Just as he had done with the complex U.S. Tax Code, he had memorized the key phrases of Ian's dissertation. "It's a brave new world for everyone, Mr. Kreshnik. Things change." He closed his eyes, which he knew was a dangerous tactic because it might make him look weak or uncertain, but it was the only way he could access the visual images of the sentences he had read from Ian's thesis. "Money-laundering techniques have evolved significantly in the past fifteen years. Political corruption has become more difficult to initiate or continue. Some criminal organizations have become so segmented that competition is beginning to look more like a standard, regulated capitalistic system than an illegal, monopolistic system, thus infringing on the advantageous profit margins realized in earlier decades."

Artani seemed confused by James's words, but Kreshnik appeared to be right in tune.

James continued, eyes open now. "All this means that criminal organizations are no different from any other international corporation of the past fifteen years. Cultural changes, political changes, technological changes, transportation and other logistical changes. But *some* fundamental human needs have not changed: the need to gamble on entertaining games of chance, the need for chemical drugs that governments have declared illegal based on legislated morality, the need for a service that an archaic philosophy or religion has condemned as a vice." James swished his hand through the air in front of his face as if dismissing a silly notion. "The point is, I've studied finance and business and economics at the highest academic levels. And I've focused solely on the economics of organized crime, so I'm amply qualified to give advice to Manchevski regarding potential strategic improvements for your organization."

James looked back at Vlastos and caught a hint of a smile, and in that moment he knew he had passed the test. He should be terrified, but instead he felt the daredevil instincts of Ian's personality still burning inside him. The quest for his brother was awakening a part of himself that he had kept dormant for years. And it had awakened in him at just the right moment. He and Vlastos were going to the next level.

# 35

———✳———

IAN LAWRENCE STUDIED the schematics for the warehouse for what felt like the hundredth time. Footsteps pounded down the staircase on the other side of the large room. Someone was calling out his name.

Still captivated by the schematics, he continued to study every architecturally scaled inch of the warehouse. This was the main entrance, and here were two back exits. One escape from the roof, three from the sides. This room was where they greeted clients; this was where they counted the money. This was where the women were kept: the large room on the first floor, these sixteen rooms on the second floor, and maybe a breakout chamber in the basement that could create thirty lower-rent rooms.

"Ian!" a voice yelled again as the man who had been the source of the pounding footsteps burst into the room.

He turned to see Marcus panting in the doorway. "Good Lord! What is it?"

"The Geryon Mafia is using someone impersonating you to meet with the Malacoda gang."

*"What!"*

"I got it from our Malacoda source."

"When do they meet?" Ian asked.

"Sometime this week, apparently—maybe even today. The timing of the information leak and the schedule would seem to imply either today or tomorrow."

"And your source thinks the Malacodas might fall for it?"

"The word is, the guy's a dead-on impersonator of you. Somehow, someone got hold of your draft dissertation. The impersonator seems to have studied it. They also seem to have gathered a lot of information about your personal life to help him pretend he's you."

"Man, those guys have some balls!" Ian murmured. Then he looked up at Marcus. "Holy shit! We could use this to help start the war."

"Use this . . . ?"

"Sure," Ian said. "If we could expose this to the Malacoda gang, let them know this impostor isn't really me, it would force them to retaliate against the Geryon Mafia."

"And then the Geryon Mafia would have to retaliate back!" Marcus said.

Ian nodded. "Each side aggressively increases its violent responses until they're officially at war."

Ian couldn't believe his luck. Some poor fool had been conned into impersonating him to get close to the Malacoda gang. And now they were going to be exposed.

"Make the call," Ian said. "Make the call and let those bastards know that they have someone impersonating me. It seems like the Geryon Mafia has planned something to try to hurt the Malacodas. So make the call and get this war going."

# 36

———————※———————

A BLACK MERCEDES drove James and Vlastos across Prague. Kreshnik was in the front passenger's seat, and Artani was behind the wheel, glancing periodically at James in the mirror. Ramos was gone. James breathed deeply and looked straight ahead without a word, just as Vlastos had coached him to do during the train ride to Prague.

The Mercedes stopped in front of what looked like a luxurious restaurant: giant windows stretching across the front of a three-story gray stone building. A valet standing outside the front doors walked toward the car.

Once inside the building, they passed through the main room of the restaurant. The smell of food, including the distinct aroma of German sauerbraten with potato dumplings, reminded James of a little grill he often lunched at on the Plaza in Kansas City, but he knew from Vlastos that this must be an Albanian restaurant. The tables were set with china on white linen. Since it was midafternoon, hardly anyone was eating, and James had the funny feeling most of the people here were part of the Malacoda gang and were probably conducting the type of business meetings that Ian had outlined in chapter 3 of his dissertation.

A man in a dark suit led him and Vlastos through the dining room and up a long flight of stairs. At the top, he led them into a private dining room guarded by two burly men in suits. Four men were inside.

The man who had led them into the room put a hand on James's chest to stop him from going farther. James noticed that no one dared lay a hand on Vlastos. The man then turned and proceeded toward the table alone. He whispered in the ear of a man who looked older than the other three.

James felt as if a spotlight were showing his every pore. For a moment he felt dizzy, as if he might pass out, and he bent his knees slightly because someone once told him that standing with locked knees increased one's chance of passing out in stressful situations such as performing in a marching band or waiting for a bride to join you at the altar, or preparing to lie to a group of made men tied to the most dangerous criminal organization in Prague.

The one to the old man's right had a bumpy shaved head and dark, dodgy eyes that reminded James of a boxer. To Boxer's right sat a man disfigured by a missing right earlobe. James was actually a little relieved when the man turned toward him and he could see that the left ear was all there. Seated to One Ear's right, with his back to James, was a tallish man who looked over his shoulder at James. He had a thick mustache.

After getting a nod from the old man, the man who had brought James and Vlastos up to the room ushered James to the left side of the room so that he stood facing the old man. Vlastos remained by the door. Until now, James had convinced himself that Vlastos would protect him if their lives were endangered, but that was before they found themselves in a room now filled with seven Malacoda gang members. If things blew up now, Vlastos was not likely to be of much use in keeping James alive—he would have a hard enough time saving his own skin.

"You're Ian Lawrence?" the old man asked.

"Yes," James said. He had been waiting for introductions that apparently were not coming. This wasn't one of the congenial business meetings he was used to having in Kansas City.

Boxer sneezed and violently shook his head the way a dog would.

"We've read your essay on improving organized crime operations," the old man said. "Do you know how we got it?"

James shook his head. He knew only of Ian's draft dissertation and nothing of any essay. He could never have known everything Ian was up to, but it seemed unfair that these men were going to blow the whole charade with their first question.

"On the Internet, Mr. Lawrence," the old man said, visibly irritated at answering his own question. "On that blog your professor keeps. That was careless of you."

*Easy,* James thought. *They don't know anything yet.*

"Careless?" James asked.

"To expose your ideas like that . . . to appear on our radar."

"Maybe he *wanted* to be on our radar," Mustache said in a basso profundo as deep as any James had ever heard.

"Why would he want that?" the old man bantered.

"Because he wants to be one of us," One Ear said thoughtfully. James now figured him for the smartest of the four.

"Stupid," the old man grunted.

"Is that true?" Mustache asked, glaring at James.

James's eyes darted to Vlastos, where they met only with stony silence. He looked back at the table. *Become Ian. What would Ian say he wanted?* His mind cleared, and once again he became the person he understood better than he knew anyone else in the world. "I want to prove that my theories work in the real world."

Boxer chuckled, and the old man laughed out loud. One Ear turned his chair halfway around and leaned back to stare at James.

"Bullshit," the old man said.

One Ear nodded. "I believe him."

This seemed enough for Mustache. "How well do you think you know our operations?"

James shrugged. "They're like any other business operations. There are certainly some industry-specific considerations, but in the end it's all about modernizing your business operations to get as much profit as possible."

"You think we aren't modernized?" the old man said.

One Ear jumped in. "We have one of the best IT units of any corporation in Eastern Europe. We have computer programmers as good as Interpol or any cybercrime division of any country's intelligence agency. Even as good as your American units."

"That's not what I'm talking about," James said, trying to backtrack. He wasn't expecting One Ear's IT rant, because he never thought the organization could be that technologically savvy. "I'm talking about management structure, principle-agent theory, game theory . . ."

"All right," One Ear said. "Tell us."

"Well," James began, "think of it like this. Your type of business has a unique strategic advantage in that once you've broken as many laws as you have, you might as well break them all. Since you're already dealing in illegal goods and services, you might as well engage in price fixing and monopolistic strategies and trademark infractions and contract violations. The list goes on."

"You're not telling us anything we don't already know," the old man said. He punctuated his statement by taking out a nickel-plated handgun and laying it on the table in front of him.

His message was clear: *strike two*.

James darted a glance at Vlastos, who was glaring back as if he, too, considered shooting him.

There was only one other point from Ian's dissertation that he could think of using. A twist on the standard data analysis technique that many blue-chip corporations used, it was the subject of many MBA case studies—cases that even James had studied while getting his master's in accounting.

"Data logistics, gentlemen," he said, trying to pretend that everything he had said so far was somehow part of a lead-up to this, his main presentation. "Wal-Mart, Siemens, Burlington Railroad—these are just a few of the companies using advanced logistical tracking systems to increase their business efficiency and profit margins. Criminal organizations have spent so much time focusing on the secrecy and security of their business operations that they have failed to invest enough in various logistical IT applications. Also, advanced data mining techniques could be used to help identify key accounting discrepancies within various business units and operating regions, which could help identify underperforming managers and even discover potential fraud activity."

"Fraud?" the old man said, then burst into laughter. "Mr. Lawrence, you don't want to know what we do to people who try to cheat us. I don't think your little numbers game will be any help to us."

"You'd be surprised," James said. "Last year, Toyota used data mining to identify eighteen fraud activities at car dealers in the southeastern United States. John Deere identified supply parts manufacturing issues from South Korea that generated savings of a million dollars. NewsCorp found franchise underbillings for advertising rights in Western Europe that landed three French bankers in jail. All these are companies that consider themselves very sophisticated, but they sat up and took notice at these discoveries and many others. Data mining techniques are one of the fastest growing methods for corporations and other large, complex organizations to better manage and trace activities across their various business segments in ways that weren't possible even ten years ago."

The room was silent, and James knew that he had finally hit upon something that piqued their interest.

"What is this *data mining*?" Mustache asked.

"You track data to look for strange things," One Ear offered.

"That's right," James said, surprised again at the man's understanding. "Trained professionals can use software to mine through an enormous amount of data looking for anomalies. Gentlemen, I'm talking about fifty thousand lines of Microsoft Access data, pulling queries and matching prices and product movements with profit margins and volumes. I'm talking about developing a robust accounting system to track and discover anomalies in large purchases, banking transaction activity, sales, money laundering, payrolls, official bribes, and so on. An organization as large as yours, with as many employees, contractors, products, services, operational locations, and daily cash flows, will by nature be rife with inefficiencies and various levels of fraud within the organization. Every large company in the world has these problems, but your organization is more prone to them than most because of the secrecy of the business transactions. International crime syndicates have become very good at using sophisticated professionals and IT systems to protect their operations and money laundering activities but have lacked the ability to monitor their operational efficiencies. What I'm offering is to take my knowledge of advanced data mining, learned from an MBA program's proven strategic management techniques, to help increase your organization's profit and monitor for internal fraud. I could potentially increase your profit margins by twenty to thirty percent over a five-year period, which—as you know better than I—could be worth hundreds of millions of dollars to your businesses. You can't lose with this, gentlemen."

*Except that it's all bullshit,* James thought after his long, excited speech. They could very well kill him where he stood!

His adrenaline had given him an alertness he hadn't known in years. And feeling this alive, focused, and energized terrified him all the more that they would take his life away from him. It all could end right at this moment when he felt more than ever that living a full, adventurous life was the cure for everything that had been slowly killing him as he slogged through his tax accounting career. This moment was about catching up and making up for all the wild things Ian had done while he sat idly by, vaguely wondering what he was missing.

"And what resources would you need to save us one hundred million dollars?" One Ear said.

"Two to three million dollars," James replied.

"How many people?"

"Ten to twenty professionals from financial auditing and IT. Maybe ten CPAs and ten CISAs." His audience might not be familiar with CISA, but the specific professional distinctions didn't matter. They were probably called something different in Europe anyway. The important thing was, he was giving them some specifics, and that would only help his *ad hoc* presentation.

A door at the back of the room opened, and a tall, rangy man entered and closed the door behind him. He held a cell phone to his ear but never said a word. His eyes had an intensity that told James something was very wrong. No one else seemed to pay attention to the man.

"What about secrecy?" Boxer asked. He directed his question to the old man.

James realized that Boxer might be smarter than he looked. For that matter, all these men were smarter than they looked.

"It's a risk," the old man said.

"*Everything* in your business is a risk," James said, feeling his strength build. When it came to business and finance, he was as confident as anyone. "Everything you do needs secrecy.

You're a large illegal organization. Secrecy is your specialty, gentlemen. Operational efficiency and cost savings are mine."

The man with the phone stepped forward and held it to the old man's ear. The old man's eyes widened as he listened. Then he looked at James.

Vlastos seemed to sense a heightened danger, for when James's eyes fell to the maple floor and followed an imaginary line to his imaginary protector, he thought he saw Vlastos sliding the silver butterfly knife out of its wrist holster. Vlastos was looking at some focal point above the table, as if to let his peripheral vision register everything in the room without looking at it directly, like a gunslinger working out how to draw and kill seven men before any one of them could kill him.

James felt as though he was going to be sick, and he couldn't stop it. He whirled about and lurched toward the corner of the room, aware of the commotion behind him: startled shouts and toppled chairs. His body had betrayed him under the stress, and all he could do was press both arms against the walls, lower his head, and vomit in the corner of the room. Tears filled his eyes, and he coughed, threw up again, spat, and moaned. After perhaps thirty seconds, he stood up straight, wiped his mouth, and turned back toward the others in the room.

Vlastos was surrounded by three men, yet he hadn't made any move to kill them. The other men were now standing around the table, staring at James. Boxer's chair was knocked over, and the old man was holding the pistol half-raised at his side.

"I'm sorry," James said.

"Jesus," Mustache said, almost laughing. He turned to the old man. "No con man or professional liar would break down like that. Still think he's false?"

The old man shook his head. "Nah, you're right. He's just a smart kid scared shitless."

"Then why is he here?" Boxer asked.

"Because he's studied the business of crime," One Ear answered. "He's spent a lot of time thinking about how he can apply his school lessons to us. He's challenging the system. He wants to turn their theories against them. And he wants to make a name for himself." He nodded toward James before turning back to the others. "I like him. And I think we can use him."

"All right," the old man said. "It's not our final decision, but we'll send him to meet the boss. But there is something I want him to see first. Something to make sure he doesn't have any qualms or compunctions that might get in the way of him working with us. Gentlemen, I think it's time to show our green business student here what it means to generate *real* blood money."

# 37

———✳———

THE TALL, SINEWY man who had interrupted the meeting walked James down the back staircase and into the alley behind the restaurant. A black Audi A8 was waiting, and through the tinted windows James could see the driver's dark bulk. James's escort opened the back door and made a circular motion with his other hand, gesturing for him to climb into the vehicle.

"What about my man?" James asked.

"He can't come with you."

James hesitated. The last thing he wanted to do was get in this car without Vlastos, but he didn't seem to have a choice.

"Where are we going?" he asked as the Audi pulled out of the alley and into the Prague evening.

The driver looked at him and then back out the windshield without answering.

The Audi drove along Wenceslas Square. James saw tourists everywhere: eating at a café outside the yellow Hotel Europa, taking pictures of the site where the huge demonstrations for the Velvet Revolution were once held, walking up the steps of the grand neoclassical Czech National Museum. He had waited too long to live life as he should have, as an adventure of discovering the world, and only now—possibly at the end of his life—could he understand the kind of happiness he had been missing.

They drove past the main railway station before turning into a parking garage and descending two levels underground. The tires gave a high-pitched squeal as they pulled through the last turn and accelerated across the empty bottom level of the garage. After speeding past several concrete pillars, the car screeched to a stop next to a dark green van with large side mirrors and no side windows after the front doors. The man grabbed James's upper arm and dragged him out of the car, pulling him toward the van. Once James and his escort were inside the back of the van, the new driver took off.

They left the parking garage.

"What are we doing?" James asked his escort.

"We're *dry-cleaning* you."

James knew from Ian's dissertation that switching to multiple vehicles was common practice when taking an outsider to meet someone high up in the organization. It was also common practice when they were going to kill someone but didn't want to do it in the city.

The van drove a few miles through Prague before pulling into the train station.

"You have a name?" James asked.

"Lucian," the man said as the van stopped. "Now, follow me." He opened the van's side door and jumped out.

James followed Lucian into the sea of people shuffling through the train station. What might they think if they knew the secret circumstances of this stranger now brushing shoulders while passing them in the crowd? What thousand other stories were quietly playing out around him in this station?

Lucian walked him through the train station to a side door, which a man in work overalls opened for them. James realized he was witnessing the inner workings of a complex, interconnected web. Lucian led him through the doorway and down a restricted-access stairway to a network of tunnels under the station. Pipes ran along below the ceiling of the long concrete corridor, which seemed to stretch endlessly until disappearing into distant shadows.

They walked down the corridor to another doorway. James figured they must have gone a hundred yards under the city, but the various turns in the dark service tunnels made it tough to keep his bearings. On the other side of the door was a stairwell. Lucian gestured for James to follow him up the steps to a restricted work platform amid a dozen rail tracks with arriving and departing trains.

They went across the rock ballast surrounding the tracks, through a chain-link fence, and into another waiting van. James got in without asking any questions, and Lucian got in beside him. He was getting accustomed to the vast organization's practices and protocols.

The van accelerated, kicking up gravel against the floor, and they were soon on a side street, heading away from the train station and central Prague. He couldn't imagine anyone managing to follow their circuitous path since they left the restaurant. The precautions seemed excessive, though he had to admit that he knew almost nothing about law enforcement surveillance practices in the Czech Republic. He knew from Ian's dissertation that the farther east one went in Europe, the more corruptible the local governments and the more rampant the bribery of politicians, judges, and law enforcement officials.

Ian had also discussed the increasing proximity between older crime families and pockets of smaller organizations from Albania. The newer Albanian crime syndicates were rapidly spreading throughout Europe because of their willingness to operate in the more unsavory illegal operations such as drug smuggling, arms dealing, and human trafficking, which many of the older criminal establishments from Ireland, Japan, or Sicily avoided. According to Ian, the Albanians were the rough, undisciplined barbarians of the modern underworld. That had been Ian's coined term in his dissertation: *underworld barbarians*. And now it seemed that James's search for his brother was leading him to their barbarous boss, Aleksandar Manchevski.

James had uprooted himself from his life in Kansas City to search for Ian and, instead, had found what Ian was looking for. And now *James* was the lost brother.

He was surprised they hadn't blindfolded him. They seemed unconcerned that he might tell anyone of the meeting afterward, and this worried him. He had read enough about the violent Albanian mafia in Ian's dissertation to know that they took security very seriously. Something wasn't right. But as long as he continued to convince them he was Ian, they wouldn't kill him.

The van drove through an industrial park. He noted the streets so he could match them to the map of Prague he had memorized on the train. They took Kristanova Strasse, then turned left onto Jicinska and right on Vinohradska before merging onto E67, which took them out of the city. Once in the countryside, James was confused by a sign saying that both Bratislava and Vienna were three hundred kilometers away. Call it two hundred miles. Budapest, at four hundred kilometers, was a little farther.

Where the hell were they taking him?

"How long will we be driving?" he asked Lucian.

His reply was an icy stare.

In front of them stretched a vast forest. The brilliant sunset was turning the sky above the treetops from a swirling dark orange to deep crimson. Driving east of Prague, it once again hit him that he was getting ever farther from Kansas. And all he could now do was watch the road in silence as they drove him into the dark woods of the Czech Republic.

# 38

---

IAN USED THE blueprints to sketch out his filming sequence as best he could, the way a movie director might storyboard a complex action sequence. But as his mind grappled with the creative aspects of how best to document the operation on film, he kept drifting back to Marcus's news of the Geryon Mafia's bizarre attempt to impersonate him.

"Apparently, he's very good at imitating you," Marcus had said when they last spoke, twenty minutes ago. "And he speaks in a perfect American accent. It sounds like he looks a lot like you, too. He's even using a passport with your name and information. It's amazing they got a good fake so fast."

How could they have found someone that looked and talked like him? And so soon?

"He even seems to have done his research," Marcus had told him. "They've asked him a lot of questions, and he apparently had some good details about your life."

*Impossible,* Ian reflected. No one could have done that. *Only one person knows me that well.*

"They completely believed that this guy was you," Marcus had declared before leaving to tell the Malacoda informant that they were talking to an impostor.

*James,* Ian realized.

The horror hit him like a sudden chill. He stood up and took slow, stiff steps, like a feeble old man struggling to walk. His fingers massaged his temples as he closed his eyes and concentrated on the puzzle pieces that were suddenly thrown at him. With each step, a new thought flashed into his mind as he imagined a story that unfolded like a nightmare.

His mom hadn't understood his last e-mail. She hadn't realized he would eventually return home. And she must have gotten James involved. But it was hard to believe that James would leave his life in Kansas City to search for him just because of their mom's concerns. Their relationship had been so strained in recent years, his eyes teared up at the thought of his brother taking on such a risk to come looking for him. And somehow, he must have come across the Geryon Mafia and been pulled into this nightmarish world against his will.

Ian felt sick. James's presence here changed everything. The plans that had consumed his life for the past few months no longer mattered. Right now his brother's safety was everything.

"Call it off!" Ian yelled at Marcus, who had just come in.

"What?"

"The information leak . . . about the imposture—call it off! Now!"

"I can't," Marcus said. "We've already sent it out."

# 39

------------------※------------------

VLASTOS WAS STANDING along the far wall in the room above the restaurant. He had been powerless when they led James from the room, able only to make brief eye contact with the American he had spent the past twenty-four hours with. Before the meeting, he had warned James that there might come a point when they would be separated. This was common practice when someone from outside a criminal organization was being introduced up the structure. The higher you got to a boss or underboss, the tighter security got.

He had warned James that Albanian criminal organizations were among the most violent in the world, if not *the* most violent. If they were to be separated, he had warned James not to resist or act concerned in any way. But Vlastos had been worried that James wasn't strong enough for the task.

Still, when the moment came, Vlastos had been impressed with how well James did. And the kid's performance had earned him an escort into a car to be driven away to an unknown location. That was nearly half an hour ago, and Vlastos had spent that time standing motionless against the wall, waiting. But behind his stony expression, he was growing worried.

He didn't like James's being with the Malacoda men without his protection. And he was edgy being in the same room as these mindless barbarians of this new, ruthless world of organized crime that had emerged from the Balkan wars twenty years ago. They were like a pack of wolves that attacked only the solitary, injured moose while avoiding any creature that still had strength.

He saw something that caught his attention. It made every hair on the back of his neck stand up. It had been a simple gesture: the old man, still sitting at the table, paused from playing cards to look at his watch, then blinked three times.

He had been watching the men closely since James was taken from the room, and this was the fourth time the old man had looked at his watch. At first Vlastos had thought it some kind of tell, but the motion hadn't been consistent with the man's cards. Then he thought it was some sort of cheat signal, because One Ear, sitting across from the old man, had returned the old man's three blinks with three blinks of his own. But that wasn't the answer, either, because a second later, One Ear had sent the same blinking signals to the man to his left—Boxer—and the mustached man to his right. This wasn't a tell, and it wasn't a cheat signal. It was a signal for all four men! And because it had started with the old man checking his watch, it was a signal of planned timing and coordination!

Because he had been forced to give up his gun when he entered the restaurant, the first thing he did when he walked into the room was note which men had guns and where they carried them. His eyes now darted around the room, measuring these seven men. He could tell they were well trained—probably some of the best soldiers this violent Albanian group had.

Vlastos lowered his head and turned away from the table. It had been nearly a year since he was in such a dangerous position, so outnumbered by competent, violent men. But it was on moments like this that he had built his reputation. He waited.

*Take the bait,* he thought. *I'm looking away, not paying attention . . . Take the bait.*

No sound came from behind him, yet something had changed. He could sense it. At least one of the men had shifted his weight in the chair.

With his head still down, his sharp eyes glared sideways and saw the old man trying to sneak a glance at him. Their eye contact held for a moment, and Vlastos saw in the man's eyes the anxiety and building aggression from whatever secret he had heard on the phone.

Something was definitely wrong. His instincts told him they were going to kill him, that he couldn't wait for their next move, that he had to act now.

He moved quickly toward them, punched Boxer, threw an elbow into One Ear's temple, and flipped the table on its side, knocking both the old man and Mustache to the ground. Cursing the foot cast that slowed him down, he grabbed the gun from One Ear and put a bullet in Boxer's left eye. Then he shot the old man and Mustache and turned to the others.

The other men in the room moved faster than he expected. The two by the main door had already crouched into a firing stance, and the man by the far window had somehow moved out of his peripheral vision. He knew the numbers, the layout of the room, the relative priority of the threats, and the odds of getting past the men and through the doorway to safety. He was focused on survival, and right now that meant killing everyone in the room.

He fired at the two men by the door. The first died immediately as the bullet ripped through the front of his neck and severed his spinal cord. The second man took a bullet through the right eye socket, near the bridge of the nose, but not before he could get a shot off. As the bullet passed by only inches from Vlastos's head, the man who had fired it fell dead on the hardwood floor.

Vlastos, having avoided a near miss while killing three men and disabling three others, would have probably enjoyed a moment of feeling lucky, but a .22-caliber bullet suddenly ripped through his right shoulder. As he staggered in pain and shock, he discovered the man he had lost by the window, now standing sideways in the dark corner, firing at him.

Stepping backward as two more bullets hit him in the side, Vlastos tripped over the unconscious One Ear and fell to the floor behind him, with his face only inches from the lobeless ear. With his good leg frantically scraping for purchase along the smooth floor, he managed to slide his hips against One Ear so that he was hidden behind him. The shooter hesitated to take a shot at him and perhaps hit One Ear. And that hesitation was all Vlastos needed as his left hand snaked under One Ear's neck and fired a shot into the shooter's forehead.

The room was suddenly silent. Vlastos pushed himself away from One Ear. Pain shot through his body when he sat up. A small pool of blood had formed under him in the twenty seconds he had been lying on the ground. He didn't feel weak, yet he knew that only shock and adrenaline were preventing him from feeling the full effects of his wounds.

The brief silence was broken by a loud commotion coming from beneath the floor. Any men downstairs in the restaurant would soon be barging into the room. With great difficulty, he stood up. His side was bleeding badly, and the more he moved, the more he realized he had been seriously hurt.

He limped across the room. Pounding footsteps and shouting were all around. He opened the back door and saw shadows sliding along the floor at the bottom of a narrow staircase. Hoping to slow or discourage anyone from coming up, he grabbed the body of the first man he had shot, and slid it a few feet so it tumbled down the stairs. It got halfway down before lodging with one leg between the banister posts.

Vlastos was angry that his injured foot had made it an uneven fight between him and all these men. In top form, he would have given this rabble the fight of their lives, but his injured foot had already tipped the scales, slowing him just enough to get shot twice before he killed everyone in the room. Now he was even slower than before, bleeding badly and, for all he knew, dying.

He hobbled back to the front door of the room and opened it, only to hear more clamor, this time coming up the front staircase. He dragged the body of the mustached man into the hall and propped him sitting up against the wall, then limped back into the room, closed the door, and rolled the bullet-riddled poker table to rest as a weight against the door.

He shuffled over to the window. The dark street below was devoid of life. He was injured, outnumbered, and surrounded, and the only way he could possibly escape was by making all hell break loose.

He picked up the body of the young man who had shot him twice, and pushed him through the window. A second later he heard a heavy thud below as the body smacked into the sidewalk. Then came the horrified screams of two women, maybe three.

He limped to the side bar and grabbed two liter bottles of vodka. The old man's lighter lay on the floor amid a scattering of poker chips. Grabbing it, he ripped the tails off the old man's flannel shirt and headed for the back door. There he opened one of the vodkas, stuck in a piece of cloth, lit the cloth, and threw it hard, aiming at the thick center baluster halfway down the stairs. The Molotov cocktail broke, and blue and orange flames flashed up, clinging to the walls and steps.

The fire spread across the bottom half of the staircase, enveloping the limp body still lodged halfway down.

Vlastos then limped across the room, pushed the table away from the front door, and looked down the staircase. He didn't see anyone, though he could hear a half-dozen men somewhere around the corner below him. What were they waiting for? Why didn't they charge up the stairs, burst into the room, and overpower him? Perhaps they hesitated because they had heard stories of some of the things he had done. They had no way of knowing how weak he was right now. His reputation for cruel, excessive violence might be his only advantage.

Vlastos wanted to keep the illusion alive. Pointing his gun at the body he had propped up in the hallway, he fired two shots into its face at such close range that it blew off half the man's mustache along with his nose, several teeth, and part of his jaw. With the effects of his barbaric cruelty visible, he shoved the body toward the top of the main staircase and watched as it tumbled in uneven pauses down the steps. Vlastos wanted the men below to imagine him doing the same thing to their faces should they came closer.

He then lit the cloth wick in the second vodka bottle and tossed it down the staircase to add to the inferno. After igniting this second fire, he limped into the hallway and clambered farther up the stairs toward a faint blue light under the metal door at the top. He was high enough in the building that this door must lead to the roof.

He threw his shoulder into the door. The metal groaned but didn't open. Voices were now shouting from the lower stairway on the other side of the raging fire, and billows of black smoke rose toward him, building into a dark cloud that was getting thicker every second.

He threw his shoulder into the door again. This time it opened, and he fell off balance through the doorway and onto the roof. Something was really wrong with his side because the injury was getting more painful by the minute.

More screams came from the street below. Sirens could be heard approaching from the distance. He also saw a helicopter against the darkening horizon.

He limped toward the edge of the roof and looked at the pavement fifty feet below. There were no external fire escapes. The closest other building was too far away to jump to. Knowing that the restaurant was right next to the river, he limped to the other side of the roof and looked down. A concrete side road barely ten feet wide separated the building and the walled-in river. If he could jump at least ten feet out from the roof and clear the stone wall at ground level, the water was probably deep enough.

He would need a running start to have any chance of making the jump. He limped back toward the far side of the roof. Trying not to think of the possibility that seconds from now his body would be crippled or smashed on the stone wall below, he lunged forward and began limping as fast as he could across the roof, toward the edge. The injured foot slowed him down, and a sharp, sudden pain exploded in his side, but he pushed on. He cried out like a wild animal unable to understand its injuries. Tears blurred his eyes, yet he pushed on, limping at a desperate, hobbling skip toward the edge of the roof. He was now only five feet from the edge.

The realization hit him that he couldn't possibly make it. This was a mistake. He would die if he tried the jump.

Collapsing just before reaching the edge, he had to grab one of the protruding pipes to keep his momentum from carrying him over the edge. He hadn't had a choice; he was too weak to make the jump.

Now what? He was at half strength and getting weaker, and boxed in.

He limped back toward the rooftop door, stepped onto the now blazing staircase, and limped down the steps toward the wild flames. Halfway down the stairs, he heard the shouts of men retreating from the building. A loud sound of sirens came from the street out in front.

He tried to move down the stairs despite the flames, but the extreme heat pushed him back into the room he had started in. Grabbing the long, low wooden coffee table along the wall, he moved it close to the doorframe and saw that the flames were now within ten feet of the top step. The smoke had grown so thick, he would soon be unable to breathe.

He pulled the small floor rug, which had been under the coffee table, over to the bar, where he drenched it using the sprayer from the sink. Then he turned the sprayer on himself. The cold water felt energizing and seemed to revive his waning energy. He pulled the rug toward the door, then flipped the table upside down and pushed it out into the hallway and to the top of the stairs. Soaking wet, he wrapped the sodden rug around him like a blanket, sat in the center of the upside-down table, and pressed his feet against the two front table legs as if leaning back on a sled. Then, staring down the long staircase walled in a tunnel of flames, he scooted the makeshift toboggan forward an inch at a time until it tipped over the top step and started its jolting slide down the burning staircase.

Sliding through the roaring inferno, he had wrapped the blanket around his body and face so he couldn't see anything, though he felt the heat of the flames curling over the front of the table as it cut through them.

Halfway down the L-shaped staircase, the table crashed into the wall in front of him, throwing him forward. Still unable to see, he tried desperately to rotate the table so that it could slide down the last flight of stairs. Flames rose all around the table and began crawling toward him as if sensing their prey.

After a few seconds of trying to rotate the table, he felt an arm fall onto his lap. At once, he realized what was stopping his progress and why he had felt a soft rocking of the unsteady table he was using as a sled. The body he had originally killed and disfigured before kicking it down the stairs and lighting the world on fire had lodged in the corner. It seemed that the man he had killed was now trying to return the favor, using the very flames he had started.

He twisted harder to make the table rotate on top of the soft flesh. It was difficult. The corpse was lumpy, making it impossible to rotate the table. Knowing he was out of time, Vlastos rotated his own body on the stubborn table and tried to force it to continue sideways down the second flight. But instead, the table flipped on its side, dumping Vlastos and dislodging the vengeful corpse.

Blinded and still wrapped in the drenched rug, Vlastos was helpless as he tumbled down the stairs with the corpse and the splintering table. He somersaulted toward the ground floor, where the table and then the corpse smashed down on top of him.

He heard shouting as men rushed toward him at the base of the stairs. He tried to reach for the gun in his inside pocket, but his left arm was jammed under the corpse. Anger sparked in him at the thought of these men shooting him down because he couldn't free his arm. He lay helpless and desperate to survive, a talented killer injured, trapped, and surrounded, cornered into the rare situation that could end the life of a man so dangerous as he. But Vlastos would never give up—not until his wild heart stopped beating. Ignoring the burning pain in his leg, he pushed against the corpse with his free hand, trying to get the dead body off him so he could aim and fire whatever bullets remained at the men closing in on him.

*Please, Lord*, he thought. *Just let me kill a few of them. Or at least let me kill one. Don't let these dogs eat me alive without my putting up a fight, without my taking at least one with me to hell.*

But he couldn't get free. It was almost as if an unseen weight lay on him, preventing him from fighting back. And as the crescendo of footsteps and shouting descended on him, he knew that he had no right to feel cheated of a fair fight, not after all the helpless men and women he had killed in his long career.

*But no children, Lord. Remember that when you make your final judgment of me. I never hurt a child. And all the women were connected with bad men. None were truly innocent.*

In fact, Vlastos had the terrifying realization that few people on earth deserved death more than he.

As men rushed toward him, he made only the effort to shift his gaze sideways so he could know which of these men might be the one to deliver the fatal blow and end his life. But looking at them, something didn't seem right. They gave commands like an experienced, organized team, not a group of wild hoodlums. Then he saw the hats and the heavy coats of firefighters.

The firefighters pulled him out from under the body, gave him a few hits of oxygen from their tanks, and carried him out of the restaurant to the bustling excitement of the street.

"What's your name?" a firefighter asked him in Czech after getting him to the ambulance.

"Vladimir," Vlastos answered.

"Okay, Vladimir," the man said. "Is there anyone else in the building?"

"I don't think so," Vlastos said. "No one worth saving, anyway." He was lying on the stretcher looking up at the curving trail of thick, dark smoke flowing from the building into the navy blue sky. *Come, thick night, and pall thee in the dunnest smoke of hell, that my keen knife see not the wound it makes, nor heaven peep through the blanket of the dark, to cry 'Hold, hold!'*

"Okay," the firefighter said, patting him on the shoulder. "Just rest here. Someone will be with you in a moment to check on you."

The man left to help his brother firefighters battle the flames that had now completely consumed the restaurant and were threatening to spread to the neighboring buildings.

Gathering what little strength he had left, Vlastos sat up with difficulty and slid his legs off the stretcher so he could stand. He zipped up his leather jacket to help hide the bloodstain creeping across his shirtfront. Then he slowly hobbled away from the ambulance and the growing chaos outside the restaurant. After he had gone two blocks, he ducked into an alley and hobbled past the shadows.

# 40

———————✦———————

THE TWO MEN from the Malacoda gang watched their target hobble away from the burning restaurant after the rescue workers had left him unguarded. Both men wore long leather coats that helped them hide in a doorway's shadows a few hundred feet from the flames. Of the twenty-two men from the Malacoda gang who had been in the restaurant, all fifteen on the first floor had escaped the fire. Once it became obvious that first responders and police had been dispatched to the fire, the mafiosi realized it would only bring trouble if they hung around the scene. So these two men had been ordered to remain and observe from a distance, while the others left. They had their marching orders: if anyone came out of the fire who wasn't a member of the Malacoda gang or a first responder, then it must be that bastard Vlastos, who had torched their restaurant.

The two men stood in the shadows of the doorway as the orange flames grew. And their anger also smoldered and caught flame as they were forced to watch their restaurant turn to ashes. They watched as the two small fire trucks arrived and masked men ran into the building. They watched as a light blue ambulance arrived, followed closely by three green-and-white police cars. And a few minutes later, they watched as the rescue workers pulled from the burning building the only person rescued from the flames: Vlastos.

They watched this dark stranger limping away in what appeared to be great pain. They followed from a distance, and after seeing him turn down an alley, they looked at each other. It was time to make their move. In unison, they both upped their walk to a run and raced toward the alleyway entrance.

Vlastos was overwhelmed by his injuries. He remembered the address of a place he had looked up this morning. Based on his memory of Prague's city map, he was only a dozen street blocks away. He didn't know what to expect at his destination, but of all the choices he had at this moment in his life, it was the one his instincts told him to pursue.

As he limped down the wide stone alley, his concerns turned to James. What had gone wrong? How had the Malacoda gang discovered their true intentions? Most of all, he was sick with concern for James.

The alley opened onto a large pedestrian square walled by centuries-old stone buildings with small dimly lit windows. In the center of the square stood a large stone fountain with water spraying from the mouths of four horses.

Since he turned down the alley, the only sounds Vlastos heard were those of his own footsteps and his own unsteady breathing. The pain from the wound in his side was getting worse. His visual focus came and went, and he felt sleepy, as if his consciousness was trying to shut down. The dark, silent surroundings, which seemed bent on soothing him to sleep, made his struggle more difficult. As he got closer to the fountain, the sound of the spraying water splashing into the bottom pool drowned the sounds of his footsteps and breathing. The roaring white noise made it impossible to hear anything else.

He sensed that he was vulnerable. Turning his head, he glanced behind him—nothing but shadows in the square, and the alley he had come from was pitch black. So he continued toward his destination.

The far side of the square opened into a wider street that forked toward a large cathedral with long steps leading to six wooden doors. A fog had risen and now moved around the corners of buildings and along the cobblestone streets like a wave of water flooding the city streets in slow motion. Just as he limped his way up to the top front step of the Gothic church, the fog engulfed the world around him.


The two men moved out of the alley into the broad square. They saw a thin cloud of mist sifting toward them from the opposite end. And through that mist, both men saw the light from an opening church door.

They jogged across the fog-shrouded square, moving at half speed with arms outstretched as if to guard against running into something. And indeed, the lead man didn't see the stone fountain in the center of the square until he bashed his shin against it, falling to the stones in pain and dropping his gun. It bounced with a loud metallic clatter across the uneven cobblestones.

Feeling blindly along the ground for his partner's gun, the second man accidentally kicked it, sending it skittering even farther. He then moved forward a few steps and found the weapon tipped up between two stones, pointing directly at his face.

Uneasy, as any man would be while approaching a gun that the ghostly mist had turned on him, he reached for it with superstitious caution. Picking it up, he stared through the mist at what looked like the blurred silhouette of a ghost disappearing into the distant rectangular light of the church doorway. Then the light went out as the door closed.

"Come on!" he hissed back at the first man, who was just getting to his feet with a groan, clasping his banged shin.

Vlastos reached the top step of the church and opened the center door. He could see a long row of tall candlesticks that stretched toward a distant altar. Above the altar rose a dark stained-glass window with a giant wooden cross hanging in front. During the day, the window, backlit by the sun, must make this room look like a way station on the journey to heaven. A journey Vlastos hadn't been on since his youth—a journey he wondered whether he could start again so late in his benighted life.

His momentary reflections were interrupted by a distant clatter of metal bouncing over rock. He turned and locked his gaze on the mist that now consumed the square he had just come from. Eyes wide and ears alert, he stared deep into the mist. He thought he heard voices or whispers, but the air around him moved in an unsteady breeze, so he couldn't be certain. But then he heard the sound of metal grating over stone once again. It was the same sound as before, only softer and briefer. A small metal object, not too light or too heavy, and not one solid piece, either, for it made different pitches as it bounced, and not too long or too thin, because the metal had no vibratory resonance, no ring, as it fell.

*It's a gun,* his instincts told him. But he couldn't know for sure.

Whatever it was, it hadn't moved on its own, and he wasn't taking any chances. He stepped inside the church and closed the door. As he limped down the center aisle, he felt the pain in his side ease the closer he got to the altar. No one else appeared to be in the sanctuary. He recalled that this church was actually a destination for the pious in Prague. There had been something honest and noble about the person who mentioned it, so it had stuck in his mind. And that was why he now found himself standing in this church, hoping to find a like-minded soul and thinking of the God he had neglected since he was fourteen years old.

He held his side as he limped toward the front of the sanctuary, looking anxiously for a familiar face, as if one might be sleeping in a pew or removed in prayer at one of the half-dozen alcoves tucked along the edges of this medieval cathedral.

His lungs convulsed, and he covered his mouth with his left hand when the coughing fit erupted. Lowering his hand, he saw round drops of blood in the center of his palm. Suddenly weak, he knelt. He looked up and saw Jesus on the cross, with the red gash on his side from the spear that had pierced him in roughly the same place that the second bullet had caught Vlastos.

He was dying, and he knew it, but his resurfacing faith was giving him the strength to face it. His eyes watered as he remembered the life he had gradually forgotten during his first few years as a runaway, seduced by the exciting life and power of organized crime. He remembered those he had abandoned: his father, his mother, and his younger brother. He had kept tabs on them in secret for years, before his life went completely dark a decade ago. But even during that time, he had never once reached out to them. He thought about how much he had loved them—about how, in the end, the relationship he once had with his family was the only meaningful thing in his life.

And he also thought about his faith.

He had been taught that God could forgive him anything as long as he asked for forgiveness. So Vlastos asked. In the privacy of this empty church at night, kneeling in front of the cross as he bled like Christ, Vlastos asked forgiveness for a lifetime of crime. He had done evil things, but for the first time in decades, he didn't feel like an evil man. He was the sheep that lost its way—so lost for so long that until now he had forgotten what it was once like to be a part of the flock.

Now, at the very end, he felt that somehow, he had found his way back to God.

But still something dark burned inside him. His instincts couldn't let him forget about potential danger. To his right, a dark passageway led to an exit from the church. Despite the promises he had just made to God while seeking forgiveness, Vlastos knew that he needed to limp away from this altar and down the dark passageway and out of the church if he wanted to do what must be done. In doing so, he feared that he may be committing an offense that even God would not forgive. But he had no choice. And so, with great effort, he stood and limped down the dark passageway to the distant door that led out of God's house.

The two men from the Malacoda gang lumbered through the mist to the church steps, guns out and pointed forward. Neither man was thrilled with the idea of entering a house of God to kill a man—even a man as bad as Vlastos. But regardless of their religious, superstitious concerns, that discomfort was nothing compared to the wrath they would experience from their boss if they didn't take care of this problem.

"What do we do if he's not inside?" the second man asked.

"I thought you said you saw him go in the church."

"I said I saw *someone* go in. In the mist."

"This was not a ghost, was it?" the first man asked, chuckling.

"No ghost," the second man replied as he reached for the church door handle. "Just a man."

"Don't be too sure about that," an unknown voice said from the thick fog by the column to their right.

Startled, both men turned to raise their guns. But before they could, two shots flashed out from the mist, killing them both on God's doorstep.

After the men had fallen to the ground, Vlastos stepped out of the mist. He stared at the bodies with his wide eyes. He knew a bad omen when he saw one. In all his years, he had never killed anyone on holy ground.

The killings left him feeling deflated. All the religious strength he had felt in front of the cross was gone. How could God forgive him his sins when he had committed the greatest sin only minutes after asking forgiveness? He couldn't change. And because he couldn't, he was forever lost to God.

The pain in his side worsened. He no longer had the strength to stand. When he fell next to the men on the steps, he thought of the danger that James was now in. James wouldn't realize he had walked into a trap until it was too late. He had failed to protect James, and now all he could do was pray that God would somehow protect the young American and reunite him with his missing brother. As he finished the prayer, he saw lights forming in the mist above him, as if the sky were opening for an angel or spirit or something else watching from above.

He thought of Shakespeare's words from Macbeth. *But I have spoke with one that saw him die, who did report that very frankly he confessed his treasons, implored your Highness' pardon and set forth a deep repentance: nothing in his life became him like the leaving it.*

Vlastos watched the changing light above him and smiled with tears in his eyes.

# 41

THE LONGER JAMES sat in the van, the more uneasy he felt. He was sitting next to Lucian, who hadn't said a word in ten minutes. It was dark now, and they were deep in the wooded Czech countryside. And he had no idea how much farther they must go before meeting Aleksander Manchevski.

The driver turned off the two-lane highway curving through the woods, onto a narrow dirt road muddied from a recent rain.

"We're meeting your boss way out here?" James asked.

"Right," Lucian replied.

James nodded, but the lump of fear in the pit of his stomach hardened. This didn't make sense. Why would they be meeting this far from the city? Ian's dissertation had outlined many operating practices of organized crime. People were taken to meet mafia bosses, but they were almost always in a city, close to all their operations. One didn't travel this far out of town just to make an introduction.

His instincts told him that something had happened, that something was wrong. Maybe he should play things out in case he was mistaken, but he couldn't get Ian's dissertation out of his mind. And according to its analysis of how people stayed alive and successful in organized crime, James needed to take a calculated course of action *now,* before he got to the fast-approaching point of no return—and assuming he hadn't already passed it.

"Lucian, there's something I need to tell you," he said.

"We're almost there," Lucian replied dismissively.

"This is important . . . I'm not who you think I am."

"You're not Mr. Lawrence?" Lucian asked calmly, with no apparent surprise.

"I am Mr. Lawrence, but not the one you think."

Lucian looked at him for the first time since they left the city. "And just how many Mr. Lawrences are there?" There was something challenging in his voice. A snide tone—he must think he was being played.

"Only two, as far as I'm concerned. There's my brother, Ian Lawrence. And there's me, James Lawrence."

Lucian's eyes widened. James could tell that the man had somehow known he wasn't Ian, but not that he was Ian's brother.

"Stop the van," Lucian snapped at the driver. "This is far enough. We'll do it here."

The tires locked, and the van slid on the muddy road before stopping. Lucian grabbed the handle, slid the side door open, and jumped out without caring how muddy his combat boots got. "Get out!"

"Wait, please," James said, eyes wide, looking to Lucian and then the silent driver.

Lucian pulled out a small black pistol and pointed it at him.

James stared at the square-cut barrel. "Okay, I'm getting out," he said. His mind raced as he slid across the seat to the door. "You want to talk with my brother? Well, so do I. I'm just trying to find him."

"Over there." Lucian motioned toward the side of the road, where the wet grass reflected pale blue in the moonlight.

"If Ian finds out you killed me, there's no chance he'll help your organization."

"He won't find out we killed you. Besides, we don't even know if we need his help."

"The things I talked about at the restaurant—they're real. These are things that can really be done. I was just outlining some of what was in Ian's dissertation."

"We've read his paper. It was very interesting, and we've taken some of his ideas, but there is nothing else we need."

"You just read his proposal of topic. I've read a draft of his complete dissertation. You have no idea what's in that, or how to implement it."

James got out of the van, and Lucian stepped back, as if he had a rule to remain out of arm's reach of anyone he was planning to shoot. "Because you have been reasonable," he said, "because you haven't tried to put up a fight or attempt any ridiculous escape—which would only have irritated me—I will give you a choice. You may be either standing or kneeling when I shoot you. Standing will show strength and courage, and I'll respect you for that. Kneeling is weaker, but it may give you a chance to meditate or make peace with . . . whomever . . . before you die."

"I'll stand," James said. "And I'm always at peace with God, so I have no need to catch up now."

"Smart choice—the grass is wet." Lucian paused. "I'll also give you the choice of where I shoot you. Your head or your heart? Neither shot will kill you instantly, but the head shot will make you lose consciousness, so you'll feel no pain. The heart shot will be uncomfortable—maybe even painful—but it will give you ten or twenty seconds of consciousness to savior the experience of fading into death. Some people have preferred to go this way."

"How can you live this kind of life?" James growled. "Have you no soul?"

"If you don't choose, Mr. Lawrence, then I shall have to choose for you."

"The heart," James said. "But listen, I'm telling you, you're making a mistake. I have things to offer that you're missing. I'm not kidding—with all due respect, you're going to regret killing me."

"Mr. Lawrence, please," Lucian said. "You were doing so well. Don't get pathetic on me at the end."

"I'm trying to help you."

"You're begging for your life."

"I'm not. I'm just trying to explain . . ."

"Down on your knees!"

"What?"

"If you want to beg, then I'll let you beg. But you'll have to do it on your knees. Or you can stand silently and die like a man with his honor intact."

"*Honor?* What are you talking about?"

"This is the last choice I'm giving you!"

"All right!" James said, falling to his knees in the mud. He was shaking and didn't know how much longer he could hold back the panic he felt inside.

Lucian shook his head in disappointment. Raising the gun, he said, "You have thirty seconds to make your case before I put a bullet through your heart."

James spoke rapidly, frantically, his words tumbling out on top of one another. With only thirty seconds to live, he had to make them count. "I can help your organization. You need me to find my brother and convince him to leave Europe. I've read his dissertation, and you can't imagine how many ideas he has for hurting organizations like yours. Everything you've heard about him is a lie. He's not trying to help you . . . he's trying to *destroy* you. And he's the type of person that won't stop pursuing something until he gets it or it kills him. He's insane. I may be the only one who can stop him. He has ideas about how to disintegrate the black market using economics. Trust me, you don't want him to try. Damn it! My brother should never have left Kansas! He should have stayed close to our parents like I did! Our father is in poor health and may not even live out the year! Ian shouldn't have abandoned us! None of this should have happened!" He took a few quick breaths, trying in vain to control his fear as his death approached. In the moment of truth, he had become a coward who would say anything to live. "The Geryon Mafia wants to find Ian, just as I do. Just as your boss does. We can help each other. I'm begging you not to do this! I just want to find my brother!"

Lucian stepped forward and stiffened his gun arm as if to fire. "I'm sorry, Mr. Lawrence. But you haven't convinced me you have anything to offer. And now your time is up."

"Wait! They're trying to start a war!" James yelled, his face contorted, tears welling in his eyes.

Something changed in Lucian. He paused. His arm relaxed, and his head tilted a little to one side. "What are you talking about? What war?"

"The Geryon Mafia! They're trying to start a war!"

"Who told you this? Vlastos?"

"No, someone else. Strobviok!" He choked on his tears. "His name was Strobviok!"

"You *spoke* with Strobviok?" Lucian gasped.

"Yes."

Lucian glanced at the equally astonished driver, then turned back to James. "You're telling me that you spoke directly to the boss of the Geryon Mafia, and he told you he wanted to start a war with the Malacoda?"

James nodded. "That's exactly what I'm telling you."

Lucian pointed at the driver and waved for him to get back in the van. Then he grabbed James by the elbow, helped him up out of the mud, and led him back to the van. "Congratulations, Mr.

Lawrence. You have just given me a reason not to kill you . . . yet."

"What's going on?" James asked, confused, off balance.

"We're going to meet the boss. He will want to hear everything there is to tell about your little conversation with Strobviok . . . about this coming war."

The driver struggled to turn the van around on the narrow muddy road, almost getting it stuck. Once they were pointed back in the direction they had come from, the van crawled steadily along in the slippery mud. They slid and jounced along, the headlights lighting up the surrounding woods, which cast long poles of moving shadows.

Beyond the van's small bubble of light lay a world of darkness into which James was now being pulled even further, and for the first time in his journey he feared that both he and his brother were forever lost from the world they once knew.

# PART THREE

*He was telling me, in case I did not know, that beyond*
*the girl's survival lay the survival of his immortal soul.*
—John le Carré, *The Secret Pilgrim,* 1990

# 42

THE FIRST TIME they switched vehicles was in an airport parking lot outside Prague. Lucian had the keys to a black Toyota pickup. James got in, and Lucian drove them toward the city while the driver stayed with the van. Once in Prague, they switched cars, again in a parking garage, this time to a boxy 1970s Mercedes. They drove across what seemed half the city before making their final switch, to a BMW 5 series parked in the basement of an apartment complex. The high-performance car must have been closer to Lucian's tastes, for he drove it faster and more aggressively than the others. Within minutes, they were pulling up to an ancient gray stone building with modern lighting and elegant neon signs. Three valets were working the front, where people in formal dress were getting out of expensive cars.

"Looks like an embassy," James said to Lucian.

"It's a casino."

Lucian drove past the entrance and turned down a narrow alley and into the massive building. Halfway down the path, they were stopped by a metal gate and two burly men in tuxedos. Once they saw Lucian, one raised the gate while the other said

something into a radio in Czech. James couldn't make out a
word of it.

The alley turned into a ramp leading down into a small
private garage under the building. Seven other cars were parked
in the garage: each a duplicate of the black BMW 5 series Lucian
was driving. When they got out, Lucian left the key in the
keyhole of the driver's door. As they walked toward the orange
elevator door, a man came the other direction and stopped at the
BMW. When they stepped inside the elevator, James looked
back into the garage to see the man changing the license plate.

"What is this place?" he asked as the elevator doors closed
and they started up.

"I told you. It's a casino."

"But why are we here?"

"I'm taking you to see Mr. Manchevski. He owns the place."

The elevator took them up four floors. When the doors slid
open, they were met by three more big men in tuxedos. James
felt suddenly tired and stressed in this world of luxury sports cars
and tuxedoed security men. He looked down at his dirty shirt and
muddied jeans and shoes. He was underdressed and looked like
hell. People would be looking at him with the same distaste that
country club members might feel at seeing a homeless man
wander into their lounge area. Still, he knew they could never
imagine half of what he had endured in the past few days.

But it looked as though the casino's patrons would be spared
getting so much as a glimpse of him. He and Lucian and their
escorts had come directly from the private garage to the fourth
floor, while the gaming areas seemed to be on floors one through
three. The security men escorted him down a lavish hallway
hidden from the public eye.

Lucian followed.

James had been a coward in the woods, and even though his
pleading had kept him alive, he had never felt more ashamed of
himself than now. He tried to think of any way he might have

betrayed Ian or put him in more danger by revealing so much about his background. He couldn't believe how terrified he had been in those dark woods. Lucian had been ready to kill him that moment, and James had broken down in a panic and betrayed his own brother. He still couldn't shake the thought of how close to death he had come. But he had also bought time to regroup, to prepare for the worst.

No matter what was to happen in his meeting with Aleksander Manchevski, no matter what the crime boss threatened him with, he would never betray Ian again.

*   *   *

"Your brother was taken from the restaurant," Marcus said as he jumped into the front passenger seat of the car.

"When?" Ian asked.

"An hour ago."

"Where did they take him?"

"Supposedly to meet Manchevski, but we don't know where."

"*Supposedly?*" Ian said, looking sick. "We both know what that could mean." He slapped the steering wheel. "Fuck!" he yelled, squeezing the wheel until his fingers went white. "So Manchevski is all we have?"

"Yeah," Marcus said.

"Okay. Manchevski's almost always at his casino when he's in Prague, right? So we go there."

"You know that could destroy everything we're doing, right?"

"It's my brother we're talking about!"

The car speeded through a traffic light turning red, and a mounted camera flashed as it took their picture.

Ian still couldn't believe that James had come looking for him, let alone followed his trail well enough to get acquainted with the Geryon Mafia and the Malacoda gang. The professor had warned him that his odyssey toward the dark heart of organized crime might go beyond anything he could control. Still, he had thought he understood the risks, but he never imagined James getting involved.

He downshifted and punched the car through another intersection as the light turned yellow. This time there was no flash from any traffic camera.

Fifteen minutes later, they got out of the car three blocks from the casino. A few other White Rose members in a van would arrive soon and await instructions. They walked beneath tall, gleaming streetlights atop candy-cane-shaped poles, toward the gilt-framed glass doors manned by greeters in long red tailcoats. When they were a few steps away, one of the men turned with a flourish and opened a door.

"Welcome to the Grande Omertá Casino, gentlemen. Enjoy your evening."

*Go to hell,* Ian thought.

# 43

———————※———————

LUCIAN ENTERED THE large office alone and saw Aleksander Manchevski looking out the glass wall above the casino floor. The Malacoda boss was a short, stocky man with dark, curly hair and a large, round face. And he still had the sharp, aggressive eyes he must have had as a street punk working for the mafiosi in Albania twenty years ago. Lucian took great pride in working for this man who had formed alliances with strategically positioned members of the autonomous gangs in the early years after the Kosovo war, when the fractured militarized units were disbanded. He had blindly followed Manchevski over the years. This included helping when his boss was sent to Prague to oversee the growing opportunities for trafficking in drugs, weapons, and human beings. Soon they had expanded into all areas of the black market. He had helped Manchevski make impressive strides in consolidating the fragmented territories operated by fifteen different criminal organizations. Prague had once been considered an "open" city, meaning that no one criminal organization had control. But Manchevski had shifted the balance of power ten years ago, and he was still the city's top mafia boss. Lucian was honored to serve such a powerful, resourceful man.

"Where is this James Lawrence?" Manchevski asked.

"Being watched in the hallway outside," Lucian said.

"And he heard Strobviok plot to kill me?"

"That's what he says."

"Maybe he heard other things, too. Does he know anything about Strobviok's plans for after I'm dead?"

"I don't know."

Manchevski turned away from the floor-to-ceiling windows, toward a long maple desk in front of dozens of video monitors for the casino's gaming tables. "He might have learned something about their operations," he mused. "Maybe even their money laundering strategy."

Lucian frowned. "I'm not sure how much of that stuff he would recognize. I don't think this is his world. He seems lost. Even scared."

"I'll explain to him what it would look like."

"Are you sure you want to tell him that much?"

Manchevski nodded. "Yes, if I have to. It doesn't matter. Do you think he realizes how much danger he's in right now?"

Lucian shook his head. "He's nervous, but I think he still believes there's a chance he'll live."

"Poor fool," Manchevski said. "After I get whatever he has to tell, I'll motion to you. Kill him quietly; then take the body back to the garage and get it away from here. The car is prepared?"

"Yes," Lucian said. "They've switched the plates, wiped the insides, and removed all manufacturer identification numbers. If there's trouble getting his body out of Prague, the car can't be traced back to us. And assuming we get it out of the city, we have a place set up where his body will never be found."

Manchevski smiled. "Good. Then it sounds like we're ready. Bring him in."

\*   \*   \*

James stood inside the doorway of Aleksander Manchevski's office. "This is a beautiful casino," he said, hoping to sound relaxed. He could see the main gaming floor a level below, through the ceiling-high tinted-glass windows. The people in the gaming area below couldn't see through the one-way mirrors, but everyone in Manchevski's office could look down on them.

"Do you know the most beautiful part?" Manchevski asked.

"This is my first time here."

"It's the same thing for all casinos."

"I don't know—the count room?"

Manchevski clapped his hands with a single loud smack that sounded like a balloon popping. "They told me you were probably smart like your brother," he said, a twinkle in his eye. "How much do you know about count rooms, Mr. Lawrence?"

"I have this client—I help manage their money."

"Where?"

"Kansas City."

"So you're what, a banker?"

"No. I'm a tax accountant."

"So you do this client's taxes?"

"In a way. The casino is owned by a Native American reservation, which is a client of my firm. They're a sovereign nation, so they don't pay U.S. taxes, but there's still paperwork."

"I thought you Americans killed all your Indians—after stealing their land, of course," Manchevski said with an icy, emotionless face.

James said nothing.

"So you know a little something about casino count rooms, but how much do you know about laundering money? Ever do *that* for any of your tax clients in Kansas City?"

"No, I haven't."

"Ever help a client with tax evasion?"

"No, it wouldn't be ethical—or legal."

Manchevski laughed. "I read a lot of history, Mr. Lawrence. And I've read about your Kansas City and its ties to the Mafia. You may be a little closer to the fire than you'd imagine. I wonder how many crime families have become wealthy in your city, in the process using the services of your firm."

James stared at Manchevski in silence.

"You're a finance man, Mr. Lawrence. So you know that illegal businesses need to launder their money so they appear to earn it through legal means. Otherwise, law enforcement will not only have proof that we are breaking the law; they will also have a clear way to measure the extent of the crimes."

"I don't launder money for clients," James said. "They're all legitimate."

"Then let me tell you how we do business, to see if you can help us," Manchevski said. "The purpose of all money laundering operations is to disguise where the money came from. If a business earns a hundred thousand a month but shows a hundred and fifty thousand on paper, it can launder fifty thousand dollars from an illegal business. If they can pull it off, who is to know that when it deposits a hundred and fifty thousand in the bank each month, fifty thousand really came from an illegal activity? As long as they have the appropriate false accounting records for the front business, the moment the money is deposited the illegally obtained fifty thousand is 'clean,' so it appears legal. This is why anyone running an illegal enterprise needs legal businesses, too."

James grinned. These men weren't the sort of buffoons one saw in the movies; they were clever businessmen who operated in illegal markets. No wonder Ian had become captivated by this dark side of economics!

"But how do you manage to falsify the bookkeeping?" James asked. "It's easier said than done."

"There are three things a business needs to launder money, and with all three in place, law enforcement will have a hell of a time matching our records with legitimate third-party records to prove we use false accounting. First, the business must provide a *service,* not a product. This is so law enforcement can't obtain matching records from the business's vendors to help quantify our sales or production figures. Second, the business must be of the type that doesn't record customer names or other identifying information about them. This is so the business can exaggerate the number of customers it serviced, without law enforcement tracking down individual customers for verification. Third, the business must conduct most of its transactions with *cash* instead of checks or bank cards. This is obviously so sales-and-revenue activity can be exaggerated without leaving a banking trail of exactly where the money came from."

"Not many businesses meet all three of those descriptions," James said.

"No, but enough do. Things like barbershops, massage parlors, or legal brothels are good examples. The only problem with these safer money laundering operations is that these types of businesses—ones that provide services for cash and don't record anything about the customers—are generally smaller businesses. It's difficult to launder a lot of money through them. So what often happens is that criminal organizations try to get more creative by using international shell corporations with varying international law. But times have changed, and the world's focus on terrorism has been both a hindrance and a blessing to the operations of criminal organizations. A hindrance in that countries' various law enforcement agencies have been working together—quite impressively, I might add—to identify the financing of terrorist activities. Because the type of financial movement and disguising of money is similar between criminal and terrorist organizations, honest criminals like me have been forced to take more precautions—just because terrorists, by their very nature, seem incapable of keeping a low profile."

"Why are you telling me all this?"

"Pay attention, Mr. James Lawrence. You said you had information I need to know about a war, and this could relate to something Strobviok told you or something you may have seen when you were with him."

Walking behind the desk, Manchevski paused in front of the many small high-definition screens zoomed in on casino tables and the countless hands exchanging cards and chips in a continuous flutter of activity. He watched as if admiring a large aquarium with a collection of exotic fish.

"So, as I was saying," Manchevski continued, "the tricky part is finding money laundering operations that can do it on a large scale."

"You'd need a lot of barbershops to launder the kind of money that your businesses must be bringing in," James said.

"So true. It was a dilemma for a long time."

"But not anymore?" James asked. He saw Manchevski's widening grin. "You've found a way of having a large money laundering operation without losing any of the safeguards? A large business that provides a service to people for cash, and you don't keep records of your customers. All cash and all service, so you can add an enormous amount of illegal cash to the pot without anyone knowing for sure where *that* cash came from." He paused, watching Manchevski's self-satisfied expression.

"Cash and services and nameless customers," Manchevski said. "Does that combination feel familiar?"

"This casino!" James said, looking around him and out at the busy gaming floor below. He took a step toward the glass wall. "Of course! It has everything you need. You provide the service of gaming for cash to people you don't keep records on in most cases. Wow, you could probably launder tens of thousands of dollars through here every night!"

"*Hundreds* of thousands," Manchevski said.

"How?"

"It's simple. Almost half a century ago, the American Mafia used casinos in your Las Vegas in skimming operations where they would take money each month from the count room, which they indirectly controlled. What I am doing here is merely the same idea working in reverse."

James understood. "So you control the men in the count room, just like the mob did in Las Vegas. In Vegas, the mob falsified the count, understating it so that a courier of theirs could remove some cash and deliver it to certain mob bosses. But you're doing the opposite—you're falsifying the count to *overstate* how much money your casino makes, so that when a courier brings cash in a suitcase from one of your illegal businesses into the casino count room, it just gets lumped in with all the rest."

"That's how we do most of it. Also, being a casino, it's very easy to have our men just come in with the cash and lose it at the tables—under supervision, of course. It has to be monitored and coordinated very carefully because we need to be able to track that specific men lost specific amounts of money, as instructed. We have people who review the video files of the tables where they are scheduled to play, to make sure they lost *everything* they were instructed to lose."

James was impressed. It was an ingenious way to routinely launder large amounts of money from illegal activities without leaving any traceable paper trail.

"So how much do you launder through this casino a month?" James blurted without thinking. He was too intrigued to realize just how dangerous all this information was to him.

Manchevski eyed him coldly. "If I tell you that, Mr. Lawrence, I might have to kill you." He smiled.

Unlike in the secluded Czech woods, James felt a bit safer here in the casino. After all, even if they decided to kill him, they couldn't very well do it here. He recalled the specific section in Ian's dissertation that described the history of Las Vegas and the fact that mob bosses always had their killing done outside the city limits—usually deep in the desert—to keep the occasional violence from interfering with the casino profits. Manchevski couldn't possibly kill him as long as he was in this casino. So he still had time to negotiate with this man for Ian's and his safe return to Kansas before this region exploded into a mafia war.

"So, Mr. Lawrence," Manchevski said, still eyeing him coldly, "Lucian tells me that you met and spoke with Strobviok in Berlin."

"That's right," James said.

"And Strobviok mentioned to you that he was trying to start a war?"

"Yes, but not just your garden-variety gang war. He wanted to start it by assassinating *you*. He wanted a war he could win quickly, and he figured it would be easy to take over your operations in Prague once your organization fell into disarray from the power vacuum you would leave behind."

Manchevski half turned from the other men in the room and looked down with arms crossed and head lowered in thought. "But it wasn't you who was supposed to kill me?" he asked.

"Look at me," James replied. "Do I look like the guy for the job? No, it was to be done by one of their men—a guy named Vlastos." How strange it felt for James to say those words, as if the short time he had been separated from Vlastos had, in this moment, erased any kind of bond he had thought he felt with the man during the past twenty-four hours.

"But you were leading this killer to my doorstep?" Manchevski asked.

"I'm only trying to find my brother, and I'll do what it takes to find him."

"Even if you could die?" Manchevski asked, unable to hide his intrigue with James's personal situation.

"He's my brother," James said weakly. "My *little* brother. I've never known life without him. And I don't want to."

"So you would die for him?" Manchevski asked, posing the question almost as a challenge.

James nodded. "Ian's the only person in the world I would give my life for."

"Noble words, and easy to say. But I do believe you. You have an honest face." Manchevski pointed at a man by the door and snapped his fingers. The man waved in two more men from outside the room and then closed the door. There were now seven in the room, including James, Manchevski, and Lucian. "You know, I, too, had a brother, long ago. He was taken from me. When I found the men who killed him, I had them thrown out of an airplane without parachutes at ten thousand feet over the Mediterranean. Oh, I could have thought of more painful ways to kill them, but I didn't want pain to cloud their awareness of approaching death. I wanted them to be frantic, horrified by the clear realization that nothing was going to save them. I've never heard men scream the way they did as I had them thrown out of an old military plane. And you know, at that altitude, they had over a minute left to live—time enough to draw another breath and scream that out, too. It was most satisfying."

James couldn't imagine the inner demons and rage that must dwell within a man to give him pleasure from doing something so horrible. That kind of rage had never burned in him, but he had to wonder whether he, too, could lose his humanity from living in this world of crime and violence.

"So tell me about your meeting with Strobviok," Manchevski said. "I said I believed you about your brother because you had an honest look when you described him. If you don't show me that same honesty about Strobviok, then I'll have my men hold you down while Lucian bashes out your teeth with a hammer. He is . . . a craftsman."

The words made James feel sick. "That's not necessary. I have no loyalty to Strobviok or anyone else in either his organization or yours. I just want to find my brother. I'll tell you everything about the meeting. And then I hope you'll help me find my brother."

"But you heard Strobviok specifically give the order to have me killed?"

"Yes," James said. "He said you were destabilizing his hold on the region's black market, that your organization was growing too quickly. He also thought your people were too violent . . . too militarized. And he feared that would encourage law enforcement to attempt a crackdown on all organized crime in the region, which would hurt his profits, too."

"That doddering old fool!" Manchevski shouted. "Where does he get off making those claims? His hands are just as dirty as mine. You know, he once killed one of his own men just so he could get the man's wife for himself. What kind of monster does that?"

"Strobviok also said you have a big sex slavery and human trafficking operation, which will eventually gain unwanted political attention because of human watch groups."

Manchevski's face flushed red. "The man is an idiot! He calls himself a businessman, but his understanding of the world is so outdated, he couldn't recognize a new opportunity if it bit him on the bum. The economics of slavery is ancient. As an American, you must understand that as well as anyone. Wasn't your country's White House built by slaves? Weren't many of your country's founding fathers slave owners?"

"I thought you wanted to know about Strobviok?"

Manchevski nodded. "Okay, you're right. Where did you first meet him?"

"Berlin."

"When?"

"Yesterday."

"And how did you meet him?"

"I was pretending to be my brother. I had gotten access to his e-mail account the day before, at the university in Leipzig. As my brother, I made him the same offer that I made you."

"And he hadn't seen you in Leipzig before that?"

"No. The day before that, I was still back in the U.S."

Manchevski appeared surprised. "You've been in Europe only three days?"

James nodded, eyes lowered. Even he couldn't believe how fast his life had been moving and how much he had experienced in the past three days. Right now his old life in Kansas City felt very far away.

"Did Strobviok ever mention anything about this casino?" Manchevski asked.

"No."

"Did you see or hear anything from him about any businesses that have the characteristics of money laundering operations? Anything at all like what we've been talking about? Think carefully. This is your quiz."

"No, nothing like that."

"What did he tell you of his plans after I was to be killed?"

"He said it would create a power vacuum and that three of your top men—your underboss, the capo of the north-central region of Prague, and your *consigliere*—would fight each other for power. He said other gangs would try to move into the territory. He said Prague was still an open city, that unlike in most other cities, no one criminal organization owned it, and that if he could take you out, he could move in on your organization, combine it with his, and take full control of the Prague black market. With control of Berlin and Prague, he thought he would become the dominant crime boss in Eastern Europe. I think he believes he can become the Lucky Luciano or Al Capone of Europe, gaining influence over the commission of other

European crime bosses, and the trade routes between Western Europe and Asia."

Manchevski seemed to realize just how ambitious Strobviok's plans were. He looked at Lucian. "I've wanted to kill that arrogant bastard for years, but we were running such profitable rackets, I didn't want to disrupt anything. But with American and European governments focused on either terrorism or economic problems, they're not as focused on organized crime as in the past. Our profits have never been greater. But now I don't have a choice: if Strobviok has become a threat, then I must have him killed. Lucian, are there ways we can corroborate what Mr. Lawrence is saying?"

Lucian stepped forward, next to James. "I think the incident with Vlastos at the restaurant shows there is much truth in what he says."

"What incident?" James asked.

"Vlastos killed about eight men and burned the restaurant to the ground."

"Is he still alive?" James asked.

"No," Lucian said, looking back at Manchevski.

James turned toward the huge tinted windows and looked out over the casino floor below. There was no question that Vlastos had led an evil life, but James had felt an odd connection with him near the end of their time together. He thought he had seen a glimmer of humanity inside the killer. But it didn't matter now. The man was dead. Whatever chances Vlastos had once had to redeem his life were now gone.

James hadn't made the same mistakes in his life that Vlastos had. Not by far. But he had made mistakes nonetheless, and Vlastos's death was just one more reason why he had to change his life by getting out of his comfy little situation, seeing more of the world, and living with a greater sense of adventure. If he ever made it home alive, he would be making some changes.

In the window's reflection, he saw Manchevski nod at Lucian. That seemed suspicious. It suddenly felt as though something was wrong. In the same moment, he recognized something briefly in the crowd of people moving along the main gaming floor of the casino. In his peripheral vision, he could see Lucian's reflection moving closer to him from behind, but what was that he had just seen on the casino floor? Stepping closer to the tinted window, knowing that no one in the casino could see through its mirrored surface into the room, he searched every face in the crowd of people below until he saw what he had half seen a few seconds ago. There, in the middle of the crowd on the far side of the grand casino room, he saw his brother walking with another man. There was Ian, less than a hundred feet away, walking past the slot machines on the other side of the green felt tables full of chips and cards, surrounded by countless people.

James raised his hand to bang on the window, even though he knew that no one could see through it from the other side. But before his hand hit the glass, something whipped around his throat and pulled him backward. His eyes briefly caught the reflection of Lucian's face in the window, with his hands tightened around the ends of a thick, white rope.

With his hand upraised to bang on the window, he had managed to throw it between the rope and his neck. Without this, he would already have lost consciousness. As he fought to keep the garrote away from his neck, his eyes briefly saw Ian and his friend walking along the edge of the casino floor, oblivious of what was happening up in this room they couldn't even see. He heard Lucian grunt while tightening the rope more. James coughed. It felt as if the rope was burning into parts of his fingers and neck. The more he struggled, the weaker he became.

The pain was too much. He couldn't keep pulling at the rope. He wasn't just going to lose consciousness—Lucian was going to kill him.

His eyes watered as he tried desperately to kick the window in one last hope of somehow alerting Ian. But Lucian reacted by pulling James backward to the ground, where he wrapped his legs around James's torso and tightened the rope even more. James heard himself gurgle like a dying animal. Looking up, he could see the cold stares on other men in the room, as if they had seen this sort of thing a thousand times before and now took only a mild interest in watching a man die.

Somehow, through all the pain, James felt something hard pressing into his lower back. He let go of the rope with his right hand and twisted his arm awkwardly to reach behind his back for the object. Once his hand was on it, he felt a surge of hope as he realized what it was. Lucian, too, seemed to sense what was happening, because he released the rope and tried to grab for the object. But it was too late. James twisted the semiautomatic handgun tucked in Lucian's waistband, thumbed the safety off, and pulled the trigger, firing a shot into the man's upper thigh.

Lucian screamed, and his body convulsed under James. He threw a hard elbow across the back of James's head before pushing him off and rolling onto his side, holding his leg in agony.

James's neck still burned from where the rope had been. He sucked fresh air back into his lungs for the first time in over a minute. He was crouched down on all fours, with his head almost on the floor, as he took another breath. With the second breath, he felt his focus return. There were shuffling sounds all around him. Someone shouted. With his third breath, he noticed that he still had the gun in his hand.

Everything seemed to be happening in slow motion.

James looked up and saw Manchevski standing behind the desk, pointing at him while he yelled at his men, who were reaching for their own guns. James, still crouched on the floor, lifted the gun and fired in their direction. Most of his shots missed, but he thought he might have hit one of them as they dived to the floor. Manchevski ducked behind the desk. Lucian crawled toward the door, where two other men lay prone. One of the men at the side of the room fired a shot, and the bullet made a sharp hiss as it flew past James, missing his head by inches before destroying one of the video monitors behind the desk.

James fired a shot back at the man, also missing. But the man jumped away from the wall where the bullet hit, and tripped over the crawling Lucian and fell to the floor.

With everyone down or distracted, James jumped to his feet and fired two shots into the corners of the huge tinted window that formed one wall of the room. The window shattered with a loud crash, followed by the tinkling of thousands of pieces of glass raining down to the casino floor below.

James saw people below staring up at the gaping hole above them and screaming at the sound of the gunshots.

He leaped from the window, landing on the green felt of a blackjack table, but his momentum carried him forward and he fell sideways through the air onto a baccarat table, knocking four of the players backward in their chairs as everything crashed to the floor.

Shaken, the first thing he noticed as he tried to get up was that he had lost the gun. Most people who hadn't fled the room simply gaped in shock. Then a big man with a beard and a shiny forehead picked James off the floor and pressed him facedown on the felt top of a blackjack table, twisting both his arms behind his back to hold him down.

"I got him!" the man shouted, looking around the room in excited confusion as if waiting for someone to instruct him.

"Hold him!" someone shouted from above. "Don't let him go anywhere! Security! Table seventeen!"

James managed to turn his head sideways enough to look up at the man shouting the orders. It was Manchevski, standing at the edge of the window frame, at the spot from where he had jumped. He looked enraged.

He struggled to get free, but the man had him pinned. He tried to kick backward against the man's shins with his boot heels, but the second he tried to shift his weight, the man just pressed his face harder into the casino insignia on the table.

James was about to try another kick when he felt the hold on his arms relax. There was a loud *"Oof!"* followed by gasps from the crowd as the bearded man fell in a heap at his feet. A hand grabbed his shoulder and pulled him up off the table. Back on his feet, he spun around and found himself face to face with his brother.

"Come on!" Ian said when he saw the approaching security men. "This way!"

James needed no further prompting. The only thing that mattered at this moment was to get far away from Manchevski, the approaching casino security people, and God knew how many other Malacoda men in the building. The man he had seen walking around the casino with Ian was now running beside them.

"Who are you?" James asked between breaths.

"Marcus . . . Met your brother through the university . . . Glad we found you."

All three clomped down a wide staircase two steps at a time. Hitting the bottom hard, James stumbled and went down. Marcus grabbed his arm to help him up.

Ian, still out in front, spun around and yelled, "What the hell are you doing! We have to get out of here—now!"

"I think I hurt something when I jumped from the window," James replied as Marcus helped him up.

Ian raced backed toward them. "We don't have time for this. Can you keep running?"

"Yeah, but I don't know for how long. And I don't think I can go fast."

Ian's face looked panicked, but then the panic turned to something worse as he looked past James, up the long stairway they had just descended.

"Shit! Run! Now!"

James and Marcus took off after Ian down the wide hallway of the grand casino, not even taking the extra split second to look behind them at whatever Ian had seen. As James hobbled at a fast skip to avoid putting too much force on his aching ankle, he saw Ian speed-dial a number on his cell phone. "Where are you?" he heard Ian yell into the phone. "Okay! We're running along the main lower corridor . . . Yes. Thirty seconds . . . They're out there? Shit! Okay, I'll count it down . . . Yes, it'll work. I'll count it down! Okay."

James still hadn't looked behind him as he forced himself to keep up with Ian and Marcus. But the pounding feet and shouts behind him seemed to be getting closer by the second.

"Okay!" Ian yelled into the phone. "Thirty seconds! Twenty-nine! Twenty-eight!"

James grimaced at the pain stabbing the front of his ankle with every step. Another loud shout came from behind them, and this time he couldn't resist turning his head to look back as he ran. He saw five burly men in suits hitting the bottom of the steps some fifty feet behind them, gaining on them.

"Twenty! Nineteen! Eighteen!" Ian continued yelling into the phone.

"Hurry!" Marcus yelled, seeing that James was still struggling to keep up.

The security men had cut the distance between them in half.

"Twelve! Eleven! Ten!"

They were approaching the six glass doors that led to the casino's semicircular driveway. Two valets were standing out front: one motioning for cars to stay back and the other standing with a gun drawn and feet spread, facing them. James could hear the men behind them almost on their heels as they rushed toward the front doors and the armed valet waiting for them outside.

"Five! Four! Three!"

James heard a loud screeching as they rushed through the first of two doors. Only twenty feet in front of them, both valets were now pointing guns at them and yelling for them to stop. But the screeching sound had turned their attention to their right, and now came the loud revving of an engine. A black van raced up the entrance to the front doors. One of the valets dived out of the driveway and up onto the sidewalk, and the other tried to sidestep the van as it came to a sliding stop, but the driver opened the door, knocking him flat.

Ian was the first of the three to make it outside, and without breaking stride, he gave the valet who had dived out of the way a boot to the head, as if place-kicking a football. The man flopped facedown on the red carpet.

Someone in the back of the van opened its sliding side door, and Ian, Marcus, and James dived inside. The driver stomped on the gas, squealing through the semicircle and back onto the street, away from the casino. The security guards who bolted through the entrance doors only a few seconds after them could only watch as the van escaped into the Prague night.

# 44

"ARE WE CLEAR?" the driver shouted as the van sped through the narrow, shadowy streets near Nové Město.

"Clear!" Marcus yelled, leaning over the back row of the van's seats, eyes searching out the rear window for anything that might be trying to catch up to them. Nothing. "You can slow down now!" he advised the driver. "We're safe. No need to draw the police."

The van backed down to a safe, legal speed.

In the middle row, James and Ian sat at opposite ends of the long seat, panting and staring at each other as the Victorian streetlights caused their faces to slide in and out of the shadows.

"You just couldn't stay put in a library like all the other grad students, could you?" James said, his eyes brimming with tears of joy. "You just had to get out and start some shit!"

"And you just couldn't stay put in K. C.?" Ian replied, reaching over and slapping his brother on the shoulder. "You just had to get out and crash my party. I can't believe you're here."

James's expression hardened. "After everything I've read and heard and seen in the past forty-eight hours, I can't believe you're still alive. Why the hell would you mess around with a bunch of crime lords just for a school paper?"

"It's my PhD dissertation," Ian said. "And it could change the world."

"Why didn't you tell us what you were doing?" James demanded.

"What was I going to say?"

"You could have told us the truth!" James shouted.

"If you had known the truth, would you have come looking for me?"

"Absolutely!"

Ian nodded. "Exactly. That's why I didn't tell anyone from back home. It wouldn't look that suspicious if I only disappeared for a few weeks. I was hoping I could finish up without anyone in the States catching on. I wanted to keep everyone I knew—especially Mom, Dad, and you—out of this. And I was worried that the bad guys had already noticed me and had tech people monitoring your communications."

"Yeah, well, you need to stop this now," James said. "You need to drop out of the PhD program and come back to the States and pray that the mafia over here isn't interested enough to follow you."

The van made a hard right, sliding its passengers leftward. Ian fell against him, but James pushed him back upright after the turn. The tires grumbled louder as the vehicle accelerated on the narrow cobblestone street lined with cars parked bumper to bumper.

"You don't understand," Ian said. "This is what I was born to do. I realized that a few months ago. I can't quit."

"Find a new destiny."

"I don't want to. Besides, the mafia here won't forget me; they won't just let me go."

"Why not?"

"He didn't tell you, did he?"

"*Who* didn't tell me *what*?"

"Strobviok," Ian said, leaning back in his seat. He looked exhausted. "He didn't tell you, because he wanted your help."

"Didn't tell me what?"

"In Berlin. The night I disappeared. It was because I killed two of his men."

"You . . . *killed*?" James asked. He looked at his brother in a new light. He had never considered that the brother he would find might not be the same one he had always known.

"So now you see," Ian said. "Strobviok has an interest in finding me far beyond just suppressing my final dissertation. He wants to kill me."

"Why did you kill these men?" James asked, praying he could understand Ian's motive. The others in the van had been silent as the brothers talked, but now he worried that they may all have contributed to some sinister transformation in Ian.

"Self-defense," Ian said, "although I can't be certain they were trying to kill me. I was trespassing to observe their operations in Berlin. They had guns and had snuck up on me. I shot and killed them. It wasn't even a thought—just an instinctive reaction."

"That's understandable," James said. "Anyone would have reacted that way."

"Not when one of the two men was the husband of Strobviok's niece."

"Shit," James said.

"Yeah. 'Shit' is right." Ian paused. "I'm just trying to do the right thing."

"What right thing would that be? Getting yourself killed? What do you think that would do to Mom and Dad? Especially after losing Jessica. How could you be so selfish?"

Ian's face tensed. "This is more important than anything else I could do with my life."

"And what do you really know of this dark world," James challenged. "Things you've read in other academic papers? Things Professor Hampdenstein fed you? Rumors you've heard and tried to verify through observations from a distance?"

"I've seen their crimes directly," Ian said, his voice cracking. "And I've seen the effects of the pain directly on families of the victims when their loved ones vanished. I've seen it in Zoe's eyes!"

"Who the hell is Zoe?"

"She's everything," Ian replied.

"What do you mean, '*everything*'? Everything to *you*?"

"You'd understand if you met her," Ian said softly. "She lost her sister, Miska, five months ago."

"You know her personally?" James asked, bewildered. "You've contacted family members of victims? All for your dissertation?"

Ian didn't reply, which gave James time to think.

"Oh, Christ! Ian, tell me you're not in love with this Zoe! I can't believe it. And now you think you can ride in like the white knight and save her sister?"

"I never said I could save Jessica," Ian snapped back.

"You said 'Jessica,'" James said, frowning.

"What?"

"You just called Zoe's sister Jessica."

Ian was silent. His expression showed confusion, then shame.

"What happened to you over here?" James asked. "What are you really trying to do here?"

The van turned down a narrow stone street between two tall buildings that looked so old they might crumble. Passing between the buildings, it emerged onto a road that ran along the Vltava River. The van moved along the riverside and drove into a small stone tunnel barely high enough for it.

James's plan had been to force Ian to return to Kansas. But now he realized that his brother wasn't the only one who had changed. His journey to find Ian had awoken something in himself.

The driver said something into his phone in Czech. Seconds later, a metal garage door clanked open. As they drove inside the building, James craned his neck to see as much as possible of the warehouse's cavernous interior. Upper levels with railed gallery walkways looked down on the open ground floor, as if they were in a small sports arena. On the ground floor, a dozen people were sitting at, or moving about between, improvised desks made of wooden crates, cable reels, or plywood laid over sawhorses. Some hunched over laptops; others stood at a table, discussing and pointing at different areas of a large paper that looked like architectural schematics. A few were packing hand radios, small satellite dishes, and other communication equipment into black duffels lined up on the floor next to three vans.

"Where are we? And who are all these people?"

"I think you know who they are," Ian replied.

"The White Rose?"

"Yeah. These are some of their members from the Prague chapter."

"How many chapters are there?"

"Forty-two and counting. We add one or two every month."

"Across Europe?"

Ian smiled. "Across the world."

The van stopped, and James could hear the garage door closing behind them. The driver killed the engine and got out to small but enthusiastic applause.

Ian opened the sliding door. "Come on. Let's go."

"Wait! I'm not done! I still have to talk to you!"

"I know." But instead of staying, Ian slid out of the van and gestured for James to join him.

Irritated—but aware of many strangers' eyes on him—James stepped out of the van.

"Well, if it isn't the prodigal son now returned to those he abandoned," said a muscular man with Chinese characters tattooed on both forearms.

Ian waved his hand in the air dismissively. "Oh, Klaus, I told you I'd be back."

James stepped toward his brother. "Ian, we really have to talk."

Ian turned to him, nodded, and held up one finger to stall him.

"Your brother?" a slender woman asked.

"Yes. Everyone, this is my brother, James Lawrence."

"We're glad you're safe," the woman said to James.

"Ian, I really need to talk to you *now*," James said.

"Just a minute," Ian hissed. He turned back to the others. "Everyone! All our planning is about to pay off. It's finally time for Devil's Night!" There were some hoots and cheers. "Tomorrow night we'll get the video that will finally show the world the brutal crimes against humanity that these organizations conduct every day. And when we broadcast it to the entire world, the outrage it creates will topple criminal empires everywhere." He paused before yelling out, "The revolution is about to begin!"

Everyone in the room cheered and applauded.

James had heard enough. He grabbed Ian's arm and pulled him away from the others, toward the nearest exit door. "I am not fucking around! We have to talk! Now!"

# 45

————————✺————————

JAMES PUSHED OPEN the exit door and pulled Ian outside. Even though he couldn't really see the black river, he could hear it lapping just a few yards away at the edge of the broad, sloping cobblestone path. He led his brother to the edge of the water.

"What the fuck are you doing?" James asked. "We're both getting on a flight back to the States! Tonight!"

Ian shook his head. "You don't get it, do you? Haven't you seen anything at all the past few days? Don't you realize there are untold numbers of people out there suffering and that maybe I can help them?"

"Because of Zoe's sister?" James asked.

"Yes. And because of Jessica."

"What does Jessica have to do with any of this?"

"She has to do with *all* of it. Every time I learn something else about the sex trafficking business, every time I think about the sixteen-year-old girls who have their lives taken from them by this sick industry, I can't help comparing it to how Jessica's life was taken from her."

The waters of the Vltava lapped up onto the sloping walkway, reaching within a few yards of their feet, then pulling back, leaving strings of water rushing back to the river through the gaps between the cobblestones.

"You're committed to doing this?" James asked.

Ian looked at him. "I need to prove that my theories work. I need to show that organized crime can be crippled."

"So once you've done this one thing and published your dissertation, you'll be satisfied? You won't continue playing Russian roulette with other criminal organizations until every one of them's put a price on your head?"

"I won't need to," Ian said. "Once we're done here, the entire world will push forward our initiatives."

James gazed forward as the river's gentle flow distorted the reflection of city lights into dancing luminous strings on the dark waters. Muffled cheers came from inside the warehouse behind them—the excited sounds of young revolutionaries who believed they were about to bring sweeping change to the world.

"And tomorrow night you're making this video for the White Rose?"

"Yes. That's why I need you to get on the next flight home. I don't want you around when we do this."

"That's bullshit. I'm not leaving here until you come back to the real world."

"James, you have to go home. I don't need you here. Marcus and I've been planning this for almost a month now. It'll go better if you're not around."

"Like hell I'm going," James snapped. "Do you have any idea what I went through to find you? I'm not about to go home now! Especially since you're about to try the most dangerous thing you've ever done. I'm not walking away now."

"James, please . . ."

"Oh, no. I can't go back to doing tax returns for wealthy clients after what I've seen the past few days. Don't you get it?

This world you've discovered over here, the things you've seen—well, now I've seen some of these things, too. You're not the only one whose life's been changed by this!"

Ian sighed. "I'm sorry you got involved in this."

"You should be. But that doesn't change what's happened. I've studied your research. I've seen things not even you have seen. I've been with people from both the Geryon Mafia and the Malacoda gang. And now I'm here with you, so maybe I can help. Either way, we need to be clear about one thing: I'm not leaving here until you finish what you need to do."

At first Ian frowned and shook his head in annoyance, but then a grin formed. "You're crazy to follow me, you know that?"

James nodded. "Yeah, crazy runs in my family."

# 46

A WAVE OF relief washed through Hanna Henzollern. After thirty-six hours of helpless anxiety and worry, the text message she had just received from James had answered her prayers that he was all right. It read, "*Met bad guys in Berlin. They took me to more bad guys in Prague. Escaped. Found Ian. We are with WR in Prague. Couldn't contact you until now. WR is planning something big. Knew you'd want to know.*"

Hanna texted back: "*Where are you in Prague? I can be there in less than four hours.*"

Within minutes, she had a reply from James. "*Internet café outside city center. Can't give location of WR but can meet you in Prague Castle at 3:00 pm today.*"

"*Leaving now,*" she answered in the final text. Then she rushed into the spare room in Victor's flat, where her half-unpacked luggage was. After throwing a few items back into her case, she rushed out of the apartment less than five minutes after sending the text. Soon she was in a taxi on her way to the main train station in Berlin.

# 47

VLASTOS'S EYES OPENED to blinding lights and a white ceiling. He was in a bed. That much he knew right away. It took him a few seconds to realize that he was in a hospital. Then he heard Czech spoken over a nearby com speaker.

He turned his head and saw a man standing by the bed, staring at him. There was something dark and dangerous in the way this man stood looking at him. "Who are you?" Vlastos asked in Czech.

"My name is Wolfgang," the man replied in German.

Vlastos's eyes narrowed. "What do you want?" he asked, switching to German.

"You're lucky to be alive," Wolfgang said. "You were shot three times. One bullet missed your heart by less than an inch. Even surviving with that miracle, you still would have bled to death if the American hadn't found you."

"What American?" Vlastos asked.

"The Christian missionary in the church. He said he knew you."

Vlastos couldn't believe it. It had to be a sign. Not only had he gotten a reprieve for a lifetime of violence, but he was also being given a chance to make up for his crimes.

"We met briefly on a train," Vlastos replied. "That is all. Talked a little over a drink at the bar. I barely know him—just a fellow traveler one meets on the road."

"You've been on the road long?" Wolfgang asked.

"All my life. You?"

Wolfgang nodded. "Most of my life. I've settled down in recent years."

"It must be tough . . . slowing down."

"Actually, I like it."

"I don't believe you," Vlastos said.

"I have no reason to lie to you."

"Fine. Then why don't you tell me what you want from me." His eyes left Wolfgang briefly, moving in a casual scan about the hospital room, though he was registering every object and found only one close enough to serve as a weapon. His eyes returned to Wolfgang, but his thoughts were on the small metal alarm clock resting on the stand an arm's length from his bed. The alarm clock was round, with a straightedged steel base. In two quick movements, he could grab it by its round top and lacerate the arteries on the left side of Wolfgang's throat with the base's pointed edge. If needed, he could even stab him multiple times in the neck should the initial strike fail.

"I'm searching for someone," Wolfgang said, moving closer to him. "And I think it's someone you've traveled with recently."

Vlastos could now see the slight bulge under Wolfgang's jacket, just below the left armpit. It must be a smaller-caliber gun, he thought. A .22, perhaps. His experience told him that only fools and practiced killers were confident enough to arm themselves with a weapon that required such precision. Vlastos himself used a .22.

"I always travel alone," Vlastos said.

"Not always," Wolfgang challenged. "Not yesterday."

Vlastos could hear the alarm clock ticking next to him. It was so close, almost calling to him. And now this man was close enough, too. This unknown man who had been waiting for him to regain consciousness in this hospital bed. This man with his dangerous questions, his dangerous weapon hidden under his jacket, and his cold, confident, dangerous assassin's eyes.

"Who sent you?" Vlastos asked.

"Someone very powerful," Wolfgang replied.

*Powerful, I'm sure. But who? Aleksander Manchevski because I killed his men and burned one of his businesses? Maybe it's even my own boss, Strobviok, who sent you to kill me because I've failed in my mission and have attracted enough attention to become a liability.* A number of guesses flashed through his mind, but of one thing he was certain: this man was here to kill him.

"Who are you looking for?" Vlastos asked.

"I think you know who," Wolfgang replied, eyeing him coldly.

Vlastos's eyes reflected the man's cold glare back at him. "Sir, I need a name."

"James Lawrence."

The alarm clock's ticking seemed to grow more pronounced, as if all the other sounds in the room were now dampened.

"And what business have you with him?"

"So you do know him."

"Yes," Vlastos said, willing to concede this much in hope of learning more about this stranger who had found him in the hospital.

"I represent someone who wants to find him," Wolfgang said.

"Because of his brother?"

This time it was Wolfgang's eyes that widened. "What do you know of his brother?"

"As much as what you know, I suppose. His brother is a bit of an enigma."

"When was the last time you saw James Lawrence?"

"I think you know the answer to that," Vlastos said. He kept eye contact with the man, but his ears were focused on the ticking alarm clock. It would need to be a precise slice to cut the artery in the man's neck. Vlastos would need to keep his eyes on the man as he grabbed the clock, so that he could adjust the placement of his strike depending on any slight last-second movement by his victim.

"If I knew that, I wouldn't be here," Wolfgang said, leaning in closer.

Vlastos noticed a hardening in the man's expression, as if he had suddenly noticed something. Wolfgang slipped his right hand under his jacket. Vlastos's right hand shot to the alarm clock, grabbed it, and flicked it like a knife toward Wolfgang's neck.

Wolfgang jerked his head back just as the sharp edge of the alarm clock's base cut into the skin of his neck. He stumbled backward and fell against the door. Stunned, he raised his left hand to his neck and must have felt the blood. Keeping pressure there, he drew his gun with his free hand and aimed it at the hospital bed. "Stop!" he yelled.

Vlastos rolled out of the bed and flipped it onto its side so it was between him and Wolfgang. He couldn't believe how fast the man had been, and he knew that even with his slight adjustment during the strike he had just missed cutting the carotid artery, making a substantial but nonfatal cut across the skin of the neck. Now he had lost any advantage and was at the mercy of this assassin. He had felt sharp abdominal pains when he rolled onto the floor. He didn't know how serious the injuries were that landed him in the hospital.

Just as when he had been cornered in the Malacoda gang's restaurant, Vlastos's only chance of escape was to create an element of chaos. He pulled all the monitors off his body, which caused a high-pitched electrical hum from the machines on both sides of the flipped bed. The machines would be centralized through the hospital's IT network and should send an emergency signal to the nurses' station. There were no other doors or windows in the room, so the only way he could escape was past this assassin.

"Stand so I can see you," Wolfgang yelled. "Slowly! I will shoot you if I have to."

*I know you will,* Vlastos thought. *But you don't know what you're up against. If you did, you would have killed me when I was still unconscious.*

Panicked shouting came from the hallway. Then the door flew open as two nurses and a doctor rushed in. When Vlastos heard Wolfgang shouting for them to get back, he stood up from behind the bed and threw the alarm clock as hard as he could at the man's head. Even though the throw was right on target, Wolfgang tilted his head at the last instant so that it just missed him. Vlastos pushed the bed out of his way and limped toward the door, knocking over the doctor and one of the nurses as the other nurse jumped out of his way.

He had almost made it out when Wolfgang slammed him against the wall. Vlastos threw a punch at his lower body, but Wolfgang countered the strike with a perfect outside block that was faster and stronger than anything Vlastos had expected. Within seconds, Wolfgang had him pinned facedown on the hard hospital floor. For a few seconds, Vlastos struggled unsuccessfully against him—the only person who had ever been able to manhandle him in his life—until he felt something jab the back of his thigh. He felt lightheaded and then nothing.

# 48

HANNA LEFT THE train station and took a taxi to Prague Castle in Hradčany just as James had instructed. She walked down the Zlatá ulička, or Golden Lane—a narrow street with tiny centuries-old fairy-tale houses lining the northern wall of the castle, beyond the east end of the Basilica of St. George. Once inside the walls, she went to the Third Courtyard, which opened up to St. Vitus's Cathedral, in the center of Prague Castle. The cathedral was the very image of Gothic architecture with its spiking towers, stained-glass windows, gilded decorations, and Romanesque rotunda.

Walking inside the cathedral, she could have mistaken it for the Vatican. The narrow nave directed all attention toward the altar fifty yards away. Sunlight fell from the clerestory windows high above the tall archways lining the path toward the ornamented altar. It was one of the most beautiful sights she had ever seen, and she felt overcome with a spiritual calmness. It was as if all the chaos she had felt in her life, all the rebellion, all the searching for her own path, her strained relationship with her father, and her guilt at being the cause of her mother's death—all these things vanished for the moment.

She stood in the center of the cathedral for five minutes as little groups of tourists drifted past her in slow motion, gravitating toward the altar. When her thoughts finally came back to the present, she moved out the side door that led to St. George's Square. From there, she walked down a narrow lane toward the Old Castle Steps, where James had arranged to meet her.

The lane sloped downhill, which pulled her strides faster than she intended, until she froze at the back side of the castle's vast grounds. Not thirty yards in front of her, a man stood on a low wall, his back to her. He was looking out at the Prague skyline, hundreds of feet below the steep slopes of the overlooking mountainside. He wore dark jeans over long, athletic legs, and his black leather jacket was zipped tight to protect him against the cold gusts that tousled his wavy chestnut hair. He seemed as mesmerized by the ancient beauty of Prague as a child seeing the endless, rolling waves of the ocean for the first time.

"Hallo!" she yelled out, and smiled when James turned and waved. She ran toward him as he jumped down from the wall, and they embraced as long-lost friends. But when he squeezed her tightly she relaxed, feeling something deeper and more heated.

After what felt like an eternity, they released each other. "I'm sorry I let them take you," she said, tears in her eyes.

"There was nothing you could have done. It was my choice to meet them. It was a desperate, reckless plan, but I knew the risks."

"I was too far away and lost you in the blackout."

He grinned. "I'm glad you couldn't do anything. I don't even want to think what might have happened to you if you had tried to stop them."

"Oh, James," she said, touching his cheek. "I can't believe you're here and that you're all right. I'm so happy. You must tell me what happened."

"I will, but first I need you to do something for me . . . It could be dangerous."

"I don't care."

He threw his arms around her again and held her tight.

"What's gotten into you?" she said, whispering in his ear as he held her.

He slowly released her. "I'm sorry. The last few days . . . I almost died."

"They tried to kill you?"

"Yes, twice. And then I found my brother. It's a lot to process, and I'm not sure I'm doing a very good job of it. That's why I wanted you here. You're the first person I really met when I got to Europe. You've been with me from the beginning, and I always feel better when I'm around you. I was hoping you could help me make sense of all this."

"All what?" She stepped closer and clasped his hand in both of hers. "James, what is it?"

"It's my brother," he said. "I've found him, but he won't leave. He says he has something planned for fighting organized crime. I can't get him to leave."

"Maybe he's not *supposed* to leave," she said.

"I can't leave him," he said. "Not after learning what he's trying to do."

Her eyes met his. "Maybe *you're* not supposed to leave, either."

They held each other's gaze, and in that moment he embraced her again. But this time their noses touched and their faces held together until their lips met. She rose up on her toes as they kissed, and he pulled her into him.

"Oh, James," she whispered, resting her head on his shoulder. "What are we doing?"

"I don't know." He ran his fingers through the ends of her long blond hair.

"We're from different worlds," she said, caressing the back of his neck. "There is no future for this."

"I haven't been living my life the way I should," he whispered. "I don't know what world I live in anymore. I just know the people who are important in my life."

"Your brother," she said. "And your parents."

"And you," he added.

"You shouldn't say that," she whispered. "What future could there be?"

"I'm through with living for the future," he said. "This could be the start of something great for us, or it could be the only chance we're ever going to have together. If we waste this moment, then we'll waste the next hundred moments like it that come along after it. If there's anything I've learned in the last three days, it's that we really should be living as if today were the last day we'll have."

"Let's get out of here," she whispered in his ear.

"And go where?"

"Someplace where we're not mixed in with all these people." She grabbed his hand and led him away from the castle wall. He let her pull him along a path that curved down a long, narrow stairway.

Twenty minutes later, they had crossed Charles Bridge and were in a hotel room on Prague's Old Town Square, making love as if they believed it was the last day of their lives.

# 49

"I WANT THE American brothers dead!" Aleksander Manchevski yelled at Lucian in the penthouse of the casino. "Put out a contract on their lives. Twenty-five thousand U.S. dollars on each brother's head. Double if their deaths are slow and painful." Manchevski could already think of four different men, each with numerous links to low-level assassins, who would be interested in the bounty.

"Yes, sir," Lucian said.

"What about the other thing?" Manchevski asked, referring to the man who had been sent to kill him and now lay helpless in a Prague hospital.

"It's being taken care of as we speak."

"Good." Now that he had addressed these few small acts of revenge, he could devote the rest of his time to planning his preemptive attack on the Geryon Mafia tomorrow, before Strobviok had a chance to hit him first in the coming war. "I want security tripled at our main operations in Prague. I want to be prepared in case Strobviok tries to hit us tonight."

After giving more detailed instructions to Lucian, he dismissed him and watched him leave the penthouse, knowing that his orders would be executed quickly. Within a few hours, all the Malacoda gang's most profitable operations would be at heightened security. If any of Strobviok's men tried to penetrate or disrupt things, the additional security would put them in dark, unmarked graves in the cold woods outside Prague—graves they would share with the American brothers.

# 50

VLASTOS REGAINED CONSCIOUSNESS and found himself secured to the hospital bed in the same room he had tried to escape. His wrists were handcuffed to the metal bars on the side of the bed, and his ankles were handcuffed to the foot of the bed. A thick leather strap was across his chest, preventing him from sitting up. When he strained to raise his head an inch off the pillow, he saw Wolfgang sitting calmly in a corner chair.

"Why haven't you killed me yet?" Vlastos asked.

"I didn't come here to kill you," Wolfgang replied.

"Why have the hospital staff and police guards allowed you to stay?"

"I told you, I work for powerful people. You seem to have assumed that meant I work for criminals. I don't. The man I work for is much more powerful than any criminal."

Vlastos lowered his head back to the pillow and sighed. "The German government," he said, knowing the man's accent.

"*Ja,* of course."

"What department? How high up?"

"I can't tell you."

"That high up, huh?" Vlastos said.

"*Ja,*" Wolfgang replied, his smile revealing his amusement at Vlastos's understanding.

"Well, I won't tell you anything. If you knew me, you would know not to even bother asking."

"I'm looking for James Lawrence," Wolfgang said. "And his brother, Ian. That's all I care about. You can talk to me about these things, I think."

"I would imagine James is probably dead by now," Vlastos said. "I have no idea about Ian, but I wouldn't be surprised if he is also dead."

Wolfgang shook his head. "Oh, I assure you, they are both still very much alive." Seeing Vlastos's head pop up to study him, he continued. "They were both spotted at the casino."

"What casino?" Vlastos asked eagerly.

"You really haven't heard? There were reports of a commotion at the Grande Omertá last night. Eyewitnesses saw three men flee the casino with security men hot on their heels. Two of them spoke English with American accents, and their descriptions are similar to those of the Lawrence brothers. I checked with a friend in Berlin who works in intelligence, and he said the casino is owned by a private equity firm long believed to have ownership ties to Aleksander Manchevski and the Malacoda gang."

"So they escaped?" Vlastos asked.

"Yes."

"James found his brother after all, and then they escaped." A wave of relief washed over him at the thought of James reunited with his lost brother.

"Yes. But no one knows where they are now. They could still be in danger. It's my responsibility to find them before anything happens to them."

Vlastos now wished he could help this man. If only he knew something, anything, that could lead the man to James. "You are right. I did travel with James from Berlin, but we were separated yesterday evening. But if he's with his brother now and they aren't trying to return home, then there is no way for me to know where they are in the city. I know places owned and operated by the Malacoda gang, but that won't help now."

"So they're on their own, probably being hunted by the Malacoda," Wolfgang said.

"Why do you assume they're being hunted?"

"Because of the description of them fleeing Manchevski's casino. Whatever happened inside there, Manchevski's men seemed to be after them—and not just to chat. You sure you don't know anything that could help me find them?"

"I already told you, I can't think of anything."

"Well, keep thinking. Something might come to mind." Wolfgang walked toward the door. "I need to make a call. Think hard. I'll be back in a few minutes."

Then Wolfgang left the room.

*     *     *

Tarkan Karadağ strolled excitedly along the first floor of the hospital. The dark, lean Turk had been a talented rising star in the Malacoda gang's select group of seven top assassins for the past three years, and now his moment had come. He wasn't sure why he had gotten the assignment. He had never failed in his twenty-two other contracts over the years, but there were other, older guys with more jobs under their belts than he had. Perhaps he had been selected because his youth made him look more convincing in a paramedic uniform as he searched through the hospital for Vlastos. He couldn't believe he had been given the opportunity to kill such a notorious man.

Tarkan didn't need to check with the receptionist or any nursing stations, for he knew where he was going. His capo had received word that Vlastos was being held in room 308. He had also received assurances that the police officer on guard during the last half of a four-hour shift would disappear from his post for the first fifteen minutes after seven o'clock. His watch showed seven on the dot, so he had just entered the kill window.

He entered a stairway and climbed toward the third floor. Taking the elevator would have meant standing still, perhaps long enough for someone to strike up a conversation, which would make it easier for them to describe him to detectives afterward.

The third floor's clean white and green checkered tiles shone under the fluorescent lights. He saw the numbered plate for 321 on the room next to the stairway. Next was 319, so 308 should be six doors down on the left side.

As he strode down the corridor, he was pleased to see no guards outside the door. His capo had told him that Vlastos would be either sedated or restrained as a prisoner, but that did not mean he should take the job lightly. He understood this already. He had worked hard and waited long to be trusted with a job this important, and he was too careful a professional to risk any slipups. After this, he would be a top consideration to get connected within the organization—a true member of the Albanian mafia. He was a young man with a bright future.

Just four doors away from him, the door to 308 opened, and a fit-looking man of about fifty came out. The man hesitated a moment before closing the door behind him and then headed down the corridor, away from Tarkan. Tarkan sensed that the man had taken brief notice of him. Being cautious, he continued a few doors past 308 and knocked on 305, on the right side of the hallway.

He stood outside 305 for twenty seconds until he saw the man disappear around the corner, far down the hallway. He then waited ten seconds, watching for any sneaky backward glances from that corner. There were none. The man was gone.

Tarkan glanced at his watch: four minutes after seven o'clock. He didn't have much time. He turned back toward his destination, walked across the hallway, opened the door to 308 without knocking, and stepped inside, closing the door behind him.

# 51

WOLFGANG WENT TO the far corner of the hospital
lounge, where he could have some privacy for his call.
He took his new cell phone out of his pocket, but instead of
dialing the number, he just stared at its black screen. It had been
too many years since he worked operations in the field, and even
then most of his experience was in mountains, deserts, and
jungles—not this urban terrain. His training hadn't been tuned
for an environment like this, but still his instincts were warning
him that something was off. He couldn't place it or even
understand it, but he had learned long ago to embrace these faint
subliminal tingles.

   He closed his eyes, trying to recall everything he had seen in
the past few minutes. Vlastos had shifted on the bed in a peculiar
manner when Wolfgang opened the door to leave the room, but
that couldn't have meant anything, since the man's arms and legs
were secured to the bed. Earlier there had been a guard outside
the door, but there was no one there a second ago. Had there
been a mix-up? Was he supposed to notify someone at the
security station on the second floor if he left the prisoner? What
about the hallway? The only anomaly was the older man who

had been sitting in a wheelchair, staring at him as if he could see in him all the violent acts he had committed in his life. The man could have faked needing a wheelchair, but not even the best makeup in the world could fake his old age. No, that guy couldn't be a threat. Who else? There had been a young paramedic. A paramedic in a hospital certainly wasn't unusual, but the more Wolfgang thought about it, the more unlikely it seemed that a paramedic would be this far from the ambulance drop and the emergency room facilities. And a paramedic's disguise would allow ample movement, with less risk of discovery by local hospital staff. After all, it was a paramedic's job to come and go from hospitals at all hours of the day and night.

He shouldn't have left Vlastos alone for even a minute without a guard on watch. Leaving the lounge, he headed back down the hallway toward the room. He would call the hospital's security office from the phone in the room and wait for the guard to return before going back to the lounge to call the chancellor.

He opened the door to 308 and stepped inside. The first thing he noticed was Vlastos's face: it seemed frozen, staring up at the ceiling. Then he noticed the young man dressed as a paramedic, standing in the far corner, almost camouflaged against the white wall. And last of all, he noticed the matte black pistol pointing at him. By the look in the man's eyes, Wolfgang was certain he wouldn't hesitate to fire at him if he tried to flee.

"Remove your gun and slide it into that corner," the man said.

Wolfgang didn't have a choice. He slowly unstrapped the shoulder holster holding his gun under his armpit and slid it into the corner as instructed.

"Who are you?" Wolfgang asked, hoping to establish a dialogue that might save his life. After all, the man had come here to kill Vlastos, not him. He wasn't even supposed to be here—he was just trying to find the American brothers.

The man didn't answer.

"He's a Malacoda assassin," Vlastos said, still staring up at the ceiling. "His name is Tarkan."

Wolfgang's eyes darted back to the hospital bed in surprise. Vlastos wasn't dead. He had just been lying there, waiting helplessly for the man to kill him. But what had Tarkan been waiting for? Why hadn't he done what he came to do?

"I'm sorry I left you," Wolfgang said. "That was a mistake."

"Yes, especially in this condition," Vlastos grumbled. "This man was just telling me what an honor it will be for him to kill me. He seems quite excited about it, actually." He turned his attention to Tarkan. "I'm afraid I don't understand what there is to get excited about, killing me when I'm like this. There is no honor in that. You may as well suffocate a man with a pillow while he's in a coma. You haven't beaten me with either your mind or your body, and certainly not with your skill. That will get around in the profession, you know." Vlastos laughed. "Honor? Good Lord, man, not even a public relations agent would stretch the word so much."

Tarkan kept his gaze on Wolfgang the entire time, and his icy expression gave no clue whether Vlastos's words bothered him. Finally, he spoke. "Either way, I am the man who will kill you. People will remember that longer than they remember the circumstances."

Wolfgang wasn't thinking about honor, but about survival. He hoped Vlastos would distract the assassin long enough that he could get to his second gun, in his travel bag on the chair just ten feet away.

"Please, don't kill me," Wolfgang said, taking a step toward the chair. "I'm not a part of anything *that* man has done," he said, pointing at Vlastos.

"You're here, so you're part of it now," Tarkan said.

"Oh, no, please, I beg you." Wolfgang took another step.

Tarkan knitted his eyebrows as if suspecting something.

"You're such a coward," Vlastos said. "Don't beg. Take it like a man."

Wolfgang felt pretty sure Vlastos was playing along with him, but he had no idea whether Tarkan was buying it.

"But I don't deserve to die," Wolfgang continued. It was easy to be convincing, since there was a good deal of truth buried in his words. He thought of his wife and son and was terrified of being taken from them.

"You shouldn't have bound me," Vlastos said.

"I know," Wolfgang replied, taking another step towards the bag.

"Stop," Tarkan said.

"Are you sorry you cuffed me to this bed?" Vlastos demanded.

"Yes, very sorry." Wolfgang took another step. He was only five feet from the bag.

"Stop!" Tarkan demanded. He stepped toward Wolfgang, aiming the pistol directly between his eyes. "You think I'm a fool? I see what you're doing. You move any closer to that bag, and I'll put a two-inch hole in your frontal lobe. Now, get on your knees, with your ankles crossed and your hands on the floor under your knees."

Wolfgang did as he was told.

"You have something in here that you want," Tarkan said, moving toward the bag. "A knife? Gun?" He felt inside the bag with his free hand while the other kept his pistol trained on Wolfgang. "I saw you leave the room. You shouldn't have come back so soon. I was nearly finished and would have been gone before you returned. But now I have to kill you, too. And I don't even know who you are. That's very dangerous for me, you understand, to kill a man I know nothing about. I hope you are not someone too important."

Wolfgang realized that raising his son during the past fifteen years had changed him from the fearless special forces soldier he had once been. He had never before felt this terrified of dying: he couldn't imagine what it would do to his family.

"Please," Wolfgang pleaded, his eyes tearing up. "I have a son."

"Then part of you will live on."

"You bastard."

Tarkan smiled, but then he frowned as his hand finished searching the bag. "What were you trying to get? There's nothing here."

Wolfgang's eyes widened. It wasn't possible, was it?

The light clatter of handcuffs was the only warning Tarkan received before the bullet blew a conical pink mist out the back of his head, spattering brain and bone onto the wall. His body collapsed on the floor.

Wolfgang didn't even try to pick up the gun that had dropped right in front of him. Instead, he slowly lifted his head to look at the man who had saved his life. Vlastos was half sitting up in the bed, his one uncuffed hand pointing Wolfgang's gun at the body, the other arm and both ankles still shackled to the metal bed frame.

"Thank you," Wolfgang whispered.

"Don't mention it."

"I mean it. You didn't have to do that. He had a silencer. You could have waited until after he killed me to shoot him."

"You seemed worth saving."

"How did you pick the cuffs?"

"These mattress springs are full of little wires just waiting to come out and play," Vlastos said. "They're not exactly prison issue."

Wolfgang smiled. "You didn't have time to pick all four cuffs, so you got one hand free and wheeled the bed to my bag, found my gun, and wheeled the bed back."

"You make it sound easy," Vlastos said. "It wasn't. I had to push off from the walls. Knocked over my IV."

"I thought this guy did that."

"No. He came in just as I got back into position. I had tucked the gun under my leg when I was maneuvering the bed back in place. He already had his gun drawn, so I couldn't make a move. I just kept my free hand close to the handcuff and waited for him to turn his back to me so I could kill him. I might never have gotten a chance if you hadn't come back when you did."

"Do I even want to ask what your original plan was—what you were planning to do with the gun before this guy showed up out of the blue?"

"Let just say I was going to try to convince you to let me go," Vlastos said.

Wolfgang nodded. "Well, you've convinced me."

They heard shouting in the hallway.

"They'll shoot you on sight if they see you with that," Wolfgang said.

Vlastos struggled to lean sideways in the bed, stretched his free arm down, and slid the gun across the smooth tile floor toward Wolfgang. Then, sighing from the painful effort, he lay back down on the bed and stared up at the ceiling. He said, "I know how to find James Lawrence."

Wolfgang stared in amazement, but before he could reply, the door flew open and a half-dozen security men rushed into the room.

"Wait!" he shouted.

But when the men saw the body in a pool of blood, they kicked the guns away from Wolfgang and surrounded Vlastos.

*   *   *

The hubbub with the hospital security staff went on for a good ten minutes before Wolfgang managed to make them understand what had happened. They moved Vlastos into another room and took Tarkan's body to the hospital morgue, and when the commotion died down, Wolfgang entered Vlastos's new room. The veteran Geryon Mafia killer was staring up at the ceiling above his hospital bed.

"How can we find James Lawrence?"

"*We?*" Vlastos asked.

"You saved my life when you didn't have to. I did that for a good man once, and he rewarded me with his trust and friendship. It was one of the best things to happen to either of us. Now, together, I think we can help the Lawrence brothers."

"I know key locations for the Malacoda's operations," Vlastos said. "If James's brother is in Prague and they are together, and if they were at the Grande Omertá Casino, then I think I know which of the Malacoda gang operations they would most likely go to next. I'm just not sure how much damage two untrained American civilians could do to these guys."

"It might not be just the two brothers," Wolfgang said. "Have you heard of the White Rose?"

Vlastos turned to look at him. "Yes."

Wolfgang stepped toward the bed, pulled a small key from his pocket, and uncuffed Vlastos's wrists and ankles from the bed. "I've received permission to release you from the hospital under my supervision. I have a few things I need to tell you about the White Rose that you may not know. And you need to tell me where we can start looking for the American brothers."

The doctors and nurses had done a remarkable job stabilizing Vlastos, but his injuries were severe. One of the bullets had ruptured his spleen, and the doctor had warned both him and Wolfgang that even after the surgery it could possibly rupture again and cause fatal internal bleeding if he didn't rest. Despite the warning, Vlastos—who still seemed not quite able to grasp that he had survived last night's hell, and hinted that he had some debt to repay—insisted on helping Wolfgang find James and his brother. Wolfgang helped him out of bed. Ten minutes later, they were in Wolfgang's BMW, leaving the hospital for the

first on Vlastos's list of Malacoda operational locations in the
city.

# 52

JAMES LED HANNA through the stone alleyway toward the Vltava River and the waterfront entrance to the warehouse. Two men he didn't know were smoking on the doorstep. They appeared to recognize him because they stood and opened the door for him and Hanna.

A dozen people were inside. Leading Hanna through the center of the activity, James noticed a familiar face leaning over a table and studying a large unrolled architectural plan.

"Marcus," he said as they approached the table.

Marcus looked up from the schematics. "James, you're back." He stared at Hanna. "Fräulein Hampdenstein! It's a pleasure to meet you. I'm a huge fan of your father."

"He's a politician, not a movie star," she said, shaking his hand with a courteous smile.

"Yes, of course. I should say instead that I have enormous respect for him and his work."

She nodded.

"Where's Ian?" James asked.

"Up there." Marcus nodded toward the vestibule.

Ian was sitting on a table, leaning back on his elbows, with his legs outstretched and his feet resting over the back of a tall chair. Another man was fiddling with something on the front of Ian's shirt collar. Next to them, a young woman worked on a laptop.

"How does it look?" Ian asked his colleague.

"It should be okay," he replied. He looked at the woman. "How's the image?"

"Still too low. It's getting cut off at the bottom. Angle up a little and pull it out more."

The man started messing with it again. "If I pull it out much more, it will show," he said.

"What are you doing?" James asked.

Ian jerked his head toward him. "Hey!" he said, grinning.

"Damn it, don't move!" the man growled.

"Sorry," Ian said, slowly turning to face forward again. "Glad you're back okay, James. You were gone longer than you said." With a big smile, he said, "Hanna, welcome to the party! I remember seeing you at the university. I've recently become a big supporter of your father, by the way. I'm so happy that you've become involved in this! James told me how much you helped him. Some of us thought you'd be a perfect fit here, but the professor wouldn't let us approach you about the White Rose."

"If I was so perfect for the group, why did the professor want you to stay away from me?" she asked.

"That's a question you'll have to ask the professor . . . or your father."

"My *father*? What does he have to do with this?"

"You mean besides being one of the few remaining founders of the White Rose?"

"What!" Hanna gasped.

"Oh . . . ," Ian whispered, apparently realizing his mistake.

Hanna's expression hardened. "What do you know about my father?"

Ian's eyes caught hers for a moment before he had to look away. "Can you guys give us a second?" he asked the others around the table.

"We're done anyway," the man said. The woman closed the laptop, and Marcus left with them. James and Hanna stayed.

"Your father hasn't told you about the White Rose back in the mid-eighties?" Ian asked.

"No."

"Then I don't know if I should be the one to tell you."

"Just tell her," James said. "For God's sake, it's her father. If you know, then she has a right to know."

Ian nodded. Then he told her about her father's revolutionary activities with her mother and the White Rose twenty-five years ago. He told her about the underground movement her parents had been involved in, which helped lead to the fall of the Berlin Wall.

Hanna got quiet, and her eyes grew moist as she listened. James hadn't realized until now how little her father had told her about her mother and their student activist days before the fall of the Berlin Wall. It amazed him to hear all that her parents had done. He couldn't imagine what was going through her mind, but he found himself admiring her more than ever.

"But my father doesn't know about your plans for tonight?" Hanna asked when Ian quit talking.

"Not yet. Professor Hampdenstein has updated him on almost everything except for our current plans. I believe he is planning to tell him tonight."

"So how can we help with tonight?" James asked.

"We can put both of you on surveillance. We have most of the area around their operation center mapped and lookouts assigned, but we can always use more watchers on the surrounding rooftops." He turned and called Marcus to rejoin them. "Marcus, I want to put them together on lookout point Delta," he said. "Move Charla to Alpha with Patrick." He turned back to them. "Marcus will explain where you'll need to go and what you'll need to do. You'll have optics and com receivers so you can hear my microphone. The team will also have radios to communicate with each other, but we want to keep the chatter to a minimum."

"Will I be able to talk to you?" James asked.

"No. It's a one-way microphone and video feed to our secured site. We're recording everything and will post it to coordinated sites and Internet news outlets an hour after we're finished. We can't stream it live, because it would jeopardize the mission if they somehow caught wind of it while we were still streaming, but we've set it up so our com receivers will hear my microphone and see the video live. You'll see and hear everything happening when I'm in there, so I can talk to all of you if I need to, but none of you will be able to talk to me."

"Well, then we'd better hope there's nothing important we need to tell you once you go inside," James said, trying not to think about all the ways it could go wrong. "Is that what you guys were messing with on your collar?"

"Yes," Ian said. "It's a button-down collar, but we've sewn it down to the shirt so it can't be flipped up. That's to keep hidden everything we have in it: a microphone inside the right opening, a micro camera inside the left opening, and a small wire running from each to an encrypted micro broadcaster the size of a pencil eraser, hidden under the back center of the collar. The entire system would be very hard to find even if they frisked me, and our intelligence shows that they don't use sophisticated signal scanners to search customers at this location. They have metal detectors I'll have to pass through, but this device won't trigger them."

"And this monitor will capture live what the camera sees?" James asked.

"Right. Then we upload it to the Internet, for the whole world to see. Where it will go viral and raise a huge outcry against organized crime."

"And that will direct governments to your dissertation?"

"Exactly. And there they can learn the necessary steps to cripple and bankrupt the criminals."

James saw others on the main floor loading equipment into vans. It seemed they were planning to leave in just a few minutes. He asked Hanna if he could have a word alone with his brother. She nodded and left with Marcus to join the others.

"You really think that after seeing the video, people will start talking about organized crime activities they have witnessed?" James asked Ian once they were alone. "You really think all those voices will come together?"

"We have to appeal to the public for information. It's more important than you realize. And online social media are the perfect tool for that." Ian paused. "Do you know who was the first American to successfully take on organized crime?"

"Eliot Ness," James replied. "He went after Al Capone. He used a tax accountant like me to put him in Alcatraz. Everyone knows that."

"Before Ness," Ian said, "there was Thomas E. Dewey, special prosecutor of New York. He went after all the names in New York in the 1930s, including Lucky Luciano. And one of the first things he did as special prosecutor was to go on the radio and appeal to the public. He asked the people for leads and tips against organized crime. And the Internet gives us the power to go beyond anything Dewey could have imagined. Tonight we'll broadcast a visual plea, which will start a revolution that will change the world."

"Come on," James said. "I'm not one of your zealots. I know you better than anybody—you think I can't tell when you're bullshitting?"

"No bullshit, bro. What we're doing is more important than you can imagine."

"I can tell you're holding something back. There's something about this you're not telling anyone. There are other ways to get an attention-grabbing video about the mafia. You don't have to take this kind of risk. You don't have to go inside the operation!"

"Yes, I do!" Ian hissed. "I have to go in there. I have to see. I have to know for myself."

"Know *what*?" James said, grabbing both Ian's shoulders. "Damn it, tell me!"

"I have to know if she's in there!"

"Who?"

"Zoe's sister!"

James couldn't believe what he was hearing. "Why?"

"Why do you think?"

"For Zoe? What even makes you think her sister will be in there?"

Ian turned away, fiercely rubbing his forehead with both hands. "I don't know if she's in there. I mean, she's probably not. But she was taken in this area, and the Malacoda control the market here. That doesn't mean they're the ones that took her, but analysts think as many as forty percent of the girls kidnapped in Prague and forced into sex slavery disappear under the direction of the Malacoda gang. And half of those remain in Prague while the other half are trafficked to other cities or countries. Because this factory is the largest forced-prostitution house in Prague, I think there could be as high as a ten percent chance she's somewhere inside."

"Do the others know about this?"

"They don't need to know. I can look for her without changing anything."

"You sure you'll have time for that?"

"I'll *make* time," Ian said.

A horn honked from the floor below. Everyone was loaded up. It was time to leave.

"All right," James said. "This is your show. I'm just along for the ride, so I won't interfere. But if we get out there tonight and things go wrong and all hell breaks loose, I'm coming in there to get you out."

"It's all right," Ian said. "It won't come to that." He wrapped an arm around James's shoulders and led him down the balcony stairs. "Come on—time to roll."

# 53

VLASTOS COUGHED PAINFULLY in the passenger seat of the gray BMW.

"You going to make it?" Wolfgang asked.

He forced a half-smile, closed his eyes in pain, and, in a dramatic English accent, said, *"My hour is almost come, when I to sulf'rous and tormenting flames must render up myself."*

"What was that?"

*"Hamlet."*

"Hamlet said that?"

"No. The ghost, his father's spirit. *'Doomed for a certain term to walk the night, and for the day confined to fast in fires, till the foul crimes done in my days of nature are burnt and purged away.'"* He started coughing again.

"You'd better take it easy on the Shakespeare. I can't find these places without you."

Vlastos nodded. "We're almost at the first one. Keep going up this hill and turn left at the top. We'll go past a few restaurants before stopping near a small factory. From there, we should be able to see whatever they have going on. It looks like a construction company, but it's actually a distribution center for opium and heroin—maybe some blue ice, also. Opium comes in from Afghanistan via Rome and Bratislava. Heroin comes in from Cambodia via Bangkok and Istanbul. Once the stuff's in Prague, it gets distributed to other cities in Europe after it's cut and a percentage for the Prague market is removed from shipment supplies."

It had been many years since Wolfgang felt near an epicenter of mankind's more malign activities. His fingers squeezed the steering wheel at the vivid reminder of the potent criminal elements lurking in the shadows of this world he was trying to raise his son in. "How do you know so much about the Malacoda gang's operations?"

"There are annual commission meetings where all the bosses of the different European organizations meet to discuss the status of underground markets, how they should be divided between the organizations, and to settle any conflicts or disagreements that may have been brewing since the last meeting. Everyone discusses all their operations so that decisions can be made to keep the peace between the organizations. Of course, the bosses always hold some things back, but we have informants who help get us supplemental information. I'm sure they have their informants, too."

"I've never understood how people can live in such a violent underworld," Wolfgang said.

Vlastos coughed again and groaned. "Do you really think we're that different? I've seen your skills: they can only have come from a life of violence."

"I was in the military. I served my country. I've killed, but only enemy soldiers or bad men. I have protected innocents who would have been forgotten victims. I've done my part to make the world a slightly better place."

"I envy you," Vlastos said as he watched the dark trees slide past outside the window. "My life has been violent, too, but nothing so righteous as yours. I have killed many, more than I can remember. Most were evil men, as you say. But some were good men. And I've killed women—seven, I think." He paused for a second as if he might start coughing again, but didn't. "And one kid that was sixteen. His father was an evil man, but I could see in the kid's eyes at the end that he had not yet been corrupted by his father."

"Then why kill him?" Wolfgang asked.

"Those were my instructions. It was decided he would be a future threat."

"And you can live with that?"

"For a long time I could, but things are different now."

"Since when?"

"Since last night."

"Because you almost died?" Wolfgang asked.

"Not because I almost died, but because I was saved when I shouldn't have been. I can't explain it, but I feel like something must be watching over me. And because of the things I've done in my life, the only reason I was allowed to live is because there is something I'm supposed to do."

"You're talking about God?" Wolfgang asked.

Vlastos nodded, then looked back out the passenger-side window. Now more than ever, he wanted to kill Manchevski. He still felt the need to earn the pardon he had received. Manchevski was an evil man, and he wanted badly to remove him from this world so that no others suffered from his actions. For that matter, he wouldn't mind removing Strobviok from this world for the same reason. Strobviok was not just his boss but also a friend— or, at least, as much of a friend as one could be in this business. But Strobviok was every bit as evil as Manchevski. And both men were dangerous to the world.

They rode in silence for the last five minutes of the drive.

"Turn here," Vlastos said as they came upon a gray factory building the size of a high school gymnasium.

Rocks kicked up under the car as it pulled up the incline and cut through the lot next to the building. Stopping near the end, Wolfgang cut the lights and engine, and the two men left the car and moved through the darkness toward the back of the building.

Vlastos was having difficulty walking, so Wolfgang carried the night vision binoculars and detached rifle scope. He seemed to have a full ops kit with him, including standard surveillance and weapons hidden in the car's trunk.

Wolfgang knelt at the edge of the rock outcropping and surveyed the world below as if he were a soldier again back in the jungles of Burma or Burundi. Meanwhile, Vlastos lay down on his stomach, grimacing in pain, to watch with him.

"What should I look for?" Wolfgang asked.

"Almost nothing is visible from the outside. Transport trucks come and go on scheduled nights, and most operations take place underground. Some security, but nothing excessive. And some construction workers are around the site."

"They actually do construction work through this facility?"

"Yes," Vlastos said. "Not much, but enough to establish the business as a front and also use it to launder money from the drug sales."

"All in the same place!" Wolfgang said. "Amazing."

They scanned the warehouse and surrounding construction site. Two men were tying marker strings around a large rock pile. Someone was operating a small backhoe, prying up the hard soil with the bottom edge of its bucket, and another man was standing near a pile of steel rebar, smoking a cigarette and talking on a cell phone.

"It looks okay, doesn't it?" Wolfgang asked.

"Yeah," Vlastos replied. Just then two vans roared along the dirt drive toward the warehouse, splashing mud as they turned into its opening. The backhoe stopped, and the two men by the rock pile stiffened, but everything eased when the man on the phone gave a short wave to the vans.

The vans' doors opened, and ten men got out.

"That can't be normal," Wolfgang said.

"It's not."

"What just happened?"

"Looks like they're adding security," Vlastos replied.

"Why? Expecting a shipment?"

"Too many men for that—too visible. They wouldn't want to draw that much attention. No, this is something else. They look like they're preparing for war."

Wolfgang lowered the binoculars. "With your boss?" he asked.

"That's what I think."

He shifted his weight to lean in closer to Vlastos as a sudden breeze washed over the hillside trees. "Is this war because of you?" he whispered.

"No, I didn't cause it. The only reason I came to Prague was because my boss gave me the assignment. And the only reason he thought he needed to assassinate the Malacoda boss, Manchevski, was because . . ." His words trailed off as the process of trying to explain *how* things had happened gave him a sudden glimmer of *why* things had happened. The tension had been there between the Geryon Mafia and the Malacoda gang for years, just as with all crime syndicates operating in overlapping markets. But the balance had kept the peace until now. Things had escalated quickly, and now they were on the verge of exploding out of control. But why now?

"I just had an idea," Vlastos mused. "What if it was this missing American brother that got the Geryon Mafia and the Malacoda gang into a war?"

"*What!*" Wolfgang whispered, again surveying the grounds and all the moving green shapes in the night-vision binoculars. "Ian Lawrence?"

"What if he planned it?"

"Could he do that . . . make two different criminal organizations go to war against each other?"

"I don't know. If he understood the economics of organized crime and exploited that knowledge to get in contact with different organizations, he could possibly impress them with his expertise and spread some misinformation. It's hard to keep the peace on a good day . . . feels like it's always on the verge of destabilizing. It might actually be feasible for someone who understands the underworld to shatter the peace and just stand by while we kill each other over a simple misunderstanding."

"If that's true, it might explain why Ian went into hiding. He didn't even try to reach out to his family back in America to let them know anything."

Vlastos nodded. "We had a man in Chicago standing by, ready to travel to Kansas to kill Ian's parents and his older brother, James, if he tried to pass information to them. We had men in Paris who hacked into his family's computers and were monitoring e-mail traffic once he vanished. Ian was smart not to try contacting them. He must have realized there was a risk we could intercept e-mails or phone calls or letters."

"His brother, James, ended up being the wild card. Why didn't Ian assume that his brother would come looking for him?"

"I don't know," Vlastos said. "According to James, something happened to them years ago that pushed them apart. Who knows?"

"But he still came looking for his brother. He's taken some terrible risks, too, even if he didn't known what he was getting into at first. You have to respect that."

"Oh, I do respect it," Vlastos said. "Especially now. I respect it more than you can know." He lowered the scope. "Come on. Let's go to the next operations site. We won't find the Lawrence brothers here."

Wolfgang crawled backward on the outcropping, stood up, and dusted off his jeans. "I was sent here by my chancellor to protect them, and I can't rest until I know they're safe."

Vlastos nodded. "I now believe that I, too, was sent here to protect them, even if I only realized it yesterday."

As they moved through the darkness back to the car, Vlastos felt a sudden sharp pain in his side. He stopped and gasped, trying to fight it. After a few excruciating seconds, it went away. Opening his eyes, he saw Wolfgang staring at him with a look of concern.

"I'm fine," Vlastos said. "Just a little tickle. Let's keep going." Irritated at his condition, he hobbled ahead of Wolfgang to show that he was ready for whatever came next.

# 54

THE THREE VANS of the White Rose separated when they were five blocks from the factory. The lead van continued straight toward the warehouse before turning down an alley and stopping. Ian, James, Hanna, and Marcus got out, and when the van drove away, James noticed that Marcus was carrying a small backpack.

"Marcus will take you to the rooftop to set you up," Ian said. "Then he'll go to his post."

"You're leaving from here?" James asked.

Ian nodded. "There's a train station two blocks that way. I'll head to it and zigzag back towards the factory. That way if anyone *is* watching, I'll look like just another customer taking the train from the city center. We believe that's how most of their customers get here."

"Be careful," James said. There was so much more he wanted to say to Ian, but in that moment he didn't know how to express all that he felt.

Ian nodded. "I'm glad you're here, James. We were just screwing around chasing twisters in Kansas, but here we can actually change something." He checked his watch. "These guys have been getting away with their shit for long enough. An hour from now, the whole world is going to see them up close. Because of us, they'll be in everyone's crosshairs." He paused. "I'll be at the entrance in twenty minutes, and I'm starting to record now."

As he walked away down the dark alley, he raised both hands and messed with the back of his collar. The recording device was now capturing everything he saw and heard.

Marcus took James and Hanna to the roof, eight stories up. There he spent a few minutes setting up the equipment from his backpack: a small SatCom unit, insertable earpieces with short-range receptors, a small video screen, a pair of handheld two-way radios with over a hundred coded scramble channels, and a black nine-millimeter Glock semiautomatic pistol.

"What's the gun for?" James asked. No one had mentioned anything to him about firearms.

"Emergencies," Marcus replied.

"Everyone's carrying weapons?"

Marcus shook his head. "Some, but most aren't. Ian wanted you to have one just in case."

James resisted the urge to ask, *just in case of what?* He took the gun, checked to make sure a round was chambered and the safety on, and dropped it into the large front pocket of his leather jacket.

All three were kneeling behind the three-foot-high brick wall lining the rooftop. When Marcus was finished setting up the equipment, he pointed out the building entrance that Ian would approach, the alleyways where the White Rose vans were parked, and the building rooftops where the other White Rose members were set up. Then he wished them luck and walked back across the dark, wet rooftop before disappearing over the edge and down the fire escape stairs.

"Come on," James said, kneeling down next to the video monitor and the small radio with its octagonal wire antenna.

"Let's see how well this stuff works." He gave one of the earpieces to Hanna and put another in his ear. Then he removed the gun from his jacket pocket and put it on the ground against the low parapet.

"You don't want that?" she asked.

He shook his head. "I didn't come here to kill anyone."

She picked up the gun and put it in her coat pocket. "Neither did I."

He turned the knobs on the two-way radios down to their lowest volume and set them on the ground. Then he turned on the SatCom receiver so they could hear Ian's audio. When the sound came into their earpieces, all they heard were steady footsteps in the night—Ian's footsteps, clomping along the dark cobblestone sidewalks on Prague's half-lit streets and alleyways, toward the factory.

And all James could do was listen.

\* \* \*

As Ian walked down the dark sidewalk, he focused to keep his breathing calm, because the recording had started. At any moment, unfriendly eyes could be on him if they weren't already. He was glad that those listening to his microphone couldn't also hear his thoughts—thoughts that had him now questioning the risks he was taking. Despite the thousands of hours he had spent studying organized crime, he had never gone this deeply into their world: walking into an operation center as a supposed customer, surrounded by the very men and activities he was determined to destroy.

James's presence gave him strength. When he disappeared from the university he had felt that the safest thing to do was to avoid all communication with his family. He knew how sophisticated criminal organizations were with IT systems, application programmers, and network hackers. He had hoped his family would get the standard runaround from the U.S. consulate as it made the standard inquiries that wouldn't get them anywhere near the truth. But instead, James had come looking for him and—amazingly—had found him. As sick as Ian had felt when he first learned that his brother was in Europe and in danger, he now felt grateful that they could be a part of something together again.

He saw the round stone tunnel at the front of the building. Surveillance had taught him that customers walked down the tunnel, staying away from the street. Shadows moved in the darkness in front of him. Someone was there, up ahead near the end, waiting for him.

"Walking toward the gate now," Ian whispered for the radio listeners. "About to enter the factory."

He took a deep breath as he kept moving forward. Two faces appeared out of the shadows. A strong hand reached out and grabbed his shoulder.

"*Mund të ju ndihmojë?*" one of the men said in what Ian assumed was either Czech or Albanian.

"*Sprechen Sie Deutsch?*" he asked, betting the man would understand the question even if he didn't speak German.

The man shook his head.

"English?" he tried, keeping the German accent he had developed in Leipzig.

"Yes," the man said coldly. "Can we help you?"

Ian nodded, acting a little drunk. "Life is short. I came here to fall in love."

"And what makes you think you can do that here?"

"I was talking to some guys from Amsterdam earlier tonight at Roxy's. They told me about this place. Said it was cool. Expensive but cool. I've been to places like this before in Bangkok and Paris, but not in Prague. Thought I'd see if it's any good. If so, maybe I become regular customer. But I need to fall in love first."

"Cash," the man said.

"Yes, of course."

The first man nodded as the other one frisked him carefully. Ian stood still as the man's large hands groped his ankles, moved meticulously up his legs, explored his crotch, concentrated around his waist, and continued feeling all around his upper body, focusing under his arms and along his upper back. He was terrified when he thought the man's fingers brushed along the back of his collar, but his fears receded when they continued down his outstretched arms.

"Take off your shoes," the first man said.

He did.

The men used a flashlight to examine both his shoes and his feet.

"You wearing a wig?" the man asked.

"No."

The man used the flashlight to look along his scalp line.

"Okay," he said, handing Ian back his shoes. "Fifty euros for one session. More if you want more."

About seventy U.S. dollars, Ian thought. Christ, that was cheap! They sold these girls as if they weren't even human beings.

New footsteps were coming down the tunnel from the street. Ian turned to see the silhouette of a man heading toward them against the faint blue backlight.

The second man said something and left them to walk toward the approaching figure.

The first man then opened the elevator gate and locked it once Ian had entered with him. With the gate secured, the old elevator clanked upward, lifting them into the factory.

Ian realized that the security layout inside the building was a lot stronger than he and his associates had estimated.

The elevator stopped. They had been going up for a long time, but the ancient contraption had been lifting them so slowly, he had no idea what floor they might be on.

When the man finally pulled back the gate and the steel door separating the elevator shaft from the building's floor, Ian couldn't believe the horror he saw. It was all he could do to resist the urge to scream out into the microphone.

# 55

LUCIAN WAS IN the front passenger seat of the lead vehicle as the four black Range Rovers tore through the narrow Prague streets. He had coordinated Manchevski's instructions to increase security across Prague, other areas in the Czech Republic, and also Dresden, where the Malacoda gang had operations or business interests. The factory wasn't the most profitable operation they had in Prague—they made much more from their opium trafficking in the east, arms dealing in the north, and pharmaceutical counterfeiting operations near the western river—but the factory was the least mobile of all their operations. After all, they could load up opium bags, ammunition crates, and pills into transport vehicles a lot easier than they could pack a bunch of drugged girls into cargo boxes. Their latest data showed that nearly thirty percent of the girls died during mass transport efforts. That was why, during these early stages of war, he, Manchevski's best man, was heading out himself to protect the factory until other arrangements could be made.

The entourage pulled up to the front of the building and turned into the dark tunnel that led into the factory.

As they approached the gated entrance at the end of the tunnel, Lucian saw a man, obviously an employee, frisking another man, who must be a customer. When the doorman saw the large group of men suddenly at the gate, he stopped frisking the other and told him to wait against the stone wall. The customer followed instructions without protest or delay.

"And what the fuck is this?" the doorman said in Czech. But his aggression withered when Lucian stepped into the splintered red light coming through the elevator's steel gate. "Oh, Mr. Novádraga, I apologize! I didn't recognize you. The shadows here are darker than the blackest night."

"Yes they are," Lucian replied, also in Czech.

"What a surprise and honor to have you here! Please go right up."

"How's business tonight?"

"It's good. It's always good here, even though it's still early. You want me to call Cyril? He will know everything."

"Yes, call him down. The boss wants us to increase security here, so I'll need to coordinate with him."

The doorman relayed the message on his radio. Less than a minute later, the elevator gate opened and a short, rotund man stepped into the tunnel.

"What an honor!" he said. "If only I had known you were coming."

"We have problems," Lucian said, cutting short the normal formalities. "Something has happened. The boss had me bring more men to increase security. I need you to walk me around the premises, inside and out, so we can best determine where to add the men. As of right now, we need to be extra careful about anyone arriving or leaving."

"What has happened?" Cyril said.

"I need current numbers," Lucian said, ignoring the question. "How many girls do you have in the building?"

"Eighty-three working," Cyril replied. "Eight more are currently sick and not working. Another four are pregnant: we're getting that taken care of next week."

"And they're all in this building? Even the sick and pregnant?"

"Yes."

"How many customers are currently in the building?" Lucian asked.

"Sixty-one."

"All men?"

"Yes."

"Two security men at the front ground entrance, and then there's you. In addition to that, how many other men are currently in the building for security?"

"Six more."

"And they're all working now?"

Cyril stiffened and revealed his first real expression of concern. "Yes, but I believe two of the men are currently taking breaks."

"Breaks?" Lucian asked.

"Yes, Mr. Novádraga. With some of the girls."

Lucian understood. One of the perks that men in the Malacoda gang enjoyed was free time with the girls in the factory. And it was no secret that the security men often took a half-dozen breaks or more each day to rape the different girls, rotating through them all until they found the ones they liked best. New girls were especially popular.

"Okay," Lucian said, counting out loud so Cyril could follow his thoughts. "You have nine security men, including yourself, and now another thirteen men just sent over, including me. That's twenty-two to control this building, the customers, the girls, the money, and protect it from any outside threats."

"No outside threats," Cyril said. "All necessary officials and law enforcement have been paid in accordance with Manchevski's agreements."

"We have new threats: the Geryon Mafia," Lucian said.

"But I thought we had agreements with them, too. They have no interests here. How can they be a threat?"

"Things change. Strobviok tried to have Manchevski assassinated yesterday. A war has begun."

Cyril shook his head. "Those bastards. We'll kill every one of them."

"I know. We'll hit them very soon. But first Manchevski wanted to make sure our business interests are secured. We have increased security teams at all significant operations. What I want now is a double sweep to make sure we know where all the girls and all the customers are in the building. We want to keep the business running well, but we need to be very suspicious of anything unusual. I wouldn't be a bit surprised if Strobviok had a few men infiltrate the building, pretending to be customers in order to do something destructive, like start a fire."

"You want to make this place a fortress?"

"Exactly. No one gets in or out unless we've done a careful check on them. Not just the standard weapons sweep your security men do now. I'm talking about an ID check and everything."

"The customers won't like that," Cyril said. "It'll be bad for business."

"Not as bad as if this whole building went up in flames because we didn't do the checks."

"Okay."

"How many foreign customers are in the building?"

"I don't know."

"Find out."

As Cyril left, Lucian motioned for two of his men to go up to the roof. He needed surveillance on the building's surrounding area as soon as possible. His heart raced at the thought that he might finally experience a great crime war, like so many legends of the past. For years he had stood next to Manchevski at tense commission meetings of the major criminal organizations of Europe—listening to compromises to maintain the peace— knowing that his boss was stronger than any of the other bosses. And now, finally, a *war* would give Manchevski and him the opportunity to show the other organizations the full power of the Malacoda Gang's pernicious might.

A fiendish grin formed as he imagined the possibility that a threat was already in the vicinity. Once he finds it, it will give them the excuse to ultimately take the dominance over the European underworld that they've deserved for years.

# 56

———————⊰✵⊱———————

SOMETHING WAS WRONG. James counted four vehicles driving into the tunnel a few minutes after Ian had disappeared into it. He radioed Marcus.

"Maybe it's a high-profile client with an entourage," Marcus replied through the radio.

"And what if it's not?" James asked. "They could be adding more security. After everything that's happened in the past twenty-four hours, it wouldn't surprise me. Four vehicles! That could be anywhere from eight to sixteen more men! How will that affect the plan? What sort of fallback plan do you guys have for something like that?"

"No contingency plans were made for anything like that," Marcus replied. "Nothing ever changes at this operation other than the routine transport of new girls in and out, or the occasional removal of a girl's body. The building's security never changes."

"We have to get him out of there now," James said. "We're not prepared for this."

"We don't have a choice—we have to keep going."

"No! It's too dangerous. We have to get him out now."

"How, James?" Marcus replied over the radio. "We can't talk to him, remember? All we can do is listen and watch."

"I'll go in," James said. "I'll find him and warn him!"

"Don't you think about it!" Marcus hissed through the radio. "You'll fuck up the whole thing. You would never get in anyway. The Malacoda people know your face."

This had been James's biggest nightmare about the operation. After only fifteen minutes, Ian was already in more danger than anyone had anticipated.

"Damn it!" James said. "We need to move people toward the exits in case he needs to make a run for it and needs our help. Expose the building if we have to."

"You have no authority here," Marcus snapped. "You're just an observer. We're sticking to the plan. If things get hairy in there, he'll sense it. He'll find a way out. And we'll be able to see and hear everything, so we'll know how best to help him."

James lowered the radio in frustration. He had wasted enough time talking to Marcus. "He doesn't get it," he said to Hanna. "He doesn't understand. Ian's not in there just to get a video. He's there because he's trying to find a *specific girl* and get her out. He's not going to run for the exits if he sees added security."

"Just one girl?" Hanna asked. "Why?"

He looked at her. "Because he thinks it'll give meaning to our little sister's death."

She looked at him with horror. "What are you *talking* about! What have the two of you been planning?"

"I just found out right before we left the warehouse. He isn't going to get out of there fast enough. He's going to snoop around for the girl."

"What are we going to do?" she asked.

"I'll tell you what I'm *not* going to do: I'm not going to sit here on a rooftop and just wait to watch them find him, and then listen to whatever they'll do to him afterwards." He removed the earpiece. "This only has a twenty-yard range to the SatCom unit. I'm taking this radio, and I'll change it to scramble channel one-seven-three. You stay here to watch Ian's video and tell me what you see and hear."

"You're leaving me here alone?"

He grabbed her and kissed her. "I have to help my brother. I need to find a way to warn him."

Then he turned and, clipping the radio to his waistband, ran across the wet roof and hoisted himself onto the fire escape. Through the grates, he saw the street a hundred feet below. Prague's lights were visible in the distance. The sky was cloudy, reflecting an orange glow that made the city less dark than usual.

He scrambled down the fire escape, his feet slipping down the steps, hands sliding down the steel-pipe banisters, descending in a sort of frantic controlled fall.

# 57

-----------·••••·-----------

IAN WAS IN a place that not even his darkest, most horrifying nightmares could have prepared him for. Silhouetted figures moved about in a foggy, dusty half-light surrounded by mists of dark shadows. The air was stale and musty with body odor and sweat.

His heart raced. He wanted to cover his mouth and nose against the smells, but he couldn't. He wanted to cover his ears to block out the moans. Nausea assailed him, but he couldn't let them see him get sick. He had to keep moving forward, looking as if he wanted this. They had to remain convinced that this was his world, too, that he thrived on others' horrors just as the men working here did.

The man from the elevator escorted him through the octagonal entrance room, toward what looked like a barred cash window at a casino. A thin older woman worked behind the bars. He had done enough research to know that every organized crime ops site had a cash count-and-storage room. This was a business, after all. But Ian kept this knowledge hidden as he affected the false expression of a man ashamed of his actions yet excited about what those actions were about to bring. He leaned into the bars until his forehead was almost touching the metal, and looked into the woman's dead, soulless eyes.

"How much?" he asked, with a half smile to let her know that price was not an issue considering what he expected to get.

"How many and how long?" the woman asked.

"As many as I can manage in two hours," he replied, giving her a confident grin. Just another lonely, searching young man with lots of energy and no conscience. Men who came to places like this never spoke of it afterward, keeping secret the debauchery of these nights so that they could blend back into their regular lives afterward.

And that was exactly what his eyes now told the woman who was accepting his money and gesturing for him to proceed down the hallway toward any of the open rooms where drugged, enslaved girls waited to be raped again. The woman took his money. The man returned to the elevator. And Ian left the barred window to move down the hallway with its dim lighting, haunting moans, and the thick, sweaty smell of sex.

He moved slowly down the hallway, ever mindful that he was getting everything on video. The hallways were narrow and zigzagged in a maze of tight ninety-degree turns. No doubt, when the Malacoda gang had purchased the building through a shell corporation they must have gutted the floor of all cubicles and nonbearing office walls so they could put up cheap walls and make as many small rooms as possible, to maximize the number of customers being serviced.

The doorways had thick red curtains instead of doors, and the curtains were pulled back in some doorways so that anyone could look inside and enter if they liked what they saw. Ian turned slowly at the first open doorway, letting the camera capture the first image of the victims of this evil world he had penetrated. Inside was a skinny girl, completely uncovered and looking half dead. She had one eye open and shifted on the small mattress that took up nearly the entire room. She whispered something he didn't understand, and reached out a long, bony arm and beckoned him to join her.

He tightened his lips and blinked back the tears. After facing her long enough to capture the sadness and horror of her plight, he stepped back from the doorway and slowly turned back down the hallway.

He stopped at each open doorway to look inside. Every room was like the first, differing only in the number of blankets on the mattress, and the color of the girl's skin. Some were Asian, some white, and one redhead with pale, freckled skin was half wrapped in a blanket and appeared to be sobbing. Ian hoped for her sake that she would stop crying before one of the mafiosi noticed and beat her for hurting business. Half the girls were blondes, which didn't surprise him, because all the statistics showed that traffickers targeted them more.

In addition to capturing images of the horrific environment for the video, he was also studying each girl to see if any of them might be Zoe's sister, Miska. Miska had no identifying marks or tattoos, but Zoe had given him dozens of pictures, so he was confident he could recognize her. And Zoe had also given him a personal question he could ask Miska in Polish so that she would know he was here to help her on Zoe's behalf. In her last pictures, taken only days before she disappeared, she was slender with short black hair and soft facial features. She also had a big, bright smile and sparkling eyes, but Ian knew he wouldn't find anything like that in this place.

After looking into ten open rooms, he decided to check out those with closed curtains. Knowing this would look suspicious and draw a lot of attention, he waited until he reached the end of the first hallway, which put him out of the line of sight with the front room. He stood in front of the first closed curtain. He didn't want to see what was happening behind it, but he knew he had to. And he knew the whole world had to see it, too. So he reached up and slowly pulled part of the curtain away to capture the images. Inside, he saw rapid movements under a thick blanket, with naked arms and legs sticking out from beneath it. The girl's head had also popped out faceup from under the blanket, but the man—obviously taking her from on top—had his head still hidden somewhere under the blanket as he continued raping her. Both were oblivious to Ian's presence.

Seeing this, Ian felt himself losing control. His hands tightened into fists, and his chest heaved. He stared intensely at the blanket, imagining where the back of the man's head and neck would be. He took a half step forward, then stopped. Still in the doorway, he shook his head and slowly relaxed his fists.

*Forgive me,* he thought toward the girl as he stepped back and slowly closed the curtain. He was glad the camera image wouldn't be blurred as his own vision was from the tears.

He had told himself before walking into this building that no matter what he saw happening to these girls, he wouldn't lose focus. He hadn't come here to save ten or twenty girls; he had come to save a million. It would mean almost certain death if he tried to save any of these girls while in the factory. Miska was the only one for whom he was prepared to deviate from the plan, and she wasn't even likely to be here. Besides, the girl behind that curtain had probably already been raped at least five hundred times in this dark world, so he could only hope she could survive a little longer, until the White Rose got this place shut down.

He moved on down the hallway. There seemed to be increased activity on the floor. More men were moving around in the distance, and they didn't look like customers. Perhaps there were more security men in the operation than usual. This didn't concern him as long as it wasn't for an emergency or heightened alert on the premises. It was possible that one of the surveillance teams of the White Rose had been spotted, but that seemed unlikely. No, he must continue as planned.

Halfway down the hallway, peering into another open room, he saw a thin, almost gaunt body with short black hair, lying with its back to him. She rolled over on the mattress and gave him a blank stare.

Something about that face seemed hauntingly familiar. But no, the eyes were too deeply set, the lips too thin, the cheekbones too sharp. He tried to imagine how that cadaverous face once looked, back when it was full of life and joy, getting enough sleep, proper food, and sunshine and without the months of horror. He tried to superimpose Miska's image on the wraithlike creature before him. Could it be . . . ? The entire world around him disappeared as he stared past all the trauma and saw the face from the Polish news article that had sent him down this dark path two months ago.

He stepped into the room and closed the curtain behind him.

# 58

———※———

JAMES SPRINTED DOWN the dark alleyway. Every second saved at this point could be the difference between helping Ian and finding his corpse. During the briefing, he had memorized everything: the area around the factory, the White Rose's observation points, the watch points for the Malacoda security men. And knowing this, he knew all the blind spots for both groups.

He raced out of the alleyway, briefly visible by the one dim corner light as he sprinted across the street before disappearing into another dark alleyway. The sudden increase in security must mean Manchevski feared an attack from the Geryon Mafia as soon as *tonight*. The White Rose wasn't ready for this; they had needed to get the video *before* things escalated. And thanks to the chaos at the casino, these new security men Manchevski had sent had a much better chance of recognizing Ian. There was now no way Ian could just walk out the entrance pretending to be a customer. James prayed that if he could just get close enough to the factory without being detected, then somehow he could find a way to warn his brother.

He stopped and stood against the cold stone building in the dark alleyway. "What's happening?" he whispered into the radio. He was a half block from the factory.

"He's been moving down some sort of hallway," Hanna's voice answered through the radio. "It's dark, but everything's still clear through the video. There are rooms on all sides. Small rooms . . . more like closets. A girl inside each one. And there are so many! It's horrifying."

"What's he doing right now?"

"He just went in one of the little rooms," her voice crackled through the radio. "He's approaching a girl inside. He's trying to talk to her. He's saying something to her, but I can't understand it. It's not English or German. And I don't think it's Czech. It sounds like maybe Russian."

"Could it be Polish?" James asked.

"Yes, it could be."

"Has he gotten enough video for the White Rose? Will it be the sensational inside look Ian wanted?"

"I don't know how much he wanted, but he has already got enough to convince anyone that this is the most monstrous crime happening on the planet today."

"Has the video shown any additional security?"

"A few seconds ago there were a lot of guys walking at the end of the hallway he was in. They were bunched together, like security searching for something."

James fought to control the panic building inside him. "Did Ian see them?" he asked, hunkered over in the damp alley, hands on his knees. He was trying to breath deeply, trying to focus.

"He didn't seem to take much notice of them," Hanna's voice crackled on the radio.

*Of course he didn't,* James thought. *He has no idea they tripled their security in the past ten minutes.* "I have to warn him right now," he said.

"How?"

He peered out of the alleyway at the darkened street leading toward the building. He had no time left to figure out the perfect plan. If he wanted to warn Ian that everything was going wrong, he had to do it now.

He came out of the alleyway and walked briskly up the street, toward the factory. Parked cars lined both curbs, but there was no traffic.

Reaching the street corner next to the factory, he stopped. Hanna had relayed to him every detail of Ian's video, including which side of the tunnel the elevator was on and every right and left turn Ian had made once he got off the elevator on the thirteenth floor. And that was how James knew that his brother was somewhere on the east side of the building on the thirteenth floor, though not along an outside wall. But this was as close as he could get to his brother while staying out here on the street.

He leaned against an old Toyota parked on the street, and kicked at a loose cobblestone the size of his fist, until it came free. Picking it up, he smashed the driver's-side window, then reached in and unlocked the door and got in. He took a deep breath for courage and pressed on the car's horn.

# 59

————————✳————————

HEARING THE LONG blast on the car horn, Hanna knew at once that it was James. She raised her head above the short wall along the roof's ledge but couldn't see where it was coming from. But she did see movement on the factory roof, then two heads popping up over the ledge, searching for the source of the disturbance. She ducked back below the parapet wall, terrified that they had seen her.

"James," she said into the radio. "There are men on the roof looking for you. Stop honking the horn. They're about to find you. James, can you hear me? James?"

When he didn't reply, she switched radio frequencies to tell Marcus what was happening.

"He's crazy," Marcus replied. "He's going to get himself killed."

"I can't stay on this channel," she said. "I've been staying in contact with him on scramble channel one-seven-three. I need to switch back to it in case he needs me. You should have the entire team switch to that channel."

"Hanna, we can't change anything in the plans until Ian's out of the building."

"The plan has gone to hell, Marcus! I can't wait any longer. I'm switching channels."

Without giving him time to respond, she switched back to the other channel. "James," she said. "Can you hear me? James, please answer. They're on the roof, and I think they've seen you. You have to stop and get out of there now. James, please answer."

She let off the talk button and waited in vain. The only sound was the continuous blaring of the car horn a block away.

*   *   *

Lucian held up a finger for silence while he listened on his cell phone. "Where's it coming from?"

"The northeast corner of Kvetinkova and Pöslova," said the man on the roof. "Gray Toyota parked four cars back from the intersection."

"And the person is still in the car?" he asked. "They haven't rigged something to hold the horn down?"

"No, sir. It's beeping on and off now, so it's even more noticeable than before."

"Stay on the roof," he said into the phone. "One of you keep watch on that car, and the other go to the other side of the roof and look for anything suspicious. I'll send men out to check the car."

Lucian lowered his phone and said to the foot soldier closest to him, "Check it out and make it stop."

"And anyone in it?" the soldier asked.

"You've seen pictures of people from the Geryon Mafia. If it's any of them, kill them. Take some men from downstairs with you."

"And if it's no one we've seen before?"

"Bring them to the front entrance. I want to look in their eyes to make sure they understand never to waste my time again.

Honking a horn like that in the dead of night in our neighborhood . . . I should probably kill them either way."

# 60

⸻✦⸻

IAN STEPPED INSIDE the room, pulled the curtain closed behind him, and stared at the girl. His mind told him he couldn't really have found Zoe's sister. The odds had always been stacked too high against him. But something else told him he had finally found her.

He stepped toward her and knelt down on the mattress. He no longer cared what the hidden camera could or couldn't see. This was personal.

"Miska," he whispered near her ear.

The girl moved slightly, trying to roll toward his voice. She was obviously high—on heroin, he supposed.

"I'm a friend, Miska," he said. "Of your sister . . . of Zoe."

The girl's eyes half opened as she tried to look at him. Her lips moved slightly, and she mumbled something unrecognizable.

"Zoe sent me for you," he said. Then, in Polish, he said the words Zoe had made him memorize. *"Zoe chciałaby, żebyś poszła ze mna pomóc jej zająć się kotkiem, którego zaadoptowaliście ze schroniska." Zoe says you need to come with me so you can help her take care of the kitten you adopted from the shelter. "Zoe tęskni za Tobą i mówi, że Fluffy też." Zoe misses you and says that Fluffy misses you, too.*

The girl opened her drug-addled eyes a little more. Ian couldn't tell if she had been able to register what he said. Then, as if to answer his thoughts, she smiled drunkenly and lifted one hand toward him, knocking aside the blanket that covered her naked body. "Fuck me, baby," she murmured.

Ian closed his eyes to focus.

"Fuck me, baby," she repeated weakly. The fingers on her outstretched hand were curling and uncurling in a gesture inviting him to have her. "Fuck me . . . fuck me."

Ian's head lowered. He hadn't wanted to think about what had happened to Miska since she went missing, but now he was forced to face the reality. He had to be strong and stay focused now more than ever if he hoped to get her out of here. He lowered the girl's arm and covered her naked body with the blanket.

She seemed to have expended what little energy she had, and gave up trying to coax him. He felt around the edges of the mattress, which came to within inches of the closet-size room's thin walls, until he found her clothes. One of the men must have tossed them there after undressing her earlier this evening, when she was first brought into this room from whatever dungeon they kept these girls in when they weren't working.

Then, in the silence of the room, he heard a new sound, one that hadn't been there a moment ago. He stopped gathering her clothes and knelt motionlessly on the mattress to avoid making even the slightest rustle. Closing his eyes, he focused on all the little nuances of sound.

It was the faint cry of a car horn—a long, continuous honk that broke into a string of short and long beeps. Listening to it, he recognized a pattern. The long beep was the system he and James had designed to get each other's attention when they were kids. At night after their parents had made them go to bed, they would send each other Morse code messages through their separate bedroom windows, like the heroes in the spy stories they had both loved so much, by aiming their flashlights at the oak tree outside and flashing them on the trunk.

Maybe he was just going crazy in this dark place of horror and evil and insanity to think that this faint beeping could be some secret message from his brother. But then, James had managed to track him down, with scant clues, in a foreign country a continent away. So if there was anyone who could get a message to him in this hellish building, it would be James.

He closed his eyes and concentrated on the short and long beeps.

*Dah-dah-dit* . . . "G." *Dit* . . . "E." *Dah* . . . "T." A short pause. *Dah-dah-dah* . . . "O." *Dit-dit-dah* . . . "U." *Dah* . . . "T." Get out! James must have seen something outside the building bad enough to risk drawing dangerous attention to himself just to warn him. He thought of the few extra security men he had seen. He needed to get out of the factory, and fast.

He crawled to the curtained doorway. Peeking out, he gave a quick glance up and down the dark hallway. No one was in sight. He crawled back to the girl. "Come on, Miska," he said. "You need to help me put these on you. We don't have much time. We have to get out of here."

But she didn't seem to understand, and turned away from him in fear. "I'm sorry," she said. "Please don't take me away. Not again. I'll be good. I promise."

"Miska, I'm Zoe's friend. I'm here to take you home. Please help me. We don't have much time."

She was unresponsive except for a single tear hanging in the corner of her eye as she lay on her back staring vacantly into the darkness above. With the drugs in her system and the unspeakable horrors she had experienced in the past five months, he couldn't begin to imagine what psychological blocks and barriers her mind had built up.

He fumbled in the darkness with her limp arms and legs, pulling her clothes onto her small body. Then he pulled her close and lifted her up. "Come on, I've got you."

She whimpered as if just being on her feet was painful.

He moved toward the curtain and stopped without pulling it back. He had been listening to the faint horn honking its repeating message: *Get out . . . get out . . . get out . . .* Ian could sense the panic James must be feeling. But just as he was about to open the curtain, the honking stopped. His heart raced even faster now because it had stopped honking after a *dah-dah-dah,* which was "O." He didn't want to imagine what could have stopped his brother so abruptly. He needed to get out as fast as possible in case James was in danger and needed his help.

But first he had to escape from the building.

"Guys," he said into his microphone. "I know you can't talk to me, but hopefully you're all still out there and can hear me. Change of plans. Now, this is going to sound crazy, but I need you to do exactly what I say. It might be the only way I can escape."

# 61

————⋇————

THE BMW DROVE through lightly trafficked streets.
   "How much longer?" Wolfgang asked. He wasn't one to give up, but they had seen no sign of the American brothers at the last three Malacoda operations. There had never been much chance of finding them anyway, and now it felt like a wild-goose chase.

   "Three more blocks and we can park," Vlastos said. "We walk two blocks after that." He started coughing violently. The coughs subsided into a few seconds of wheezing; then he leaned his head against the window.

   "You're not doing well," Wolfgang said. "We can stop if you need to."

   "I'm fine. We need to keep going. There's a good chance they might be interested in watching this next place."

   "You said that at the nightclub we just came from."

   "This place is better," Vlastos said. "Maybe we should have come here first."

   "Right. You said this is a prostitution ring."

   "*Forced* prostitution."

"That makes me sick," Wolfgang said, grimacing. "Is there no honor?"

Vlastos smiled between wheezes. *"Set honour in one eye and death i' the other, and I will look on both indifferently."*

He pulled the car into an open parking space. "Two blocks? Are you sure you can make it? You don't look like you're doing so well."

"I'll make it," Vlastos said, wincing as he reached for the door handle. He pulled on it and pushed against the door as if moving a heavy stone slab. When the door opened, a faint car horn could be heard in the distance.

"You hear that?" Wolfgang asked.

Vlastos nodded.

"It's in front of us," Wolfgang said. "Not far. Maybe a few blocks. Close to the factory, you think?"

Vlastos nodded as he unbuttoned the gun in his shoulder holster.

They headed toward the factory and the blaring car horn. Vlastos was definitely hurting. Wolfgang could have moved much faster on his own.

They had gone only half a block when the honking stopped. With a new sense of urgency, they kept moving as fast as they could toward whatever lay ahead.

# 62

JAMES HAD BEEN cycling through the message on the horn for probably two minutes when he saw four men emerge from the factory and come barreling toward him. Their heavy, rapid footfalls bounced off the surrounding buildings. James stopped honking, jumped out of the car, and took off running.

"I need help!" he said into the radio, but he could hear the footfalls behind him getting closer, so he tossed the radio aside and ran as hard as he could.

Some of the men were shouting—in Albanian, he supposed—and he could hear the others' heavy breathing.

He made the mistake of jerking his head back to see how close the men were, only to see that they were barely twenty feet behind him and closing fast. He couldn't believe how fast they were, and he cursed his tax accounting job in Kansas City for letting him get so soft and out of shape over the years.

But desperation and fear made him run harder than ever before in his life. He knew what would happen if they caught him.

He was running through the second intersection when the closest man caught him. It happened so fast, James couldn't tell whether the man had tackled him by the neck or the shoulder, not that it mattered. He went down hard on the cobblestones. By the time the man had gotten in the first few punches, the other three men were on him, taking turns kicking him and shouting in that cursed language he would never understand.

It occurred to him that he was about to die, stomped to death in a street while being yelled at in a foreign tongue.

\*   \*   \*

Hanna screamed down at the clump of men beating James. When they ignored her she pulled the gun from her pocket, aimed it at a car near the group, and fired a shot. The bullet missed the target but somehow ricocheted off the brick building and shattered the opposite side window of the car.

The men jumped back from James and searched for the source of the shot. "*Deri atje!*" one of them yelled, pointing toward her. He pulled his gun and fired two shots up at the roof.

Hanna ducked below the brick parapet. She hadn't really thought past her instinct to help James by firing a shot, but now the realization that they were actually shooting at her snapped her back to reality. She could hear the bullets smack into the brick wall protecting her. She closed her eyes, too terrified to move.

Then the shooting got much faster and didn't seem directed toward her anymore. It sounded as though a gunfight had broken out on the street below.

# 63

IAN HELPED THE girl down the dark hallway as the sound of gunfire erupted outside the building. He didn't know what the hell was happening—only that James was out there somewhere, along with many of Ian's friends, and he had to assume that the Malacoda gang had found them. He had to get outside and find out what was happening to James.

"You're doing good, Miska," he said, half carrying and half dragging her down the hallway. "Keep moving your legs. We'll be out of here in a few minutes."

"We can't leave Sasha," she mumbled.

"Who's Sasha?" he asked without slowing. He was afraid she might pass out, and wanted to keep her talking.

"She's my friend." Her words were slurry.

"She's in here?" he asked.

"Um-hm."

"Where?"

"In here."

"But where?"

"I don't know."

"We'll have to get her later," Ian said.

"No. Please help her, too."

"I have to help you first. I'll come back for her soon. She'll be okay until then."

"No . . . Sasha."

But she was too weak to protest further, and Ian wasn't deviating from his plan. He was getting the hell out of here with Miska first; then he would do what he could to help Sasha and all the other girls in the factory. More gunfire went off somewhere outside, and Ian knew that if Marcus had heard his message, there would soon be a new dimension to the chaos out there.

*Dear Lord,* he prayed as he pushed through the door to the stairwell, half carrying the girl with him, *please help James and Miska and me get through the next ten minutes. If you give me this one wish, I swear I'll devote the rest of my life to doing good. Give me ten minutes of your help, and I'll give you ten million minutes of mine.*

Ian shifted Miska around to the right side of his body so that he was on the inside of the stairwell. His left hand was on the railing, and his right arm was wrapped around her. Somewhere several floors below, he heard a metal door bang open, and angry, shouting men start rushing up the stairway.

*Here we go, Lord,* he thought. *Ten minutes . . . starting now!*

# 64

ON A ROOFTOP two buildings away from the factory, Marcus looked anxiously over the shoulder of a tall blond kid pecking away on a laptop connected through a USB port to a large black box.

"It's almost ready," the kid said. The black box had a dozen wires running from it to other boxes lined along the edge of the roof.

"We need this to happen now!" Marcus said.

"I'm trying!" the kid yelled. "We hadn't planned to do this until much later. We've had to reset everything in the program."

"How much longer?"

"Sixty seconds."

"That's too long," Marcus said. "Ian's expecting it now."

"I'm still waiting on the other unit to reprogram."

"Start this one if it's ready now. Then start the other as soon as it's ready."

The kid nodded, looking uneasy, and relayed the message into the radios. "Okay! Everyone, get back!" Then he entered the final command into the laptop and turned to run toward the fire escape on the far side of the roof.

"All right," Marcus said into the radio, "everyone watch your back. This place is about to go supernova!"

And then, just as he promised, the skies lit up.

# 65

WITH THIS MANY men kicking him at once, James believed he was as good as dead. He curled up into a ball, covered his head with his arms as best he could, tucked his knees to his chest, and tightened his muscles to provide some shielding for his internal organs. But there was only so much he could do to protect himself.

Then a single gunshot rang out, shattering a car window just twenty feet away. The men stopped beating him to pull their guns and fire up at the rooftop. Then it registered: that was Hanna shooting down at these men, using the gun Marcus gave them.

He tried to stand up and fight the men shooting at her, but his body wouldn't cooperate. They must have hurt him worse than he thought.

As he lay on the stone road, he looked up sideways to the roof's edge, where Hanna must be ducking behind the narrow brick parapet. Eventually, the men would go up the back stairs to her rooftop, and he prayed she would be gone by then.

Then the head of one of the men standing over him just exploded. A bullet from somewhere had hit him in the back of the head and blown out half his forehead when exiting.

Then another of the Malacoda men had his ear shot away, and by the time he stopped shooting and raised his hand to the side of his head, another bullet went through his chest. The man grunted and collapsed to the ground without another sound.

Seeing the second of his four assailants die, he knew that the Malacoda gang and the White Rose were not alone in this dark neighborhood.

*　*　*

"Something's going on up there," Vlastos said, pointing toward the shadows running through the street a block ahead.

"Stay to the side," Wolfgang replied, always the special forces soldier considering position and line of sight. He had seen the movement, too. At first, he thought the group of men had somehow learned of their presence and were running at them, but then he saw the running figure they were chasing. "Get down. I don't think they've seen us yet, and they're heading right at us."

The men were only half a block away when they caught up with their quarry, tackling him to the ground and then kicking him repeatedly.

"We need to intervene," Wolfgang said.

"No," Vlastos said. "We can't expose ourselves."

"But they might kill him."

"Maybe. Or maybe it's just a well-deserved beating."

"It has to be related to the Malacoda gang," Wolfgang guessed.

"Yes," Vlastos replied. "They're running a whorehouse. Men get out of line all the time. We deal with the same thing in Berlin more than you would imagine. We'll just wait until it plays out."

Then, without warning, a gun fired.

The men stopped beating their victim and fired up at the rooftop.

It appeared that this was not merely a case of an unruly customer. Whoever was on the roof had disappeared in the darkness without firing another shot.

Suddenly, gunshots went off next to Wolfgang. He looked over in alarm to see Vlastos methodically aiming and firing at the men.

"What are you doing!" Wolfgang shouted.

"It's him!" Vlastos said. "It's James Lawrence on the ground."

"You're sure?"

"I just saw his face! It's him!"

Wolfgang joined Vlastos in shooting at the men standing around James, making sure to aim high.

Together they advanced on the men. Vlastos stood tall and hobbled in spurts while firing, moving as if the battle always went to the boldest.

Whereas Vlastos's attack style seemed rooted in bullheaded, overconfident daring, Wolfgang advanced on the men like the trained, seasoned fighter he was. He crouched low, pistol forward as he scampered across the shadowy street. The men had initially focused on Vlastos, which made it easy for Wolfgang to drop one of them with a clear shot to the head.

Vlastos's shots had hit a man as well. But the last two men dropped to the ground next to James. Using him for cover, they turned their fire on Wolfgang, forcing him to dive over the trunk of a parked car and land hard on the other side. Bullets popped into the steel bodies of the cars around him. He was pinned down. There was nothing he could do but stay hidden behind the cars.

Then, out of the corner of his eye, he saw movement. It was Vlastos, moving faster now along the opposite building's shadowed wall. The man seemed reinvigorated by the violence.

Inspired by Vlastos's boldness, Wolfgang stood up from the shelter of the cars and raced out into the open street, charging at the two men lying low near James.

Then something happened that Wolfgang could never have expected: the skies erupted with fire and explosions, so distracting the men he and Vlastos were fighting that they looked up. And in that moment of confusion, they both died.

The dark skies above the factory exploded into a massive fireworks show so loud and bright, it could be seen from anywhere in Prague.

# 66

IAN HEARD THE fireworks exploding outside the building. *Thank you, God,* he thought. Someone was still out there. But all the help in the world on the outside wouldn't mean anything unless he could escape from the building.

He heard footsteps stampeding up the stairs, very close. They were moving fast. Or maybe *he* was moving *slowly*. It was awkward holding Miska on her feet while trying to get down the stairs.

"Come on," he whispered to her. "Help me get you out of here. We're almost there."

She moaned something incoherent, and he worried that she was so far gone she couldn't understand him anymore.

He counted the landings as they descended. They had made it down four flights, starting at the thirteenth floor. The men were maybe five flights below them and coming fast.

"Just two more levels down," he whispered to Miska, struggling to help her down the stairs. "We're almost there."

They were close enough to the men below that Ian could now hear their shouts.

At the landing to the seventh floor, he opened the door and pulled Miska inside. Standing against the wall in the faint light coming through the door's small wire-meshed window, he pulled her close to him and covered her mouth with his hand. "Don't make a sound."

A few seconds later, light flashed through the window as the men in the stairwell rushed past the door, heading toward the upper floors. All it would take was for one of the men to open the door, and they would be caught.

Once the hammering sound of footsteps faded, he whispered, "Come on, Miska," helping her along the hallway through the dark seventh floor. "You're doing well. We're going to make it. Just a little bit farther . . ."

But as they moved down the hallway, he realized that they had entered the dungeons of the factory. Girls lay everywhere, coughing on mattresses spaced along the floor.

At the far end of the dark hallway he could see the flashing glow of fireworks. Even the confused eyes of the drugged-out girls stared in amazement at perhaps the most beautiful thing they had seen in months.

Ian rushed toward the exploding fireworks, pulling Miska along with him while trying not to think of all the other girls he was leaving behind. As they reached the end of the hallway, a huge silhouette stepped out of a doorway and blocked their path.

"Co tady děláš?" the figure asked.

Ian felt the girl go rigid in his arms. She seemed to have learned long ago to fear voices that spoke as this man had.

"Speak English!" Ian demanded, knowing that he had to make this man believe he was on his level to win power over him. "Who are you!" he demanded before the man had time to ask the same question of him.

"Gregorik," the man replied. "And just who are you?"

"Only Manchevski is allowed to know my name. He's the one who hired me from America to fix this business. But your capo, Cyril, the one in charge here, was instructed to let me study what's wrong with your operations. The name you are to call me is "the Ghost." This is the name I work under. Manchevski already communicated this to Cyril. And Cyril should have communicated it to all his men, including you." Ian paused. "Perhaps you have bad memory? Maybe you forget who's in charge?"

"Cyril is not in charge right now," the man said. "We have crisis. Lucian Novádraga has taken over to fight crisis."

Ian recoiled inside. Lucian Novádraga was a legendary monster even within the dark underworld of Eastern Europe.

"A crisis because of the low standards of quality for your business, no doubt," Ian said, staying in the character that he had invented a week ago as a precaution for just such an encounter. "Just look at this place! Look at these girls, how poorly you keep them. What do you think the customers feel when they are with women who are kept in such filth? You think the customer doesn't notice? You think the men who come here are so desperate to feel the insides of a woman, they don't care how dirty she is? You think this doesn't hurt business. Well, think again! Even a farmer knows to keep his cattle comfortable, to keep them from getting so stressed their meat toughens and doesn't taste as good."

The man laughed at Ian's words. And Ian joined in his laughter, though he wanted more than anything to throw his weight into the man and, with any luck, knock him through the window to the cobblestones seven floors below.

"Cattle," the man said, still laughing. "Slaughter. Like this place. Perfect. I like you."

"You won't like me when I tell Manchevski how much money I think he's losing because you and the other men are careless with these girls."

The man stiffened. "We do only what we are told."

"Oh, I think you do much more than that," Ian said. "You and the other men take advantage of these girls when it pleases you. This alone is not a problem; it is expected. But you don't keep them clean. And that is bad for business."

"We still have good business here," the man protested.

"Ah, but think of the rates men would pay if these slaves were clean, if they smelled the way a man wants a girl to smell."

Gregorik was silent. "What can I do?" he finally asked.

"Tonight?" Ian said. "Nothing. Tonight is crisis, like you said. It is chaos. Look—even the skies are on fire." He gestured toward the window. The giant turned to look out, and both men watched the exploding pyrotechnics illuminate the black skies surrounding the factory.

"Watch the stairway," Ian finally said. "Make sure none of the girls escape into other parts of the building."

"But the windows," the man said. "I'm supposed to watch the windows."

*Of course you are,* Ian thought. "Not tonight. Because of the new threats, we've had to take men away from regular posts. This means we're having more openings than usual in the security, and right now the biggest hole is the stairwell. Protect it, while I evaluate the rest of this floor. If we can get through this night, then I may not be as inclined to report to Manchevski *all* of the deficiencies I've noticed here."

The man nodded and walked past him toward the stairwell.

Ian half carried Miska down the rest of the hallway, around the corner, and toward the far window, which flashed with every burst of fireworks exploding in the night, revealing before them the silhouette of a fire escape. It was the same rusted old fire escape that the White Rose's surveillance team had noted their first night scouting the building—and that he had prayed he would never have to use.

"Come on, Miska," he whispered to her in between the crack and boom of fireworks as they moved toward the windows and the decrepit fire escape. "It's time for us to see if there is a God in this world."

He threw an elbow into the pane of glass, shattering the window that had been nailed shut. "You can do this," he said, pushing away the glass shards. "Come on." He helped her out onto the fire escape, whose metal groaned under their weight. The skies above them blossomed with gaudy light, and the cold, dark street below seemed waiting to crush them.

Holding Miska around the waist, Ian felt her shiver in the cool night air. This was probably her first time outside the factory in months.

Gunshots crackled across the area. He heard someone screaming in the distance, or perhaps yelling—he was too far from the source to know. A car engine revved, and tires screamed somewhere in the darkness below. The world seemed to be exploding and breaking up all around him, with bedlam erupting in so many pockets around the building, it was impossible to judge which spots were worst. The White Rose people would be moving away from the fireworks, to avoid being targets for the Malacoda. And the Malacoda men were also undoubtedly on the move, trying to secure the area or flush out the customers or get the girls out—anything to contain the threat. And wherever James was in all the chaos, he was likely in a potful of trouble.

The fire escape metal was cold and slippery, the steel-pipe railing rusted almost through in places. The whole structure moaned under their moving weight, and Ian prayed that it would hold them until they reached the street below.

# 67

A S GUNFIRE EXPLODED all around him, James staggered
to his feet and ran out of the street. Reaching the corner of
the building, he looked up at the roof just in time to see Hanna
peering over the ledge, backlit by the sudden eruption of
fireworks in the skies above. Shots from unknown sources killed
the two remaining men who had attacked him. All shooting
stopped after the last man went down, and the only sound
remaining was the crackle and pop of the brilliant fireworks
above.

Then, out of the shadows, the two men who had saved his
life approached. One was tall and strong looking; the other had a
bad limp. As they drew closer, he recognized the limping man,
who was smiling.

"Vlastos!" James shouted.

Vlastos limped past the four bodies in the street, looked up at
the smoke from the ongoing fireworks, and said, "*So foul and
fair a day I have not seen.*" He ended the line with a ragged
cough.

James couldn't believe Vlastos was alive. In the casino, Lucian had said he was dead. Judging by his condition, Lucian hadn't been far wrong.

"I'm sorry you didn't get a chance to kill Manchevski!" James yelled over the fireworks. They were standing far apart, as if things needed to be said before they could approach each other as men now freed of earlier obligations. It was as if their paths had only momentarily aligned before they were forced onto different paths again, only now to arrive on the other side of an abyssal darkness.

Vlastos nodded. "It's not your fault. Somehow they found out. Someone betrayed us to them. I'm glad you still breathe."

"It wasn't easy," James said.

"And you found your brother."

"Yeah, I found him. But he's jumped back into the fire like he always does . . . So who is this?" James asked, looking at the man next to Vlastos.

"Wolfgang!" Hanna's voice said from behind James. She was still breathing heavily from rushing down the stairs from the roof. "Oh, my God! I can't believe it! Papa really did send you." Tears were in her eyes as she ran to him and threw her arms around him.

Wolfgang seemed less thrilled. "Hanna! *You* shouldn't be here! It's too dangerous. Your father would die if something happened to you."

"Then it's a good thing you're here to protect me."

Wolfgang turned to James. "Where is your brother?"

James looked at Hanna, deferring to her for the answer.

"He's taking the fire escape from the factory. He was hoping the fireworks would distract the Malacoda gang. If all goes well, he should be on the ground in the next few minutes. And there's something else." She paused. "He's not alone."

James looked at her with excited disbelief. "My God, he found her," he said. He could only imagine the thrill Ian must be feeling at this moment, even though they were still in great danger.

"Found whom?" Wolfgang asked.

"A girl. It's a long story. Right now we need to help make sure he gets away once he's on the ground." He turned to Hanna. "What side of the building is he climbing down?"

"He said into his microphone he was taking the northeast side."

"Come on!" James said. "We need to be there when he gets down."

"Wait," Wolfgang said, stepping forward and grabbing James's arm. "We can't just go charging in there. We need to think this through."

"We don't have time," James said, a little surprised at the strength and speed with which this older man had grabbed him.

"You in a hurry to get killed?"

"I'm in a hurry to keep my brother from getting killed," he said, stepping over and taking the pistols from two of the dead bodies in the street. "I don't care what the rest of you do, but I'm going to go help him." Then, after checking the magazine of each pistol, he rushed back to Hanna. "I want you to stay here so there's no chance of something happening to you."

"But I want to fight with you," she said. "I'm a freedom fighter—it's in my blood. I can help."

"Please, just stay," James pleaded.

"Forget it," she said. "I'm coming with you."

"And so are we," Wolfgang said, scavenging an extra pistol from one of the dead men and giving it to Hanna.

"Thank you," James said, moved that three foreigners, one of them a complete stranger, were willing to join him on something so dangerous. Whatever sheltered life he had once lived in Kansas City was now gone.

He, Hanna, and Wolfgang took off running toward the factory, with Vlastos limping after them.

# 68

LUCIAN SENT MEN to move all the customers into a locked room on the thirteenth floor. They were then to move all the girls to the basement, which connected to a network of underground tunnels built during the war. From there, he had an escape route mapped to the basement of a shipping company a half mile away. There the girls would not be found.

"Where is he now?!" Lucian yelled through the radio.

"Looks like the fifth floor, sir," said the Malacoda soldier who had noticed a man—obviously part of the team attacking them—climbing down the fire escape with one of the girls.

"How soon until more men get here?" he asked another soldier next to him.

"Six minutes, sir. And they said Manchevski himself is coming with them."

Six minutes, Lucian reflected. Not a lot of time to capture the fleeing man. He knew how badly his boss wanted to spend time with this person who had caused him so much trouble. And if Lucian could personally deliver him to Manchevski when he arrived, he would seem to have the situation well under control.

"And the police?" Lucian asked.

"Manchevski took care of it. Between both the dispatchers and the night captain, we've been given an extra fifteen minutes before any police attention gets directed this way."

That was not much time for everything he needed to do, but it beat having to work around the normal police response time of four minutes for reported gunshots.

Climbing down the inside stairwell, Lucian was nearly down to street level. Over the radio, he coordinated other soldiers to accompany him down the stairs or meet him at the exit. He bounded down the last flight, a pistol in his right hand and a submachine gun strapped over his shoulder and bouncing against his back. Hitting the last step, he barged through the exit door and was out in the street on the north side of the factory. Five men were right behind him, and three more were already outside.

"Hurry!" Lucian said in a low voice. "He's coming down the fire escape. He's only at the fourth floor, but he probably doesn't know we've seen him. We've got him! Hurry! This bastard is about to get the surprise of a lifetime!"

Lucian ran from the exit toward the northeast corner of the building, with eight soldiers ready to kill on his command.

*    *    *

Manchevski, in the third of five black Range Rovers racing through the Prague streets, was seething over how fast his empire was blowing up in his face. He was a businessman, and there was nothing he hated more than interruptions to routine operations that, under good conditions, generated healthy profits for him. Even the idea of losing one hour of business made him sick over the lost profits. That the Geryon Mafia had targeted the factory was unforgivable—hypocritical, even, for he knew how many similar businesses they had scattered throughout Eastern Europe. This was drawing entirely too much attention to operations that needed to stay as far out of the public eye as possible.

But now things had exploded, and as the leader of his organization, he needed to see firsthand whoever was daring to disrupt his income stream.

"How much longer until we're there?" he demanded from the driver.

"Five minutes, sir."

"Tell the lead car to make it in four!"

"Yes, sir."

# 69

⸻⸻⸻✳⸻⸻⸻

ONLY THREE FLIGHTS of stairs remained, but it took half Ian's energy just to keep the semiconscious Miska on her feet. The fireworks had ended with a brilliant finale, and now the skies were filled with pale smoke drifting above the rooftops. Everything else was silent: no more gunfire, no screaming, nothing.

He told himself he had already succeeded. The video must be riveting. And he had finished his dissertation and delivered it to Professor Hampdenstein with all his ideas laid out. His life's masterpiece was finished and now in the hands of the man best able to get it published. And despite the long odds, he had found Miska and pulled her out of the darkness, and soon he would return her to Zoe. He only prayed that she could recover from the horrors she had been through. It would be a long, hard road, but if there was anyone that could help her heal, it was Zoe.

"Only two more flights, Miska," he said, helping her down the stairs. "Come on. We're almost there."

She moaned in reply, and he couldn't help smiling as he helped her down the steps. They were almost home free.

# 70

————◦✳◦————

MARCUS SAT IN the van with two other White Rose members. "Upload it now!" he said.

"But what about the others?" the kid with the laptop said.

"Ian said to upload the video as soon as possible if things went bad," Marcus replied. "We can't risk going through all this only to be stopped from uploading it. Once it's out there no one can stop it. The only reason we had for waiting was that it could expose Ian when he was still in the factory, but that doesn't matter anymore. So do it! Give it to the entire world—now before it's too late!"

The kid's fingers began to fly across the keys, sliding across the mouse, clicking and double clicking, dragging, tabbing between screens, typing again, clicking some more, and then waiting as the software uploaded the video to various sites—all tagged with links to the White Rose site stored on the IT Cloud through four different university servers hacked by the group over the past few months with backdoor subcodes. When the kid completed the final command, everyone in the van waited, watching the final green-and-white stripes rotating on the toolbar like a horizontal barbershop pole. Everyone knew the significance of what they were doing: speaking through a digital megaphone across the entire world to, eventually, untold millions of people. They would watch the video of Ian walking through the valley of the shadow of death, witnessing an evil that the world would no longer be able to ignore.

"It's done," the kid said.

"It's completely uploaded?" Marcus asked.

"Yes."

"To each site? Already?"

The kid nodded. "Oh, it's out there. The whole world has it now. We just got our first hit."

"We already had a hit?" Marcus said as the reality hit him. He could almost sense the cyber world turning its billions of eyes toward them. Somewhere, someone was watching the beginning of Ian's video.

"Make that fifty-five hits," the kid said.

"You're kidding me. So quickly?"

"Uh, make that three hundred and sixteen."

"Good God!" Marcus said. "In less than thirty seconds? No matter what happens now, we've already won."

Tears welled in his eyes as he envisioned the digital wildfire of shock and anger that was now spreading across the world, and the hope that would follow.

# 71

A S VLASTOS RAN down the street with the others, a pain worse than any he had ever felt suddenly shot through his head. He couldn't understand it. It felt like high-voltage electricity, setting off every screaming nerve in his body at once. It wasn't the kind of pain a man could fight. And it brought him to his knees screaming, both hands holding his head, before he collapsed on the sidewalk.

*   *   *

James was sprinting toward the factory when the scream from behind stopped him in his tracks. He spun around in time to see Vlastos collapse to his knees and then fall to his side, curled up in a ball.

James stood motionless with Hanna, unsure what to do or what Vlastos's collapse meant. But Wolfgang, who seemed to have a better understanding, rushed to the man's side.

"What's wrong?" James asked, concerned.

"He's dying," Wolfgang said.

"Right *now*?" James asked, shocked.

Wolfgang nodded.

Vlastos, still holding his head, seemed to have gotten at least a brief reprieve from the pain. He said, "*As flies to wanton boys, as we to the gods; they kill us for their sport.*"

"What did he say?" Hanna asked.

"It's Shakespeare," James said. "He does that." He rushed toward Vlastos. "I need your help," he said. "My brother needs your help."

"*I am tied to the stake, and I must stand the course,*" Vlastos said.

James could see the bitterness in Vlastos's eyes. This was a man struggling to contain his anger at dying, but perhaps also a man who had come to terms with the evil he had done over most his life, and who knew that by all rights he should have been struck down decades ago.

"I'm sorry," James said, grabbing Vlastos's hand. "I'll never forget what you did for me tonight, and I'll never forget our journey together from Berlin to Prague. You're a better man today than your reputation would have others believe. I'm sorry, but I have to go help my brother."

"*Every inch a king,*" Vlastos said. "If only I had had a brother like you."

James squeezed his hand, then let go. Jumping to his feet, he ran toward the factory, with Hanna running at his side.

"Hang in there," Wolfgang said to the fallen man. "We'll come back for you as soon as we can."

Then he ran after James and Hanna toward the factory, leaving Vlastos to die alone on the cold, dark sidewalk.

# 72

---◦❈◦---

IAN AND MISKA were almost on the ground when he saw two groups of men running toward them. Realizing he was surrounded, he felt fear grip him. Miska was in no condition to make a run for it, and they couldn't climb back up the stairs. They were trapped.

He thought of Zoe, who would never learn the truth about everything he had done to try to help her sister.

Just when he thought the situation couldn't get any worse, the lead man in the closest group pulled a pistol and fired at them as he ran. The bullets zipped and whined off the steel staircase, a ricochet hitting Ian in the shoulder, spinning him around and sending him sprawling down the last half flight of steps. Suddenly without support, Miska stumbled down the steps and landed on him.

Stunned, he didn't know what he could do. There was a throbbing pain in his shoulder and arm. Their pursuers were closer now. Miska was moaning more than ever, and he wondered if she, too, had been shot. He sat up and scooted onto the sidewalk, pulling Miska with him toward a bricked-in doorway only a few feet away on the building's outside wall.

More bullets came, clanging against the fire escape and whining off the brickwork. With his remaining strength, he dragged Miska into the small doorway, pulled her past him with his good arm, and leaned sideways to cover her with his body, giving her what little protection he could.

"Close your eyes, Miska!" he yelled over the gunshots. "Think of your sister! Know how much she loves you! Remember the life you had before this!"

Her body trembled, but she made no sound. He wondered how much she understood of what he was saying, and how much strength she had left.

And then he heard a voice shout out through the gunfire. He didn't understand it at first, didn't believe it. But then he heard it again, shouting desperately. It was James, yelling amid the gunshots. This meant that he and Miska might not be surrounded after all. The only group that had fired at him was to his left. The other group rushing toward him, from the right, could be James, with others from the White Rose. And that gave him some hope, although he knew there wasn't a single person in their group with the weaponry or skills to take on the force of this many killers from the Malacoda gang.

Then, to his astonishment, a hail of bullets flew past his doorway from the right, attacking the Malacoda men to his left.

\*  \*  \*

Lucian snarled. He had shot the man and had him pinned down, but now he and his men were under fire from a small group rushing toward them from the other corner of the building. The fools had no idea of the force that would be arriving any minute. They had no idea that they had just killed themselves.

He ducked behind one of the brick cutouts along with his men and fired at the group from his covered position. Manchevski and his men were less than a minute out. Once they arrived on the scene, completely surrounding this small group, Lucian would dash in and slaughter the interlopers.

*   *   *

James inched along the wall with Hanna just behind him, while Wolfgang ran in the shadows, hunkered down and alternating his rapid shots between the men in front of them and a few others up on the roof.

James yelled for Hanna to stay back and dashed toward his brother. He ducked low, terrified of the bullets, as anyone would be. He was no hero. And it wasn't until he saw Ian, pinned in a doorway, getting shot at while trying to protect the girl, that James's concern for his own safety vanished. Ian was willing to die for his causes: saving Zoe's sister, helping the White Rose's fight against slavery, and contributing to the international debate on governments' policies for crippling organized crime. But James was different: the only thing he was willing to die for was to protect Ian.

He darted forward, into another doorway some twenty feet from Ian. The bullets were coming faster now. As he ducked behind the brick doorway, he was mesmerized by the sight of Wolfgang, racing along in the darkest part of the building's shadows, firing on the run and killing everything he aimed at. A submachine gun smacked into the sidewalk not far from James and broke into pieces. It must have fallen from the roof.

This was his chance. He darted out from his cover and sprinted toward Ian. Because of the heavy fire Wolfgang was laying down, none of the Malacoda men dared take a shot at him.

"Are you all right?" James shouted, diving into Ian's doorway.

Ian looked pale. "Help me get Miska out of here," he said. "I think she's hurt."

With bullets ricocheting off bricks outside the doorway, they each wrapped one of the girl's arms around their neck and lifted her to her feet. But her body was so limp, they had to carry all her weight.

"We won't make it," Ian said.

"Wolfgang will cover us," James insisted.

They moved out of the doorway, into the field of gunfire. Wolfgang was still laying down suppressing fire, which kept the Malacoda gunmen in check for the moment. And as the brothers carried the girl between them down the sidewalk, it seemed they would make it—until a bullet ripped through Miska's back. She gave a short, high scream and fell silent. The impact made her lurch in pain, throwing both brothers off balance, and all three stumbled to the ground.

James was the first to remove her arm from his neck so he could sit up and look at her. She lay motionless on the ground between him and Ian, just as their sister had lain slumped between them in the pickup when she died. And James could see his brother's face when he looked at the motionless girl between them. Ian's expression was that of a man whose psyche had contained a boiling rage as long as it could.

James stared in shock as Ian grabbed the gun from him and charged back toward the Malacoda men, firing at them. But it was the fury in Ian's scream that shook James out of his shocked state.

"Ian!" he yelled at his half-mad brother. "No!"

He scrambled up and ran after him. His brother had snapped loose from reality, and he had to pull him back. James had always been faster than his brother, and now he would have to be again. In his desperation, he tuned out the sounds of gunfire and the bullets whizzing by and pinging off the street and walls around them. He was twenty feet from Ian, closing the gap faster than he imagined, because Ian was firing the gun as he ran at the men. Ten feet . . . five . . .

He was almost there when a sharp pain exploded in his left leg and he tumbled to the ground. A bullet had caught him in the thigh. He couldn't stand. Less than a second later, he watched helplessly as his brother was hit and fell.

Then, out of the corner of his eye, he saw a pack of black SUVs racing around the corner toward them. It must be the reinforcements for the Malacoda gang.

*We're dead,* James thought. *We never had a chance. It was always our destiny to die tonight.*

He thought of his parents, old and waiting back in Kansas for the return of their two remaining children.

He remembered the first words of Ian's dissertation: "There are dark places in the deep ocean—places where light cannot penetrate—but there is nothing darker than the hearts of evil men whose souls have been poisoned by a life in organized crime."

Now they were going to die in a place of such darkness.

# 73

———————✳———————

VLASTOS FELT A flicker of life pulsing back into his body. Not much, but enough for him to stand. And once he stood, he fought to take a step while leaning on the building's brick wall. Then he took another step. Every breath was agony, and his face was rigid with the pain of his broken, dying body. His eyes looked down at the sidewalk in front of him as he struggled to take another slow step toward the pop of gunfire a block away. He took another step. Then another.

*   *   *

Manchevski's dark eyes glared with rage through the windshield of the Range Rover. Fifty yards ahead, the factory loomed out of the night. He could see two groups shooting at each other along the building. He made out Lucian on the right side with some men, and another two or three men lying motionless on the ground. On the left side, a man was in a crouch, shooting and running toward the center, where other men lay on the ground. The four other Range Rovers in his convoy raced toward the fight, while Manchevski's vehicle stayed back for his security, even though he wanted desperately to charge into the violence and kill whoever was attacking his business. He had not become the boss of the Malacoda gang by hanging back—or, indeed, by being anything other than aggressive, violent, and merciless. In the course of his career in the mafia, he had probably risked his life more boldly and more often than any other man in his organization.

"Kill them!" he yelled into his radio, talking to his men in the other vehicles. "The ones on the left! Kill them all!"

Just as he shouted the command, he saw a white van race around the corner, close to the group on the left. The top-heavy van leaned rightward as it made a hard left turn into the plaza. It darted toward the two fallen figures in the middle and stopped, shielding the little group from the line of fire. The back doors opened, and three people got out and started shooting pistols at the four Range Rovers barreling down on them. One of them even had a shotgun.

Bullets riddled the first two Range Rovers, causing all four to slam on their brakes. Manchevski watched as his men jumped out of their vehicles and engaged the group. To his surprise, two of his eight men went down. Then his surprise turned to concern when another three fell.

"Fatherless, dung-eating swine!" Manchevski yelled to the driver and two bodyguards in the vehicle with him. "Someone out there can really shoot!" He turned to look into the back cargo space of his SUV. "Let me out! We need the guns from the back!"

"We should stay in the car, sir!" one of the men said.

"Let me out now! We're going to show these motherfuckers what happens when they fuck with me!"

The bodyguard got out of the front passenger door and, after scanning the area, opened Manchevski's door in the backseat. The other bodyguard climbed out the opposite door and scanned his side of the vehicle for any threat to Manchevski. There was nothing—all the action was directly in front of them.

The driver swung open the back door, and Manchevski began pulling out one of the two cases that each contained a Yugoslavian Zastava M84 machine gun. It could fire eight hundred 7.62x54mm cartridges per minute, and he couldn't wait to unload it on the group in front of him. His favorite tool of death, he had used it often during the Balkan wars in his youth. It would take him about thirty seconds to assemble the seven separate pieces. Then he would unleash hell itself.

# 74

WOLFGANG WAS STARTLED by a white van that came racing around the corner. He turned his attention away from the advancing convoy of SUVs and was about to fire on it when Hanna screamed that it was from the White Rose. Spinning back toward the Range Rovers, he knelt on one knee and fired double pops into the driver's side of the first two windshields. Countless military assaults had taught him well the first imperative in an open encounter with the enemy: give a show of force sufficient to reduce his confidence and slow his charge or stop it altogether.

The van raced past him and screeched to a stop next to the American brothers, who both had fallen after being shot. They looked in bad shape: James had been struggling to drag himself toward Ian, who wasn't moving.

He didn't think he had hit any of the drivers of the Range Rovers, but once the White Rose members had jumped out of the van and started shooting at the SUVs, the Malacoda soldiers piled out of their vehicles to engage them. And that made them easy targets for Wolfgang, who began dropping them with unnerving precision. Despite all the shots being fired by the members of the White Rose, it was Wolfgang who dropped five of the eight men from the SUVs right away.

He saw that the fifth Range Rover in the group had stayed back and not attacked them. However, he didn't have time to focus on it. After dropping most of the newcomers, he turned his attention back to the original group they had been fighting.

As he ran behind the van, he saw Hanna rush toward James and hold him down. Ian was still motionless, and so was the girl he had rescued from the building.

As Wolfgang ran toward the north side of the building, he saw that only two men were still shooting at them. Slowing his steps as he had been trained to do in the *Bundesnachrichtendienst*—the German version of the CIA—he leveled his shoulders and steadied his outstretched arms so he could accurately fire each shot. He had rarely missed during his military training exercises, and tonight was no different.

Both men fell. The first was still moving when he got to them, and showed impressive strength of will in trying to raise his gun. But Wolfgang shot him again, this time in the throat, and the man stared wide-eyed for a couple of seconds before falling slack.

Now that he was closer, Wolfgang recognized the man as Lucian Novádraga, a top Malacoda assassin who had captured headlines across Europe for years with at least a dozen high-profile murders. Prosecutors had never been able to obtain eyewitnesses or any other incriminating evidence that would hold up in court. Looking at the dead killer, Wolfgang realized for the first time the potential of what he was doing here in Prague, which went far beyond trying to protect the American brothers. He could never know how many future deaths he had prevented by killing such a dangerous man who was untouchable by the law.

Just as he turned back to the remaining threat from the Range Rovers, a loud scream of high-powered machine-gun fire split the night. The rounds ripped into the van, dropping another of the White Rose members. Wolfgang again dropped to his distance-firing stance and unloaded his clip at the fifth Range Rover, which was the source of the machine-gun fire. But it was too far enough away, and his shots missed. Then the machine gun turned from the van toward him, obliging him to dive behind the corner of the building as the rounds ripped into bricks and concrete.

The White Rose people were sitting ducks against such a weapon. Their only hope was for Wolfgang to double back around the opposite building and get close enough to the Range Rover to take it from behind. But that would take at least two minutes, and by then he feared that the machine gun would have killed all those still alive in or around the van.

And then he saw something he could scarcely believe. Across the square along the wall of the far building, struggling with each step, was Vlastos, limping toward the Range Rover from behind.

*   *   *

Lying on his stomach and firing the low tripod-mounted machine gun, Manchevski felt the old thrill of killing surge through him as he riddled the white van from front to back. Then he turned the weapon on the bastard firing at him from the corner of the factory. He laughed seeing pieces fly off the van as the rounds chewed through the body metal, and at least one person went down beside the van. Even the talented shooter by the corner of the factory was no match for him at this range, with this firepower. He would cut them all to pieces, and he loved it.

Then he heard a quick succession of loud snaps from his left and realized that something was terribly wrong. Jerking his head left, he saw both his bodyguards fall to the pavement. Then something invisible hit his kneecap hard. He yelped as pain shot through him. Releasing the machine gun, he twisted sideways and rolled on the hard cobblestone square, holding his knee with one hand and searching for the source of his pain. Another snap came from beside him, and his driver fell gurgling to the asphalt while Manchevski tried to sort out what had gone wrong.

All the gunfire had now stopped. All was silent but for the soft, slow scratch of halting footsteps dragging toward him. Breathing hard from the pain, he felt the rage well up in him at the realization that after all these years of surviving everything that came at him, he had been beaten. He looked up and saw a man now standing above him who looked as close to death as any man could while still standing on his feet.

"Whoever you are," Manchevski hissed, "I'll see you in hell!"

"Perhaps not," Vlastos replied. Then, raising his gun, he fired three shots into the man's head.

Lowering the gun, he looked at the mangled face of the Malacoda boss. Then, after staggering backward a few steps, Vlastos collapsed. He had fought off death as long as he could, and now he felt himself beginning to slip away forever. There was no coming back this time, and he knew it. He had been given a brief second chance at life, and though it hadn't been much, he was grateful that he had at least been able to live a good life at the very end.

But he still had one last thing he wanted to do to ease his soul—something he would never have the chance to do now. Something that would have made the world a better place and would have made both his father and Shakespeare proud. A final good deed on earth. If only he had had more time . . .

# 75

J AMES SENT HANNA to help Miska while he crawled toward Ian's body. Turning his brother over, he held him in his arms. The shooting had stopped. Wolfgang ran from the corner of the building and dropped to all fours next to them.

"He's not moving!" James yelled frantically. "Ian! Can you hear me!"

Wolfgang checked Ian. "He's still breathing," he said. "We need to get him to a hospital fast. Just keep holding him and talking to him! I'll check on the others, and we'll get out of here fast!"

"Please hurry," James begged, an unnerving fear flooding over him at the idea that Ian could be slipping away from him even as he held him. He had never seen his brother so helpless.

Wolfgang took off running toward the van. It looked as though one of the White Rose members had been hit, maybe killed. Hanna was kneeling next to Miska. All the van's tires had been hit, and James watched as Wolfgang finished giving instructions to Hanna and then ran out into the square, toward the Range Rovers.

After pausing at the first four Range Rovers, he stepped over the Malacoda soldiers and ran to the fifth one, where he knelt down next to someone lying on the ground. Could it be Vlastos? James wondered. Then Wolfgang lowered his head so that his ear was right up against the man's mouth. He kept it there for a while, then raised his head to look into his face for a few seconds. Then he rose to his feet and rushed over and jumped inside the fifth Range Rover. James saw the vehicle shudder to life and the headlights come on. A second later, it was racing toward them.

"Stay with me, Ian," James yelled to his unconscious brother, holding his head in his arms. "Don't you dare leave me."

The Range Rover raced around the white van and came to a screeching stop. The muscular White Rose member with the tattooed arms helped Hanna lift the fallen man into the back. Then they lifted Miska in as well. Then Wolfgang raced the vehicle toward them and stopped. For the first time in minutes, a few gunshots came at them from the factory roof. Wolfgang jumped out and fired a few well-placed rounds at the edge of the roof as Marcus jumped out of the passenger side and helped James get Ian into the SUV. Then Wolfgang jumped back in and stomped on the accelerator. The Range Rover lunged forward and roared across the open square as a few more shots came from the factory roof.

Once across the square, the Range Rover disappeared into the shadows of a narrow street, away from the factory. Seconds later, its headlights and revving engine blended into all the other lights and sounds of the city. Those in the vehicle who were still alive and not dying had survived the chaotic assault on the factory. But the larger war was just beginning.

# 76

JAMES LAY IN his hospital bed at the Landstuhl Regional Medical Center and stared up at the ceiling, as he had done for much of the past three days. After Wolfgang's madcap drive from the factory to the Prague Central Military Hospital, he had contacted German chancellor Henzollern. Because of the rapidly spreading global Internet sensation of Ian's video, and concerns about retaliation against the brothers, the U.S. Secretary of State had gotten involved. Instructions were issued to have the brothers flown via a medical transport jet to Ramstein Air Base in Landstuhl, Germany. From there, they were transported to LRMC, where they joined thousands of injured American troops from Afghanistan at the largest overseas military hospital operated by the U.S. Army.

That was three days ago, and since then James had spent most of his time staring up at the pattern of holes in the acoustic ceiling and waiting—waiting to heal, waiting to go back to being a tax accountant at the firm . . . waiting to return to a life in Kansas City that he was no longer sure he wanted.

The past three days had given him time to think about everything he had experienced since first setting out to find his brother. It all had rushed by so fast that he had no time to reflect on things in the moment, and now that it was finished, everything felt like a blur. It had been a wild, nightmarish adventure over four days. But it had also been exhilarating. He had helped in the fight against at least one criminal organization, and perhaps others. In just four days, he had been a part of something that he could be proud of for the rest of his life. And that sense of meaningful accomplishment to help make the world a better place, as corny as it sounded, also gave him a real high—a high that he wanted to repeat again. And he was pretty sure he could never get this feeling from doing tax returns. And yet, his job at the firm was waiting for him back in Kansas City.

"Did she make it?" a voice asked from beside him. "Is she alive?"

James was tired and weak, but he managed to turn his head to look at Ian, lying in another hospital bed, ten feet from his. They had been put in the same room, but this was the first time his brother had been awake long enough to speak. "Did *who* make it?" James asked.

"Jessica," Ian answered.

"Jessica died eight years ago."

There was a short pause. "Miska," Ian said.

"Yes. She lived. Zoe's with her at the hospital in Prague."

"You saw Zoe?" Ian asked.

"Yes," James said, remembering the half day he and Ian had spent in the hospital in Prague. Ian had been unconscious the entire time, but all the doctors had assured James and Zoe that he was stable, the surgery had been successful, and he should regain consciousness in a few days. "She wanted me to tell you she loves you."

"Was anyone else hurt?"

"Yeah," James said. He hadn't wanted to volunteer the news, but since Ian had asked, he wasn't going to lie. "Sebastian was killed, and Patrick was in critical condition at the hospital in

Prague. Marcus was also shot, but it was relatively minor, so he's doing well."

"Sebastian? *Damn it!*" Ian hissed.

"What we did will save many. A lot of people in the world have been inspired by what we did."

Ian shifted in his bed to look at James. "We need to create a memorial for Sebastian on the Web site. And Patrick, too, if he doesn't pull through. The world needs to know what they sacrificed."

James nodded. "We will."

"The video?" Ian then asked. "It came out all right?"

James nodded. "Over fifty million hits on the Internet so far. It's amazing. Captured everything. It's all over the place in the media: CNN, BBC, and everywhere else. You're actually kind of a celebrity right now."

"Shit," Ian said. "Just what I need."

"Yeah, well, you can't fight it now. The White Rose is on the map, and you're in a perfect position to be their spokesman."

"Yeah, we'll see about that. What about you? What are you going to do once we get back to the States? You going back to doing taxes the rest of your life?"

"That was always my plan," James said.

*"Was?"*

James sighed. "I don't know. To be honest, I'm having some doubts now."

"Join me," Ian said. "Devote yourself to something greater than yourself. I could use your help. You've seen parts of organized crime that not even *I've* seen. This thing is building momentum. You've seen the horror. Can you honestly think of a more valuable way to spend your life? We were *born* to do this!"

"I don't know," James said. "I have a job waiting for me, a career I've worked hard developing."

"But you don't love it. It'll never excite you the way this will. It wouldn't be so crazy dangerous like it was this time.

We'd focus on academics and policies with various governments and law enforcement divisions. We'd administer and organize and train the growth of the White Rose across the globe."

James smiled. His brother was right, of course. He had felt more alive in the past week than in the past five years. He tried to imagine continuing in the life his brother was describing. "I need to think about it."

"Think about it while you take a trip with me," Ian said. "The professor had an international exchange student a few years ago who's been working on identifying economic weaknesses in drug cartel supply chains. He says she's brilliant, and he thinks her strategies could be helpful on a new special project he's working on: strategies against the Russian mafia's black-market operations in Moscow."

"You're thinking of taking a trip to *Moscow*?" James asked.

"Not Moscow. She's studying economics in Mexico City. Her brother's a policeman there, and she's been researching the links between corruption of officials and cost reductions of narcotics distribution. The professor thought she could help the White Rose with the project in Moscow. Apparently, there's something she needs to show us, and the professor thinks I should be the one to meet with her."

James shook his head vehemently, then groaned with pain. "You promised you wouldn't be involved in anything else dangerous."

"And I won't. I'd just be going to talk with her. To see what she's discovered. Please, come with me. We started something with the White Rose. And this could be a great next step."

"I'm not even sure when they'll let us out of here. We could be here for weeks."

"She'll wait for us."

"We need to get back to Kansas. Mom and Dad'll want to see us. They would have flown over here if it wasn't for Dad's health."

"We could fly into Mexico City for a half day on our way back home, then continue on up to Kansas after meeting with her. Just a half day there, that's all. And then we're home."

"Unless something goes wrong."

"What could go wrong?" Ian asked. "She just wants to show us something in her research."

"All right," he said. A half-day detour on the way home couldn't be that bad. "Mexico City it is."

# Epilogue

————————※————————

STROBVIOK WALKED OUT the front of his hotel into the rainy Berlin night. Three bodyguards accompanied him, even though his struggle with the Malacoda gang was rapidly winding down since the murder of Manchevski. A meeting of the European bosses had been called for next week in Zurich. Fourteen other bosses would be there in addition to Strobviok and whoever was going to replace Manchevski as boss of the Malacoda gang. A power struggle within that weakened organization was still going on, which was exactly why he was moving fast to further disrupt it. He planned to make the grab for the best business segments before the meeting with the other bosses, who would want to carve up the Malacoda gang's profit centers for themselves in exchange for peace within the Commission.

Strobviok could hardly believe how fast the region's criminal organizations had fallen into disarray. But as luck would have it, Manchevski had been killed. So it was he, Strobviok, who had the best chance to unify much of the black market in the region. And he was ready to move fast to consolidate his power and expand the operations of his growing criminal empire—to become one of the top crime bosses in Europe.

A sudden snap came from the building's shadows behind him, and pink mist exploded from his lead bodyguard's head just as he reached to open the door of the armored limousine. Then more bullets riddled the side of the car, and the second bodyguard fell backward, bounced off the trunk, and slid to the street, where he lay motionless and wide-eyed in death. The passenger-side door opened as the driver, who had slid across the seat to get out on the side away from the shooters, rolled out holding a Heckler and Kock MP5A3 submachine gun. He crawled across the ground, popped up from behind the trunk, and held down the trigger to send a long burst of gunfire out into the night, in the direction of the attack. As the percussive metallic sound ripped through the night, the last remaining bodyguard pushed Strobviok to the far side of the car and held him down despite his furious eagerness to join the firefight.

Then all the firing from the shadows stopped.

Strobviok's own men, however, kept firing into the shadows. The submachine gun's loud chatter bounced off the surrounding building walls. The men attacking him either were pausing to reload or—with luck—had been hit. Strobviok determined that they were either a small faction of the Malacoda gang—in which case he had carelessly underestimated their strength and ambition during this time of transition—or men from one of the other major criminal groups in Europe. Perhaps it was the Montreui gang from Paris, or Serbian mafia in Amsterdam, or the Tambov gang from Hamburg, or Sicilian Mafia out of Athens. It could even be one of the major groups from Moscow. Either way, this attack on his life was a sign that a new war was only just beginning.

No sound had come from the building's shadows for nearly two minutes. Both Strobviok's remaining bodyguard and his driver told him they couldn't be sure they had hit all the men attacking them, and that they should try to slide into the car to escape.

He nodded—they would make a run for it. The driver crawled back toward them to open the door, while Strobviok peeked over the hood of the car to survey the building. Nothing moved, but his instincts told him that the attackers were still there in the darkness, waiting for a chance to hit them again. This seemed strange, though, because hit men for organized crime were not generally this patient and calculating. When they hit something, they hit hard, with all their force, until it was finished. Men like that didn't take intermissions; they didn't wait.

Then Strobviok realized that something was wrong, that he had made a mistake. "Wait," he said, turning back to his bodyguard and the driver. But he saw that he was too late when the driver stopped reaching for the door handle and stared with wide eyes into the shadows beside the vehicle.

The bodyguard spun around just as a figure emerged from the shadows with a semiautomatic assault rifle. But he never had a chance. The attacker blew a hole through the bodyguard's cheek and then took off the face of the driver with his next shot. All that was left was a rattled, blood-spattered Strobviok.

Stepping completely out from the shadows, Wolfgang slung the rifle over his shoulder so that its strap held it to his back, as it had during so many jungle treks in his past. He then pulled a Walther PP9 semiautomatic pistol from a Velcro holster in his vest and pointed it at Strobviok until he got close enough to kneel down in front of the man.

Strobviok had no words for this man. He knew what was now in store for him. He had beaten the odds during a life of crime and violence, until this rainy night in Berlin. He breathed heavily, staring with icy eyes at this man who had somehow, single-handedly, taken out his entire security force.

With the hand that wasn't holding the pistol, the man pulled a military knife from another Velcro pocket in the vest. Then, in a move so fast that Strobviok could hardly see it, he stabbed deeply into Strobviok's left lung. Then, after giving the knife a sharp twist, he pulled it out and stabbed him again, this time in the gut.

Strobviok tensed, then slid sideways along the bottom of the limousine's door until he lay in the gutter, between the sidewalk and the front tire.

Wolfgang placed his mouth to the dying man's ear. "Mr. Strobviok, do not feel ashamed. I'm a son of Germany, and I've killed hundreds of men in the name of my country and to protect my people from the evils of the world. I was with your assassin Vlastos in Prague when he died. Before he died, he made a request to me, which I promised him I would fulfill. What he requested was that, upon returning to Berlin, I find you and kill you. He told me that you had been like a father to him for decades, but that he had found a new light and that he finally understood the terrible harm you have caused the world. And he asked me to give you a message from him. What he wanted me to tell you were his final words before he died. What he said was this: *'Not that I loved Caesar less, but that I loved Rome more.'*"

A tear formed in Strobviok's eye, and he growled like an injured animal making one last attempt to scare away the predator that had taken it down. And then, without another sound, he died.

Wolfgang stood up from the body and walked away, toward the glittering skyline of Berlin, the shadows of Europe, and the hope that he could now enjoy a peaceful life with his wife and son. He had seen hell and traveled through fire, and now he could finally go home. He had killed his last man in the name of peace. As far as he was concerned, it was now up to others to fight the evils of this world. He had done enough and had nothing left that he was willing to sacrifice for the greater good.

A war was coming, and others would have to make sacrifices for it, but not he. He was a soldier no longer.


THE END

# About The Author

Bryan Devore was born and raised in Manhattan, Kansas, and received his Bachelor's and Master's in Accountancy from Kansas State University. He also completed an exchange semester at the Leipzig Graduate School of Management in Leipzig, Germany. He is a CPA and lives in Denver, Colorado. He welcomes comments and feedback, and can be contacted at bryan.devore@gmail.com.

Novels by Bryan Devore:
The Aspen Account
The Price of Innocence

Made in the USA
Lexington, KY
02 February 2017